BENNETT R. COLES

LIGHT
—— IN THE ——
ABYSS

BLACKWOOD & VIRTUE

PROMONTORY
PRESS

To the crew of His Majesty's Canadian Ship EDMONTON
and
United States Coast Guard Law Enforcement Detachment 407
Spring 2023
Hacia La Grandeza

Also by Bennett R. Coles

The Blackwood & Virtue Series

Winds of Marque
Dark Star Rising

The Astral Saga

Virtues of War
Ghosts of War
March of War
Fog of War: The Battle for Cerberus (interactive novel)

LIGHT

IN THE

ABYSS

CHAPTER 1

"The solution is simple: more rum."

Commander Lord Liam Blackwood noted the approving nods around the small, round table. His four companions were making a show of looking relaxed, lounging as best as the uncomfortable wooden stools allowed. Around them, the tavern was bustling with late evening energy and he doubted anyone was paying them the least bit of attention, but nevertheless he leaned forward.

"Keep them drunk; keep them happy. And keep them looking at you. Hopefully we're in and out before anyone notices."

"Hedgie and I," Petty Officer Amelia Virtue said at his side, "already have a plan for the distraction. But more rum will always help."

Amelia grinned at Able Rating Mia Hedge, who smirked back and lifted her mug. Downing the contents in a single, long gulp, Hedge slammed it down and reached for the bottle in the center of the table.

"More rum!" she shouted to the distant barmaid.

"Easy there," growled Chief Petty Officer Harper Sky. Her powerful frame hunkered against the table, incapable of relaxing.

"You heard what the boss said," Hedge replied triumphantly, refilling her cup. "This is the simple solution."

Liam assessed his team again. They were all, like him, children of the Halo and as a group they were probably the palest in the room. On a planet this far into the Hub, where the countless stars closed in and daylight was perpetual, most patrons of the tavern had darker complexions ranging from olive to brown to deepest black. Skin tone didn't matter amongst common folk like these – as it did amidst the nobility – but it would certainly catch the eye.

Amelia and Hedge, in their worn, tapered, busty dresses, looked like any random pair of fairly young, fairly pretty, fairly poor girls out for the night – they'd blend in just fine with the growing crowd in this working-class tavern. They even complimented each other: Amelia was the sweet brunette; Hedge was the sultry blonde – a rarity in these parts that would prove useful if Amelia's plan worked.

Chief Sky wore a practical, form-fitting tunic that highlighted her broad shoulders and powerful arms. With her cropped hair – although she'd let the top grow a bit – and cold eyes she looked as always like an enforcer. That would be particularly useful when the time came, and right now it kept any would-be suitors far away from the table.

Lieutenant Mason Swift was dressed in local working clothes that masked his lean build, and in this crowd of laborers he almost looked skinny. He matched the girls for style and was supposed to be their companion for the evening, but his dour expression and shaved head made him look more like their grumpy uncle than their friend.

"Try to look like you're having a good time, Mason," he chided.

"When you and Chief Killjoy here get moving, it'll be a lot easier."

"Fair enough." He scanned the room again, noting a trio of serious-looking men making their way between the tables toward the dark stairs at one end of the room. "I think our contact is almost here, anyway."

"I see him," Sky muttered, nodding toward the near end of the bar. "Purple coat and gold buckles, talking to the barkeep."

Liam let his eyes drift casually in that direction, spotting the target easily in the sea of drab browns and beiges. He always wondered what drove petty kingpins to show off their wealth – it made them so easy to spot. Sure enough, there was Max Strongback, a merchant who had come to His Majesty's attention over the past few years for a few questionable business deals – and more than a few sudden, mysterious deaths of competitors. His network of influence in this small corner of the planet Sapphira was growing, as was the amount of surveillance His Majesty's diplomatic corps applied to him.

None of this was of any interest to Liam or the Navy, but that steady surveillance had revealed Strongback's connection to a recent incident here on Sapphira that most certainly was. And the meeting Strongback was about to have in the tavern's upper room was one that Liam intended to drop in on.

"You all clear on the escape plan and the rendezvous?" he asked quietly, eyes mainly on Hedge. She wasn't a usual member of the ship's reconnaissance team, but Amelia had convinced him that, given the setting, she'd be a natural asset.

Hedge was busy adjusting her dress to show off her two best natural assets, but she nodded to him. His glance around the table confirmed his confidence in the rest of his team.

Strongback was now making his way through the tavern, gazing benevolently at the seated patrons who glanced up at him. He was a force to be reckoned with, and he knew it.

All the more reason, Liam decided, to take him down a peg. He rose slowly from his stool. "It's time."

Sky stood as well, eyes scanning the room. Liam smoothed out his long, black coat and adjusted his high collar. His outfit was subtle, but to the discerning eye was clearly from the finest tailor. No-one here on the tavern floor would give it more than a second glance, but in the upper room he knew it would speak volumes.

He gave Amelia's shoulder a squeeze.

"Be careful, darling," he whispered.

Her hand reached back to brush against his leg as he passed behind her. Her eyes lifted to meet his, but other than a sly smile she said nothing.

Following Sky, he weaved his way to the outer edge of the tavern and started closing the stairs.

Amelia watched Liam depart, still smiling as she admired his tall, lean form. He'd made a big deal about how his outfit would only be noticed by those wealthy enough to appreciate fine tailoring – but, come on, how could anyone not notice a man that handsome and stylish sidling between the tables? Not that she hadn't drawn a few admiring glances herself with this dress. She felt the coarse fabric between her fingers, recognizing the skill some local seamstress had used to take cheap materials and turn them into something practical and fun. She had a sheathed dagger strapped high inside her thigh, just in case things got really bad. Liam had worried that folks seeing a weapon like that might raise suspicion, but with her hems dropping all the way to floor, she knew this dress would have to be hitched up pretty high for any revelation to occur. And if that happened, she thought with a snigger, she doubted anyone would be looking at the knife.

"Hedgie – Mia!" She reminded herself that on missions they had to use each other's first names only. "Stop playing with yourself."

Hedge cackled as she adjusted her cleavage one more time. "I love wearing dresses – so much more freeing than our uni… What we wear at work."

Mia downed the remainder of Liam's mug of rum and half-rose from her stool, sliding across to land next to Mason Swift as she collected Sky's untouched drink along the way. She draped her arm, crooked at the elbow, on Swift's shoulder.

"Care for a drink… Mason?" She lifted the cup toward his lips with a smile.

Amelia scooted over one stool, resting a hand on Swift's opposite shoulder. "I think the rum is intended for anyone who joins us."

"I'm hoping *you'll* join me," Hedge said to Swift with a smolder. "Back at my tenement."

"Mia!"

"It's fine," Swift said, a smile creeping across his face. "Honestly we're trying to gather a crowd."

She looked around and saw that an entire table of local men had turned their attention toward them, drunken gazes watching as Hedge traced her finger up Swift's cheek.

"Hey," Amelia said, making a show of tapping his shoulder, "eyes over here, jerk."

Swift turned to give her a sympathetic smile, then looked over to where their sudden audience was watching. He gave the men a quick toast with his mug. They all toasted back, downing their drinks.

"Bar wench," Swift called out loudly, motioning the serving girl over. "Another round for my friends there. And a shot of rum for each of them."

The men cheered in sudden appreciation. Other tables looked over in curiosity, and more than one new gaze rested on this pale, bald stranger with a young woman on either side. Swift gave the nearby table a gracious nod and looked back at Amelia.

"I think our distraction is starting to take hold." She felt his arm brush along her back. "Do you mind playing along? It's nothing personal, Amelia."

"That's right," Hedge breathed, rising on her stool to trace her fingers along Swift's scalp. "Nothing personal."

Amelia let her lips curl into a sultry smile as she shuffled closer, leaning into him and feeling more eyes fixate on her. It was actually kind of fun to see the dour Lieutenant Swift transforming into a lady's man and she ran her hand up his arm. She just hoped Liam couldn't see the specifics from all the way across the room.

Hedge reached over to gently push Amelia's shoulder. She knocked Hedge's hand aside, noting the sudden rush of attention from their audience.

"Okay, I think they'll be hoping for a fight, soon." She scanned the distant staircase, and just spotted Liam's tall figure loitering near it. "The others are in position."

"We need a good reason to fight," Hedge said with a grin. "And we need to give them a good show."

She rose from her stool, leaned in and put her head between Amelia and Swift. Then she laid a wet, lingering kiss on his ear.

"Mia," Amelia whispered. "This is pretend, remember?"

"I've never kissed an officer before," she whispered back, directly into Swift ear. "I bet it's fun."

"You can't-"

Hedge's powerful hand suddenly shoved Amelia, knocking her backward. Her stool tipped and she crashed down onto the sticky floor. She heard a gasp from the crowd.

Hedge rose and threw one leg over Swift. She straddled his lap and pressed herself against him as she ran her hands up and down the sides of his head. His hands came up to caress her waist, but when he looked sideways toward Amelia, Hedge gripped his chin and turned him back to her.

She kissed him full on the lips, holding his face with both hands. A drunken cheer went up all around them.

Amelia climbed to feet, fighting the folds of her dress. "Mia, stop!"

She grabbed Hedge's shoulder and wrenched her clear of Swift. Her friend's face was one of triumph, but her eyes gleamed expectantly.

Amelia threw her punch, harder than she'd planned. Hedge fell backward, bouncing off the table before tumbling to the floor. Amelia felt the rush of adrenalin, fuelled by the roar of approval around her, and she backhanded Swift and sent him tumbling down as well. The surprised cheer drowned out the words she snapped down at him.

"That's for enjoying that so much!"

Hedge was already on her feet, face twisting in rage even as her eyes shone with humor. "Let's do this, bitch!"

Amelia screamed and threw herself into the fight.

Liam glanced at Sky as the noise growing at the far end of the tavern swelled into a roar. Half the room was on its feet, and those near him were starting to rise. Whatever Amelia and the others were doing, it was working.

After another loud cheer, the chant of "*Fight! Fight! Fight!*" started to swell around the room.

"Ahh," one of the tavern bouncers currently guarding the stairs groaned as he gestured at his colleague, "come on!"

They started pushing their way through the cheering crowd.

Sky was already up the stairs and Liam followed quickly, eyes adjusting to the shadows as he padded along the landing. A pair of guards – likely Strongback's own, based on their merchant house tunics – stood by a closed door. They stepped forward immediately.

"No visitors," the first one warned, raising his hand.

Sky grabbed his hand and twisted it. He collapsed to his knees in a cry of pain that was silenced as she slammed her fist into his face. She threw him down and raised her arm to block the strike of the second guard, palm snapping out to drive his face upward. Her second hand formed a knife-edge and drove against his throat, sending him gargling down. Any momentary sounds were swallowed up in the cacophony on the tavern floor. By the time Liam reached the door, both guards lay unconscious.

He tested the door latch – it was unlocked. Nodding to Sky, he pulled back his coat and drew his short sword and a pistol. She did the same. He pressed down on the latch again, and she kicked it open, disappearing through the opening.

Liam was right behind her, slipping through the doorway and scanning center to right with his pistol while Sky covered the left. Detecting no movement, he kicked the door shut behind him and took a better look.

Max Strongback sat in a padded armchair, half-turned and frozen in shock as he stared wide-eyed at the intruders. One guard stood behind him, slowly raising his empty hands as Liam's pistol trained on him. Close on the left was another guard, who stood motionless with Sky's blade against his neck.

And facing Strongback in the center of the room, resting on a luxurious stool, was a Theropod.

The reptilian alien was motionless. The small, wedge-shaped head was ridged, indicating a male, and it turned on a long neck toward the newcomers even as his body remained upright, facing Strongback. Dressed in plain working clothes he clearly meant to draw no attention to himself, although his long, powerful tail was impossible to hide. His small forearms still gripped a cup of tea, his legs bent in a crouch with backward-bending ankles extending down elongated feet to triangular boots that Liam knew hid wicked claws on the three toes.

"Please," Liam said with a smile, "don't get up. In fact, why don't you two guards lie down on your stomachs, hands on heads."

Strongback's eyes narrowed in anger, but he nodded to his goons to comply. Sky shepherded them both to the side of the room where she could cover them easily. Liam sheathed his sword and moved into clear view of both seated men.

"Apologies for interrupting your meeting. My friend and I just want some information and then we'll go."

"What kind of information?" Strongback muttered.

"Not from you," Liam turned his eyes to the Theropod, "but from your visitor."

"I know nothing about this world," came the response from the translator that hung around the brute's neck as he hissed and growled in his own language. "I have only just arrived."

"That last bit isn't true," Liam said airily, "but we'll ignore it for now. What we won't ignore is the fact that you have dealings with a Theropod art… let's call him an art *dealer* named Shordar."

"Who?"

"Perhaps your translator isn't quite up to the task, or perhaps I simply can't pronounce his name properly. Shordar. An infamous thief who preys upon the nobility of this peaceful Empire, stealing only the finest treasures and selling them to," he turned his gaze back to Strongback, "unscrupulous buyers."

"I would never buy stolen goods," Strongback protested.

"That also isn't true," Liam said, letting his tone harden. "As a certain two-story warehouse with faded blue paint and a mild infestation of rats in the eastern dock region can currently prove."

Strongback's face went carefully neutral, but he said nothing. Liam appreciated the few tidbits of intelligence the diplomatic corps had provided earlier but hoped he wouldn't have to pull out many more – he only had one for each of them. He didn't like bluffing, so he decided to just move forward. Reaching into his belt pouch, he pulled out a purse heavy with coin and tossed it on the table between Strongback and the Theropod.

"I just want information about Shordar. And I'm willing to pay. Then my friend and I will leave you to whatever you were discussing."

He was met with silence.

"Who wants to go first?"

"I know nothing about whom you speak," the Theropod said.

Liam lifted his pistol. His finger pulled back on the trigger and the teacup still in the Theropod's hand shattered. Shards of porcelain and lukewarm liquid spattered over both seated figures.

"Let's all stop lying, please," he said, any trace of a smile gone.

The Theropod lowered, legs visibly flexing.

"Very well," it hissed. "I will *tell you* nothing about whom you speak."

"Then we'll burn your ship. The pinnace with the four red stripes currently docked at the western end of the public terminal."

That was his last trump card, but he kept his expression stony.

The Theropod barked a laugh. "Do you think that's worse than what will happen to me if I give you information?"

Liam turned questioning eyes to Strongback. The merchant glowered back in silence.

"So be it." He turned to Sky. "Come, my friend. We have to burn a ship and a warehouse tonight."

Still, no-one caved. It was, he realized, time to bluff.

"Gag them," he ordered. "And shoot them all in the legs. I don't want anyone raising the alarm until we're gone."

"All right!" Strongback interjected, raising his hands in acquiescence. "Yes, I was looking to buy an artifact from Shordar."

"Where is he?"

"Not here," the Theropod interrupted. "Far away from this stinking world."

"But he's going somewhere. Tell me, and keep that purse of coins."

"Never."

"Okay, my friend, let's get started." Liam stepped forward, aiming his pistol at Strongback's thigh. How far could he take this bluff?

"Morassia!" the merchant cried. "He has a house on Morassia where he keeps many of his artifacts."

The Theropod lunged forward, hissing as his jaws went for Strongback's throat. Liam's weapon flicked over and a crack thundered through the room. The Theropod stumbled, collapsing through the table as he clutched at his bleeding leg. Shooting a defenceless prisoner was forbidden. But shooting an alien trying to silence his informant... That was allowed.

Strongback recoiled, then stared in fear at Liam.

"Morassia, you say?" he prompted the merchant.

"Yes, in the town called... something unpronounceable that starts with an R. It's in the center of the southern continent."

"How does a Human know that?"

"Because Shordar invited me there, when we met. He wanted to show me all his wares." Strongback took a long breath. "And I think he wanted to show off a little."

That sounded like the thief Liam was hunting. Famously arrogant, and rightly so. Morassia was the perfect place for a Theropod interested in Human culture to hide in plain sight.

"Tell me everything you know," Liam said, "no matter how unpronounceable it is. Leave nothing out."

Amelia was pulling the lustrous black hair of some local girl when the bouncers finally grabbed her. As planned, her fight with Hedge had expanded very quickly as they both threw as many wild punches at random female onlookers as they did each other. This had roused the crowd even more, bringing more combatants into the fray and pitting drunken onlookers against outraged boyfriends. It was pure chaos.

Releasing the woman's hair she slipped free of one bouncer, spinning around the other and kicking out the back of his knee. He stumbled down, but his iron grip still held her arm.

"Ow!" she cried, letting big tears well in her eyes as she looked up at him pleadingly. "You're hurting me!"

"Don't give me that," he scowled, standing up and lifting her clear into the air as he stepped over a stool and kicked aside discarded cups. This entire end of the tavern was littered with broken furniture and overturned tables. The bouncers were advancing like grubby musketeers in a war zone, breaking up the worst of the fighting and hauling people toward the doors.

Two others pulled Hedge off a man she'd knocked down to the floor – fighting him or kissing him, Amelia could rarely tell – and ignored her screams of protest as her feet lifted into the air and kicked impotently.

She glared at both of them, then twisted to grin at the bigger one. "Hey, you're cute."

"Shut up," he muttered.

They heaved her out the front door. Beyond, the deep blue twilight that was the closest this planet came to night revealed a crowded street.

Moments later, Amelia felt herself being flung through the opening. She landed heavily on the cobbled street, righting herself quickly amidst the groaning, cursing patrons in various states of pain all around her.

The narrow road was busy with people out carousing. A single carriage clattered by, the driver shouting at people to keep clear. On one side of the tavern was a stall selling meat pies, and on the other was a stable. The doors were open and straw spilled out as a servant pushed out a wheelbarrow and dumped her load of dung into an open sewer hole. She glanced at the crowd of drunken louts and dropped the wheelbarrow before running back inside.

Many eyes were on her, Amelia noticed, and she realized that her dress had somehow been torn and hung loosely off her left shoulder. It revealed quite a bit more flesh than she intended, and in this part of town at this time of night, it might give the wrong impression.

Hedge rose to her knees and brushed off her dress. It appeared intact, although her blonde hair was a matted mass with strands dancing in the breeze.

Amelia helped her to her feet but then dodged back as Swift came hurtling through the door.

"And stay out!" yelled the bouncer.

Swift picked himself up, examining his shirt that was torn half open from the collar while he hitched up his trousers.

"Where's your belt?" Amelia asked.

"I dunno," he said, looking around at the drunken crowd starting to climb to their feet. "Some woman took it off me."

What she'd thought were bruises on his face were, she realized as she got closer, lipstick.

"The same one who planted these on you?"

"No, another one." He looked around. "And where's my shoe?"

"That was awesome," Hedge said, wrapping an arm around Amelia's shoulders. "Is it always this much fun when you guys go on missions ashore?"

"Hey!" a stranger shouted, struggling to his feet and stabbing a finger at Swift. "You were kissing my wife."

"I don't think I was," he said, blinking to clear his head as he backed away.

"He's mine!" Hedge retorted, moving between them and balling her fists. "You keep your little home-wench away from him!"

His eyes widened in shock and anger.

"Hedgie, no," Amelia hissed, grabbing her arm and pulling her back. "The distraction's over."

"This your belt?" another man said, holding it up to Swift.

"Oh, yeah," he said, stepping forward to grab it. "Thanks."

"Get him!"

A mug smashed against Swift's skull, shattering and sending him toppling forward as his eyes rolled back. Amelia caught him, dragging him backward as a trio of angry men started to close in.

"Don't know where you pasties come from," one of them slurred, "but you're gonna learn some manners."

<hr>

Liam wandered over to the window of the room, looking down on the bustling street below. He sensed that Strongback had truly told him everything he knew, and the discussion had become much more relaxed, almost amiable, once the positions of power had been properly established. Strongback was a survivor, and so long as there were no embarrassing witnesses he was happy to comply with this mysterious stranger.

"I think we're done, then," Liam said, as much to Sky as to Strongback.

She hadn't moved from where she covered the two prone guards, but her nod confirmed that she'd digested everything Strongback had said. The only question remaining, he knew, was how to silence and detain all these people so that he and Sky had enough time to leave unhindered.

The passage of a carriage in the street below caught his eye, the pedestrian crowds moving to make way as it rumbled up and down the street. If he and Sky could grab one of those, they'd be blocks away in moments. He recalled them passing fairly regularly while he and his team had surveyed the tavern earlier.

The crowd below parted again, but this time it was a pair of pale women – one blonde, one brunette – each with a hand on a wheelbarrow they were frantically pushing. In that wheelbarrow was the unconscious form of a man. Close behind them, a trio of men angrily chased them, a growing crowd of men and women following along behind.

He looked quickly around the room one last time, then pushed open the window. The noise of the crowded street rushed upward as he leaned out, noting the series of iron-grilled gardening ledges under each window stretching away until this building joined another with a flatter roof.

"Out we go," he ordered, climbing through the window frame and scrambling across the sills until he jumped to the next building. He slid along the rough clay shingles until he could see the street below.

Sky joined him, her expression more curious than anything.

"It seems the distraction is continuing," he said, "and our friends are in trouble."

"What else is new?" she asked. "What's the play?"

The wheelbarrow rumbled over the cobbles, Swift's deadweight keeping it grounded as Amelia lowered her handle and Hedge raised hers, turning the whole contraption to the left as they weaved onto a new street. Amelia knew the boat was waiting for them in the docks, but a single glance back proved that they'd never make it, even with their pursuers as drunk as they were. The street widened out into a courtyard, quiet at this time of night, with roads leading off on all four sides.

"The boat is just a few more blocks down there," she gasped, pointing to the right. "You go and get them and come back for us. I'll hold them here."

"How?"

"Trust me."

Hedge, to her credit, didn't hesitate, letting Amelia take both handles of the wheelbarrow and then dashed off toward the docks. Looking back,

Amelia saw their pursuers pause in confusion for a moment. Then, after a quick, drunken debate, two of them went after Hedge and the third followed her. Perfect.

She scanned the courtyard, spotting an open gate that led into what looked like a private garden with an awning over it. With a surge of energy she pushed the wheelbarrow through the gate, slamming it shut behind her. She had enough time to park the unconscious Swift and stand in front of him before the gate burst open and a panting, red-faced, jealous drunk stumbled through.

"That's far enough," she said firmly.

"Your man," he gasped, "kissed my wife."

"There was a lot of confusion in that room," she said, keeping her voice calm. "I'm sure it was a mistake."

She could take him if she needed to, but ideally this evening could end without real violence.

He looked past her, eyeing up Swift's limp form. "No mistake. He's the only bald pasty I've ever seen. Don't even know why she wanted to kiss him."

"What?" she said, seeing an angle. "You don't think pale skin is attractive?"

She took a step toward him, brushing her torn dress to reveal a bit more of her shoulder, and just hint of the curve of her breast. His eyes were automatically drawn down, his drunken thoughts swirling.

"If it was a kiss that caused all this fuss," she said with a smile, "maybe another kiss can put it to rest."

His eyes took on a dangerous gleam. "It'd need to be more than a kiss. A lot more."

She kept her smile seductive, but inwardly she sighed. Any good man could be jealous, but no good man would cheat on his wife. This idiot had just revealed his true character.

"So," she said, "you want to see what's under my skirts?"

"For a start."

She reached down and grabbed her hem, slowly lifting it up with one hand as she reached beneath and gripped the concealed dagger with the other.

"That's close enough," boomed a new, deep voice from above.

The man's eyes jerked upward, then widened as he backed away. Amelia stole a glance over her shoulder.

Liam stood on the roof of the building, pistol out and pointed at the man. She let her hands go loose, ignoring the dagger and letting her dress fall back to her feet. The drunk ran off, and after a moment Liam lowered himself to the awning, slid along the smooth surface and dropped down beside her.

"I had him right where I wanted him," she said with a scowl.

He glanced at Swift, then gave her a wink. "You're welcome, darling."

"Did you get the info we needed?"

"I did. We need to get back to the ship and on our way, before the info goes cold." He took both handles of the wheelbarrow and leaned it toward the street. "What happened to Mason?"

"Too many admirers," she said, holding open the gate and then shutting it behind.

"I knew that would catch up to him one day."

"A problem you both have, no doubt."

She smacked him on the butt, spotting the ship's boat as it soared into the courtyard and settled down in the center. Hedge and Sky were both already aboard, she saw. Her plan had worked.

They reached the boat. Sky climbed out with the bowsman, Able Rating Hunter, to load Swift through the transparent canopy and onto one of the benches. Sky gave him a quick exam.

"Still breathing," she reported to the boat coxn, Master Rating Faith, "no blood. He's just going to sleep it off."

"I'll be happy to join him," Hedge said, rolling her shoulders and wincing. "I'm beat."

Sky frowned as she stepped out of the boat, eyes automatically scanning the deserted courtyard for threats before she sized up Amelia. "You okay, Petty Officer Virtue?"

"Fine. Just some bruises and bloody knuckles."

"You're lucky," she said quietly, glancing back to where Hedge sat in the boat. "And now Hedge is going to tell everyone on board that all our missions are just good, clean fun."

"I'll take lucky and good, clean fun any time, Chief."

"Just next time," Sky muttered, flicking a loose corner of Amelia's torn dress, "try to come up with a plan that doesn't involve you and your team taking half their clothes off."

She didn't argue – there was no point in arguing with the ship's assaulter, who had more experience than all of them put together. But who also, Amelia knew, only had one style. One brutal, effective style. After all this time together, she'd hoped that Sky might appreciate her more flexible approach to missions.

"I think Petty Officer Virtue performed brilliantly," Liam declared.

Sky gave him the ghost of a look. "Yes, sir."

The assaulter gave Amelia another once-over, then climbed into the boat.

"You know," she said, turning back to Liam, "I really was fine. You should have focused on completing the mission and getting that info transmitted to the ship."

"You're much more important to me than any mission," he said, turning fully to her.

The look in his eyes spoke the truth of his words. She both loved him and hated him for it.

"Well, I'm fine. And you got your info, thanks to my plan."

"Your plan? I'm the one who figured out that Strongback was meeting a Theropod contact of Shordar's."

"And I'm the one who ensured you had the chance to speak with him."

He gave her a strange smile, then nodded. "I suppose so."

"So next time," she said with a smile, gesturing for him to precede her into the boat, "let me execute my plan the way I want."

He regarded her for a moment, his smile softening.

"Very well."

CHAPTER 2

Liam glanced around the confined, narrow bridge of the fast cutter *Freedom*, and then up through the bridge's clear canopy, to where the glow of a thousand suns in the Hub was briefly dimmed by the silhouette of the ship they were rapidly approaching. It had been a fast run away from Sapphira, but even so it had taken more than a day to collect their passenger, and then nearly two to make this rendezvous. Meeting a ship in deep space was nothing unusual, but what they were about to attempt certainly was.

"Lord Blackwood," came a cultured voice behind him, "it is acceptable for me to observe you?"

Liam assessed *Freedom's* wide turn as the Hub fell out of view to starboard, replaced by the more scattered stars of the Halo, and decided he had a few moments. He turned to face the owner of the voice, who stood in the shadows at the rear of the bridge.

Sublieutenant Lady Julia Sungate looked every inch the Naval Academy graduate. Deep skin tones matched the noble accent expected of an officer. Her blue coat was spotless and her thick black belt was almost reflective with its shine. Her ruffled white shirt was perhaps a bit fancier than Liam would have chosen, but her crisp white trousers were without adornment, tucking into her knee-high boots that shone as much as her belt.

"Do you mean to inspect my attire," he quipped, "or my handling of the ship?"

Her large eyes sparkled in amusement, then turned downward for a moment.

"I have no doubt as to the quality of both. I simply wish to learn."

"Then by all means…" He gestured her forward to a spot on the deck just ahead of him.

She advanced with sylvan grace, nodding her thanks to him as she clasped her hands behind her back as any good cadet was taught to do.

"Are we close?" she asked. "I can't see any other ships."

"You'll learn to see them soon enough," he said, "but until then you can refer to the tactical table here." He indicated the information displayed on one of the consoles. "You can see the contact is fine on the port bow, closing on a steady bearing."

"Doesn't that mean we're going to collide?" she asked with sudden concern.

"Only if we're careless."

She stared at him for a moment, then her lips curled in a smile. "You're jesting with me."

"Just trying to get you to think."

She did, then nodded as her eyes scanned forward again. "If we're going to rendezvous, we have to close them on a steady bearing to get as near as possible… And then carefully come alongside."

"Quite right."

"Thank you, Lord Blackwood."

"Just one thing, Sungate…"

She turned back, mild curiosity lighting her serene face.

"On this ship we use military rank, not noble titles. You will address me as XO or sir."

Surprise flashed through the sparkle in her eye, but her expression shifted only into an apologetic smile.

"Of course, sir."

Liam stepped forward, separating himself from the new noble officer and giving himself a better view of the ship's masts visible beyond the canopy.

"Sailing officer," he called quietly, "how's our speed relative to target?"

Barely three paces forward of him on the cramped bridge, Sublieutenant Charlotte Brown stood over the sailing table. In the tight space even her middling height was enough to force her to stoop as the clear canopy overhead closed in above her to conform to *Freedom's* pointed bow. Brown's careful gaze flicked between monitoring the status of the sails and glances out through the canopy toward the top, port and starboard masts, ensuring the sails were properly trimmed as *Freedom* turned into the solar wind.

"Increasing, sir," she reported. "Recommend reducing to two masts for final approach."

Brown had worked for years to lose her common accent, but having just listened to Sungate's musical speech Liam's ears twitched at the thin veneer of noble pronunciation strapped onto Brown's words like loose-fitting armor.

But he offered her nothing but an encouraging smile. "Yes, please."

Liam's eyes rose again as Brown issued orders to the crew. *Freedom's* hull was narrow and built for speed, but her length allowed for towering masts that shouldered acres of sail. Here on the bridge the small crew was practically motionless, but Liam knew that sailors were even now scrambling up the port and starboard masts to haul in the sheets in preparation for stowage.

He looked out to both sides of the ship, at the port and starboard masts extended outward horizontally into space. The sails were pressed by a brisk solar wind, and he saw the first evidence of furling as the sailors worked inside the masts to bring the sheets in.

Against the darkness of the Halo it was difficult to spot their target, but a steady pattern of eclipsed stars indicated movement ahead. He lifted his telescope – there she was, as expected.

Light from the nearest stars glowed off her stubby, dusty hull still festooned with detachable cargo pods, except for a single stretch of dark brown hull awaiting *Freedom's* arrival. Her four sailing masts extended outward in a cross shape, but Liam could see that the starboard mast was bereft of sheet and was even now starting to slowly retract against the hull.

Most noble officers from the Hub would scoff at her appearance, say she was a washed-up old tub that should have stayed in the testing grounds until she finally rotted out. But she'd been Liam's home for the better part of two years and had proven her worth countless times. Out here in the Halo, this little frigate was gaining a huge reputation.

His Majesty's Sailing Ship *Daring*.

"Starboard ten," he ordered. "Sailing officer, status?"

The helm responded to his order and *Freedom's* nose drifted to the right.

"All sheets stowed on port and starboard masts," Brown replied, not looking up. "Just starting to retract port mast now."

Liam glanced left and saw the dark, empty form of the port mast as it started to move. Heavy creaking echoed throughout the ship as the huge structure folded inward.

"Midships," he ordered, "port ten."

Freedom steadied and reversed her turn, bleeding off some speed and now approaching *Daring* at a wider angle. Liam took a bearing to his target and gave the helm a new course to steer. There was a deep thump as the port mast secured against the hull, followed by new strains as the starboard mast began to retract.

"Speed?"

"Reducing, sir, but we're still gaining on *Daring* handily."

"*Freedom* really flies, doesn't she?"

Brown looked up from her sailing table long enough to flash him a proud smile. Of all the officers, she knew this captured ship the best and never missed an opportunity to take her out.

Daring's hull now dominated the view outside the bridge canopy, closing fast.

"Secure top and bottom masts," he ordered. "We'll coast from here."

"Yes, sir." Brown quietly issued more orders.

High above, Liam saw the sails of top mast begin to furl. Reports on the sailing table confirmed that the sailors inside bottom mast, three decks beneath his feet, were following suit.

"Stand by thrusters," he called out.

Freedom was slowing in relation to *Daring* as the frigate maintained her course and speed. With her own starboard and bottom masts stowed, *Daring* was struggling to remain steady, making Liam's task somewhat more challenging. The frigate wasn't considered a particularly large vessel by Naval standards, but as Liam assessed his approach he was suddenly very aware of her solid bulk, and how *Freedom's* lighter hull could easily dash itself against those robust planks. He needed to roll his ship just so to line up for docking, and get rid of her remaining speed.

"Bottom mast secure," Brown reported.

Liam gave a few quick thruster commands, and the view outside slowly spun as *Freedom* twisted to line up her lower hatches with *Daring's* cargo port. The frigate slipped beneath the canopy, and the view filled with the naked stars of deep space. Liam used the thrusters to rob *Freedom* of any last speed, and slowly, slowly, the two ships came together. Distant clanks indicated the coupling of airlocks.

"We're in position," Brown confirmed, "initial docking complete. Permission to send lines across?"

"Yes, please."

Liam stood for a moment with his hands clasped behind his back, an oasis of calm as his crew diligently performed their duties.

"You're so serene, sir," Sungate said behind him. "I thought docking two ships was a perilous undertaking."

"It's never routine," he said, turning, "but an officer's job is to make it appear so."

She nodded, a smile playing across her lips. "And if one manages a touch of panache?"

He couldn't help but smile back. "Then one gets to brag at supper."

———•———

"Liam sure does like to show off, doesn't he?"

Amelia noticed the sudden surprised glance her way and regretted her outburst. She had an officer beside her, and the captain herself was only a few paces away.

Lieutenant Mason Swift turned toward her, looking fully recovered from their adventure ashore three days past. He blocked the captain's view of her as he leaned in. "Bold words, Quartermaster…"

From where Amelia stood on *Daring's* bridge, *Freedom* was now obscured beneath the hull, but she gestured downward anyway.

"I mean," she whispered, "I'm not a ship driver like you folks, but that looked like a pretty fast approach."

"*Freedom* doesn't like to go slow," Swift said, his usually dour expression becoming almost wistful for a moment. "I reckon the XO was just trying to keep her reined in."

"Or showing off for that new, noble officer he's delivering to us."

Try as she might, Amelia couldn't shake the twinge of jealousy she felt. Not that she doubted Liam's loyalty to her, but… Maybe it wasn't that kind of jealousy. Glancing at her fellow commoner Swift, she realized he didn't look too pleased at the reminder either.

"Just what we need," she muttered almost under her breath. "Another self-important snotter."

"Well," Swift growled, "I for one am *glad* we have a new officer fresh from the Academy. Think of all the wisdom they can impart to us."

"Sarcasm," came a sudden, icy tone, "is not a tone for the bridge."

Amelia instinctively straightened as Captain Lady Sophia Riverton stepped down from her command chair and strolled over to the officer of the watch station. Tall and willowy, with dark hair and deep skin tones, she was every inch the ideal vision of the aristocrat. On her a uniform was somehow as elegant as the finest ball gown and she moved with a serene confidence. Even after all this time Amelia was a little in awe of her. She cast cool, appraising eyes over them, and Amelia felt Swift stiffen.

"His Majesty sees fit, from time to time, to send us new officers," she stated. "It is up to us to mold them into effective shipmates."

"Yes, ma'am," Swift replied.

"As the more senior officer, Lieutenant, I expect you to set the example."

"Yes, ma'am."

Riverton's gaze passed over them both again.

"But in this instance, you're correct: the executive officer brought *Freedom* alongside as best as anyone could." Her expression warmed enough to hint at a smile. "She's a fast ship and needs to be handled with respect."

"Thank you, ma'am," Swift mumbled.

"Have Sublieutenant Sungate report to my cabin after supper."

"Yes, ma'am."

Riverton glided away, pausing at the bridge's aft door as a newcomer held it open for her. She exchanged a few quiet words with the man, whom Amelia recognized as the ship's new propulsion artificer, Petty Officer Ethan Narrow.

"Oh, boy," Swift grumbled. "And now the captain's talking to my PO."

"What's wrong with that?" Amelia asked.

He let out a long, slow breath and ran a hand over his shaved head. "I don't like being away from my masts, but before he left the XO suggested it would be a good idea to let my new artificer have some space to establish his authority with the team. So I let him oversee getting our masts ready to receive *Freedom* alongside. That's why I'm hanging around up here."

"I'm familiar with how the XO makes suggestions," she said with a sympathetic smile.

"It's a good idea," Swift admitted with exasperation. "I just hate it."

"Trust," she said, "is a difficult thing to give. But it's essential."

"Yes, yes… yessss," he hissed. "Stop reminding me that the XO is always right."

She laughed. "Lord Blackwood is hardly that."

"Just most of the time."

Her humor faded into genuine affection, and she couldn't quite suppress a warm smile. "Yeah."

Her conversation complete, Captain Riverton disappeared through the aft door. Petty Officer Narrow closed it behind her and strode forward.

He was at least as tall as Liam, but with broader shoulders. Perhaps a few years older than Amelia, he moved with a powerful grace, expression set in an easy smile under a shock of brown hair. He approached with purpose, eyes dancing as he held Amelia's gaze for a moment before turning to the propulsion officer.

"Lieutenant Swift," he said, knuckling his forehead. "*Freedom's* alongside and I have the starboard and bottom masts aligned for extension, ready for your inspection, sir."

"I'm sure you've done the calculations properly, Petty Officer Narrow," Swift replied, although Amelia could hear the tension in his voice. "No need for a formal inspection."

"The lads will appreciate that, sir," Narrow replied, his voice lowering. "But if it's not too much trouble, I'd appreciate your sober second opinion. This is my first time extending masts with another ship lashed alongside, and *Daring* has some… unique aspects to her."

"That she does," Swift replied, the relief palpable in his tone. "I'll be happy to stop by once my watch is over in an hour."

"Thank you, sir." Narrow knuckled his forehead again and made as if to turn away, but then paused as he faced Amelia. "Quartermaster, are there any loading issues with *Freedom* alongside that you're worried about? It's quite a shift in mass."

Amelia was impressed that he'd thought outside his own part of the ship enough to consider that. "The re-stocking we did yesterday will help, but honestly we're so full right now there isn't much more to do. We're just going to have to sail imbalanced for a while."

"But in time you'll be able to rebalance to account for *Freedom*? I'm concerned about the stress on my masts."

"Likewise. Let's talk every few days and I'll move things around as consumables get used up."

"Thanks, much appreciated."

He offered her a lop-sided grin that offered both sincerity and the sense that they shared a secret. They were the only two petty officers on board and she was still getting used to having a true peer around her. As far as she could tell, in the few weeks since he'd joined the ship, he was a good fit to this happy crew.

With a nod to Swift, Narrow turned and strode aft. Amelia found herself wondering if he'd earned that butt through hard work, or just inherited it through good breeding.

"He seems nice," she said.

"Nice and competent aren't the same thing," Swift growled.

"That's true," she said, turning to face him fully. "I mean, you're very competent."

His brow furrowed, then a wry smile split his rugged features. "Shut up, Amelia."

"Yes, sir."

Liam was accustomed to climbing through airlock tubes when transiting between ships, so it was a welcome surprise to stand inside *Freedom's* roomy cargo hold, wait for the doors to slide open and then simply step through into one of *Daring's* cargo holds. It was like walking from one part of the same ship to another. Sungate followed to his left and Brown to his right.

"Confirm all the lines are properly secured between ships, Ms. Brown," he said, "and then start shutting down *Freedom's* systems. Keep her at two hours notice to sail."

Brown's expression brightened at those final words and with a quick acknowledgement she hurried off to her duties.

"That's kind of you," Sungate said, "to give so much responsibility to a commoner."

Ensuring they were alone, Liam stopped abruptly. Sungate matched his movement, turning smoothly toward him.

"I'm going to say this once," he said, keeping his voice calm. "There are no noble titles on this ship, and no difference between the classes. If you want to be treated with respect, *Sublieutenant* Sungate, then you must give it first. And if you want to keep it, you must earn it. If this doesn't sit well with you, I'll let go all lines and sail *Freedom* right back to the station where we picked you up."

Liam had dealt with many entitled toffs who masqueraded as officers in the Navy. Some did it because of family legacy, some for a break from the boredom of courtly life, and some – the young men especially – simply for the uniform and the right to attach a military rank to their name.

Sungate's expression stiffened in a moment of frustration. But not, Liam sensed, directed at him. She lifted her chin in a courtly gesture of reluctant submission – but then lowered it again, her features wrinkling in an odd frown. An entire drama seemed to play out on her face in barely a moment.

"My apologies, sir," she finally said. "So fresh from the Academy, one struggles to shake off the prevailing opinions of the herd."

And occasionally, Liam reminded himself, there were exceptions. Some nobles still understood their founding obligation to serve. Or at least, were open to learning how.

"You'll find this ship and her crew," he said, "very different from anything you saw at the Academy."

She kept pace as he began to walk again. "I'm very appreciative of Captain Riverton accepting me at such short notice. I'm here to serve this ship and her crew to the best of my limited ability."

It was so hard to tell when an aristocrat was actually being sincere, but Liam sensed no duplicity in Sungate. He softened his tone.

"I'm sorry to hear about the robbery in your family home. Was anyone badly hurt?"

"Thankfully, no," she replied. "My brother and his friends were knocked unconscious and tied up, as I was, but my own dear friends were allowed to flee. It seems those brutes were more interested in seizing our valuables than causing real injury."

The fact that she used the vulgar term "brutes" to describe her Theropod attackers spoke to the emotion she was suppressing. Theropods were smaller than Humans, but they were quick and vicious, and those reptilian eyes were utterly alien.

"It must have been frightening," he said.

"It all happened so fast," she admitted. "I barely had time to realize what was afoot before I was hit from behind."

He led her through into the main passageway of Three Deck, nodding at a couple of sailors who passed by.

"Then you have something in common with our sailing officer, Lieutenant Swift," he mused.

"Do I?"

Memories of the mission three days past still made him smile. Amelia's plan had been gloriously unorthodox, and Mason Swift had suffered no permanent damage except to his ego.

He gave Sungate a new smile. "We've been gathering as much info as we can on the thieves. Those brutes are led by a mastermind named Shordar, and we're hot on his trail."

"I'm grateful that His Majesty has taken such an interest in my family's troubles."

"And we're grateful to have another officer on board." He started to ascend the steep stairs up to Two Deck. "I hope you paid attention in your Academy training, because we're sailing into harm's way."

"I'm ready for anything, sir."

They stepped past a gaggle of sailors in Two Deck's main passageway, many of whom cast curious glances at the new officer. Sungate nodded politely to them all, then smiled anew at Liam as they strolled clear.

Then she stopped cold. Her eyes went wide and her hand instinctively reached for a sword that wasn't there. Liam looked ahead, spotting her source of unease.

Two reptilian forms in pale clothing padded side by side down the passageway, bodies lowered in the walking stance on powerful hind legs with long tails extended backward to balance their light frames and S-curved necks that ended in wedge-shaped heads. In their delicate hands they carried mesh nets holding neatly stacked crockery.

Liam smiled and gestured for the two Theropods to join him. As they approached in near-silence, vertically slit eyes peering at the newcomer, Liam reached back to place a reassuring hand on Sungate's shoulder.

"Sublieutenant, may I introduce Sam and Bella, *Daring's* chief cook and chief steward." His words were repeated in the snarls and hisses of the Theropod language by the translators hanging around their necks.

Sungate simply stared.

The Theropods stared back. Sam's long nose ridges were pale, indicating no alarm, and Bella lowered her smooth head as she gazed upward at the newcomer. Liam knew them well enough to sense their friendly body language, but their utter stillness could be unnerving.

"Sam and Bella," he continued, with as much reassurance as he could muster, "this is our new officer, Sublieutenant," he slowed to pronounce her name carefully, "Julia... Sungate."

Bella set down her netting and stepped forward slowly, lowering her head further to indicate no aggression.

"It is a pleasure to meet you," came the translated words, followed by her best attempt to pronounce Sungate's name, "*Joo-lee-arr.*"

Sungate's dark cheeks had paled, Liam noticed, and he kept his hand firmly on her shoulder.

"How... How nice to meet you," Sungate finally managed. Her hand began to rise as if to receive a kiss, but the movement barely started before she gripped both her hands tightly in front of her.

"Welcome to the ship," Bella said, before gathering her crockery and backing several steps away. With a nod from Liam, both Theropods swung their horizontal bodies around and retraced their long strides toward the galley.

Liam watched them disappear, and watched the friendly greetings of the sailors who passed their Theropod shipmates. When Sam's tail finally disappeared from sight, Liam gave Sungate's shoulder a gentle squeeze.

"You okay?"

"I guess I wasn't quite ready for everything, sir."

Amelia was glad that her cabinmate was absent as she packed up the last of her things. It wasn't that Chief Petty Officer Sky had ever made life in their cabin unpleasant, but even after all this time and all their adventures together, Amelia knew they'd never clicked as personalities. If Sky had been here when Amelia finally vacated, the goodbye would have been awkward at best.

Packing up her belongings had been mercifully quick, and this was the final of only three trips. Amelia took one last, careful look around the cabin, then hefted the two small satchels in one hand and reached for the ball gown hanging on the wall.

There was a quick knock on the door. Setting down her bags, she grabbed the latch and pulled.

The ship's doctor, Sublieutenant Lady Ava Templegrey, swirled into the room like it was a grand ball. Amelia had never thought of a physician's white coat as elegant, but somehow on Templegrey's noble figure it was transformed into a veritable gown. The doctor's long, blonde hair was secured efficiently in two braids tight against her head, but all that did was reveal the sleek lines of her neck. Her blue eyes lit up as she spied Amelia.

"Oh, hello, darling! I was looking for Chief Sky, but you're a delightful surprise."

"Just about to leave," Amelia sighed, gesturing at her two bags and the dress. "This is the last of it."

"What a divine frock," Templegrey said, running a hand along the smooth silk of the ball gown. It was green with gold highlights that had shimmered in the dancing lights of the ball. Amelia knew that Lady Ava was just being polite – and that she had dozens of dresses of finer quality – but Amelia still loved her gown all the same.

"Maybe I should wear it when I get to my new cabin," she said. "Appropriate attire to greet my new, noble cabinmate?"

"Something more subdued would be better," Templegrey mused, "and perhaps not silk…"

Amelia frowned, her lips curling as she saw comprehension dawn on Ava's face.

"Your dry wit fools me once again," the doctor said with a sudden smirk, batting Amelia lightly.

"Sarcasm is my only weapon," she said. "Without it I don't stand a chance in your courtly wars of words. Although I suppose I'll soon be well-practiced, what with my new, high lady cabinmate."

"Darling, you're wonderful," Templegrey said with sudden sincerity, resting both her hands on Amelia's shoulders. "Don't ever change."

Amelia suddenly realized she needed a hug, and she pulled her friend into a tight embrace.

"I guess," she sighed, "I'm just trading one kind of unfriendliness for another. Chief Sky and I didn't exactly party it up in here."

"Beer and wine are very different," Ava said into her ear, "but both can be appreciated if you have the right mindset."

"I just hope Lady Sungate is the right vintage," she said, releasing Templegrey to unhook the gown and lay it over her arm. "I hear she's from an even more noble house than yours."

"The Sungates are held in high esteem at the Imperial Court," Lady Ava said with a slight tightening of her features. "But you know that on this ship we're all equals."

"I hope she knows that."

"I'm sure Liam has explained it to her."

Amelia shrugged. "From what I saw of *Freedom's* reckless approach, I think he was too busy showing off. Lieutenant Swift says that *Freedom* always comes in fast, but…"

"Oh, I'm sure that he was showing off," Templegrey scoffed. "But he'd do that no matter who was on board. He always wants to give people a bit of a thrill."

"I just hope he doesn't mean to give our new noble officer *too* much of a thrill. I really don't want another one of you hanging off him with your courtly manoeuvres."

Templegrey's face twisted into an expression that somehow captured amusement, annoyance and sympathy all at once. She glanced down for a moment, then met Amelia's gaze again.

"Lady Sungate is here because it was the robbery of her family home that inspired our mission. She has a personal interest in our success."

"I suppose I should be impressed that she bothered to show up in person at all, and not just order us to our deaths trying to recover her family trinket."

Lady Templegrey clearly bit down her response. Then a new smile split her features.

"How was Lieutenant Swift on the bridge? I hear he left Petty Officer Narrow in charge of the masts for the docking."

"Grumpy as usual. But credit to Narrow: he did come all the way to the bridge and ask Mason to inspect his work."

"I think they'll get along just fine," Templegrey opined. "They complement each other."

"I hope so."

"And if not, I hope they sort things out in a shirtless wrestling match."

Amelia froze, staring at her noble friend in shock.

Templegrey shrugged, a new sparkle in her eyes. "What? I may not be inclined that way, but I'm not blind."

An image of Swift and Narrow, shirtless and greased for combat, flooded Amelia's mind. It was funny, but also not.

"Me neither," she admitted.

"I'm just sorry I'm going to be late for supper tonight – I'm covering Lieutenant Swift while he comes down to eat. I'll have to inspect our new lady officer afterward."

"I'm sure she's blandly perfect."

"How dull."

"Here's hoping."

"On your way then," Templegrey said, opening the cabin door and stepping clear. "Time to meet your new cabinmate."

CHAPTER 3

Amelia felt silly carrying her ball gown along the main passageway, and she ignored the smirks of the sailors over the deep green folds of the dress. She still loved the dress and couldn't wait for a chance to wear it again, but it just seemed absurd in the utilitarian confines of the ship. It was with no small relief that she reached her new cabin.

Opening the door proved quite a fight as she tried to balance the dress and the two small bags holding the last of her things. One bag slipped free of her fingers but as she moved to catch it she tripped over part of the gown's train that had dangled loose. Slamming into the bulkhead to avoid tumbling over completely, she was about to utter a most unladylike phrase when a strong hand suddenly stabilized her.

"I got you there, PO."

Amelia looked up gratefully as *Daring's* coxn, Chief Petty Officer Oliver Butcher, helped her regain her balance. The ship's senior sailor was respected and feared by the crew, but in their time together Amelia had come to view him more as a stern uncle. His weathered face was topped by close-cropped silver hair and his eyes were always assessing. But there was a kindness beneath his gruff exterior, and even his grip on her shoulder had a gentleness unexpected from such powerful hands.

"Thanks, Coxn," she said. "Could you get the door for me?"

He opened her cabin and she stepped gingerly inside, throwing everything down on the lower bunk with the rest of her gear. It frustrated her to be so disorganized, especially with her new cabinmate's imminent arrival.

Butcher leaned his head in through the door, admiring the tiny space. "Can't believe this was a storage locker when we sailed from port. Your storesies do good work."

"Thank the hullwrights," she said, running a hand along the stacked wooden bunks, the frames blotched with discoloration and fine joins. "They cut and carved these from discarded planks destined for the oven."

"The ingenuity of sailors," he marvelled.

"Sorry you had to move cabins, too. And get a cabinmate – I guess you thought you were done with those days."

He shrugged. "Chief Sky is the same rank as me. She deserves her own cabin for a while."

"At least she won't have to fight her way past my ball gown anymore," Amelia laughed, looking around at the close walls. "But I think it might be moving back to the stores office."

"Your new cabinmate will likely have her own fancy wardrobe," he said with a grimace. "You might want to save her some room in stores."

"We'll see."

Amelia understood that *Daring* was bound to get new officers eventually, and that very few graduates from the Academy were commoners like Charlotte Brown. But she was annoyed at the sudden change in cabin assignments.

"Why isn't the new officer going with Lady Templegrey?" she blurted in sudden frustration. "Me and Charlotte Brown would make better sense as cabinmates."

"It helps senior mess unity by mixing noble and commoner as much as possible," he replied carefully. "We have a unique setup here and we need to encourage a classless arrangement."

If his slow delivery hadn't tipped her off, the choice of words made it clear that Butcher, as the loyal coxn, was echoing the words of either the captain or the XO. Amelia suspected that his own opinion was something different, but if so he'd never let on.

It was a quality she knew she struggled with. Maybe living with a young, noble officer would give her a chance to exercise her professionalism. And she could start, she decided, by getting her stuff put away.

"Thanks for the help, Coxn," she said, "but I need to start unpacking my things."

"No problem," he said, retreating through the door. "If you like, I can send *my* new cabinmate to help you."

She looked up at that, but Butcher was already disappearing, a bit of a smile lightening his features. Why would she want Petty Officer Narrow to help her? Her cheeks reddened slightly at the thought of him in here, helping her stow underclothes. Banishing the thought, she pulled the first of her chests from under the bunk and emptied her two bags into it. She could fold everything later, when her cabinmate was on watch. Looking around for a place to hang her gown, she realized that this tiny cabin had almost no free bulkhead space. Ethan Narrow's broad shoulders probably wouldn't even fit in here…

She blinked away the thought and held the gown up against the door, figuring they were about the same width. If she could find a nail to hammer in, the dress could hang there for now.

A knock on the door made her jump back, and she banged her legs against the bunk. The dress fell to the deck and she cursed, rubbing her calves. The door opened, forcing her to retreat further to not get hit on the head. She tumbled back onto her bunk, wincing as her head cracked against the bulkhead.

Sprawled on her back, she looked up and saw Liam peering into the cabin. His warm eyes met hers, sparkling with amusement.

"Good afternoon, Amelia. Am I interrupting anything?"

The sight of her beloved washed away all the frustrations of the day.

His handsome face softened with affection and he held out his hand. Grabbing it, she clambered to her feet, rubbing the bump on her head. "I need someone to kiss this better…"

His eyes widened and he stepped back, pushing the door fully open. Behind him was a young officer, her face set in an expression of mild curiosity.

"Sublieutenant Julia Sungate," he announced, discreetly letting go of Amelia's hand, "may I introduce *Daring's* quartermaster, Petty Officer Amelia Virtue."

Amelia straightened her uniform, suddenly very aware of her own many failings of dress as she sized up Sungate. The officer stepped forward in her perfect uniform, smiling demurely as she lifted a hand, fingers curling down.

Amelia grabbed the hand and shook it vigorously, forcing a smile to her own lips.

"Julia, is it?" she said, just a little too loud. "Nice to meet you."

Sungate's smile barely faltered as she briefly gripped Amelia's hand in return, then released. She was taller than Amelia, eyes bright against her dark skin as she peered into the cabin.

"Thank you for sharing your cabin with me. Is the bottom bunk yours?"

"I hope that's okay."

"Of course." She turned back to Liam. "Sir, thank you for escorting me here. When can I expect my bags to arrive?"

Liam fought down a smirk, but Amelia felt her own mouth fall open.

Sungate, to her credit, picked up the cues immediately. She reached out to touch Liam's arm. "I was only jesting, sir – I'll collect my things as soon as I have a moment."

Liam squeezed out of the cabin. "There'll be plenty of time later. We don't have you scheduled for your first bridge watch until tomorrow. And supper is in a few minutes – shall we dine, ladies?"

"Thank you, sir," Amelia replied. "I'll be right there – just need to put away some clothes. Extensive wardrobes are so tiresome. Don't you agree, Julia?"

Sungate's smile was only slightly crooked. "Quite so, Amelia."

At Liam's gesture the young officer departed the cabin and they headed for the senior mess. As the door shut behind them Amelia frowned, scooped up her gown from the deck and, after a moment's consideration, tossed it on her bunk. Ava Templegrey had seemed an ice queen when they'd first met, she reminded herself. She could handle Julia Sungate.

Liam opened the door to the senior mess and invited Sungate to precede him in. It was a cozy space, with wood-lined walls giving it a warmer feel than most spaces in the ship and decorated with a few paintings that had been scavenged over the years by various officers. A built-in bar immediately to his left was already prepared with the evening's rum, and across a few strides of open space the dining table was set for supper. Bella's long form stretched out at the head of the table as she made final adjustments to the last setting.

She glanced over at the arrivals, curling her tail down to rest against her booted, three-toed feet. "Good evening *Lee-arm*," she said through her translator. "Welcome, *Joo-lee-arr*, to the senior mess. I hope you feel at home here."

"That's very kind of you," Sungate said, stepping forward with none of her former unease. "If I may ask, what curious series of events brought you to serve aboard one of His Majesty's sailing ships?"

Bella barked a laugh and began to tell the story. Liam knew it well and turned as the door opened behind him to reveal Petty Officer Ethan Narrow.

"Hey, good evening, XO," the artificer greeted with a smile.

Narrow had only joined the ship in their last port but already seemed very much at home. Liam had met many a sailor who made their way through life on good looks and charm, but already he sensed that Narrow had a lot more going for him.

"Good evening, Artificer. How did your mast supervision go today?"

"Well enough, I think," he said with a laugh as he stepped past Liam and opened the bar cabinet. "But I need a little something to rebuild my confidence. Lieutenant Swift is… sparing in his praise for my work."

Liam laughed sympathetically and grabbed the decanter of wine that Bella had already prepared. "This is our typical pre-dinner drink, Ethan. I'll certainly join you."

Liam poured three glasses of wine, handed one to Narrow and then offered the second to Sungate. The young officer accepted it with a smile but kept her attention on Bella, who was just in the process of describing how Amelia had used a sack of coffee as a deadly weapon.

"I love this story," Narrow exclaimed, moving to stand next to Sungate. She turned slightly to him and offered her hand. "Julia Sungate."

"Ethan Narrow."

He took her fingers in his and, after a moment, kissed them. Or rather, Liam thought, practically smooched them. For all his roguish charms, Narrow hadn't mastered the courtly art of manners. Sungate withdrew her hand a bit quickly, then returned her gaze to Bella. The Theropod continued her story, eventually drawing laughter from both listeners as she laid out the rest of the escapade.

Liam retreated to pour out more glasses of wine, meeting the rest of his mess mates as they trickled in for the supper hour. Sublieutenant Brown was the first to arrive, barely taking the glass before telling him all about *Freedom's* readiness to sail. Chief Butcher was close behind, downing half the glass before acknowledging the others with a nod.

"Coxn," Liam said, taking Butcher a few steps away from the others, "how did the disciplining go?"

"Without incident, sir," he said. "The two defaulters took their lashings without complaint and Dr. Templegrey assures me they'll both heal quick enough."

"Did you have Petty Officer Narrow administer the punishment?"

"No…" Chief Butcher glanced at the tall man, who was in the middle of a joke that apparently held Charlotte Brown and Julia Sungate enthralled.

"He's still new, and well-liked. I didn't want to end his honeymoon with the crew quite that soon."

Liam hated it when discipline demanded physical punishment, but it was a reality of Navy life and everyone had to buy into it.

"The sooner a senior sailor demonstrates their resolve," he said, "the sooner they're respected by the crew."

"So when is Petty Officer Virtue going to execute a set of lashings?" the coxn replied, a touch too sharply.

Liam had no answer to that, and they both knew it.

"The crew are already terrified of Chief Sky," Butcher concluded firmly. "She administered the punishment."

"Very good, Coxn."

Amelia arrived in the mess, taking a glass of wine from the bar and toasting Liam silently.

"I'll leave you to your evening, sir," Chief Butcher said.

Amelia grinned as she stepped close beside Liam.

"XO," she greeted.

"Quartermaster."

As he lifted his glass to drink, he suddenly felt a tiny hand grab his butt and squeeze. Wine dribbled down his chin as he fought down his surprise. Her giggle was drowned out by the laughter in the center of the room as Narrow finished his story.

Lieutenant Swift arrived just as the bells sounded for supper, waving off the proffered drink. "I have to go back on watch. Permission to get started eating, sir?"

"Of course."

Swift grabbed the plate at the foot of the table and helped himself to the serving dishes arranged down the center. Bella noticed and immediately excused herself from the conversation to serve him, but he waved her away.

The door opened and Liam greeted Chief Sky. The ship's assaulter took the glass of wine with a stoic expression, her gaze passing between Liam and Amelia, who still hovered close at his side.

"Thank you, sir," she said simply.

"How goes the training of the new boarding party members?"

"They're generally fit and strong, but hardly a brain among them." She took a thoughtful sip. "I can work with that."

"Are they ready for Sam to give them some Theropod training?"

She ran a calloused hand through her short hair. "No. But I'm going to get him down to help anyway. I gather we don't have much time."

"No, we don't." Liam gestured toward the table. "Let's discuss it while we eat."

At his call everyone took their seats at the table, joining Swift who was already well into his meal. Liam took his usual seat at the head, noting with interest just how much closer everyone had to sit now that there were two more permanent seats at the table. Alternating men and women seemed to be the best way to fit everyone in reasonable comfort, but as they all started reaching for servings and using their cutlery, Liam noticed a lot of subtle jostling.

As always, the wine flowed freely and the friendly banter even more so. Liam was ready to discuss the mission but he was happy to let his mess mates socialize. A happy leadership team made for a happy crew and he was pleased how both Narrow and Sungate integrated themselves – he with good humor and she with reserved charm. Swift excused himself quickly and disappeared to take back the watch. Several minutes later Templegrey arrived and squeezed in at the table's far end.

"You must be Lady Julia," she said, offering a dazzling smile as she extended her hand to Sungate at her side. "Dr. Ava Templegrey."

Sungate's expression lightened in sudden recognition and she took the doctor's hand. "Charmed to meet you, Lady Ava. The Templegreys have been sorely missed at court this past season."

"A failing my father will shortly rectify. He sails for Homeworld within the fortnight."

"How splendid! I'll send word to my brother to host him for dinner."

"How kind."

The Sungate family weren't actually high nobles, but they seemed to command wealth and influence as if they were part of the inner court. The fact that *Daring* had been ordered to recover their property wasn't lost on anyone, but no-one had expected an actual member of the family to show up in person. And although Ava's smile hadn't faltered for a moment, even Liam could sense that she'd been effectively slapped in the face twice.

He tapped his glass for everyone's attention.

"Ladies and gentlemen, I'd like to explain our mission."

All eyes turned to him. Bella discreetly served Templegrey at the end of the table and the doctor quietly ate while gazes were elsewhere.

"There is a notorious thief at loose within the Empire," Liam announced. "A Theropod named Shordar. He's been active for years and has gained a reputation for stealing only the most valuable of treasures, but his latest theft has crossed a line and has drawn His Majesty's full attention."

"Did he steal a princess's chastity belt?" Narrow quipped, to a few guffaws.

"No," Sungate said firmly, "he stole my family's most sacred heirloom: the Suncatcher."

Her quiet voice cut through any rumblings of conversation and silence fell again.

"Sorry," Narrow offered.

"We have a solid lead on Shordar's whereabouts," Liam continued, "but he rarely stays in one place for long. We're making best speed for Morassia, where we intend to recover the Suncatcher before he finds a buyer."

"What exactly is it they took from you, Julia?" Amelia asked. "This Suncatcher."

"An object of exquisite beauty," she said, lowering her eyes for a moment. Her face split in a wry smile. "I'm sure my bias is clear when I declare it the most beautiful object in the galaxy, but even the Imperial Archives record it as an ancient treasure."

"Ancient?"

She lifted her gaze to scan the entire table. "The Suncatcher is more than a thousand years old. Legend says that it was crafted by Master Goldbright himself, but in fact it was created by his apprentice, the first Lord Sungate."

"So I get that it's old," Chief Butcher said, "and no doubt beautiful. But with respect, what makes it special?"

"Master Goldbright was a legendary creator," Liam replied, "and any remaining artifact of his is considered a royal treasure. Even something made by one of his apprentices is almost priceless."

"Almost," Sungate added gravely, "but not quite. The Suncatcher will be highly sought after by many criminal collectors, and possibly even by the Sectoids themselves – simply as a trophy."

"Any foreign power who can show they have it can claim that the Empire is weak," Templegrey added. "In these troubled times, the Emperor will not abide anything that could make us look weak."

Liam scanned the table, judging the reactions of his senior crew. The two aristocrats were clearly on board with the importance of the mission, but the expressions of Brown, Narrow, Butcher and Sky were decidedly skeptical.

He looked to Amelia for help.

<hr>

Amelia caught Liam's stare and sighed inwardly. Listening to Ava and the new girl, Julia, she now had an idea why the Emperor had taken a personal interest in seeing this Suncatcher recovered. She didn't necessarily agree with His Majesty's thought process, but she knew where it would lead.

"We should do anything we can to reduce the likelihood of war," she declared. "We all know that the Sectoid threat is still looming, and don't kid yourselves into thinking that there aren't criminal factions from our own race looking for leverage. If a Theropod kingpin can tout this ancient artifact as a propaganda win, others might try to follow suit. That'll require a response from the Emperor, and most likely a show of force. Any show of force with the Sectoids massing on the border could easily lead to war. And I for one don't want to see thousands of us die in an unnecessary war."

She looked around the table, forcing herself to stare down Brown, Narrow, Butcher and even Sky.

"Catching pirates and thieves is what we do. If we can do it one more time, thousands of our fellow shipmates can keep leading their happy, wretched lives in peace."

Sky rolled her eyes and drained the rest of her wine. Butcher sighed. Brown looked thoughtful.

"Well said, Amelia," Narrow suddenly added. "I may be new here, but this ship is legendary for exactly this sort of mission. Why would they call on anyone else to do it?"

"Because we always say yes," Sky muttered.

"And so we should," Brown added, her clipped words banishing any hint of a common accent. "None of us can claim to know what's going on in the highest halls of power. If the Emperor tells us to go, we go!"

Her sudden ferocity startled everyone into silence.

"Of course we go," Butcher replied, looking around the table. "And we uphold our oaths of loyalty to the crown with honesty and integrity."

"Of course we do," Sky echoed, without enthusiasm. She gestured to Bella, who hovered near the bar. "XO, shall we do the toast?"

"Yes, please," Liam said. His expression hadn't shifted, but Amelia could just make out the subtle relaxation of his shoulders.

Bella handed down the decanter of rum and everyone took turns pouring their own glass and passing the bottle along the table. Even Sungate expertly kept the decanter in contact with the cloth, Amelia noticed.

Liam raised his glass. "Quartermaster, the toast of the day, if you please."

Amelia rose from her seat, quickly thinking of how many days it had been since they'd departed Sapphira. Realizing it was three, she smiled: this was her favorite toast.

"On this, our third day in space, I toast our loyal and hard-working sailors. Long may they serve and long may we serve them. To the crew."

The words of the toast echoed around her as everyone downed their rum. People then began excusing themselves from dinner. Butcher, Sky and Brown were gone almost immediately, and after only a few minutes of polite chatter Narrow excused himself as well.

"The captain wanted to meet you after supper, Julia," Templegrey said. "I'll take you to her cabin."

Sungate slipped her hand into Templegrey's offered elbow and the two ladies exited the mess like old friends.

Amelia watched them go, then noticed that Liam was also watching.

"Hey," she said, swatting his tunic, "eyes over here."

"Want to show me your new cabin?" he said with a sparkle in his eye.

Amelia stole a glance at Bella, who was no doubt listening but who was also one of the few people on board who knew the full extent of their romance.

She slapped Liam's butt and ran out of the mess. Slamming the door behind her she strode down the passageway with as much dignity as she could with a smirk on her face, then opened the door to her cabin. She waited just long enough to see him emerge from the mess, then stepped through into the tiny space.

He appeared at the open door, glanced both ways down the corridor, then stepped into her cabin and shut the door. In the confined space they were pressed against each other, and she luxuriated in his nearness. Wrapping both arms around his neck, she pulled him in for a passionate kiss.

"Hello, darling," he said finally. "I like your new cabin. Very intimate."

"I'm happy to make it more so," she said, keeping him close.

Pressed against him she could tell he loved the idea, and was pleased at how he was getting better at spontaneity. He kissed her again, unbuttoning her uniform coat and sliding it off her shoulders.

"But my lord," she whispered in his ear. "Lady Julia might return at any moment."

"Don't worry," he whispered back, "this won't take long."

Her laughter broke the tension, and she stepped back slightly to thump his chest. "Seriously, though, she'll be back soon. Captain Riverton will eviscerate her with a few choice words and she'll be back here, sobbing into her hankie. You need to get her on that watch rotation so she has to stay on the bridge for a solid four hours."

"Starting tomorrow, darling, I promise."

She gathered up her coat from the deck and draped it over the single chair. Her gown was still laid out on her bunk and her bags cluttered what little free space there was.

"I should probably finish unpacking. I don't think I made my new cabinmate feel welcome last time."

"Yes," he replied, eyeing her curiously. "That was a bit aggressive. *'Julia, is it?'* I think you've been taking lessons from the captain on how to insult with a smile."

She knew she was rough and unrefined, and it bothered her every time he compared her to one of the noble women on board. Even when it was meant as a compliment.

"Whatever." She pressed her head against his chest. "It's taken long enough to get used to Ava Templegrey – now I have another noble tart to break in."

His deep chuckle echoed through her.

"It's good to have you back," she said. "Can we get this mission over and done with? That lead we uncovered won't last forever."

"It only cost us a few days to break off and pick up Sungate. I'm sure that nefarious master thief is still on Morassia."

"Well then," she said, tapping his chest decisively, "let's go catch ourselves a thief."

CHAPTER 4

Amelia remembered the heat on Morassia, but she'd forgotten just how thick the humidity was. She'd picked up some lovely, practical hot-weather clothing during one of their recent port visits, adoring how lightweight the fabric was and how it flowed along her limbs. But in the hot soup of Morassia's air, it clung to her in ways most uncomfortable.

"Are you hurt?" Bella asked through her translator as they made their way through the crowded streets. "You are limping."

"Not hurt," Amelia said with a mild frown, reaching down to free the fabric between her legs, "just trying not to chafe."

"There is plenty of water in the air," Sam added on her either side. "You Humans should not add more on your skin."

"It's not by choice," she laughed, charmed by the simple truths of her Theropod friends.

The Theropods were both dressed in drab, brown and green outfits, blending easily into the sea of reptilian forms around them. Morassia was the only world where significant populations of Humans and Theropods mixed freely, and no-one glanced twice at the three of them. She glanced back once to ensure that Liam was still behind them with Swift in tow, but otherwise left them to keep up as she pushed her way through the throng.

Morassia had several large settlements, each one indistinguishable to Amelia's eyes. There were no large civic structures, no ancient monuments or grand palaces – just block after block of low buildings, usually dried mud or stone, with colorful stalls blocking the frontages as less-reputable merchants hawked wares from all over the galaxy. Most of it was innocuous enough, and some possibly even legitimate, but rumors always swirled of fabulous treasures to be had, if one knew where to look.

Amelia didn't know where to look, and nor did her Theropod friends. But Captain Riverton, it seemed, had connections everywhere. She'd received an update just that morning that the elusive master thief Shordar was still in town and possibly open for business.

"This is the street," Sam said, pointing to the left with his nose.

"I see *Harr-perr*," Bella added, neck extended fully upright to give her a better view of the crowd.

Amelia scanned the sea of Theropods lowered in the walking stance and the Human figures that stretched above. There, loitering in the shadows of a yellow and white-striped awning next to carts of fruit, stood *Daring's* assaulter, Chief Petty Officer Harper Sky. She leaned against the cool pillar of an archway, powerful form never quite looking relaxed as she kept watch. Meeting Amelia's gaze even from thirty paces away, she stood up from the wall and strolled out into the crowd.

They met by the large well in the center of the intersection, mingling with locals lining up to draw water. Amelia stood nearly as high as Sky's nose, but the older woman dwarfed her in every way. Her bare arms were like steel rope wrapped in sandpaper, body thick and powerful under a pale, padded tunic. A translator hung from a cord around her shoulders. Sweat trickled down from her hair but she seemed unaffected by the heat as she greeted them all with a glance.

"Shordar isn't there," she said without preamble. "But his lackeys are.

If we can convince them we're serious about buying from him, they'll arrange a meeting."

"Smart of him to stay hidden," Liam said.

"Staying hidden is our natural way," Sam replied.

Amelia looked down at Sam's powerful form, open-toed sandals allowing his hind claws free access if necessary. Theropods were originally ambush predators, she'd heard, and they knew how to disappear. She looked around at her team, considering her assets as she weighed the options.

"What's the plan, sir?" Sky asked.

"It's Amelia's plan today," Liam replied.

She appreciated that he'd agreed to let her devise every aspect of this mission on her own, but did he have to sound like such a condescending fop when he said that? Sky frowned as well, but probably not for the same reason. The assaulter folded her arms and looked at Amelia expectantly.

"Okay," Amelia said, "I'll take Sam and Bella with me up front. It makes sense for me to have them available as translators, and they can read the Theropod body language. I'll wear your translator."

She gestured to Sky, who removed the device and handed it over. Amelia draped it around her own neck, under her pony-tail. The device weighed little, but the pressure of the rope was uncomfortable against her raw skin.

You three," she indicated her fellow Humans, "can stand in the back and look mean. If I'm some kind of buyer, or even the representative of one, it makes sense that I travel with a guard."

All eyes went to Liam. It irked her, but they'd all done enough cloak and dagger missions together that even she had to admit that he was an expert. The fact that he was also the ranking officer mattered, too. Amelia found that she needed to keep reminding herself of that – having enjoyed a couple of months away from the ship after their last mission, she was used to just thinking of him as 'Liam' and not as 'Commander Blackwood'.

"Are you clear on your fake identity?" he asked. "And why you want the Suncatcher?"

They had all debated at some length about who they should present themselves as. They couldn't admit that they were in the Navy, but there was no hiding the fact that *Daring* had visited this world before and had been involved in more than one adventure likely to have earned them notice. In the end, it had been with some irony that they'd concocted a near-truth that might actually fly.

"I am," she said in her best imitation of the noble accent, "Lady Amelia Silverhawk."

"Don't use the accent," Liam said with an eyeroll. "You sound like you've been hit in the head too many times."

"Any woman willing to accept that title would have to be a few jugs short of a barrel," she retorted, dropping the poncy voice.

"They will not know the difference between accents anyway," Sam interjected.

"Let us speak to them first," Bella said. "It would be strange if you did."

"My local agents establishing their role?" she said with a smile. "And securing their commission?"

"Yes."

"Okay, let's do this," she said, loud enough for everyone to hear. It wasn't exactly the sort of inspiring words of command Liam might utter, but she'd never pretended to be something other than she was.

The street was crowded with Humans and Theropods going about their days, mostly with eyes down and strides quick. There were a few glances at Amelia's flowing clothes but other than the standard hails from the merchants no-one seemed to pay much attention to her little group.

"Open door on the left," Sky muttered by her ear, "just past the blue and white awning. That's where they're hanging out. I assess at least four of them."

Amelia followed Sam and Bella as they slipped through the crowd, watching the dark opening of a single wooden door hanging off the plastered white surface of the building. There was an open window to the left, with a space cleared of any stalls to give it a bit of frontage on the street.

"A dive bar?" she asked.

"More a private lounge," Sky replied. "Our presence will be immediately noticed."

"And challenged?"

"Likely."

Sam disappeared through the door, Bella right behind him. Amelia kept pace, but forced her shoulders to relax as she passed through the opening.

Her senses were assailed by the sudden heat, the smell of scaly skin and sour liquid, and the sudden rush of tiny movements all around that fell silent. Her eyes scanned the dim room, the only light coming from the window to her right. Shadows danced as her Human companions walked through the door behind her. Sam and Bella advanced several paces then paused, rising into the resting stance as their heads darted left and right, assessing.

The room was a bit bigger than *Daring's* senior mess, with small round tables spread across the rough floor. On the far wall was a shabby bar with something that looked like kegs mounted behind it. One Theropod hunkered behind the bar, conversation with another brute obviously interrupted by the newcomers. Two others crouched on stools around one of the tables, and one more stood in the corner by the window, oiling the massive blade strapped to its tail.

No, Amelia corrected herself – *his* tail. The ridges on the noses of all these Theropods indicated that they were male. Those ridges had shades of red coursing through them, she saw, indicating a sudden heightening of tension.

"Hail the heat of the sun," Sam said in his own language, the translator echoing his words. "We come to do business."

All heads snapped to the Theropod standing on the near side of the bar. He didn't move, other than to raise his central hind claw and strike the floor slowly.

Tap. Tap.

One of the seated brutes raised his neck, meeting Sam's gaze as he spoke.

"We're not interested," he said, taking a slow sip from the long straw protruding from his cup.

"Shordar will be."

"Who?"

"Shordar. Your leader."

"Never heard of him."

Sam's nose crests flared and he stepped back to lower into a ready stance. On Amelia's other side, Bella suddenly did likewise.

Both seated Theropods pushed off from their stools, long tails stretching out as they flattened their bodies, lips curling back to reveal razor teeth. The brute with the tailsword shifted his weight but didn't lower his stance.

Behind her, Amelia heard her Human friends slowly spread out to fill the room. She suspected their hands were moving toward weapons. Bella had warned her that this sort of display was normal between Theropods, but she could feel her heart racing.

"Friends," she said loudly and slowly, the translator picking up her words, "we are here to buy something. We have money."

"We have nothing to sell," the brute facing Sam replied.

"Just a Suncatcher."

The room remain frozen in a tense tableau. Then the Theropod at the bar raised his claw.

Tap-tap. Tap.

Bella's head tipped toward Amelia just enough for her closest eye to meet the Human's gaze. She winked, indicating progress. Amelia took a step forward, staring down both Theropods before her. A show of dominance, Sam had told her, was necessary to establish the relationship. This was going to be tricky, but she knew she could do it.

This was going nowhere, Liam thought, hands clasped on his belt next to his hip holsters. Maybe Sky had found the wrong gang. He surveyed the room again, assessing the best escape route if things went sideways. The brute with the tailsword was the most obvious threat, but who knew what weapons were hiding behind that bar.

As Amelia stepped forward, Liam watched the two nearest Theropods lower in their stances, powerful legs coiled to spring. He knew that she now had to make a show of dominance, but questioned again why he'd let her lead this negotiation. She was the smallest Human in the room, and quite frankly the least intimidating by pretty much any measure. He chided himself for letting her take the most vulnerable position. He knew she felt she had something to prove with this mission, but getting herself killed wouldn't prove anything.

Glancing left and right to where Swift and Sky held their positions, he knew they were ready. Raising his own shoulders, he made himself as big as possible and shuffled to get a better view of Amelia's opponents.

The brute facing Amelia snapped his jaw at her, hissing. Amelia bent her knees and raised her fists.

"Back off," she said, shuffling forward another step.

On the right side of the room, the brute with the tailsword took a single step, blade lifting slightly off the ground. In front of Amelia, the two brutes held their ground, beady eyes watching her every movement. At the bar, neither Theropod had shifted, but their gazes missed nothing.

Amelia shuffled forward again. The first brute matched her, crouching lower even as he raised his head to be level with hers. Sam and Bella both raised their heads, hissing. The brute's head flicked left and right, then slowly lowered as he glared at Amelia.

Liam checked the tailsword-wielder. He'd taken another step forward and the blade was higher. Sky was watching the giant sword, but her body was still turned toward Amelia and the stand-off.

Amelia unclenched one of her fists, her fingers crossing the open space between her and Theropod until the tips nearly touched his nose. Liam felt his pulse quicken, and moved his hands along his belt.

Teeth flashed as the brute bit Amelia's hand. She suppressed a cry of pain as she yanked her hand back, blood splashing with the movement.

Liam's pistols were in his hands before he even registered.

All Theropod eyes flicked to him, then motion erupted everywhere.

The tailsword was suddenly swinging. Sky leapt clear but staggered and fell as the blade skidded off her leg. Amelia tumbled back as one of the brutes pounced on her, claws from all four limbs tearing at her. Sam threw himself onto the attacker as Bella leapt forward and grappled the other brute at the table. Swift dove into the fray, grabbing limbs as Amelia desperately defended herself.

Liam's right pistol was up and he emptied his bullets into the tailsword brute. The creature collapsed backward. Liam couldn't fire at Amelia's attacker as the scene degenerated into a mass of limbs, fists and claws. Beyond, the two Theropods at the bar were already running for what must be a rear exit. Liam fired at them, bullets smashing through the barrels and spraying dark liquid.

"I will follow!" Sam shouted, leaping over the toppled tables to pursue.

Swift managed to pull Amelia's attacker clear, but the brute's rear claws still ripped into her legs.

Liam drew his long, ceremonial dagger and charged forward. Amelia was down, her clothes shredded and dark with blood. The brute screamed as it raked Swift with his foreclaws, hind talons slashing at air as it fell backward. Liam stomped his foot down on the brute's nearest leg, pinning it, as Swift fell forward to hold back its jaws. The Theropod's chest was exposed as it wriggled desperately. Liam didn't hesitate. His jewelled blade plunged into the brute's heart. Its limp form sagged on the floor and went still.

Bella had the other brute down, but there was too much blood to see who was winning. Swift kicked downward to pin the brute's head, giving Bella a moment's advantage. Her own jaws clasped down on her opponent's neck. There was a savage tear and the brute went limp beneath her.

"Follow Sam," Liam ordered Swift. "We'll get everyone back!"

Bella was already tearing fabric from her dead enemy's clothing and pressing it against the worst of Amelia's wounds. Liam turned to Sky, who was conscious but pale as she grimaced up at him and held a long, ugly slash down her leg.

"Bastard," she muttered. Blood poured through her fingers.

Liam tore off his shirt and wrapped it around her leg, tying the sleeves as tightly as he could above the wound. The thin material was soaked through in seconds, but Sky had removed her belt and cinched it above his sleeves to cut off the circulation.

Bella helped a barely lucid Amelia to her feet. Amelia's legs were wrapped in multiple rags and her loose outfit was shredded and sodden from the assault. Both her eyes were blackening and she could barely focus as Liam lifted her arm around his shoulders.

"Come on, darling," he whispered. "We have to walk."

"A mistake," she mumbled. Her eyes rolled back and she sagged against him.

He scooped her up into his arms, gaze turning to Bella. "Are you healthy?"

"Yes," she said, sliding past him to help Sky.

Sky shook off Bella's attempts to support her, but her right leg could barely hold weight. Her eyes were hard as she stared down Liam through short, sharp breaths. "Let's get out of here."

Without waiting for Liam, Sky drew one of her pistols and limped through the door. Liam hustled after her and Bella brought up the rear. The assaulter simply pushed past anyone who got in her way, and many eyes lingered on Liam as he carried the unconscious Amelia through the crowd. One brute tried to peer closer, but backed off at Bella's defensive hiss.

It was an exhausting hike through the crowd. Liam blinked sweat from his eyes as he concentrated on putting one foot in front of the other, keeping pace with the limping Sky across the market and down the main road to the docks. When the long jetties finally came into view, Bella dashed ahead.

"I will get help," she called back.

Minutes later she returned with the boat's crew, Faith and Hunter. The big boat coxn took Amelia from Liam's leaden arms while the bowsman wrapped Sky's arm over his shoulders and took her weight. The assaulter grumbled but didn't resist, and together they made it quickly back to the boat.

As they were loading up, Liam heard running down the jetty and turned to see Swift. Red-faced and drenched in sweat, the propulsor ran up and lay a hand on Liam's shoulder. Between gasps, he managed to report.

"Sam and I think we've found the gang's real hideout. He's staying to watch until we can return."

"Is he hiding?" Bella asked.

"Yes."

"Good." She climbed into the boat. "He will be safe."

"I'm going to do a wider recce," Swift said. "Find out if there are any more surprises."

Liam reached into the boat and grabbed one of the portable radios, handing it to Swift. "Call if anything goes wrong. Stay safe."

Swift nodded, accepting the radio. He turned and walked with purpose down the jetty, still breathing hard.

Liam untied the boat and climbed in, signalling for Faith to take them home. Hunter was already pressing fresh bandages to Sky's wound. Amelia lay motionless, most of her clothing stained red.

"Full thrusters," Liam ordered. "Get us back to the ship."

The boat shifted as Faith pointed her upward and pushed the throttles open. Liam grabbed the radio and hailed *Daring*. He recognized Dr. Templegrey's voice on the other end.

"Get Brown up to relieve you on the bridge," he said. "And meet us at the airlock with full medical support."

"Are the wounds life-threatening?" came Templegrey's calm reply.

Liam looked down at Sky, who snarled in pain as she squeezed her own leg. Her face was white, her eyes glassy.

And Amelia wasn't moving.

"Yes. Life-threatening."

CHAPTER 5

Amelia's world was reduced to two things: pain and weight. Pain lanced through her body, everywhere and nowhere specific. Weight pressed down on her, constricted her, trapped her. She couldn't see or hear anything, or even guess what was happening. There was just the pain. And the weight.

Panic welled up, but she fought against it. For a moment she thought she was back on Passagia, just a kid who'd fallen into a pond. Nightmare images of being pulled down into the murky waters by the bulk of her basket flooded her mind. She tried to move her limbs, to swim and kick her way upward. She shook her shoulders to help the basket slip away, knowing that if she took even the tiniest breath her lungs would fill with water and she'd die. She shifted again, trying to lose the weight even as she swam upward.

Breathe.

It was all she wanted to do, but she knew she mustn't. A faint glow appeared ahead of her – the surface! She steered toward it, forcing sluggish limbs into motion. Her legs were leaden, her arms thrashing desperately. A distant roar grew in her ears, the rush of water around her, pressing on her.

Breathe.

Her lungs were on fire, but she dared not use them. Not until she reached the light. Her arms flailed, her legs useless as they trailed behind her.

"Come on, darling, breathe."

The woman's voice was faint, almost otherworldly. Amelia's limbs were exhausted, but she had to get to the light. She fought upward through the water, the way she had when was just a little girl. Who loaded little girls with heavy baskets so close to ponds, anyway?

"Please, Amelia, breathe."

And since when did people on Passagia speak in noble accents?

She gasped for breath, feeling the cool, blessed relief of air in her lungs. The weight constructing her suddenly lifted, and her ears filled with the sounds of voices and machinery.

She opened her eyes, blinking against the harsh lights. A mask lifted off her face and the shadow of a person moved into view. She couldn't see the face, but the light from behind made the blonde hair glow like an aurora.

"That's it, darling," Dr. Ava Templegrey said with relief, "just breathe. You're safe, back on the ship."

Amelia realized she was lying on a bed in sickbay. Templegrey hovered close, her professional expression melting into a friendly smile. One bed over Chief Sky was on her back, mostly covered in a sheet as Master Rating Song applied dressing to her exposed leg. The assaulter was conscious, but pale as she stared upward blankly at the deckhead. The rest of the small medical team busied themselves around the room.

"Where's Liam?" Amelia asked, surprised at the effort to do so.

"He's briefing the captain," Templegrey replied, giving her hand a little squeeze. "He's fine."

"Sam and Bella? Mason?"

"Bella's with the XO. Sam is still on the surface. Lieutenant Swift is returning in the boat as we speak." Amelia felt the squeeze of her hand again. "Everyone is okay, Amelia. Just relax."

She looked around again, gripping Templegrey's hand to test her own extremities. She could wiggle her toes, but her legs didn't want to move.

"My legs…"

"Are still there," Templegrey said, "but I've immobilized them because the slash wounds need to knit and if you start moving around they'll just start bleeding again."

Lifting her head, Amelia confirmed that her body was intact. Bandages wrapped around most of her legs and much of her torso. Even the slightest pressure stung, adding to the overall ache from her shoulders to her ankles. She lifted her free hand to touch the cloth over her breasts.

"You're going to have some impressive scars," Templegrey said with a touch of amusement, "but yes, they're both still in one piece."

"I guess my new outfit is ruined…"

The doctor nodded toward a bucket of bloody rags. "I'll get you something nice when we're next at Emperor's Reach."

"No big loss – they were starting to chafe, anyway." She looked down again. She was covered in so many bandages they were practically a full set of clothes. "Theropods aren't precision killers, are they?"

Templegrey sat down on the edge of the bed, professional gaze scanning the damage. "I think your attacker panicked, and just started slashing at whatever he could reach. You have about two dozen slice wounds, but most of the upper ones are superficial – lots of surface blood so they look nasty, but nothing I'm worried about. The brute's hind claws did carve a few deep trenches in your legs… But we got you back in time. I've been giving you new blood for an hour, now."

"Don't take it all," Sky suddenly growled from the next bed. "I might need some."

"Chief Sky," Templegrey added, raising her voice slightly, "took a tailsword to the leg. It thankfully didn't cut deep, but rather scraped along her thigh."

"Bastard carved off a steak," Sky quipped. "I doubt I taste good."

"You're both going to be staying here for a while," the doctor said firmly. "No more adventures until you can each walk without a limp."

"I'll be up by the dog watch," Sky said.

Templegrey rolled her eyes and turned back to Amelia. "You, too, darling.

Just relax and let your body heal."

Amelia nodded, in no mood to fight the doctor's orders. As her mind cleared, though, she started replaying the events on the surface. How had they misjudged the scene so badly?

"You're generally very good at this," Captain Riverton said, leaning forward in her chair. "So explain to me why this mission failed so completely."

Liam kept his expression neutral, fighting down the old anger. Riverton might be good at diplomatic engagements, but she clearly didn't understand the chaos inherent in street-level negotiations. They stared at each other for a moment across the table in the captain's cabin.

"We misread the Theropods," he said finally. "We thought their actions were just posturing, but then one of them attacked Petty Officer Virtue."

Riverton's eyes narrowed slightly at the mention of Amelia's name. She turned her gaze to the Theropod crouching at Liam's side.

"Bella, your thoughts?"

Bella's head pivoted between the two Humans, her alien eyes unreadable. She blinked several times, then cocked her head as she turned to Riverton.

"My people are always unpredictable. I thought negotiations were going well, but then suddenly everything changed."

"Why?" Riverton asked.

The question hung in the cabin for a long time. Liam was still sorting through the sequence of events and Bella had offered little commentary since their return.

The silence was interrupted by a sharp knock at the door. At Riverton's call, the door opened and Swift stepped inside, covered in grime and dust.

"Captain," he greeted, saluting. "We've found the main hideout."

"Where is Sam?" Bella asked.

"He's stayed on the surface to observe. He has the boat radio."

"Do you know if Shordar is at the hideout?" Riverton asked.

Swift took a slow breath. "We don't know for sure, ma'am, but there's a fast sloop moored outside. Common thugs don't usually have that sort of ride just hanging around."

"And he may not stick around after this incident," Riverton added. "We have to move quickly."

"Yes, ma'am," Liam said, mind already racing. "I recommend we take *Freedom* and the entire boarding party as backup."

"His Majesty's Navy," she retorted, "does not simply sail down to a free city and start shooting at private citizens. We need to know that Shordar is there."

"As you said, ma'am, there's no time. We'll go in force but leave the bulk of the team in reserve. We can try negotiations one more time, and in so doing discover whether Shordar is there in person or not."

"Bella," Riverton said, switching her gaze, "will negotiations have any chance of success after the last encounter?"

"Yes. My people are always looking to make money. And grudges are rarely held."

"And do Humans hold grudges, Commander Blackwood?"

He was surprised at the question, and at her sudden icy stare. "No, ma'am. It's all about the mission."

Riverton nodded. "Then assemble your team and proceed."

Liam rose, following Swift and Bella out of the captain's cabin.

Once in the corridor, Bella suddenly swirled around, her head rising to stare up at Liam.

"I like you, *Lee-arm*," she said, "so I did not speak in front of your captain. Those negotiations failed because you drew your pistols. That crossed a line and said that we were treacherous."

"Why? They had a tailsword in motion."

"It was not. And you used a faraway weapon. Shows of dominance always – always – used close-in weapons. You were stupid."

Before Liam could reply, Bella spun around and stalked off.

Liam stared at Swift, who stood in grim silence. The anger on his face was clear. The two of them had done countless shore operations over the years and had seen many of them go less than according to plan. They'd endured injuries, loss and even capture. But never, ever, had they turned on each other. But something in Swift's expression said that today was different.

Liam opened his own cabin door and gestured for Swift to enter. The propulsor stepped through and Liam shut the door behind him.

"Speak your mind, Mason."

Swift pursed his lips, clearing considering his words as he took a long, tight breath.

"Bella's right," he said finally. "When two groups are posturing with each other, it's all just a show… until real weapons are drawn."

"That brute attacked Amelia," Liam retorted hotly. "They crossed the line first."

"It was the Theropod equivalent of a slap in the face," Swift snapped. "It wasn't a real attack."

Liam considered his reply, but before he could speak Swift suddenly shouted in his face.

"And you *know* that!"

Liam was stunned into silence. For all his grumpiness, Swift had never lost his temper in Liam's presence.

A long silence held in the cabin, broken only by Swift's eventual sigh.

"Sir, I've seen you talk your way past Humans, Theropods, Sectoids and even Aquans. You know the ways of our enemies… But as soon as Amelia is threatened, you lose all restraint."

The accusation hit Liam like a slap. "How dare you…"

Swift glared at him, not backing down.

"Mason," Liam said carefully, "I care for all of my sailors, and I take their safety seriously."

"But you also recognize that there's risk whenever we go into a situation. You accept that risk for yourself, and for each one of us. Except Amelia. And that makes you a liability."

"I think you overstate your case."

"The situation today was still under control," Swift pressed on, "and would likely have worked its way to us being taken to Shordar. But then you drew your pistols as soon as Amelia was threatened, and all hell broke loose. And now-"

Liam held up his hand, his own anger growing. "Okay, I get it…"

"And now," Swift snapped, swatting Liam's hand away, "we have to start all over, and two of our best sailors are lying in sickbay with serious wounds."

Liam's hand stung, and he wanted to punch Swift in the face. But through his frustration he glimpsed the truth in his friend's words. He looked away, clasping his hands behind him.

"Sam took off in pursuit of the gang members," Swift pressed, "and Bella didn't drop everything to chase after him. She knew that her place was with us, fighting the brutes still in front of us. Her mate ran off alone into danger and she let him – because it was the right thing for the mission."

Swift stepped back in the small cabin, fighting down his anger.

"And Bella is just a civilian who chooses to work with a people not even her own," he concluded. "You are a professional Naval officer."

Liam clenched his fists at his side. "What are you saying, Lieutenant Swift?"

"Sir," he said finally, "you're the best there is at surface missions. But your protectiveness of Amelia is a danger to us all."

Liam replayed those critical moments in his mind, reliving the sudden fury he'd felt as Amelia cried out in pain. In that instant he'd truly believed that they were all in danger, but as he reconsidered he realized that no other Theropod had attacked. Indeed, no-one had moved until his pistols were up and pointed.

"I made a mistake," he admitted.

"I often tell the crew that you're always right," Swift said quietly. "But you aren't."

The simple words cut deep. But Liam couldn't deny them.

"So," Liam said finally, "I should just remove Amelia from our landing team? She's invaluable."

"I don't know, sir. That's something you need to think about. And maybe discuss with the captain."

Admitting weakness to Riverton was still anathema to Liam, and this topic in particular was fraught with peril. The captain knew about his relationship with Amelia and had quietly turned a blind eye all this time. But she tolerated it only because it hadn't created any complications.

Complications. They were the death knell for military discipline, and it seemed he was the only officer on board unable to avoid them.

"Thank you, Mason. I'll consider your words."

"Yes, sir."

Liam opened the cabin door. "Gather the boarding party and get replacements for Sky and Virtue. I'll prep *Freedom* for departure."

Swift slipped past him and through the door. "Yes, sir. Anyone in particular you want as replacements?"

His thoughts were still in chaos, and he shook his head.

"Bella suggested we bring the biggest people we have," Swift offered, "to help with intimidation."

"The coxn, then, if we want to intimidate. And perhaps that new sailing artificer of yours."

Swift nodded curtly.

Liam shut the door. He stood alone for a moment, then leaned against the soft wooden surface as his body finally let go of the tension. He had a lot to consider.

But now wasn't the time. First, he had a mission to complete. Allowing himself a deep breath, he straightened, assumed the stern expression of the executive officer of HMSS *Daring*, and opened the door.

Amelia could hear the quiet hum of sickbay around her, but kept her eyes closed as she tried to doze off. Templegrey had given her a dose of poppied rum to ease the pain, and now that her body merely ached she knew the best thing to do was just sleep it off and wake up when she was healed. But amid the quiet voices and shuffling movements, she heard a distinct set of sharp footsteps that abruptly stopped. And she felt a distinct presence.

Opening her eyes, she saw Julia Sungate staring at her. The young noble's gaze moved up and down her form, and she blinked as she realized Amelia was staring back at her.

"Oh, Petty Officer Virtue," she whispered, stepping closer. "I'm so sorry."

Amelia doubted the sincerity of any words uttered by a noble she didn't know, but in the moment she appreciated them nonetheless. She tried to nod but it was little more than a dip of the eyelids.

Sungate clasped her hands together in a show of concern. "Lady Ava – Dr. Templegrey – tells me that you'll be fine."

"It looks worse than it is," Templegrey said, sidling up to Sungate. "Chief Sky is merely sleeping it off and Amelia is made of tough stuff. They'll both be back on their feet in no time."

"Still," Sungate said, turning fully to Templegrey, "I hate to see such injuries in the name of recovering my family's treasure."

"This Shordar is a first-class rogue who has wronged many families," Templegrey replied smoothly. "His capture is His Majesty's priority and we are all pleased to serve."

"I'm honored that our captain deigned to include me in the hunt. I hope to earn my place here."

"Captain Lady Riverton is an officer of the highest order, and demands the same from all of us."

"I'm certain you will outrank me soon enough, Lady Ava."

Templegrey glanced at the sublieutenant symbol on her shoulders. "On this ship we are pleased merely to serve. Our reputations mean more than rank."

"Then I'm certain your reputation is one to aspire to."

Amelia had grown used to Ava Templegrey's courtly manner, but to see two young aristocrats interacting was quite something. As their conversation moved smoothly away into a more general discussion of Imperial affairs, both women smiled and gestured with a sense of affable confidence clearly designed to both disarm and assert control. It was something to watch, and Amelia tried to guess when the first of them would make physical contact with the other. Liam and Ava touched each other so often Amelia had actually once thought they were an item, but had eventually learned that flirting was just part of the noble game. Knowing what she did about Ava's romantic preferences, Amelia wondered if courtly manners allowed for…

Templegrey gave Sungate's arm a squeeze as she laughed, her brilliant blue eyes alight. Sungate's face melted into a warm smile, her own hand brushing over Ava's as she turned toward the door to regard the man just now entering sickbay.

"Good afternoon, Petty Officer Narrow," Templegrey said, dropping her hand from Sungate.

Amelia's gaze flicked over, drinking in the sight of Ethan Narrow. His face and hands were streaked with grime and he'd clearly abandoned his uniform coat some time ago. His smudged, white shirt clung to his broad chest, muscles rippling as he hastily wiped his hands on his trousers.

"Doctor," he greeted, nodding next to Sungate, "ma'am. I just heard that we took wounded. Is there anything I can do?"

Templegrey stepped forward, eyeing him up and down. "I had no idea you were hiding medical skills amongst your many talents. Would you care to assist me in a double amputation of Petty Officer Virtue's legs?"

"What?" he cried.

"What?" Amelia blurted.

Templegrey's laughter rang through sickbay and she rested a hand lightly against Narrow's chest, turning amused eyes to Amelia.

"Oh, both your faces!" She stepped back and moved to sit on the edge of Amelia's bed. "Fear not, dear friends; there are no body parts being removed today."

"A bit of a cruel jape, Lady Ava," Sungate said with a smirk.

"One develops a gallows humor in my line of work, Lady Julia," she said, giving Amelia a wink. She then patted the bed. "Come over, Artificer – come and see that both my patients are on the road to recovery."

Amelia felt herself blushing as Narrow's gaze met hers. She was fully covered in a sheet over her many bandages, but even so she imagined that her figure was rather visible. Narrow kept his eyes on hers as he approached, though, clearly respecting her modesty.

"How are you feeling?" he asked.

"Wrapped up tight and relaxed with rum," she said as airily as she could.

He leaned his hand on the bed and lowered himself, keeping a respectful distance. "Can I get you anything, Amelia? A book, some food, or coffee?"

She considered, not really knowing what she needed.

He seemed to misinterpret her silence. "Is it all right if I call you Amelia?"

His sudden bashfulness was endearing.

"Of course, Ethan. We're all messmates and, hopefully one day, friends." She nodded toward the two noble officers who were chatting once again. "In the mess, her ladyship is just 'Ava'. Although it took a while."

"I don't know if I'll ever get there," he said with a lopsided grin.

"I didn't either. But you'll figure out soon enough that the nobles are just people."

He scoffed in a show of disbelief, but didn't argue.

Their attention suddenly shifted as the jostle of armor filled the door to sickbay. Chief Butcher's broad form was encased in a charcoal breastplate and from beneath his helmet he scanned the room until he spotted Narrow.

"Artificer, we're returning to the surface in strength. You're needed for the landing party."

"I also wish to go," Sungate declared.

"No, ma'am," Butcher replied. "You'll be staying aboard *Daring*."

"This is my family's treasure," she insisted, glaring with new intensity at the coxn. "I will be there for its recovery."

"That's exactly why you're staying put, ma'am." Butcher's voice was soft, but everyone in sickbay could heard the hard finality behind it. "This is tricky business, and the last thing we need is someone with a personal interest messing things up."

His eyes flicked quickly to Amelia before snapping back to Sungate. Was he sending her a message?

"I understand," Sungate said with obvious reluctance.

"There will be many more missions," Templegrey offered quietly.

"Narrow," Butcher snapped, "let's go."

The artificer gave Amelia once last glance, his lips curling up in a tiny grin, then he rose and followed Butcher out of sickbay. Sungate said brief farewells to Templegrey and then followed.

Amelia closed her eyes, suddenly exhausted. So the mission was continuing, even without her and Sky. It made sense, and no doubt Butcher and Narrow would do well in their places.

But what had Butcher's glance meant?

Amelia's ruminations faded as she drifted off to sleep.

CHAPTER 6

Liam gripped the side of the officer of the watch console as the atmosphere buffeted *Freedom* once again. With her solar sails stowed she was like a bullet in the air, plummeting toward the surface with only thrusters to fight the pull of Morassia's gravity. By stellar standards she was a small vessel, but she was easily one of the biggest ships capable of crossing the threshold from space. Through the bridge canopy tiny flames licked over the nose as the gases thickened around the ship and compressed. A steady roar rumbled through the hull, matching the shudder of the deck.

At his side, Charlotte Brown hung onto the console, her eyes darting between the few readings on the sailing table that meant anything. All of *Freedom's* sailing ability was battened down – the thickening air would rip masts and sheets clean off – and Brown's job was comparable to steering a cannonball onto target.

"Forward thrusters, half power!" she shouted over the racket.

Master Rating Atticus Flatrock repeated the order from the helm position, his burly form struggling to maintain control as he released one hand from the helm to push two of the throttles. *Freedom's* hull rippled as she changed vectors. The nose tipped up, shifting the brunt of the compressed air against the bottom of the hull.

"Speed over the ground dropping," Liam reported calmly, keeping watch on the critical gauges as Brown checked her thruster fuel status. "We're moving into the lower air."

"All thrusters, full power!"

As Flatrock let loose all six thrusters, *Freedom's* deck jolted violently. Liam staggered, but clawed his way back to Brown's side.

"Reduce thrust," he said.

"But we have to slow our descent," she said, hanging on as the ship lurched again.

"Do it gradually," he said, "we still have the time and space."

"All thrusters, half power!"

Flatrock obeyed and the shuddering diminished. *Freedom* was still descending, but it was less a plummet and more a glide. "Navigation, how's our course?"

Swift had a land chart – or "map" – spread out on the table to starboard.

"We're on course for intercept," he reported.

"We're a little high," Liam suggested. "But we can still afford to shed speed."

Brown considered for barely a second. "Stern thrusters, three-quarters power!"

The extra thrust dipped the nose slightly, increasing *Freedom's* rate of descent while also bleeding off additional speed. Liam gave Brown a reassuring nod, then stepped forward to survey the scene ahead.

The green and brown landscape below was growing in detail. Liam's eyes traced the lazy blue line of the river visible on the port side until it crossed into the city and started to turn brown. There was a sharp turn in the waterway, and inside that turn there was a broad white shape that he knew to be a large house. Lifting his telescope, he confirmed that there was a sloop tied alongside the tower that rose up from the central dome. Shordar was likely still in residence.

The deck shook again as Brown adjusted her thrusters. The view of Shordar's compound descended from view for several moments, then reappeared as *Freedom's* nose dipped again. Wispy white clouds flashed by as the ship turned to point toward the city.

"We're at a safe speed, sir," Brown reported. "I'm starting my final approach."

"Very good," he replied, setting down his telescope and motioning for Swift to follow him. "We'll board the boat."

"Don't grab all the loot before we get there, sir," Flatrock called from his seat.

"This is an exchange, Master Rating," he called back. "Don't put your grubby fingers anywhere near our chests of gold before we hand them over."

"Wouldn't dream of it, sir."

Liam climbed down through the hatch at the aft end of the bridge, descending the ladder to *Freedom's* main deck below. Swift was close behind him and Liam ducked as he moved forward along the ship's central passageway. The main accommodations aft were large and luxurious, but everything forward was tight and efficient. Built for speed and luxury, this cutter could hold barely a quarter of *Daring's* crew. With a skeleton sailing team under Brown's command, the entire boarding party under Swift's command plus Liam's own negotiating team, there was little room to spare. As Liam and Swift descended another ladder to the lower deck, they were greeted by a packed crowd of armored sailors.

Chief Butcher towered over the seated sailors, keen eyes surveying their gear and weapons. As Liam approached, Butcher steadied one of the padded back-plates on a sailor and reefed on the leather strap. The plate pressed snugly into the sailor's body.

"Comfort is not the goal, people," the coxn boomed. "Keeping you alive *is*."

In the middle of the crowd, Mia Hedge sat on a large chest, her feet resting on a smaller one. She looked very different from when Liam had last seen her, practically falling out of her dress in that tavern on Sapphira. Now she was bundled up in the same padded armor she'd picked up on their first mission, numerous hacks and shreds revealing how many times it had saved her. Her helmet was split by an obvious weld line, and wisps of blonde hair peeked out from beneath. She grinned up at Liam.

"I like my new chair, sir."

"Don't get too comfortable," he replied with a smile. "If all goes well, we'll be trading that today."

"For something better, I hope."

"Much better."

"Ready, sir?" Chief Butcher asked.

Liam had never seen him in armor before, as his role of coxn always kept him on the ship. But the craftsmanship of his breastplate revealed both good taste and a sense for the practical. Liam had grown to rely on Chief Sky at his side, but if the assaulter couldn't be there, the coxn was a good substitute.

"Ready, Coxn." He made eye contact with Bella and Petty Officer Narrow. "Negotiating team, board the boat."

As they climbed through the narrow airlock, Liam turned back to Swift.

"After the second pass, loiter close and be ready to land. I don't want them to expect any treachery on our part."

"Yes, sir." Swift suddenly extended his hand. "Fair winds, sir."

Liam clasped his friend's hand firmly. "Following rays, Lieutenant."

Liam climbed through the airlock, crawling down the cylindrical tube. He missed the zero-gravity that usually allowed for easy passage: his weapons hung awkwardly on his belt and the padded armor plates hiding under his civilian clothes were heavy and bulky. But with minimal fuss he emerged into the boat, clambering up onto the edge of a seat as Hunter reached past him to shut the hatch. The transparent top of the boat revealed the Morassian landscape far below and the wind howled against the hull. The boat had no artificial gravity and everyone hung on where they could while Hunter decoupled from *Freedom*.

The boat lurched as it fell free. Liam wrapped both arms around the back of a chair and gasped as the boat spiralled downward. The air roared against the hull as the blue of the sky interchanged with the colors of the ground. Liam heard the firm hissing of thrusters and the spinning slowed. The boat finally settled out into a level course and descended toward the city. *Freedom's* dark form was already diminishing ahead, still descending as Brown aimed for a low pass over Shordar's compound.

Liam settled himself in a seat next to Butcher, sensing Bella's head peering between their shoulders. Narrow sat forward next to Hunter, watching the landscape rush by beneath them. *Freedom's* distant hull levelled out, rocketing over the city.

The radio crackled with the excited growls of a Theropod. Liam glanced at Bella.

"That is Sam," she replied. Liam grabbed the microphone and held it up to her mouth. She spoke into it.

"Yes," her translator squawked, "that was *Free-dorm*. We are coming in the boat and will land soon. Are the gang members responding to *Free-dorm*?"

Sam's snarls and barks sounded through the boat.

"Yes," Bella reported, "the ship's pass created thunder, and everyone is running outside to see."

"Good," Liam said. "That will get their attention."

"Let's hope Sublieutenant Brown can time her next one just right," Butcher added.

"Sam is staying where he is," Bella said. "He will join us when we land."

"Tell him that *Freedom* will do another pass just as we land."

Bella's lips curled back in what might have been a smile, except Liam knew it was a sign of menace. But her eyes were focused on the large white residence that the boat even now descended toward.

"We will make a good show of force," she said.

The boat cruised over the rooftops at a brisk speed.

"Compound is approaching, sir," Hunter reported from the bow. "Do you want to do a sail past to survey the place first?"

Liam grabbed the radio. "*Freedom*, this is *Rapier*: how long until you pass over again?"

"*This is* Freedom," Brown replied. "*Estimate two minutes.*"

"This is *Rapier*: proceed. We're starting our landing now." He glanced back to Faith, who nodded.

The boat banked as Faith fired thrusters to start a turn, then dropped as he killed their speed. Liam watched as the white house with the moored sloop loomed ahead. The boat floated over the white outer walls and he saw a half-dozen Theropods watching from the compound. His eyes were drawn to sudden movement as Sam scrambled up that wall, hunkering down as the boat settled to land. As soon as the boat touched down, Sam leaped down from the wall.

Butcher unlatched the side door and climbed out, hands on weapons. Bella was a second behind him, lowering into a ready stance as her head snapped around to survey each Theropod in the compound. Sam loped over to Butcher's other side. Narrow squeezed his bulk through the boat door and took position beside Sam. The compound was surrounded on three sides by the human-height wall, the fourth side dominated by the white house. A large portico stretched away from the central structure, mostly dark in the shadow of the sloop moored overhead.

"Rapier *this is* Freedom," Brown's voice echoed, "*on final approach.*"

Liam rose from his seat and made a show of leisurely stepping out of the boat, slipping a translator around his neck.

"Stand outside the boat," he ordered Faith and Hunter. "Look mean, but do not draw weapons unless the coxn or I order it."

He stepped out, breathing in the hot, fetid air. Just as he straightened to his full height, the air began to shake as a distant rumble grew quickly into a roar. A moment later, *Freedom* flashed overhead in a wave of thunder, stern thrusters blasting. The Theropods in the compound all ducked their heads, teeth flashing as they shifted uncomfortably.

"Hail the heat of the sun," Bella greeted their reluctant hosts, her voice almost lost in the dying echoes of *Freedom's* wake. "We are here to conclude our friendly business."

The Theropods shuffled uncertainly, heads snapping back and forth as they sought direction. There was movement in the shadows of the portico, but in the bright sunshine Liam couldn't make out details. Then a Theropod voice rang out, the translator around Liam's neck crackling to life.

"Then let the light of all the moons shine upon our good fortune."

Bella turned her head, winking at Liam.

Liam remained motionless. He sensed Butcher's tension beside him. Narrow shifted his weight and rolled his shoulders expectantly. Both men were in full armor, looking every bit the bodyguards, and as Liam felt the alien eyes focused on him all around the compound, he suddenly wished for his own breastplate. But the expensive tunic and fashionable trousers he wore proclaimed that he was here to talk, not fight. He shifted the weight of the pads protecting vital points on his arms and torso, ensuring they were hidden beneath the fine clothes.

"Let me demonstrate our resolve, sir," Narrow growled.

"Steady, gents," he whispered. "We're here to negotiate."

"Aye, sir," Narrow muttered.

"We'll follow your lead, sir," said Butcher.

"Bella, Sam?"

Sam gestured for them to advance toward the portico, then trotted forward ahead of them. Liam moved to follow, keeping his hands empty even as they brushed across his sword and pistols. Butcher fell in beside him, a step behind, as his breastplate clinked softly against his belt. Narrow lumbered up on Liam's other side, scabbard thumping awkwardly against his padded armor. Bella's sandaled feet padded along at the rear.

Two Theropods emerged from the shadows beneath the portico, both unarmed and unarmored. They took up positions on either side of the opening, lowering into ready positions as Sam approached. Sam slowed to a halt, tail swishing slowly as he eyed both of them. They shifted their feet but otherwise remained still.

Seeing no signal from Sam to stop, Liam continued his easy stride forward.

"At least three more in the shadows ahead," Butcher said quietly.

"And a dozen around us," Narrow added, "including four new ones on the wall."

Liam barely nodded. He resisted the urge to look around, instead keeping his expression and movements carefully neutral. He and his fellow Humans towered over the Theropods, and he was confident *Freedom's* show of force had seized everyone's attention. Planting his feet next to Sam's, he waited.

An eddy of wind carried a whiff of foul air and a swirl of dust. Liam took his lead from Sam and remained motionless. For a long moment the compound was frozen in tableau.

A single Theropod stepped forward from beneath the portico. Clearly bigger than the others, his crests were flushed red and he strode forward with menacing power. He stopped half-way to Liam, lowering into a ready stance and bearing his teeth. All around him, the other Theropods growled.

"You must assert dominance," Sam whispered.

Liam looked left and right, keeping his movements casual. Narrow shifted his weight as if to step forward, but Liam snapped out a hand to still him.

"Let me take him, sir."

"This will not take me long," Liam said, loud enough for the translator to pick up his words.

Liam strode forward, locking eyes with the Theropod. The brute lowered his body, hind claws raising, even as his head and neck lifted in challenge. Liam kept his pace steady, watching for any movement. Then, at barely four strides, he suddenly burst into a run.

"I'll crush you!" he roared, raising both his fists to strike.

The Theropod roared back. The translation was lost as the brute reared back and snapped his jaws forward, teeth snapping down on Liam's left forearm.

Except Liam's forearm was no longer there as he flicked it up and out of the way. His right fist slammed into the Theropod's skull, right below the eye. The brute's head rebounded from the blow, teeth sinking into Liam's fist before he could withdraw it. Pain seared through his knuckles but his left fist slammed down from the other side, this time directly into the brute's eye.

The pressure eased as the Theropod's jaw released, and he shuffled back. His injured eye blinked continuously, and a snarl escaped his lips.

"Nice move, ape," came the dutiful translation.

"I won't go so easy next time, brute," Liam snarled back.

The Theropod stepped back, tilting his head toward the portico. Nothing visible moved, but Liam heard a distinct sound as claw smacked against stone.

Tap-tap... Tap-tap.

The big Theropod gave him one last look, then loped off to take a position in the ring of guards.

Then, from the shadows, a pair of female Theropods trotted into the sunshine, each carrying a stool. They set them down at a distance apart roughly the length of a Theropod in the walking stance and stepped to each side, lowering their heads. Another pair of females emerged, each carrying a low, circular table that was placed next to a stool. A third pair of females walked into view with trays of refreshments that were rested on the tables. And finally, four young males jogged out through the doors, each carry a thin pole supporting a wide, light canvas between them. The Theropods stopped in a square and planted their poles, the colorful canvas stretching out overhead to create a shaded area over the tables and stools.

Liam heard the padding of feet behind and glanced back to see Sam approaching him.

Sam nodded for Liam to step forward. "Approach the stool, but do not sit until your host does."

Liam walked forward into the shade, allowing himself the freedom to glance around once before fixing his eyes on the portico. He could just make out the stone tiles of the floor, and the dark arch of a doorway leading into the house. From that archway a Theropod emerged, moving into the sunlight with long, steady strides. Sunlight seemed to glitter off his deep green skin, and as he lifted his eyes they sparkled with a piercing iridescence. Liam couldn't help but stare for a moment, and his reaction seemed to earn him a respectful nod as the Theropod ordered his guards to step back.

All the Theropods obligingly retreated, and Liam looked over his shoulder at Sam. Sam's hands lifted up and his tiny fingers gestured backward, even as he shuffled back a few steps.

"Give us some room," Liam called back to Butcher and Narrow.

Both Humans retreated a pace, flanked by Bella and Sam. Beyond them, Faith and Hunter stood by the boat. Hunter made a show of lifting the boat's radio microphone to his lips. *Freedom* was nearby, and Liam glanced upward before locking gazes with his host once again.

"Master Shordar, I presume?"

"I am honored to be known to your kind," the Theropod said, gliding over one of the stools and resting his weight upon it. "Please bring similar honor to my kind."

"I am Lord Liam Silverhawk," he replied.

If he was going to lie about his identity, he might as well do it in style. Even after all this time the brazen attack on a Human high lord was well-remembered on this world.

Shordar let out a long, hissing breath. "My condolences on the insult to your clan. I assure you: no-one in my clan or service was responsible."

"I know."

"Did you ever catch the culprits?"

"No. But the hunt continues." He sat down. "If you have any information to offer, my family will pay handsomely."

"I will turn my attention to helping you, *Seel-var-hok*. Avenging the honor of a clan-mate is the highest calling."

"Thank you."

Shordar took his drink and sipped from the straw. "Please, refresh yourself on this hot day."

Liam picked up the glass and looked carefully at the contents. The clear liquid had no odd smell.

"It is simple water," Shordar said with a bark that Liam knew to be laugh. "You think I would poison my guest?"

Liam sipped the straw, appreciating the cool wetness against his tongue. He let out a contented sigh. "I was merely hoping for something stronger."

Shordar barked again. "Usually I wait until the sun sets."

Several quips came to Liam's mind, but he doubted any of them would survive translation. He merely nodded and took another sip before replacing the glass.

"I understand," Shordar said, "that your clan has grown in power and influence."

Shordar selected a piece of meat from his tray and popped it in his mouth. He swallowed it whole and then turned his polite gaze back to Liam.

"My clan is one of the greatest among Humans," Liam continued, "and we wish to become even greater. You can help me with that today."

"What would a humble Theropod have that would interest your mighty clan?"

"A particular work of art. A classic piece of both historic and cultural value. It was originally created by a member of my clan but was stolen by a rival clan many years ago. My clan wishes to thank you both for stealing it from them, and for safely returning it to us."

"Who says I have done either of those things?"

"Do not be modest, Master Shordar. Your exploits are legendary across all cultures."

The Theropod suddenly looked past Liam, then lifted his fingers to beckon. Liam heard the familiar padding of feet as Bella trotted to his side.

"Tell me, pretty one," Shordar said, "does this Human speak with good faith?"

"He does," she replied. "Or else you will have to get in line to rip out his throat."

Shordar barked another laugh. He waved his hand in dismissal. Bella winked at Liam and retreated.

"What is it you seek, my honored guest?"

"I'm sure your clan-mates have already told you what I seek. The Suncatcher."

"Those clan-mates of mine who lived to tell the tale," Shordar said, his lips opening to reveal a flash of teeth. "I lost three of them today."

"As did I," Liam said, gesturing vaguely back toward his crew. "I had to bring new friends to this meeting. I believe we're even on that score."

Shordar considered, then waved his hand again as if dismissing the thought.

"How did you find my home?" he asked.

Liam pointed up at the sloop berthed above them. "You are far from subtle, Master Shordar."

"It is hard to be so, when one is becoming a legend."

"Sell me the Suncatcher," Liam said, leaning forward, "and I will help you move unnoticed through Human space."

"I have yet to name a price, and already you sweeten the deal."

"I have yet to agree to any sum of gold, but I have many things to offer."

"I prefer gold."

"Then you can have it. Name your price."

"Assuming I even have this Suncatcher. Perhaps you confuse me with another Theropod."

"Then if so," Liam said as he rose, "I thank you for your hospitality."

"Sit, sit," Shordar said, waving him back onto the stool. "I see you are no fool. Very well. Let us talk truth. I will gladly sell you the Suncatcher for… thirty thousand of your Human gold coins." He lifted another piece of meat, then paused. "Plus another twenty thousand for returning it to your clan."

It was an absurd amount of money, worth more than *Freedom* herself. And certainly more than what was carried in the two chests aboard the ship circling overhead. But it was also just the first offer.

"I think perhaps you are still coming to appreciate the benefits of aligning with the Silverhawk family," Liam said. "We can get you access to the highest halls of Human influence, where you can find the greatest treasures our species has created. I'll consider the Suncatcher a token of our new arrangement, and I will immediately get you inside the royal vaults on Honoria. All I ask is ten percent of the value of anything you free from those vaults."

"I always appreciate an offer of mutual benefit," Shordar purred, "but such a relationship works only with trust. And we have yet to establish that."

He sipped his water.

"I will step out in trust and remove my fee for returning the Suncatcher to you. All you have to do is lay thirty-five thousand gold at my feet, and the treasure is yours. After that, we can discuss working together."

"You said thirty thousand."

"I find my attachment to the Suncatcher's beauty has grown."

"As a gesture of our new friendship," Liam said carefully, "I will offer you ten thousand gold… Plus another five for the loss of your clan-mates."

"Five thousand each."

"Less as much for my lost clan-mates."

Shordar sniffed. He took a sip of water and glanced up at the sky.

"Twenty thousand, and we trade ships as a sign of our new friendship. My sloop, *Emerald Crown*, for that magnificent vessel that has twice roared overhead."

"Fifteen thousand, and I'll let you use *Freedom* for your visit to Honoria, under my supervision."

"The first stirring of trust between us." Shordar raised his cup. "To honor that, I'll bring you the Suncatcher for only twenty thousand, plus the use of your ship at Honoria."

Liam knew he had fifteen thousand gold under Able Rating Hedge's butt, and the other five under her feet. The promise to use *Freedom* for another raid would be the perfect chance to bring this rogue to justice.

"Agreed, Master Shordar. Just bring the Suncatcher out to the courtyard and I'll bring *Freedom* in to land. Your gold is aboard."

"Splendid." Shordar emptied his drink. Liam raised his own and took as long a sip as he could.

Shordar rose from his stool and gave orders to his people. Liam also stood and moved a few steps into the sunlight, motioning his own crew around him.

"The deal is made," he said. "Signal *Freedom* to land and be ready to bring out the twenty thousand once the Suncatcher is clearly in the courtyard."

"Yes, sir," Butcher replied before retreating to the boat.

"Do you trust these brutes?" Narrow whispered.

Liam turned off his translator. "No, but I trust their desire to walk away with twenty thousand gold coins. They're a lot easier to spend than an ancient family heirloom."

"I've heard that Shordar doesn't sell many of his prizes. He genuinely appreciates them and keeps them in a private collection somewhere."

"I doubt a Theropod has any appreciation for Human treasure. He just knows how much we appreciate them – and how much we'll pay for them."

Narrow nodded, his eyes scanning the relaxed Theropods still filling the courtyard. "As you say, sir. But I'll still be ready for anything."

"Very wise, Petty Officer Narrow."

Shordar walked leisurely past the ring of his supporters, speaking quietly with each one as he passed. As he approached Sam and Bella, Liam casually made his way over, flicking on his translator again.

Sam inched closer to his mate as Shordar neared. Bella gave his neck a quick rub.

"And who is it who brought this mighty Human clan to my doorstep?" Shordar asked, head weaving as he surveyed them both.

"We were hired by them off-world," Sam said, "to make introductions."

"I don't believe we've met before." Shordar looked them both up and down, appraising.

"We've worked several sectors," Bella said, her gaze dropping slightly, "and have heard of your many exploits. We were curious to meet you."

Shordar bowed his head, fixing Bella with a steady gaze. "I hope that I live up to the stories."

"You do indeed."

Sam also bowed his head. Bella dipped hers before giving Sam's neck another rub.

Shordar assessed them both, eyes bright. "Perhaps we can all work together another time. I always need good partners."

"Perhaps, Shordar," Sam said.

"We appreciate your offer," Bella added.

Butcher walked over to Liam, keeping a respectful distance away from Shordar.

"Sir, ship's inbound."

"Master Shordar," Liam called out, "*Freedom* will be here shortly. I look forward to gazing upon my clan's ancient treasure."

"It is being brought out immediately," Shordar replied. "It will warm my blood to see it returned to its rightful owner."

A distant rumble deepened the air, and as Liam looked up the sleek, bullet-like shape of *Freedom* moved slowly over the nearby buildings. Thrusters fired as she maneuvered closer, until she was holding position right above the compound. Liam sensed Narrow at his side, the bigger man watching the Theropods even as Liam watched the ship. Butcher hurried over with the radio and handed it to Liam.

"*Freedom*, this is Lord Silverhawk," he said smoothly. "Prepare the gold and please land as soon as our prize is brought out to the courtyard."

At Brown's curt reply, Liam handed back the radio and nodded politely to Shordar. The Theropod nodded in return, flicking his chin to an underling who ran under the portico and into the house. Moments later, four Theropods emerged. They were lowered in the walking stance, each one supporting a crossbar with their crooked forearms. The crossbars supported a small platform, and nestled on that platform was a golden bowl wide enough that Liam doubted he could wrap his arms around it. The jewel-encrusted gold was exquisitely formed into swirling patterns and ancient symbols and scenes. It was clearly the work of a master.

Servants rushed to clear the tables and stools out of the way as the Suncatcher was carried under the awning, only to emerge again in the sunlight.

For a moment, Liam forgot all about his mission. He suddenly understood why the Emperor himself had taken an interest in getting this artifact back into Human hands. It was, Liam realized, perhaps the most beautiful object he'd ever seen.

"You appreciate it," Shordar said, sidling up next to him. The Theropod's eyes gleamed, and this close Liam could see the cunning intelligence behind them.

"As I hope you appreciate the twenty thousand gold coins I'm about to present you."

"For certain," Shordar said, backing away in the Theropod version of a bow.

At Liam's nod, Butcher ordered *Freedom* to land. The cutter was just too big to fit into the compound, but Brown managed to lower her until the hull was touching the tops of the wall – barely a man's height above the ground.

A single door opened, and a scramble net fell down. Swift climbed down, adjusting his weapons belt as his feet touched dirt. He met Liam's gaze, then scanned the area. Finally, he signalled upward. Hedge appeared at the door, having rigged a simple pulley, and she hooked on the smaller chest. As it lowered to the ground, Liam made an inviting gesture to Shordar.

"Would you care to inspect the gold?"

Shordar held his ground. "I prefer to gaze upon the magnificence of the Suncatcher one last time. One of my people will collect the gold."

Liam nodded, and gestured for Swift to open the first chest. The large Theropod who had challenged Liam loped forward, lowering his head to snuffle about in the gold. He twisted his head back toward Shordar.

"There is only five thousand or so in here."

Liam had anticipated Shordar's questioning stare and he turned with an apologetic look. "I wanted to show you some of our gold to prove my honesty. Before we bring down the rest, I ask that the Suncatcher be brought closer to my ship."

"Of course." Shordar motioned for his four litter bearers to bring the artifact another ten paces closer. The Suncatcher gleamed in the brilliant daylight about half-way between the awning and the ship's shadow.

Liam surveyed the scene. There were perhaps a dozen Theropods in the compound, forming a loose circle around the Humans at five to ten paces distant. Liam had seven allies on the ground with him, including Sam and Bella, plus an entire boarding team inside *Freedom*. It was too early to declare victory, but he finally allowed himself a glimmer of hope that they might pull this off without bloodshed. He signalled to Hedge. She began to lower the second, larger chest.

"It has been a pleasure to meet you," Shordar said with another bow. "I look forward to raiding Honoria aboard your ship."

He cleared to several paces away, and at his signal the Suncatcher was lowered to the ground. The four Theropods backed away from their burden, heads low. Liam motioned for Butcher, Narrow and Swift to join him – the four of them could hustle the Suncatcher to the ship in moments.

The Suncatcher was larger than he'd expected, and as he stepped close enough to touch it, Liam's eyes moved hungrily across the detailed scenes of ancient heroism wrought in the gold surface, swirling lines and shapes catching them up like dreams. The Morassian sky was hazy and diffused the sunlight, but even so the Suncatcher lived up to its name: a dazzling, almost mesmerizing artefact. Around him, Butcher, Narrow and Swift all took their places at the support poles, each eyeing up the treasure with barely concealed awe.

The second chest from *Freedom* hit the ground and the big Theropod flicked the latch open to confirm the wealth inside. He nosed through the coins, spilling a few on the ground, then lifted his head to stare intently at Shordar.

"It's all there," he roared.

"Victory!" Shordar shouted, and the Theropods all around the compound roared in what Liam guessed was a response his translator couldn't pick up.

Shordar turned toward the portico, shouting again and receiving another roar in reply. He shouted a third time…

And dozens of Theropods charged forward from inside the house, tailswords swinging.

Amid the shouts of surprise around him, Liam simply cursed.

"Stars and damnation."

Sword already sliding free, he drew his left pistol and started firing.

CHAPTER 7

His pistol cracked five times. Three brutes staggered and fell, but too many tailswords still bore down on him. Stepping away from the Suncatcher to cover Narrow's flank, Liam slammed his empty pistol back into its holster and raised his saber, shuffling back as the reptilian charge descended upon him.

The first tailsword clanged against his blade, the ring of metal matching the shudder down his arm as he held off the blow. As the first Theropod pulled back another swung into the attack, and Liam barely shifted his sword to defend again. Beside him, Narrow held his cutlass up in pure defence, both hands gripping the hilt as he blocked the mighty blows.

Liam side-stepped a low, upswinging attack, feeling the rush of air as a brute took another swing at Narrow. The Theropods had the power, but they needed space to swing those tails, and as Liam and Narrow backed against the Suncatcher itself, the fighting got very close.

Which was exactly how Liam preferred it.

Parrying another heavy attack, Liam deflected the brute's entire tail down toward the ground, unbalancing his attacker. He stomped his left foot on the sword and hacked to his right, his blade slicing into the exposed tail of the latest attacker pushing Narrow back. Blood sprayed as he cut to the bone, and his saber wrenched free to swing inside the tail of the next brute in the line. Liam cut the beast at the neck, blade slicing clean through flesh and out the other side to block another heavy blow.

Narrow danced back, clutching his left arm as blood trickled through his fingers. His lips were twisted in pain but he kept his sword up.

Liam stepped forward, swinging his blade simply to put the Theropod attackers on the back foot. In the close quarters his wild attacks did no damage but gave them a moment's reprieve.

"Still with me, Artificer?"

Narrow stepped forward, new determination in his eyes even as his left sleeve dripped red.

"Ready, sir."

They hacked their way forward as their smaller, quicker blades danced past the giant tailswords, finally gaining open ground. The Theropods roared new challenges and curses at them, but seemed content to fall back and protect their wounded. Several paces away, Swift and Butcher had also fought free. All around the compound, Theropods were running and diving for cover as Hedge and the boarding party rained down musket balls from *Freedom*'s open door.

Just below *Freedom*'s hull, the big Theropod who had challenged Liam looked up, his long nose twitching as he assessed the scene above. He paused in a crouch, then leapt upward clear through *Freedom*'s door. All firing stopped as shouts of alarm mixed with shrieks and roars inside the ship.

Gasping for breath, Liam gave Narrow a quick glance. The artificer nodded, his face streaked with sweat and blood. Beyond, Swift and Butcher were both on their feet. A quick scan confirmed Sam and Bella were hunkered down at the ship's boat with Hunter and Faith. For a moment, he thought Shordar's goons had made a tactical mistake and failed to use their superior numbers to isolate and overwhelm the Humans.

But then he saw the four litter bearers scamper through the crowd of tailswords, and watched as the Suncatcher rose in the center of the pack and began to retreat. They hadn't cared about him or his people – they just wanted the treasure. As one, the armed Theropods spread out in a defensive wall as the four litter bearers hustled toward the portico.

Liam drew his right pistol and took careful aim. The awning's nearest pole shattered, the canvas collapsing on the bearers. The Suncatcher disappeared in a tumble of fabric, all progress momentarily halted. Snarls and hisses rose like wildfire from the retreating Theropods, and Liam emptied his pistol's remaining rounds into the nearest brutes.

"Attack!" he ordered. "Recover the Suncatcher!"

Liam ran forward, saber raised. Narrow was close behind him, Swift and Butcher steps away. Liam glanced back and saw Hunter and Faith taking up the charge as well, as Bella frantically grabbed a tailsword from the boat for Sam.

The brutes were distracted trying to free their prize and its carriers, and barely saw the Humans rush toward them. Knowing Theropods were easily panicked, Liam hacked down as fast as he could, screaming in feigned fury. The others followed his lead and swung crazily, adding deep battle cries to the close-in chaos.

As expected, the Theropods fled the attack, falling back toward the portico. Liam bashed his sword pommel into anything that moved beneath the awning. The four Theropods trapped beneath desperately clawed their way free, abandoning their prize as they limped away. For a long moment, the courtyard was still. Perhaps a dozen Theropods stared from the portico as half a dozen Humans gathered around the tattered awning still draped over the Suncatcher.

A series of sharp roars focused the Theropods. Liam's translator was hacked away and lying in the dirt somewhere behind him, but he sensed a rallying cry. The brute line parted as Shordar emerged, a gorgeous tailsword extending down his armored body. He slapped a crested helmet over his eyes and roared again.

He staggered back as a bullet pinged off his breastplate. Liam stole a look over his shoulder and saw Flatrock holding a smoking rifle. He shuffled aside as Hedge pushed the big Theropod's limp, lifeless body forward. It fell heavily, awkwardly, hitting the ground with a hard crunch.

Shordar roared again, raising his tailsword. His followers did likewise, murder in their eyes.

"Get back to the ship," Liam ordered, already stepping away from the reptilian horde.

The Theropods raced forward with inhuman speed. Liam pushed Narrow back behind the rumpled awning for cover, raising his sword as shots whizzed over his head from *Freedom*. He looked back again and saw Hedge riding the pulley rope down to the ground, more sailors lining up behind to follow her.

Then the Theropods arrived, tailswords lashing down with new fury. Liam blocked and parried, stepping back as he tried to hold the flank. Shordar himself led the charge, close enough for Liam to see the serrations along his massive blade. Shordar slammed down against Swift's sword, knocking the propulsor to his knees with the force. Butcher was there in an instant, shouldering Shordar back before hacking down another brute coming in from the side.

Liam ducked under a tailsword swing and stabbed straight ahead, skewering one opponent. He leaned into the thrust and grabbed the dying Theropod's tail, using their combined momentum to push the tail into the next brute on the line. The blow didn't land, but it knocked the Theropod back enough to give Liam space. Ripping his saber free he danced away from another big tail swing, then cleared to the outside.

The Humans had naturally formed a line to defend, each man watching the flank of his mate, and the initial Theropod surge had been a tight push against that wall. But mere moments into the renewed battle all structure was falling away as brutes darted and apes swung. It was a melee of the most vicious kind and Liam used his sudden distance to assess. More of *Freedom*'s crew were racing into the battle and the numbers were tipping against the Theropods.

To his left, Liam saw the awning finally being ripped clear as the four litter bearers doggedly worked at their task to free to Suncatcher. Liam ran toward them, saber up, but barely caught a flash of steel in the corner of his eye.

Swinging his sword in defence he clanged against the serrated edge of Shordar's massive weapon. Both blade and armor gleamed as the Theropod sidestepped Liam's counter stroke. The big sword reared again, and again Liam barely blocked its titanic force.

"You are a most ungracious guest," Shordar's translator said, the words almost comically calm as the Theropod hissed and snarled.

"You are a very rude host," Liam countered, leaning left to avoid a blow.

His saber struck down on Shordar's tail, but armored scales wrapped the thick limb and his blow skittered free. Shordar stepped clear, tail retreating for another attack.

Then the brute lunged forward with his arms, daggers gleaming in each. Liam hissed as one of the blades sliced through the gaps in the padded armor beneath his shirt, felt the burn of torn flesh and the heat of flowing blood. He spun to clear the range, bringing up his saber to block the tail swing he knew was coming. He dropped to his knees to get under the swing, feeling the rush of air as the serrations whisked over his head. His deflection unbalanced Shordar and Liam was already back up on his feet, saber slashing down at the break between Shordar's breastplate and skirt armor.

Shordar roared in pain, daggers flashing up again in defence as he backed away.

Liam could feel the hot, sticky blood seeping down his shoulder and could only hope that his own strike to his foe was drawing blood more quickly.

"It is a shame, *Seel-var-hok*," Shordar said, continuing to retreat, "that we couldn't actually be allies. You fight with courage."

"Then why betray me?" Liam asked.

"There are some treasures too precious to give up. The Suncatcher is one."

"Then why even have this discussion?"

If Theropods could shrug, Shordar did so. "You offered me twenty thousand gold and your ship. It was worth a gamble."

Before Liam could reply, Shordar bolted for the portico. The Suncatcher was just disappearing into the house. Overhead, Liam could hear the preparations for *Emerald Crown's* imminent departure. Those Theropods still on their feet had broken away and were sprinting for the house, their long legs easily outpacing any Human pursuers.

Liam assessed the scene. At least four of his people were down, but both treasure chests were still resting untouched on the ground and *Freedom* still loomed over them. He looked again at the dark opening to the house beyond the portico. Charging headlong into there would only get sailors killed, and wouldn't stop Shordar from loading the Suncatcher into his sloop.

"Back to *Freedom!*" he shouted, jogging toward his crew. "This is now a ship battle."

Hoisting the wounded was the natural priority, but it took far too long. *Freedom's* crew threw down scramble nets from the other doors for sailors to climb up, but Liam stood impotently as he watched *Emerald Crown* let go all lines and thrust away from the tower.

"Shall we pursue with the boat, sir?" Butcher asked, pointing to where Faith and Hunter had climbed into their small vessel and were watching expectantly.

"There's no point," Liam replied. "Tell them to dock with *Freedom* as soon as we slip. We need to pursue with our cutter."

"Can *Daring* intercept?"

Liam glanced at the coxn, appreciating the fresh perspective. He made for the nearest scramble net.

"Coxn, supervise the last of the personnel and get those chests aboard; I'll get on comms with *Daring*."

Liam struggled up the thick rope of the net, appreciating the strong hands that grabbed him and hauled him aboard as he reached level with *Freedom's* deck. With barely a glance outward to watch *Emerald Crown* pull away, he raced for the bridge.

Brown turned as Liam climbed the ladder up onto the bridge, her youthful expression set for duty. Beyond her, through the low canopy, Shordar's sloop slowly gained altitude as its thrusters fired.

"Sir, we're loading the last casualty and will be ready to push off in sixty seconds. The boat reports ready to slip and will come alongside as soon as we're clear of the compound."

"Very good," he said, striding to the comms panel. "Make ready to push off as soon as able. Steer a course to pursue Shordar's vessel."

"Yes, sir."

He grabbed the handset for inter-ship communications.

"*Daring* this is *Freedom*, over."

Through the crackle of atmosphere, Riverton's voice came back. "*This is* Daring."

"This is *Freedom*. Prize sighted, currently in target vessel leaving our location with thief embarked. *Freedom* will pursue but assess capture unlikely. Request *Daring* move to intercept target vessel."

There was a pause, likely as Riverton sought confirmation from her lookouts. From orbit, details on the surface were too indistinct to capture in detail.

"*This is* Daring, *understood. Pursue as best you can to help us localize.*"

As expected, *Daring* did not have a visual on the situation. Traffic over Morassia was sparse compared to many other worlds, but the sheer volume of space made finding a single ship in good time a tricky endeavor.

"Everyone's aboard," Brown announced. "Commencing push-off."

Liam's mind raced as he felt the deck shudder. *Freedom* was a big ship to be this deep in a gravity well and getting her off the ground took effort. *Emerald Crown* was also struggling to rise, but it was smaller and lighter – and likely had augmented thrusters that the master thief routinely used for surface thefts.

"Are the cannons loaded?" he asked.

"Yes," Brown replied, "but the crews aren't ready to fire. Shall I close them up?"

It would take several minutes to make the guns ready, Liam knew, and Shordar was pulling away every second. Once both ships reached the edge of space, *Freedom* would need everyone on board to extend the masts and set the sails.

A quick measurement showed the sloop already at the edge of cannon range. And unlike in space, any cannonball that missed its target would eventually rain down on the planet's surface below. Morassia was barely under Imperial control as it was – the last thing His Majesty's Navy needed was reports of stray fire destroying houses.

"No," he said finally. "Get that boat recovered and make for open space. We're going to have to catch her."

Brown couldn't quite hide her grin. "Yes, sir."

As *Freedom* gained altitude, Liam was joined on the bridge by Swift and Butcher. Both looked worn and tired, but thankfully intact.

"Any bad casualties?" he asked.

"We're running out of bandages below," Butcher replied, "but most wounds are superficial. Narrow took a bad hit to the arm, but Song tied a tourniquet to stem the flow."

"I'd like us to save his arm, sir," Swift growled. "He's more useful to me with two of them."

"You should probably get that looked at, sir." Butcher pointed to where blood was staining Liam's tunic.

"Take care of the others first."

Liam looked ahead to where *Emerald Crown* was moving through wisps of clouds. Its thrusters glowed like mini-suns as it pushed upward. *Freedom's* deck rumbled as she pursued at full power.

"*Daring* is going to try and intercept." Liam said. "Should we put Narrow in the boat and send him home while we conclude this chase?"

"I'll check on his wound," Butcher said, heading for the ladder.

Liam was used to ship engagements taking hours to unfold, but those always took place in deep space with no immediate reference points. Watching the surface of Morassia slowly drop away gave this chase an immediacy that made him pace the small deck. *Emerald Crown* was a dark shape in the pale sky, slowly growing as *Freedom* pushed upward.

"Thruster fuel down to fifty percent," Brown reported.

"We're closing," Liam countered, "continue on full thrust."

The sky was fading to the black of space when the radio crackled to life again.

"Freedom *this is* Daring," Riverton said. "*We're tracking multiple ships outbound. Can you localize?*"

Liam grabbed a telescope and scanned upward through the canopy, searching for *Daring*'s squat, dusty form. There were dozens of ships in motion, and none close enough to clearly identify.

"Charlotte," he said, "do we have signal flares ready?"

"Yes, sir," Brown replied, a puzzled frown creasing her forehead. Flares were used to signal other ships with basic messages. "What shall I prepare?"

"Mason, load flares in the forward gunports. Point them at Shordar as best you can."

Swift nodded. "A little fireworks display for *Daring* to close?"

"Exactly."

The propulsor departed the bridge.

"*Daring* this is *Freedom*," Liam said over the radio, "Look for two fast vessels moving together. We're astern and we're going to light up the target with flares."

"*Understood.*"

The distant glow of the Hub began to shine as Morassia's atmosphere faded below, a deep golden sector of the sky to *Freedom*'s port. Liam raised his telescope again and spotted the glow reflecting off Shordar's hull. The sloop was altering as it climbed, no doubt searching for the first of the solar winds.

"Come ten degrees to port," Liam ordered, trying to get *Freedom* pointed directly at their quarry.

Brown gave manoeuvring orders and the view through the canopy shifted, centering the sloop ahead.

The internal phone whistled and Liam picked it up. "Bridge."

"*Four flares loaded forward,*" reported Swift. "*Twenty in reserve.*"

"Continuous fire: fire at will."

It was odd to give cannon commands for flares, but Liam knew Swift would get it right.

The first flare rocketed outward, looking like a dazzling green comet at it sailed past Morassia's limb and against the black backdrop of space. Seconds later a red flare followed, then a yellow, then a white. The brilliant balls of fire stretched forward, finally fading just short of Shordar's fleeing sloop. The pattern repeated itself only seconds later. The fireworks lit up the sky, no doubt catching the eye of every ship in sight.

"Freedom, *this is* Daring," came Riverton's voice, "*we see you. Closing to intercept.*"

Liam trained his telescope upward, scanning the vessels nearby. There! What looked like a tubby transport ship suddenly hauled to starboard, sails fluttering as it shifted tack and began to descend.

"Thruster fuel status?" Liam asked.

"Twenty-six percent," Brown replied. "We're closing the gap."

Clear of the atmosphere, Liam would usually be thinking about extending the masts and switching to the ship's natural form of propulsion, but the brilliant sparks of Shordar's thrusters indicated the thief still considered this a sprint. Liam smiled, knowing *Freedom* was up to the challenge.

"Steady as she goes, Ms. Brown."

The flares faded away as Swift depleted his stock, but Liam knew *Daring* had her target. He watched as the bigger ship tacked again, sails flush as she rode a favorable eddy through the maelstrom of close planetary solar winds. Riverton was steering ahead of Shordar, and Liam was closing from behind. He couldn't help but smile again. He doubted even a master thief had much experience against the officers of His Majesty's Navy.

The distances continued to close, until Liam could clearly see the stern windows of the sloop, behind which was no doubt a luxurious cabin. The bridge bulged upward just forward of that, but otherwise the sloop's smooth lines were marred only by the four masts still pressed firmly along the hull. *Daring* was farther ahead, dropping across the view as she cut off the escape route.

Then, the sloop's thrusters sputtered and died. The ship was still hurtling forward, but had suddenly lost her ability to manoeuvre. If Shordar wanted to evade now, he'd have to extend his masts and sails, and that made him vulnerable.

"Time to intercept," Liam asked.

"Two minutes," Brown replied.

Liam reached for the main internal broadcast. His voice echoed through *Freedom's* interior.

"This is Commander Blackwood. We are closing to intercept the enemy ship in two minutes. All boarding party members report to the lower airlocks: prepare to board."

Daring had positioned herself in front of the sloop and was retracting her starboard mast to open cannon arcs.

"Freedom *this is* Daring," Riverton said calmly over the radio, "*I'm preparing grapples.*"

"This is *Freedom*," he replied. "My boarding team is ready."

Freedom continued to close, her thrusters still burning as the sloop sailed helplessly ahead. *Daring's* bulk blocked the way. Even from this range Liam could see the gunports opening all along her side.

"All teams," he ordered throughout the ship, "prepare to board."

One of the sloop's masts began to extend, as the thieves finally seemed to realize the trap they were in. But Liam knew it was too late. *Freedom* was practically on top of the target. The sloop's extending mast was on the side closest to *Freedom*, almost like an arm trying to push them away.

"Reverse thrusters," Liam ordered. "Match her course and speed. And keep clear of that mast they're trying to point at us."

"Yes, sir."

"Just get us lined up with their airlocks," Liam said, as the sloop's dark hull filled most of his view. In the glow of the distant Hub he could even make out sinewy lines of green running the length of the sloop and circling a painted crown of gold. *Emerald Crown*. A subtle extravagance befitting a master thief.

In the near distance, a line of smoke burst forth from *Daring's* side, obscuring the ship as the cannon fired their grappling hooks.

Liam was suddenly blinded by a burst of light outside the canopy. Instinctively shielding his eyes, he sensed movement ahead, and peered up just in time to see the sloop's hull vanish from view, a line of small thrusters lighting up its entire side. The sloop lurched away, displacing itself neatly from the trap, but before Liam could utter a word, he realized the mistake they'd made.

Freedom clanged as *Daring's* grappling hooks smashed into her hull. The deck heaved as the grapple took hold, and *Daring's* gunners began to heave in. Liam scrambled for the radio, watching as *Emerald Crown* thrusted further clear and all four of her masts began to extend with surprising swiftness.

"*Daring* this is *Freedom*, release your grapple," he signaled. "You've got us!"

The pull didn't relent as *Daring's* gunners, unaware of what target they'd hit, diligently did their job and hauled in their catch. Liam repeated his hail, watching in impotent frustration as *Emerald Crown* unfurled sails and began to open the distance.

The hull creaked under the force of the grapple, and Liam could practically see people moving on *Daring's* bridge as the bigger vessel closed in. Finally, the pressure eased as the hooks released and began to retract.

Shordar was already clear and under full sail, his ship no doubt capable of high speed. But the Theropod hadn't had a proper race against *Freedom* yet.

"Ms. Brown, prepare to deploy all sails, racing configuration."

"Yes, sir."

"*Daring* this is *Freedom*," he said over the radio, "I'm prepping for a high-speed chase. Keep up as best you can."

"Freedom... *Confirm you're equipped for a long voyage?*" Riverton's voice was calm, but Liam could sense the weight behind her words.

Was he equipped for a long voyage? *Freedom* might be small, but she was fully capable of independent travel between the stars. He was about to answer in the affirmative, but something made him glance at Brown.

"Thruster fuel at twenty percent," she said simply.

That was well below what any ship should deploy with, he knew, and his mind suddenly made the shift from tactical to logistics. *Freedom* hadn't been stocked with food. She hadn't been topped up with air reserves, or extra sails, or anything a good captain made sure they had before departing into the unknown. And, he had wounded on board, at least one of whom definitely needed Dr. Templegrey and her sickbay. Liam the warrior watched in frustration as *Emerald Crown* continued to flee… But Liam the sailor knew that he shouldn't follow.

"*Daring* this is *Freedom*," he said, suppressing a sigh. "Negative. Prepare to receive us alongside. Medical team requested at the airlock."

"*Ready to receive.*"

"All positions," he said over the internal broadcast, "stand down. Prepare to come alongside *Daring*. Priority disembarkation is the wounded."

He resisted the urge to thump the console, merely leaning both his hands on it and letting out a long, slow breath.

"That was a tricky move by Shordar," Brown muttered, her young face dark with a mix of anger and embarrassment. "He caught us all by surprise."

Liam was tempted to snap at her, but she only spoke the truth.

"I think we need to re-assess our adversary," he said finally, looking up at the looming bulk of *Daring*. "But first, let's get these ships secured."

"Yes, sir." Brown turned to confer with the skeleton bridge crew, then did a visual sweep of her sailing table.

Liam forced another deep breath and allowed himself one last look at the diminishing form of *Emerald Crown*.

"Damnation."

CHAPTER 8

Amelia awoke with a gasp, cringing in pain as she tried to sit up. The sheet felt like lead pressing her down, but all the slashes and cuts up and down her body lit up like fire with every movement. She blinked her vision clear, breathing heavily as the sensation of being smothered finally faded.

There was a distant rumble all around her, which she quickly recognized as the fading thunder of a cannon broadside. All fog of pain and bad dreams instantly faded: cannon fire wasn't part of the plan.

Sickbay was filled with personnel and the steady, professional chatter of medics tending to patients. Templegrey herself worried over a large form propped up on a bed directly in front of Amelia. The doctor's steady hands were stitching a nasty wound in Ethan Narrow's arm, her eyes down and focused. His shirt was smudged and bloodied, cut away from the wound and hanging across half his chest. Narrow's face was set in discomfort, but he noticed Amelia and gave her a withering smile.

Amelia vaguely recognized the forms of her colleagues, relieved to see that Mia Hedge wasn't among them. Hedgie tended to be the first into battle, and had probably spent more time in sickbay than anyone but Dr. Templegrey herself.

She lifted her bedsheet and started shuffling herself to the edge of the bed.

Master Rating Song approached her, his face and hands obviously scrubbed clean and in stark contrast to the muddy, spattered armor peeking out from under his white medical coat.

"Are you all right, PO?" he asked with clinical concern.

Amelia propped herself up on her elbows, surveying the room. "How did the mission go? Why are we firing?"

Song shrugged, dropping his eyes. "We almost had it, but then the brutes turned on us and the fighting started. I think we're chasing them now."

"Where's Liam?"

"Who?"

She cursed herself inwardly. Even a long-serving crewmember like Song probably didn't know Commander Blackwood's first name.

"Nothing," she muttered. "Just shaking off a bad dream."

The deck rattled at the thunder of another broadside. Song steadied himself against Amelia's bed.

"Do you need something for the pain?" he asked.

Her instinct was to refuse the offer, but the entire front side of her body stung and her legs ached right down to the bone. And she was not going to just sit while the ship went into battle.

"Yes, please. Something to get me moving."

"You really shouldn't-"

"Well I am."

Song dutifully provided her a shot glass of poppied rum. She downed it, enjoying the way the thickened liquid coated her throat as it burned all the way down.

"Help me up."

"This isn't a good idea," he warned, even as he steadied her arm and lifted the sheet to clear her legs.

She eased her feet off the bed, shifting her weight down as Song steadied her at the elbow. Dressed in nothing but a nightgown over her many bandages she felt the rush of air as she moved. Her bare feet pressed against the cold deck and her legs took the strain. Pain lanced through her and she shivered, but she didn't collapse. Shaking off Song's hand, she looked toward the door.

Templegrey looked up at the movement, her face hardening in a frown. Her fingers moved with expert swiftness as she concluded her sewing work on Narrow's arm. She gave him a few words of encouragement then strolled over to Amelia.

"Hello, darling," she said quietly. She nodded to Song, who retreated to tend other patients. Templegrey's noble features were set in a pose of refined ease, but Amelia could see the clouds of concern deep in her eyes. "You shouldn't be moving yet."

"We're in battle." The roar of another broadside punctuated her words. "I'm no use to anyone lying here."

"You're no use to anyone lying collapsed and bleeding a deck away from here, either."

Ava Templegrey rarely displayed anything other than serene contentment. Her sharp tone and stern glare gave Amelia pause. But she knew that she couldn't stay in bed.

"I have to help. The ship needs me."

"We need you healthy."

Amelia gripped the edge of the bed, knowing that the poppied rum would take effect soon. If she didn't get moving she'd fall back asleep, and that was worse than the pain.

"Ava," she whispered, "please. I can't do it anymore."

The doctor's expression softened. "Another nightmare?"

"I was being smothered this time, like under a pile of sand."

Templegrey nodded, lips pursing in thought. "You feel helpless?"

"Maybe."

"It's an uncomfortable feeling for anyone like you," she said with a kind smile, "who's used to being in the center of the action."

"I guess the mission failed."

Amelia hung onto the bed as the deck tilted. Templegrey leaned into the ship's turn with long practice.

"I haven't heard all the details yet… But we don't have the Suncatcher on board and we're starting to chase the thief's ship."

"Is Liam okay?"

"He's fine. I think he's briefing the captain."

Relief flooded through her, a wave of emotion she didn't realize she'd been holding back until it broke. Shutting her eyes to hold back the tears, she nodded.

Templegrey's hands brushed against her elbows in reassurance. Amelia reached out and wrapped herself around Ava, burying her face in the doctor's collar. Delicate arms embraced her, holding her tight.

"I need to get out there and help," Amelia said into Templegrey's shoulder. "I can't just lie here."

"I could order you back to bed."

They were still embracing, and Amelia could hear the resignation in her friend's voice. "But you won't."

"No…" Templegrey released her arms and took a single step back, eyebrow arched as she gave Amelia a once-over. "But I *am* ordering you to put on a uniform. You're no good to this ship if you distract all our sailors from their duties, traipsing around in that negligée."

Amelia scoffed as she looked down at the shapeless nightdress. But it was sheer enough that her bandages were just visible through it. She felt herself redden.

"Hedgie would happily go into battle wearing one of these."

"Able Rating Hedge would pull it off, tear it into strips and use them to tie up her prisoners," Templegrey countered with a growing smile.

"So, I can go?"

Templegrey stepped back, sighing slightly as she gestured toward the door. Amelia nodded her thanks and stepped past.

In the facing bed, Song was snipping away the wreckage of Narrow's shirt. The artificer rolled his broad shoulders and glanced down at his sewn arm. Amelia's eyes did not linger on the wound, but on the broad shoulders and chest exposed next to them.

He caught her gaze, smiling with a bit more strength than before. She curled her lips upward in return, but then headed for the door and turned her mind toward battle. But the image of Ethan Narrow, half-naked in bed, lingered for a while.

Liam felt half-naked as he stumbled onto the bridge, his civilian clothes in tatters after the desperate fighting in Shordar's courtyard. He might not have cared, except the bridge was currently under the watch of Sublieutenant Julia Sungate, who turned at his approach with an elegance refined by a lifetime of always being observed. Her uniform was crisp and correct as always, the weapons belt of the officer of the watch cinching her waist just enough to reveal the hourglass figure beneath her long blue uniform coat.

Her eyes scanned up and down him just once, her expression carefully neutral as she met his gaze. "Commander Blackwood, sir. I've come hard to starboard as the captain ordered, but in so doing the target vessel is moving out of cannon range."

"I've just briefed the captain," he said, mind still racing, "who is even now preparing queries for her contacts about where Shordar might be headed. If you have any connections in your personal network who might be able to help, now's the time."

Her expression didn't waver, but he could sense the mental activity behind her gaze. This was no dilettante, as proven by the fact that Captain Riverton already trusted her to be on the bridge alone with hostiles nearby.

"I'll reach out, sir," she said finally, "but I don't know what else my family's network could offer that hasn't already been provided."

"Very good." He looked beyond her to where he estimated Shordar to be. The thief was fleeing further out into the Halo, away from civilization and Imperial influence. "His ship isn't as fast as I feared."

"No, sir. Even with two masts retracted for cannon fire we've been able to keep up. Shall I extend the port and starboard masts?"

"Not yet. For now, our orders are to maintain tracking on Shordar and pursue."

"Are we preparing *Freedom* to follow?"

"It's an option, but one of several. For now, we're gathering information."

She nodded. Her lips parted slightly, but she hesitated to speak.

She was really trying to recognize her place as a junior officer, he could tell, and he appreciated the effort. But hers was a keen mind and he didn't want her to feel stifled.

"Do you have a recommendation, Sublieutenant Sungate?"

"*Freedom* is one of the fastest ships in the Empire, and surely can outgun that sloop in a quick battle. If we load *Freedom* with chain shot we can shoot out Shordar's sails, allowing *Daring* to close at her leisure."

His first recommendation to Riverton had been almost word for word the same. And in other circumstances he'd already be actioning that plan. But, as always, Captain Riverton had kept her eye on the big picture.

"Look at this," he said, directing her attention to the navigation table, which showed the local area of space and all the other ships that *Daring* was tracking. "Here we are, and here's our target. There are more than a dozen other ships nearby – do you see anything unusual about them?"

She studied the plot, eyes narrowing in thought. He held back, seeing if she could see what Riverton had assessed immediately and had tracked from the moment the intercept failed.

"These three ships," she said finally, pointing them out. "They're all heading away from Morassia… and converging ahead of us."

"Bit of an odd coincidence…?"

"They're working with Shordar," she concluded.

"Possibly. Nothing we know of this thief suggests he has his own fleet, but I think he may have more resources than we thought."

"And sending *Freedom* out by herself would put her at risk."

"One-on-one, *Freedom* could take that sloop. But four-on-one, she'd be in trouble."

"So we watch, wait, and see what those three ships do."

"Exactly."

Her face lit up in a smile, and Liam sensed the genuine satisfaction behind it.

"Thank you, sir," she said, hand brushing against his bare arm. "I understand fully now."

"This chase will require patience. So maintain this course, observe and be ready for anything."

She nodded with quiet determination. "Yes, sir."

Amelia's new cabin was thankfully less than two dozen paces from sickbay and she made her way down the passageway mostly unobserved. There was a tension in the ship's air and those sailors she saw moved with focus that stopped any eyes from lingering on her half-naked form.

Also thankfully, her uncomfortably attractive new cabinmate was absent from the tight space. Amelia shut the door, stripped down to her bandages and pulled out a fresh uniform. The shirt was simple enough to don, its loose fabric giving her space to move, but the trousers were agony to slip up over her shredded thighs. She was sweating by the time she buttoned the waist and slumped down onto her bunk to pull on her boots. Eyeing up her uniform coat, she took a few deep breaths and decided maybe just to carry that.

The deck heaved, but she honestly wasn't sure if it was the ship, the pain coursing through her, or the poppied rum doing its work. She sat for a moment longer, forcing herself to focus on where she'd be most useful.

The deck rolled again, not as violently, and she recognized the motion of the ship turning to catch a better wind.

Forcing herself to her feet, she stepped out into the passageway again. Five sailors were ascending from Three Deck, the last being the coxn himself. Chief Butcher's armour was battered and scratched, and Amelia got a new sense of the brutality of the battle the landing party had found themselves in. She tried to stride forward, but the shooting pain through her thighs reminded her only too well of how dangerous Theropods were up close.

Butcher had reached the galley and knocked on the door. It swung open as Sam poked his small head out.

Even Theropods who were her dear friends could be dangerous, she thought, as she limped her way down the passageway. Sam and Bella were wonderful people, but were no strangers to deadly violence if necessary. As she closed in, she saw evidence of battle streaked across Sam's skin and clothing.

Butcher noticed her approach. "Quartermaster, good to see you up."

"Trying my best, Coxn," she replied, leaning against the galley door.

"I was just telling Sam that we need to start preparing food that can be delivered to people at their battle stations. This is going to be a long chase."

"And I was saying that I can do this," Sam replied. "But I have already given all my prepared food to *Shar-let* for *Free-dorm*. Apparently she will be sailing independently."

"So you need me to open stores," Amelia concluded. Feeling into her coat pocket, she found her keys.

"Yes."

She slipped one key off the ring and handed it to Sam. "This is food stores. Get what you need."

Sam handed the key to one of the sailors, along with a scrap of paper. "Here is the list of what I need. I will join you in a moment."

Butcher ordered two of the sailors to go and they disappeared down the ladder.

"This is water stores," Amelia added, giving another key to one of the two remaining sailors she recognized as a long-time shipmate. "You two go and draw a couple of pony kegs; we can distribute it around to all the stations."

At Butcher's nod the two sailors departed.

He turned a bemused face to her. "Taking charge of my people? Maybe I had something else planned for them."

"If you need food, you need water."

He tried to frown, but not very hard. "I'd have thought of it eventually."

Bella emerged from the galley, carrying trays of biscuits. Her clothing was torn and stained, and she limped slightly, but otherwise her usual poise was intact.

"These will do for now," she said, stopping when she spotted Amelia. "I am pleased to see you up."

Amelia regarded her Theropod friends with a new sense of wonder. They'd volunteered to be in the middle of these negotiations, they'd clearly fought alongside the Humans, and now were doing what they could to support their friends in a ship battle.

"You two are amazing."

"It was all worth it," Sam said, "to meet the infamous *Shorr-dahr* in person."

"He lived up to the stories, then?"

"Oh yes," Bella replied. "If I wasn't life-mated to *Sahrm* I would have switched sides immediately."

Sam barked in laughter. "I was tempted myself."

"Really?" Amelia asked.

"He is very charismatic," Bella explained. "A natural leader of our kind."

"Still just a thief," Butcher grumbled. "And now we've got him on the run."

"I will deliver these," Bella said, slipping past with her trays.

Butcher eyed up Amelia. "I suppose you want to be useful?"

"Here," she said, handing him her coat. "Help me with this."

He held it up and eased the sleeves over her arms. The familiar weight of the uniform was reassuring and she quickly buttoned it up, feeling protected by it.

"Are you sure you should be up and about?" he asked.

"I'm not sitting out a battle," she said. "Maybe I can't fight, but by the stars I can deliver food and water."

He appraised her for a moment, then nodded. "All right, stick with me for now. Sam will need some time to get food prepped – let's tour the ship and assess what we have to work with."

"You doubt the crew?"

"No," he replied, gesturing her forward, "but people are people, and battle brings chaos. I want to discover early if there are any potential weak links."

She recalled many a coxn suddenly appearing at her battle station during a quiet moment before the shooting started. Sometimes that coxn would make a bit of small talk; sometimes they'd just pass through without a word. Never had she felt like she was being assessed. In fact, it had never felt like it had been about her at all.

"And the crew seeing you," she realized in sudden clarity, "can help strengthen any weak links. Reassure them that they're being supported from the top."

"Never underestimate the power of simple presence," Butcher said, glancing down at her. "It's something the officers don't understand – so it's our job to do it."

———

Liam stood next to the captain's chair, raising the telescope to his eye once again. "The first target is turning inward again."

"Come right," Riverton ordered, "into the cannon arcs."

"Yes, ma'am," Sungate replied, issuing orders to turn the ship.

Liam watched as the small ship closed, sails leaning heavily into the wind as its bow pointed toward *Daring*. It was one of three vessels that were harassing them, trying to slow *Daring* as *Emerald Crown* pulled away. *Daring* could only have top and bottom masts extended in order to keep the cannon arcs clear, and she just wasn't displaying enough sheet to close Shordar.

"They're in range," Sungate reported, monitoring the tactical table.

"Full broadside," Riverton said, "fire."

The order was relayed down and seconds later *Daring* shook as her entire port side exploded with cannon fire.

Watching the target, Liam saw the nimble vessel suddenly haul to port and open again.

"They've turned away," he said.

Although impossible to see at this range, he knew that their broadside would sail harmlessly past the target. There wasn't much in deep space to slow a cannonball down, but the constant pressure from solar winds reduced accuracy to nothing over distance.

He turned to assess the target closing them on the starboard side. It had also turned away, just outside engagement range.

"I think they've figured out our effective weapons range," he sighed.

"They're just trying to harry us," Riverton replied, face set in stone. "Forcing us to alter so that Shordar can gain distance on us."

Liam looked directly upward, past the billowing sails of top mast and toward the third vessel haunting them. Through the telescope he could see its starboard bow as it closed them on a slow intercept course. It was still out of range, but not by much.

"Third target still closing," he said, pointing upward.

"Maintain course," Riverton replied. "Let them get well within range before we alter again."

There was a long moment of silence on the bridge and Liam surveyed his team. The sailors crewing the forward stations were a mix of veterans and new recruits, the difference easy to spot in the restless shifting and whispered questions of the newcomers. At his side he sensed Sungate's nervous energy, but discipline kept her rooted in place at the officer of the watch console. Riverton was a pillar of calm as always, and Liam had sailed into more than enough battles to know that this one was probably not going to amount to much. It was more nuisance than threat… until the enemy did something unexpected.

"Can we increase the range of our cannon?" Sungate asked suddenly.

"If you can figure out a way," he replied lightly, "you'll find yourself posted to the Imperial Armory as master gunsmith."

He expected her to smile at the gentle retort, or perhaps be embarrassed by her question. But she simply looked down at the navigation table again, eyes narrowed in thought. With Templegrey busy in sickbay, Swift overseeing the sailing team and Brown supervising frantic repairs and restocking in *Freedom*, Sungate was the only officer of the watch on the bridge. He was surprised to realize that this didn't worry him.

"Target three is in range," she said suddenly.

Liam glanced up, scanning with his telescope to confirm that the ship was still pointed at *Daring*. As he watched, she hauled sharply to port. A series of fire bursts rippled down her side.

"Incoming fire!"

"Hard roll to port," Riverton ordered.

Thrusters on *Daring's* hull burst to life and the starscape beyond rotated swiftly. Seconds later, the clangs of cannonballs striking the ship echoed through the deck.

"Starboard broadside," Riverton snapped, "fire."

Sungate relayed the order and *Daring* shook as the starboard guns unleashed their power.

Liam found the target in his telescope and watched as multiple impacts battered the small ship. It turned away, a shimmer distorting the stars beyond in its wake.

"Several hits," he reported. "We might have punctured their hull – I think I see air escaping."

"Very good," Riverton replied.

"Target three is retreating," Sungate reported. "That leaves only two."

"I wouldn't count her out yet. I'm sure they can patch a hole and stay in the fight." He grabbed a handset and rung down to sailing control. Swift answered.

"Did we take any damage?"

"*A few dents, maybe,*" Swift replied over the line. "*Both masts are good, all thrusters functional, no leaks detected.*"

"Very good."

He hung up and surveyed the scene again. The small vessels were manoeuvring independently on three sides of *Daring*, and Shordar was still pulling away. He walked over to Riverton.

"No damage, ma'am, just harassing fire."

"It's all they're capable of," she replied. "And all they intend to do."

He leaned in closer, meeting her eyes. "I don't like the way this is playing out. We need to change it up."

"How long until *Freedom* is prepped?"

"She's stocked with stores, but Brown is still assessing damage from the atmosphere run."

"Go and find out." Riverton sat back in her chair and glared outward. "I can handle these knaves."

⁕

Amelia opened the small, reinforced door of the last gun compartment, climbing through ahead of Chief Butcher. The air was laced with the lingering smell of burnt powder, with cannon balls and powder bags piled up and ready for use on opposite sides of the gun. The crew looked back curiously, but she was quickly greeted with friendly smiles.

"Bringing cupcakes, Quartermaster?" Hedge quipped.

"Or an extra tot of rum," offered another sailor.

"Just coming to take dinner orders," Amelia called out with forced good humor, fighting down the pain as she rose to her feet in the crowded space. "We have roast leg of Sectoid or poached filet of Aquan."

"How about Theropod shanks," Hedge said, gesturing her thumb out toward space. "I can probably reel in a few."

"Not sure Sam and Bella would approve."

"But if anyone could make Theropod taste good, it'd be Sam!"

Amelia smiled at the nervous laughter around her. Hedge was the gun commander, the other three sailors all new recruits. In the past, many of *Daring's* crew had known Amelia when she was one of them, and she'd been able to move in and out of her petty officer role as appropriate. But time marched on, and as she looked at these fresh young faces she realized that she was a distant figure to them, a figure of authority.

And then all eyes moved past her toward the coxn as he eased his bulk through the tight door. Expressions turned serious, almost solemn.

"How's the gun crew, then?" Butcher asked, as he'd done fifteen times previously.

"Good, coxn," one of the sailors replied automatically.

"We were just deciding which kind of alien meat would taste best," Hedge added.

Butcher moved in next to Amelia, nodding thoughtfully as he cast his gaze around the compartment. "My favorite is Sectoid hatchling, dipped in chocolate."

"Yes!" Hedge said, trying to hide her smirk as she watched the shocked expressions of her sailors.

"Really?" one of them ventured.

"Some people like to mash them up into a paste and mix in syrup," Butcher replied, face still remarkably serious, "but I like the crunch as my teeth break through their little shells."

The sailor shuddered.

Butcher finally laughed. "I'm just messing with you, Leaf. We don't eat other intelligent species."

"Although," Amelia suddenly added, "everything tastes better with chocolate."

"Yeah," Hedge said, "make sure to store extra chocolate, in case we're ever marooned and the only thing to eat is alien."

"Except Sam and Bella."

"Oh, yeah – I'd eat an officer before I ate Sam or Bella."

Amelia tried to hide her sudden blush as the sailors laughed.

"How are you feeling, PO?" Rating Leaf asked. "I heard you were a little beat up in that mission ashore."

"Nothing too serious," she said with an easy smile. "My legs are just a little sore. But I'll be happy to take some Theropod loot in exchange when we catch them."

This drew a chorus of agreements, and some chatter about the infamous treasure thief Shordar. Whatever tension had been lurking in this gun bay diffused into space as the chatter turned to how everyone was going to spend their share of the loot, led mostly by Hedge and her crazy ideas for new armor with huge, molded breasts.

"They'll never see my swing coming," she declared triumphantly, "if they're too busy staring at my gazungas!"

Amelia couldn't help but laugh, even if it rattled her torso and made her many slashes itch.

Butcher, she noticed, said very little, but his presence filled the room. All the sailors kept a close eye on his reactions, especially as Hedge wandered more and more into the bawdy, but slowly, slowly, they relaxed. One of them even dared to ask him a question about his earlier service life, which he answered smoothly and with just a touch of humor. It had the perfect effect, she realized, making him seem approachable but not giving anything away.

After only a few minutes, Butcher motioned for her to exit.

"You folks stay sharp," he said as Amelia began to climb out. "This might be a waiting game and it might seem boring. But when the captain needs you to fire this gun, you bet your butts she means business."

"Yes, coxn," came the chorus response.

"Leaf, Blue, Beach, you listen to Hedgie here. She knows what it's all about."

"Yes, coxn."

Amelia stepped out into the One Deck central passageway and breathed through the pain of movement as Butcher climbed out and shut the door.

"You know every one of their names," she said, incredulous.

"Of course I do. I signed every one of them to this crew. And each one of them is my responsibility."

"Still… wow."

"Do you know exactly what's in each in your storage bays, Quartermaster?"

"Of course."

"Of course," he repeated as he stepped onto the ladder leading down. "Because that's what you're responsible for. I'm responsible for people."

"And you know them all," she finished in wonder.

"And I care about them all… Even if they don't realize it."

As he descended the ladder and disappeared, Amelia felt certain that every single sailor on board realized it.

Liam found Brown in *Freedom's* sailing control room, hands buried in a mess of circuitry under the raised sailing table display. The low space was crowded with dark consoles and equipment, and a single bright lamp hung above the young officer, her white uniform shirt practically glowing in contrast to the shadows. Her blue coat was uncharacteristically abandoned and her sleeves were rolled up as she pulled out a burnt fuse.

"I need a new fifty-five," she called, her common accent in full force.

"What color is that?" came a response from inside the top mast access tube.

"Green."

"I don't have one."

The muttered curse died on her lips as she spotted Liam. She straightened, glancing down at her disheveled appearance.

"Repair status?" he asked calmly, looking her in the eye.

"Hull friction scoring forward has weakened some of the plates," she replied, her voice settling into the low, precise, modulated tones of her Academy training, "and I need to get technicians suited up to apply external patching."

She gestured down into the open panel before her. "We've also blown three relays that send remote signals up the masts. They should be easy to repair, if we have the right equipment. If not, we'll need extra hands to crew the masts manually."

Freedom, they'd discovered, was a state-of-the-art vessel with many automated features that made it possible to effectively crew her with minimal sailors. It also made her vulnerable to extreme conditions, though, and her systems failed when *Daring's* simpler but more robust architecture simply kept going and going.

"Time to repair?" he asked.

They both suddenly gripped their nearest consoles as the deck swung heavily. Lashed to *Daring*, *Freedom* did a barrel roll every time the bigger ship did a heavy turn. Brown's cheeks were distinctly pale and perspiration trickled down her temples.

"The hull patches will need several hours at least," she said, clearly fighting down sudden nausea. "And that's just to apply a temporary fix. Real repairs will take days. If we have the parts we can fix the sailing system in minutes and maintain minimal crewing. If we don't, there's no fixing it and we need more crew."

"So two hours to make basic repairs, and possibly some additional sailors."

"Three hours, more like." She brushed stray hair out of her face, leaving a faint smear of grease on her forehead. "Sir."

"Sending people outside the hull when the enemy is firing at us isn't my favorite idea."

"Nor mine, but any direct hits to the bow would risk a breach if we don't."

Liam considered the options. "Keep working the problem here, but don't suit up anyone yet. I'll get back to you."

"Yes, sir."

Liam climbed up the ladder to *Freedom's* main passageway, looking forward and aft down the clean lines of what had originally been built as a luxury yacht. She was many things, but a front-line combatant she was not. And certainly not without the right preparations. He made his way to the airlock and strode back into *Daring*. The large space was guarded by a single armed sailor and Liam nodded briefly to her as he sought out the nearest communication panel. He switched to the bridge channel and spun the power handle. Seconds later, Riverton answered.

"*Captain.*"

"Captain, ma'am, XO. *Freedom* has forward hull plate weakness that will need at least three hours to repair, or several days to replace. She may or may not need additional crew to control her sails, depending on whether we have the right circuitry parts to repair the automated system." He paused for breath. "I recommend against deploying *Freedom* on her own into battle."

"*Understood. Return to the bridge.*"

"Yes, ma'am."

He hung up the phone and exited the cargo bay swiftly, ensuring that he kept his stride steady in sight of the sailor on sentry duty. *Officers never run,* he'd been told many times in training, *for it panics the crew.* He didn't know how true that was for the many veterans aboard *Daring*, but there were just enough new recruits on board that he didn't want to test the old chestnut today.

Emerging into the main passageway of Three Deck, he started aft, mind whirling with possible courses of action to get *Daring* out of this combat stalemate.

And nearly strode straight into the coxn. Chief Butcher's powerful hands caught him.

"Whoa, there, sir."

"Coxn," he greeted, his next words fading as he spotted who was behind the chief.

Amelia. Slumped in her stance and clearly hurt, but on her feet. His heart swelled, but still feeling the coxn's hands steadying him, he simply stepped back and straightened.

"Quartermaster, how nice to see you up and about."

Her eyes were clouded with pain, but he could still see the sparkle in them as she met his gaze.

"I hate to miss a good battle, sir. I'm helping the coxn with his rounds."

The distant rumble of cannon fire echoed through the hull, followed by a gentle sway as *Daring* turned. The deck movement was subtle, but Amelia leaned her hand heavily against the bulkhead.

"And how is the ship?" His words said one thing, but he knew she'd get his real meaning.

"She's been through the wars, but she's ready for more."

"I'm happy to hear that."

"Sir," Butcher interrupted, "we're just heading to sailing control. I'm sure we're keeping you from your duties as well."

He wanted nothing more than to take Amelia into his arms, but even with only the three of them in the passageway he knew he couldn't. Chief Butcher and Chief Sky were neither blind nor stupid, and were both no doubt aware of the "secret" romance in the senior mess. But even after all this time, and the tacit approval from the captain, neither had ever warmed to the idea of a romance between an officer and a sailor. And as executive officer, the last thing Liam wanted to do was antagonize his coxn and assaulter.

"Carry on, then," he said simply. With barely a glance at Amelia he moved past, headed for the bridge.

Amelia kept her mouth shut as Liam hurried away. He was still in the tattered civilian clothes he'd worn on the mission, blood-soaked bandages hinting at multiple wounds that he was clearly ignoring in his devotion to the ship. She wanted nothing more than to run after him, but her legs were barely holding her up.

And Chief Butcher was staring at her.

"To sailing control, then," she said, forcing her legs into motion.

The coxn said nothing as they took the last steps to their destination, but his expression was cold as he pushed open the door and motioned her through.

Sailing control was packed with sailors. Some handed across tightly packed sheets of sail to waiting hands in the four access tubes. Some stood by monitoring stations that carefully tracked the pressure angle and furl level of each sail. Lieutenant Swift stood in the center, coordinating everything. And behind them all, creaking under the constant pressures, was the cross-shaped thrust block – the massive join of all four masts coming together to transfer their captured wind power to the hull and propel the ship forward.

Swift looked up immediately at her arrival, assessing her in a second and motioning her toward him. She eased her way past the sailors, using consoles as support, and stepped down to the central sailing table. Swift rose from his seat and gestured for her to take it.

"I'm fine," she muttered.

"Shut up, Amelia."

She sat down, sighing at the relief.

The sound powered phone warbled and Swift picked it up. "Sailing control... Yes, ma'am."

Replacing the handset and turning, he addressed the room.

"Listen up!" The general hubbub faded. "We're about to make a prolonged tight turn into the wind, so shorten what you need to. Then get ready to deploy port and starboard masts. Go."

The room erupted into motion as sailors scrambled into the two active mast access tubes, disappearing upward and downward. Signals were sent from the various panels and very quickly replies started coming back. Amelia watched as the sailing table in front of her began to change as top and bottom masts were reefed. She felt the ship begin to turn, and heard the creak on the thrust block as the titanic forces driving *Daring* shifted.

Chief Butcher was quietly working his way around the room, not interfering in the work but still managing to offer quick encouragements. His presence was noted by everyone, Amelia could tell, and appreciated. She'd enjoyed touring the ship with him, but she was beginning to realize that Dr. Templegrey actually knew what she was talking about – maybe walking around hadn't been a good idea after all.

The poppied rum had held off the worst of the pain, but as she sat in Swift's chair, her warm uniform coat wrapped around her, she felt her eyes start to get heavy. Maybe if she just leaned her elbows on the sailing table she'd be okay. The hubbub of noise around her was surprisingly soothing, as Swift and his crew of mast monkeys guided *Daring* through her turn. It did seem strange that Captain Riverton would turn sharply into the wind when they were in the middle of a chase, especially if they were about to extend the other two masts. But Amelia was confident that the captain knew what she was doing. Especially if Liam was there with her.

Liam… she thought as her eyes closed.

"Listen up!" Swift's voice shocked her awake. He was holding the phone again and looking around at his team. "We're going to extend port and starboard masts simultaneously. I want steady movement on both sides – keep that balance. Keep talking to each other and for star's sake keep an eye on the pressure shifts."

"Perhaps," came a new, deep voice, "I might be able to assist, sir?"

The cheer that swelled up from the sailors startled Amelia anew, and with wide eyes she turned to the door. Petty Officer Narrow was filling the entrance, a big grin on his face as he stepped in. He was still wearing the same, half-wrecked shirt from the battle, his shoulder bandages clear. He nodded to the sailors around him, even shaking a few hands as he descended to the sailing table and knuckled his forehead to Swift.

Swift slapped Narrow on his good arm. "Good to have you back, Artificer. Supervise the port mast, if you please."

Narrow nodded his acknowledgement and took a few steps to port, but paused to lay a surprisingly gentle hand on Amelia's shoulder.

"You thinking of taking my spot, Amelia?" His easy smile robbed the words of any malice.

"Your boots are far too big for me to fill, Ethan. I'm just here to watch the show."

With a wink he climbed up to the port mast controls and relieved the master rating in the control chair. Swift positioned himself on the starboard side and with a few technical shouts back and forth that went right over Amelia's head, they began the tricky process of extending two masts at once.

Butcher loomed next to her, leaning forward on the sailing table to bring their faces level.

"It may not seem like it," he said, "but the sailors appreciate you being here."

"I think they've forgotten all about me since Ethan Narrow returned."

Butcher chuckled. "He has a natural leadership style that's working really well. Lieutenant Swift is the smartest person I've ever met, and tough as nails in a crisis, but he lacks the common touch."

"He *is* a commoner."

"Yes, but the officers are all forced to act like nobility, no matter their origins. I feel bad for young Brown, and how hard she tries to fit in with the noble crowd."

"She does try hard. But I don't think Swift does."

"Maybe. I hope so, because I guarantee you this: neither Swift nor Brown, no matter how hard they try, will ever fit in with the aristocracy."

"Brown will do okay." She gave him a sudden, wry grin. "Swift is just too much of an ass."

Butcher smiled in agreement, but his expression became serious again.

"Whatever the reason, though, they're both destined to be on the outside. They'll never command their own ships. Because the nobility always look after their own. The nobility will never accept people like us."

"Coxn…" The conversation, already mildly uncomfortable for Amelia, was suddenly feeling like an assault.

"It's all a game to them," he continued quietly. "Everything. And when they've had their fun, we're the ones who lose."

Amelia wanted to argue, wanted to fight the prejudice that poisoned this whole Empire, but the poppied rum was slowly winning. A hundred words tried to fight their way up her throat, but all she could do was sigh.

"I think it's more complicated than that."

"I don't think it is," he said with a shrug. "They look after their own kind, and we look after ours."

Any further discussion was suddenly cut off by Riverton's voice over the speakers.

"Do you hear there, this is the captain. Daring *is temporarily withdrawing from our pursuit in order to effect necessary repairs to* Freedom *and to position ourselves with advantage. We will stand down from battle stations as we open the distance from our enemy, but I do not think it will be many days before we move to strike again. Remain vigilant. Rest when you can. Keep your equipment and your hearts ready for battle. That is all."*

Moments later, the call went over the main broadcast to secure from battle stations.

The tension dropped in the sailing control room, but only slightly as the dual extension of masts was still underway. Amelia wasn't sure if the tension remained between her and the coxn.

"I think," she said finally, "I'm going to go and lie down."

"Amelia…" Butcher's face softened. "You remind me of my daughter, and I'm very fond of you. I just don't want you to get hurt."

"I appreciate that."

"I'm not telling you what to do. Just…" he glanced over to where Narrow was expertly coordinating the movements of port mast. "Be aware that you have other options."

With a friendly clasp of her shoulder, he departed.

Amelia registered his words but was still processing them through the cloud of poppied rum. She only realized that she'd been staring blankly when she noticed Narrow waving at her. She blinked her vision clear, noting his friendly grin before he turned his attention back to his work.

Sliding out of the chair, she headed for her cabin.

"Okay," Liam said, watching the two masts complete their extension on either side of the ship, "watch for the green locking signals here."

Sungate looked down to where he was pointing. "Port locked… Starboard locked, sir."

The deck was rocking as *Daring* steered into the wind, punctuated by a sudden jolt. Liam steadied himself against the officer of the watch console. Sungate lost her balance and pressed against him for a moment.

"Sorry, sir," she said, glancing up shyly.

"No worries. You'll get your space legs soon enough." He cast his hand over the sailing table. "You'll start to see sails being deployed on the masts now, but reefed because we're still heading into the wind."

"How long will we maintain this course?"

"Look at our three harassers," he replied, pointing at the tactical table. "Are they still closing us?"

She studied the plot for a moment. "No, sir."

"They can't follow us into the wind very well, so they have no choice but to fall back. Hopefully they'll interpret our move as a retreat."

She turned to face him fully. "Isn't it a retreat though, sir?"

He offered her a wink. "Trust the captain."

She offered him a small smile. "Yes, sir."

Riverton turned in her chair. "XO, you said three hours to effect hull repairs to *Freedom*?"

He strolled over to her side. "At a minimum, ma'am. Sublieutenant Brown would prefer to replace the panels completely, but that will take days."

She studied her own tactical screen and nodded to herself.

"Tell Brown to make the full repairs. We have the time."

"Several days, ma'am?"

"Time for our multiple wounded to recover, and *Freedom* to be ready for a fight. We can track Shordar's ship from at least a day behind her, and with full sails and a stern wind we can catch her handily. But I want all our people and equipment in full fighting order when we launch our next attack."

Liam nodded. "I recommend we maintain this upwind course for twelve hours, then turn and start the pursuit. It'll take us at least three days to catch up enough to draw their attention."

"Agreed." She stepped down from her chair. "Officer of the Watch, I'll be in my cabin if you need anything."

"Yes, ma'am," Sungate replied.

Riverton reached the aft door just as Templegrey arrived on the bridge. The doctor held the door open as the captain passed through wordlessly. Templegrey entered and tossed Liam the tiniest of glances as she approached. The captain's trust of the doctor was still shaky, Liam knew, and it was the kind of wound that would only heal with time.

"Good afternoon, Doctor," he greeted her.

"Good afternoon, sir." She turned her gaze to Sungate, expression perfectly composed into one of professional curiosity. "I'm ready to take the watch at your convenience, Julia."

"No rush at all, Ava," Sungate replied smoothly. "I know you've been very busy down in sickbay."

"This is a pleasant change. At least as officer of the watch I know that everyone will actually obey my orders."

"Do you have difficult patients?" Liam asked.

She came as close to rolling her eyes as a trained noble could. "The sailors are fine, and even Chief Sky has remained in her sickbed. It's those insolent petty officers who refuse to get the rest they need."

"I saw Amelia up and about – she looked a bit shaky."

"Yes… And Ethan practically snipped the end of my stitches himself before bounding out of sickbay to return to duty."

"Devotion to duty is admirable," Sungate offered carefully, "is it not?"

"I suppose. But if they hurt themselves even more because of their stubbornness, it just makes more work for me."

"I'll have a word with both of them," Liam said.

"Thank you, sir. They might actually listen to you."

Sungate unbuckled the weapons belt of the officer of the watch and offered it to Templegrey, but held it even when the doctor went to take it.

"Well… I don't wish to impose, nor do I wish to be seen as being overly devoted to duty, but I was hoping to remain on watch." Sungate raised a reassuring hand. "I'm happy to relinquish charge, Ava, but I'm still eager to learn. I was hoping I might stay up and observe you for a bit longer."

Templegrey's sudden smile was warm, and Liam assessed that it even touched her eyes. "Of course."

"I'll leave you to it, then," Liam said. If Sungate wanted to continue with extra training, good for her. He had other priorities that needed his immediate attention.

———

Amelia winced at every brush of fabric over the wounds still knitting in her thighs. But as she hobbled along the passageway she set her expression into one of steely resolve.

"Afternoon, PO," greeted one of the gunners as he passed.

"Good afternoon," she replied airily.

She moved to one side as a trio of propulsors struggled along with a rolled-up sail. The translucent material practically shimmered in the multiple lanterns illuminating the passageway.

"Need a hand?" she asked automatically.

"No thanks, PO," the lead sailor said. "We got this."

She gave them all an encouraging smile as they guided their awkward load past her. She reached the door to her cabin, but suddenly realized that the last thing she wanted was to isolate herself again. Up ahead was the door to the senior mess: she figured a coffee and a nice chat with Bella was what she needed to get started as a useful member of the crew again. Another sailor hustled past, nodding quickly to her. It was still strange to be considered a senior member of the crew to be respected and even feared, but she finally felt like she was growing into her role.

She hadn't yet released the handle to her cabin door when she heard someone descend the after ladder. There was something immediately familiar about the gait and she turned.

It was Liam. Still dressed in his tattered clothes from the mission.

His face lit up as their eyes met, an uncharacteristic grin splitting his features.

Amelia stopped, a sudden rush of emotion overwhelming her. After everything that had happened, it was all she could do not to run forward and throw her arms around him. Her vision blurred as tears streamed forth, and she immediately opened her cabin door, gesturing for him to follow.

The door fell open and she stumbled into the dim space, vaguely hearing the rapid footfalls behind her. A moment later she sensed his presence. The door clicked shut and his powerful arms were around her. She knew his touch, his scent, the familiar rise of his chest as she leaned her head against it. Her hands slipped up under his coat to wrap around his body.

"Amelia…" he whispered, holding her close.

She buried her face into his chest, not understanding where the sobs came from, or the river of tears that soaked his shirt. She just knew she wanted to hold onto him forever. He simply stood, arms wrapped around her. But as she listened to his heartbeat, her mind flashed with images from her recent nightmares. Of drowning. Of being buried alive.

She lifted her head, noting that his eyes were as wet as hers.

"Hello darling," he whispered.

"Hello…" She hugged him anew, then eased herself back so that she could see him properly.

He was perfectly ragged in his slashed, dusty clothes. The bandages over several sword cuts were stained but not yet soaked through. She studied his face, noting the familiar lines of fatigue.

"Are we giving up the chase?" she asked.

"Just for a few hours," he sighed, leaning against the door and folding his arms. "We're not able to catch them with only two masts, but Shordar's escort ships kept harassing us, forcing us to keep the side masts stowed and the cannons engaged. I gather you've been doing the rounds."

"Just following the coxn around."

"How's the crew?"

"Eager for a fight." She eased herself down onto her bunk, wincing at the movement. "But personally, I just need a nap."

He crouched down in front of her. "The doctor wasn't happy that you left sickbay. How are you feeling?"

"Like I've been through a harvester."

His eyes closed. "I'm sorry."

"For what?"

"I started that fight on Morassia." He sighed. "I didn't mean to. But when that brute put his teeth into you… I just wanted to keep you safe."

She remembered the sting of the Theropod bite, and shuddered at the chaos that followed. She'd thought the negotiations were under control, and in her few clear moments of thought since she'd been puzzling over why things went so badly so quickly. It was because Liam had messed up?

"You don't have to keep me safe," she said. "I can do that myself."

"I know…" Tears welled up in his eyes. "This time, though… I thought I'd lost you."

"Hey," she said, lifting his chin with her fingers, "I'm okay. It's nothing permanent, except for some wicked scars."

"You truly are unstoppable," he said with a shuddering laugh, resting his hands on her knees.

"You want to see some of my scars…?" She gave him a smirk as she unbuttoned her coat.

"Only if I can show you mine," he replied, moving to slip off his own.

The door suddenly opened, banging into Liam's back in the tiny space. He turned with a start, shoving his face into the opening.

"Oh…" Amelia heard a cultured voice say, "Commander Blackwood."

Amelia rebuttoned her coat as Liam slowly opened the door wide.

Sungate stood in the opening, eyes moving between the two occupants of her cabin with great interest.

"Sublieutenant Sungate," Liam said stiffly. "My apologies – I was just checking in on our recovering quartermaster."

Amelia waved weakly, still sitting on her bunk.

"How kind of you," Sungate said, resting a hand on Liam's shoulder as she slipped past him. She knelt down in front of Amelia and offered a warm smile. "So good to see you out of sickbay, Amelia."

"Thank you," Amelia replied.

"Yes, so good indeed," Liam echoed.

There was an awkward moment of silence in the cabin. Sungate kept her bright eyes on Amelia, but there was no doubt she was very aware of Liam's presence.

Amelia cast her eyes up to him. He held her gaze for a moment, offering an apologetic smile, then turned for the door.

"I'll take my leave, then."

Sungate shut the door behind him, still smiling as she removed her coat and hung it up. "So nice of the executive officer himself to stop by. He really takes an interest in his crew, doesn't he?"

"He's a good man," Amelia offered, pulling off her coat, tossing it on the deck and laying down stiffly on her bunk. She considered reaching for her boots but couldn't be bothered.

Sungate didn't reply, setting herself down in the cabin's sole chair and reaching for a book on the shelf. But her smile didn't quite fade.

CHAPTER 9

Amelia sat back in her chair, coffee cup in hand, as Bella cleared away the last of the dinner dishes. Part of her said she really should get up and help her friend, but a bigger part of her realized that, for the first time in days, she was feeling comfortable. And that was something to cherish. Sighing quietly, she took another sip.

The senior mess was quiet with just the two of them, even more so because Bella's movements were so close to silent. Only the chink of serving dishes being piled onto a netted tray disturbed the peace.

"Do Theropod children play hide and seek?" she asked suddenly. "I figure you'd be pretty good at it."

"It is one of our favorite games," Bella replied, closing the net and slinging the tray of dishes under her claws. "But it too often ends in injury."

"The seeking gets a little rough?"

"We call the game 'hunt'… if that makes things clearer."

"Yup." Amelia gestured vaguely outward. "So is Shordar enjoying the game we're playing right now?"

"Very likely. He thinks, with his smaller ships and superiority in numbers, that he has the advantage. In Theropod tactics, bigger is rarely better: it comes down to who has more assets."

"Have you shared this insight with the captain?"

"Of course. You are my family."

"I just haven't seen any change in our tactics."

Bella opened the door with her free hand, long neck reaching back to keep her eyes pointed at Amelia. "The captain has something that Theropods do not… patience."

She slipped out the door, long tail still brushing through the frame when Human hands took hold of the door and pushed it open. Ethan Narrow entered, heading straight for the coffee before he even noticed Amelia.

As she took another sip, she couldn't help but notice him. There was no denying that he was handsome, but after Butcher's none-too-subtle chat the other day she'd taken to watching how Ethan interacted with the crew. He was a natural leader, for sure, who set the example and lifted everyone's spirits with his boundless optimism. When he turned and spotted her at the table, his eyes lit up. And she felt an easy smile spreading across her own lips.

"Amelia," he greeted, coming to sit across from her. "Still on the mend?"

"Never better. You?"

He rolled his shoulder easily. "Barely a scratch. Ready for the next round."

"Me, too. And something tells me we won't be negotiating this time."

"Oh, no," he laughed. "That time is long gone. I just hope you can join us for the fun."

"Why wouldn't I?'

"Oh, I heard the doctor and the XO discussing you in sickbay when I got my last dressing replaced." He reached across the table, resting a strong hand on her forearm. "Don't worry: the doctor said you were fine to return to duty."

Meaning Liam was leaning in the other direction, she thought with sudden frustration. Her legs were still wrapped in bandages, it was true, but she was more than capable of doing her job. She didn't need to be protected. She also didn't move her arm, and let Ethan's hand rest on it for a long moment.

The moment was broken only by Brown's voice over the main broadcast. *"All senior personnel to the bridge."*

"I guess that's us," Ethan said, giving her arm a squeeze before downing his coffee and rising.

Amelia followed him up the two decks to the bridge. He bounded up the ladders easily, waiting at the top of each with a grin as she labored up them. By the time they reached the quarterdeck her muscles were burning, but she refused to show weakness and offered him a triumphant smile.

"No ill-effects whatsoever," she declared.

"I had no doubt."

He opened the forward door and she stepped through onto the bridge. Liam was already there, as was Captain Riverton in her command chair. Brown had the watch and was already flanked by Templegrey and Sungate. As Amelia approached, the bridge hatch popped open as Sky, Butcher and Swift climbed up.

Liam surveyed the group and motioned them to encircle the command chair. "We're all here, ma'am."

Riverton brought up a tactical display next to her chair and pivoted it so that everyone could see.

"Ladies and gentlemen," she said, "the time has come to move against Shordar."

Amelia did her best to interpret the screen, judging that *Emerald Crown* and three escort ships were in a loose group ahead of *Daring*.

"We've been closing Shordar's formation for five days," Liam began, "easily keeping pace with some shortened sails, even as we made the appearance of being at full sheet. Compliments to the sailing officer for maintaining the deception."

"It was mostly the sailing artificer," Swift said. He offered a most uncharacteristic look of praise to Ethan, who nodded humbly.

"Why the deception?" Amelia asked.

"We wanted Shordar to think that we were barely keeping up," Liam replied, "to give him the sense that he still has many more days before we close into range. So when we make our move, he'll be caught unawares."

"Love it," she said.

"The attack plan is complex," Riverton interjected, bringing up new symbols on her display. "Theropods prefer pack tactics, as we saw when they harried *Daring* during our departure from Morassia, and no doubt they expect to use them again if we close in our single ship. Which is why we're not going to do that."

At her nod, Liam took up the explanation again. He moved the symbols on her display as he spoke. "*Freedom* will launch when we're just outside cannon range and open wide to approach on a different vector. *Daring* will come to full sail and close at speed. Both boats in *Daring* and the boat in *Freedom* will all have boarding parties embarked, and as soon as we close to boat range we'll launch all three."

"Five against four," Riverton concluded, "will render their usual pack tactics ineffective."

"But our boats are unarmed," Chief Butcher objected. "They're no use in a cannon fight."

"Nor do we intend for them to engage in one," Riverton replied. "With *Freedom* manoeuvring swiftly to provide covering fire, each boat will board one of Shordar's escorts. Capture or neutralize the vessel – take it out of the battle and leave *Emerald Crown* alone against *Daring*."

Butcher nodded. Amelia liked the plan and sensed support all around her.

"Who's taking which boat?" Sky asked.

"Lieutenant Swift, Chief Sky and Petty Officer Narrow will each lead a boat," Liam replied. "I'll command *Freedom* with Sublieutenant Sungate. Sublieutenant Brown will remain in charge of *Daring*, with Sublieutenant Templegrey assisting unless she's required in sickbay."

Riverton would obviously remain in command of *Daring*, Amelia knew, and the coxn's place was also here. But that still left one person unaccounted for.

"And..." she said carefully, "me?"

"You'll be in *Daring*," Liam said quickly. "We need one experienced boarding team member in defence."

"Since when?" That was never how they'd played it in the past. Amelia suddenly felt very hot under her coat.

"Since we have to split our boarding party across three boats," Liam retorted. "We're going to be pretty thin on the decks here, and we can't afford to leave *Daring* vulnerable."

"I hardly think the most powerful ship in our little armada will be vulnerable."

"Is that your expert tactical assessment?" Sky snapped suddenly. "Do you have a different mission plan you've created all on your own?"

"That's enough," Liam said sharply, glaring at them both.

Amelia glared back at him, trying to think of a polite way to say what she was thinking.

"I recommend Petty Officer Virtue lead the third boat," Butcher said suddenly, "assisted by Petty Officer Narrow. She has the experience and he has the muscle."

"I'm sure the artificer is capable on his own," Liam said coldly. "And the quartermaster is still recovering from wounds."

"I'm fine," Amelia insisted, turning to Templegrey. "Isn't that what you said?"

The doctor's face was carefully neutral, but her eyes flicked between Liam and Amelia. With a flash of apology to Liam, she spoke quietly. "Petty Officer Virtue is fit to return to duty, if she so chooses."

"Your courage is beyond question, Quartermaster," Riverton said, suddenly turning in her chair, "so do not feel obliged to go into combat if you need more time to heal."

"I'm ready for combat," Amelia said, staring at the captain so that she didn't have to look at Liam.

"I would prefer," Riverton said to Liam, "the most experienced boarding leaders we can muster."

"Very well," he said, face stony. "Petty Officer Virtue will lead the third boat, with Petty Officer Narrow supporting."

"Gather your teams and equipment," Riverton concluded. "We strike on the middle watch."

As the meeting broke up, Amelia kept her eyes down, stepping away from the cluster of people. She'd barely made it four paces, though, before she felt a hand on her shoulder.

"Hey, Amelia, a moment?"

She spun around, half-expecting Liam to be behind her, but the sharp words died in her throat when she saw Ethan, flanked by Swift. Ethan gave her a friendly smile, but Swift's face was an expressionless mask.

"No-one's arguing with your decision," Swift said, "but we figure you should have the pick of the boarding team to support you. Take your top three."

She genuinely appreciated their support, but the anger was burning too hot for niceties.

"Hedge, Flatrock, Song," she snapped.

"I'll let them know," Ethan said. "How about we muster at midnight?"

"I'll take *Freedom's* boat," Swift added. "You and the assaulter take the regular ones."

"Fine."

Liam had finished saying whatever to the sublieutenants and passed her on his way aft. Amelia ignored him and gave her boarding party shipmates her best attempt at a smile.

"Thank you, sir. I'll have my team ready by two bells past midnight."

Swift nodded. Amelia spun on her heel and walked away. She grabbed the bridge door and ripped it open, only at the last minute thinking to not slam it behind her. She was a senior leader on this ship, she reminded herself, and anger in front of the crew was never a good look.

No, this anger was best directed at a private audience.

The door to Liam's door was open. She rapped her knuckles against the wood in two sharp strokes and strode in, swinging it shut behind her.

He hadn't even sat down yet, and he stepped back to offer her the chair while he sat on his bunk. "I'm not surprised to see you."

"What are you doing?" she demanded, looking over him. "I am not going to sit out the most important engagement of this mission."

"I never intended for you to do that. But I wouldn't send any of our sailors into combat on an enemy ship if they're not in fighting form."

"We do it all the time, if we need to!" She stabbed her finger in his chest. "I've seen you cinch down the bandages and run in swinging plenty of times."

"With Narrow available, we have a backup. And this way you'd be fresh if there was a follow-on engagement."

His tone was so calm, so reasonable, that part of her just wanted to believe it. But she knew it was just his noble charm taking charge of the conversation again.

"Don't give me that. You can throw all the reasons in the Halo at me, but we both know why you did this. To protect me."

He gestured again for her to sit. She finally did.

"Is that so wrong?" he asked quietly.

"Yes, when it takes away my freedom to make my own choice."

He chewed on that for a moment.

"I'm not some porcelain doll for you to put on a shelf," she continued.

"I know-"

"Do you?" she leaned in, looking into his eyes. "Do you really?"

"Yes, Amelia. Why would you think otherwise?"

"Because I feel sometimes like I'm being smothered by... by your love."

His handsome face twisted in a frown, and she could see him processing her words.

"After Morassia," she said, "I was having nightmares about drowning, or about being smothered, or buried alive – in every case I couldn't breathe. And that's how I feel when you get like this: like I can't breathe because you're smothering me."

"I'm... sorry I make you feel that way."

"But there's more to it than that," she said, realizing an insight that she'd been trying to grasp ever since the first dream. "There's something fundamentally different about how you and I view death."

"Oh?" He sat back, a guarded expression clouding his features.

"When I was a kid," she continued, "I was with my family bringing in the harvest from the orchard we worked on. It was getting late and my mother wanted us to finish before nightfall. She piled us up with as much as we could carry and told us to cut through the ponds to deliver our baskets.

"It was getting dark and I took a wrong step. I fell into the pond and was dragged down by the weight of my basket. I couldn't swim, and… It was all I could do to get the basket off my arms and claw my way upward."

"I'm sorry," he said with sincerity. "That must have been terrifying."

"It was. But the worst part was getting to the surface and hauling myself onto ground… and then realizing that my little brother was gone. He'd been following close behind me, and slipped in the same spot I did." She closed her eyes, steeling herself. "And my mother's biggest worry? That we'd lost two baskets of fruit in the water."

"Your brother?"

"Never found him. Never went looking. We just kept going with our work and got paid enough to eat the next day."

Liam was silent. He leaned forward, clasping his hands on his knees.

"Death of a loved one came quick and brutal in my life," she said. "Something tells me you didn't have the same fears growing up."

He started as the conversation suddenly focused on him.

"Well, no…" he said. "We had our worries and challenges, but…"

"But you never thought you were going to die. Or that your parents or siblings might get snuffed out that day. You worried about stuff, but never about losing the ones you loved."

"That's fair," he said cautiously.

"I assume your entire family is still alive?"

"Yes."

"I had nine brothers and sisters. Four of us made it to adulthood."

"I'm sorry."

"Don't be – it's not your fault." A sudden outrage about the inequality of the Empire's class system screamed in her mind, but she fought that down. "But I learned early on how to deal with the death of people close to me. You never did."

"But that obviously changed when I joined the Navy. I deal with death all the time."

"With your crew, yes. And while I know you care for every sailor under your command, you don't make strong attachments to any of them. Because you know you might lose them."

"That's a burden of our profession."

"But now," she concluded, "it's different. I'm not crew to you anymore. I've made that great leap into that tiny part of your heart that really, truly cares. And you can't handle it."

"I think," he said, his face twisting in insult, "you oversimplify."

"Do I?"

He sat in silence, contemplating her words. He clearly didn't like them, but to his credit he was at least willing to absorb them. She watched as he turned them over in his mind, as he examined them for every angle. Slowly, his expression lightened.

"It's true," he said finally. "I never want to lose you."

"You won't. If you let me be me."

"I wouldn't want you to be anything else."

It was, she suddenly realized, a typical, charming thing for a noble to say.

She looked at him anew, at those eyes she knew so well, and suddenly she felt like she was in a fencing match. Each phrase was a deft strike, each statement a reposition to gain the advantage. She'd watched Liam and Ava conduct their smiling, flirting wars of words many times in the senior mess and elsewhere. She'd seen the same games play out just recently with Julia Sungate and both her noble colleagues. Every interaction was a contest, an opportunity to either score points or to play some long game.

She was, she realized, getting very tired of playing.

"What do you really want, Liam?"

"What do you mean?"

"For me. For us. For our future."

"I thought we'd agreed to not really discuss it. To just let things play out."

"Well, I don't like how they're playing out right now. I want to know what's really in that noble heart of yours," she tapped her finger against his chest. "No spin, no games. What do you want me to do?"

"I love you. And I want you to be safe."

Her heart warmed at his words, but she knew it wasn't an answer.

"I love you, too. But you know I won't always be safe in this ship. And you know I'm not going to shy away from my duty."

He sighed. "I know. And it's hard."

"So what do we do?"

She could tell he was considering his words carefully. Too carefully.

"Just spill it, Liam!"

He leaned forward, taking her hands in his. "Honestly, Amelia, I think it would be best for both of us if you retired with your riches, and lived the life you want on Passagia."

It was, he realized the moment the words were out of his mouth, the absolute worst thing he could say. Amelia's eyes widened, but not in the cute way they did when she was surprised by a bawdy joke. They hardened as they widened, turning to flint as she withdrew her hands from his.

"No," he stammered immediately, mind racing, "what I meant was-"

"Oh, no," she said, voice low and dangerous, "I don't want to hear from Lord Blackwood. I want to keep talking to Honest Liam. Let me guess… you want me to go and sit in a little castle, all safe and pretty, while you continue your grand adventures across the stars?"

This was getting out of control very quickly. Especially since Liam knew it wasn't that far from a truth he rarely even admitted to himself.

"Amelia, please. Just because I have a desire it doesn't mean that's what

I think we should actually do. I know that you wouldn't be happy just sitting around."

"But it would be best 'for both of us'… isn't that what you said? It would be best 'for both of us' if I just retired and disappeared."

"I misspoke-"

"No, I don't think you did. But here's what I think: I think it would be best 'for both of us' if you just kept to your own stern wind and let me chart my own course."

She had a full head of steam and experience had taught him that she often said things she didn't really mean, but that last phrase was too much to let slide.

"Chart your own course?" he repeated back. "And what, pray tell, do you mean by that?"

She paused, suddenly hearing her own words. The silence extended in his cabin.

"I meant," she said, much more quietly, "that I don't like being handled. We both have our roles on this ship and I need to be free to conduct mine fully."

"I love you," he said again, feeling the ache in his heart as he said it. "And I can't help but worry about you."

"And I love you," she said immediately, the anger melting away. "And I worry about you, too. But I know how to manage those feelings. I don't tell you to stay here in the ship. And I certainly don't tell you to stay in your little castle and be a handsome dilettante for me to come home to."

"No." He could see her point. But it wasn't that easy. "I just don't know how to stop worrying."

"Neither do I. I just live with it."

"Then I guess I have to do so, as well."

She let out a deep breath, and he could see the fatigue in her. "Look, I should go. I need to get to bed for a few hours and," she gave him a touch of a smirk, "I actually need to sleep. It's going to be an exciting night."

He reached out and took her hands again. She squeezed his fingers and then pulled him forward. They both rose to their feet and she pressed herself against him, sliding her arms up to his shoulders. He held her tight, relishing her warm proximity. He kissed her hair and felt her tighten her grip.

He lost track of how long they just held each other, but eventually she loosened her grip and stepped back.

"I should go," she whispered.

"Goodbye, darling. See you tonight… after you capture a ship for us."

She flashed him a tired grin and exited his cabin.

He sighed, tapping his fingers on the desk. Orders had been given and ship preparations were now out of his hands as his senior personnel would make their necessary preparations. Liam knew he could always do another tour of the ship, but after Amelia's outrage he didn't want to come across as smothering to the ship's leadership. But he couldn't just sit in his cabin.

Instinct took him forward to the bridge, where Brown had the watch. To Liam's surprise, Sungate was also present, and the two sublieutenants were engaged in a focused conversation.

"The explosive power derives from the liquid?" Sungate was saying in barely concealed astonishment.

"Yes," Brown replied. "The missile propellant burns far more evenly and powerfully than our gunpowder."

"Discussing our weapons?" Liam inquired politely.

"I'm curious, sir," Sungate replied, "why we have different ranges between our missiles and our cannon. Sublieutenant Brown, I've just learned, studied chemistry at the Academy and is quite the expert in such matters."

Brown shrugged modestly, but Liam could see the slight flush in her cheeks. "I was explaining how there are many things that can burn, both liquid and solid, and it's both the rate and intensity that we study."

"And the cost," Liam added. "Our missiles are invaluable both in combat and on His Majesty's financial sheets. It's why we reserve them for Sectoid engagements."

"That," Brown added, "and were we to fire one at Shordar, it would obliterate his ship."

"Not the outcome my family desires," Sungate agreed. "Unless, of course, the Suncatcher was safely aboard *Daring*."

"An outcome we're singularly focused on," Liam said. "But to do so we'll have to use our reliable cannon. Enough damage to cripple his ship and an easy way to fire across our grapples."

"And enough ammunition to keep up the fight for weeks at a time," Sungate agreed, her eyes lighting up. "They really are the perfect weapon – I find myself fascinated with them."

"You should compare *Freedom's* cannon to *Daring's*. Ours are Navy standard, but *Freedom's* are a smaller caliber – shorter range but more accurate up close."

"Really?"

"You and I will have some fun in the upcoming battle."

"Thank you for allowing me the opportunity to serve under you, sir." She lowered her gaze and looked up through long eyelashes. "I'm sure you can teach me a great deal."

"We'll use everyone to the best of their ability," he replied, holding her gaze for just a moment.

Then he turned away, offering Brown a warm nod before opening the bridge hatch and descending downward. He passed through the Gun Deck and down to Two Deck, noting the quiet activity of a ship's company only now being alerted to an upcoming battle. He found his way aft to sickbay, where he was surprised to see Ava Templegrey alone in the shadows of only a few lamps.

"Good evening, Doctor," he greeted. "It must be a relief to have no-one under your care."

Templegrey cast him a sad smile as she finished dropping bandages into a basket and washed her hands. "It would be more of a relief if they were all completely healed. But you know how sailors are."

"Yes," he said, feeling a sudden rush of irritation. He glanced around to ensure the room was empty. "I thought we'd decided that Amelia was not ready for combat."

She turned fully toward him, folding her arms. "*You* decided that. I merely advised on my patient's condition."

"And then you contradicted me in front of the captain and the entire senior leadership team."

She stared him down, arms still folded. "Am I addressing the executive officer right now, or Lord Liam Blackwood?"

"The XO."

"I'm sorry, sir."

"And now," he said taking the nearest chair and gesturing for her to sit across from him, "you're addressing Liam."

She lowered herself into the chair, shoulders slumping. "Could Amelia use more time to recover? Of course. But so could Chief Sky, Petty Officer Narrow and the rest of the sailors who were in here. We're a small ship with limited crew – we work with what we have."

He nodded. "The thing is, had you and I disagreed about, say, Chief Sky, I probably wouldn't have given in during the briefing."

"Oh?"

"If I didn't think Chief Sky was ready, I would have vetoed even her most vehement requests to return to duty. But with Amelia… I second guess myself. I truly don't think she's healthy enough, but I know that there's more coloring my decision. So, against my better judgement, I let her sway me."

"Even though putting her in danger is the last thing you want."

"I want to protect her… but I want to give her what she wants." He smiled. "Love is complex."

Ava's expression softened. "And difficult, in your situation."

"Most difficult." He glanced up at her. "Later, in my cabin, I suggested that maybe she should retire and live on her riches."

Harsh laughter rang through sickbay. "And how well did that go over?"

"About as well as you'd think. It was a silly thing to say."

"But heartfelt, I'm sure."

Liam shook his head. "There's little room for heartfelt gestures in our line of duty."

"Yes, duty…" She let that word hang in the air between them. "It's what people like you and me are born into. It permeates every decision we make, and rarely for our own personal favor."

"A new twist in your love life?"

Something flashed across her expression, just before the noble mask slammed into place. "Whatever do you mean, darling?"

"Are you facing another marriage proposal?"

She sighed. "So long as I stay in space with the Navy, I appear to be safe. But my father has informed me of several interested suitors. For whenever I'm ready."

"Perhaps he'll give up one day. My father has."

"You Halo houses are so charming," she said with a condescending smile that was laced with sadness. "Family duty will never escape me. I must marry and produce an heir."

They sat in silence. Liam's mind churned and he knew Ava was lost in her own thoughts. He glanced up once, appreciating that he was perhaps the only person on board who she ever let see her true self. In that moment Ava simply sat in the shadows, slumped with fatigue, absently fingering the hem of her coat as she pondered a fate she would do anything to avoid. For all their differences, they understood each other remarkably well.

"Well," he said finally, slapping his knees and rising to his feet, "let's focus on the duty right here in front of us. To our ship, to our crew, to ourselves."

"Quite right, sir," she said, rising as well.

"Everything may be uncertain," he added, "but in our ability to deal with what comes, I have no doubt."

"Good. Now go give Amelia a kiss, you idiot, then get back to work."

"Yes, Doctor."

CHAPTER 10

"Let go all lines, Ms. Sungate," Liam ordered. "Get us clear."

"Yes, sir," Sungate replied, moving around *Freedom's* low bridge to issue various orders. A skeleton crew of sailors were spread throughout the little ship, all *Daring* could spare for the upcoming battle.

"Shame you can't join us for the boarding tonight," Swift muttered at Liam's side.

"The burden of senior rank," Liam replied. "But I'm sure the drinks and canapes will make up for me missing the fun."

Liam glanced at his friend long enough to catch the propulsor's wry grin, then returned his gaze ahead as he felt the gentle shift as *Freedom* detached from *Daring*. At Sungate's order, thrusters fired and the space between the two ships opened.

"I thought you'd at least wear your armor so that I might think you were going to work hard."

Swift had recently invested in personalized armor and the plates clinked softly as he stepped forward. The breastplate was a deep blue, and across it was etched a faint, silver outline of *Daring's* forward silhouette, all four masts at full sail. It was understated, but clearly top quality – much like Swift himself.

"I'm ready to defend the ship if necessary," Liam replied, pointing to the aft corner of the bridge where his own polished black armor was prepped for rapid donning.

"Sir," Sungate called, "we've opened to more than two mast lengths: permission to extend masts?"

"Yes, please." Liam clasped his hands behind his back and watched the sailing table to his right, noting the quick progress of the mast deployment.

"She's good," Swift admitted, glancing forward to where Sungate moved with purpose between bridge stations. "But I'm curious to see how well *Freedom's* automation works under duress. You know I won't be here to fix things if they break."

"I promise to be careful," Liam said quietly. "But I'm making you sign for that boat."

Swift scoffed. "I'll have it back in one piece."

As the masts extended and the sails unfurled, *Freedom* opened from *Daring* on a course that kept the fleeing Theropod armada hemmed between them.

"Sir, permission to deploy forward spritsail?" Sungate asked.

"Yes, please."

Liam sensed Swift's attention focus as *Freedom's* unique forward sail was loosed – a huge, square wind catcher that was useless in any headwind but was like gunpowder to the hull in a tailwind. Through the low canopy he saw the great sheet deploy ahead of the bow, fluttering as it unfurled but becoming taut as it caught the steady winds from the Hub astern. *Freedom* noticeably shifted as she picked up speed. Liam checked his tactical table and watched *Daring* fall rapidly astern and the Theropod ships draw left ahead of them.

"This is a beautiful ship," Swift muttered.

Liam watched the relative positions of the ships change, waiting for Riverton to make her move as planned. Sungate did one more sweep of the bridge systems and joined him.

"Should we signal when we're in position?" she asked.

"The captain can see us," he replied. "We just keep flanking and wait for her to start the attack."

A soft exhalation of breath was Sungate's only response. Liam stole a glance at her, noting the nervous glimmer in her eyes that no amount of noble training could quite hide.

"Just follow my orders," he said. "Trust your training."

"Yes, sir."

Swift had wandered forward and was peering to port through the canopy. He lowered his telescope. "*Daring's* at full sheet."

Liam studied the tactical table and confirmed that *Daring's* speed had increased. Riverton was making her move.

"Come hard to port and close the Theropods at full speed," he ordered Sungate. "Boarding officer, it's time."

Swift joined Liam at the tactical table.

"This is your target," Liam said, pointing at the nearest small ship.

Swift lifted the telescope again. "I see it. Yellow stripes down its hull. And the biggest of the three escorts."

"I hardly think 'big' is an applicable term for any of them. But yes."

"I appreciate the challenge."

"Just don't tell Sky."

He extended his hand to Liam. "Fair winds, sir."

Liam shook his hand. "Following rays, Mason."

Swift descended through the bridge hatch and Liam turned his full attention to manoeuvring. The Theropod ships were fast approaching, and had no idea what was about to hit them.

***

"I have no idea," Hedge said with a shrug.

"And you don't care, do you?" Amelia persisted.

"Nope."

Amelia shifted in her armor and shook her head as Hedge shrugged and checked her gear one last time. She turned in the crowded passageway to take in the rest of her boarding team. Master Rating Flatrock met her gaze.

"I don't care either, PO," he said. "Just so long as there's loot waiting for us."

Amelia sighed, noting that at least Song seemed to have a professional interest in what she was trying to explain.

"The target we're taking down," Ethan Narrow said over her shoulder, "is like the guard post outside a vault. We have to take it out before we can get to the treasure in the vault."

"So no loot today?" Flatrock grumbled.

"One step at a time."

Flatrock nodded.

A few strides away, Chief Sky hung up the phone.

"Listen up," she called. "It's time to deploy. My team is boarding port and our target is the ship with midships bridge and the blue scales painted on it. The quartermaster's team is boarding starboard and your target is the ship with the aft bridge and black hull."

She strode into the center of the crowd of armed and armored sailors with a powerful grace. As they shuffled clear of her, all chatter ceased.

"Our mission is to capture the targets if possible, scuttle them if not. There's probably valuable stuff on board each ship, but our main target remains *Emerald Crown*. Our job is to get rid of these escorts so the captain can close Shordar and capture his ship."

She cast a glare around the assembled crowd.

"Any questions?"

If there were any, Amelia doubted any sailor would dare voice them.

"Good luck." Sky grabbed the airlock opening to her boat and swung through.

"Let's go, team," Amelia said, gesturing for her sailors to board their boat.

Hedge, Flatrock and Song swung down through the airlock tube with practiced ease. Narrow took a bit more time but moved with competence. Amelia was the last sailor in the passageway. She checked to ensure Sky's airlock door was sealed then climbed down into her own, pulling the hatch shut behind her. She floated in the freezing zero-gee of the airlock tube as she cranked the hatch down tight, then pushed herself down into the boat. Hands grabbed her armor and guided her down to a seat. Able Rating Hunter sealed the boat hatch and took his position forward.

"Push off," she ordered Master Rating Faith behind her.

The view through the transparent boat top was surprisingly dark as the slow chase had taken them many days further out into the Halo. The Hub was little more than a glow astern and pinpricks of light all around revealed the thinning stars in the outer part of the galaxy. Wherever Shordar hoped to go, it was far from any civilization.

The boat jostled with the thruster movements as Faith launched them clear of *Daring*. Hunter handed Amelia one of the telescopes before leaning forward to stare outward himself.

"We're looking for a black hull, right PO?" he asked. "Not the easiest to spot in these night skies."

"The other targets have yellow stripes or blue scales," she replied. "If we steer clear of them, by process of elimination the only other one is ours."

"Got it," he said with a grin.

The great bulk of *Daring's* masts and sails blocked the view as Faith carefully steered the boat clear, and Amelia could tell that the ship was moving at speed. Even at full thrusters it took the boat a hundred-count to get forward of the sails and give Amelia her first good look at their quarry.

The four Theropod ships were surprisingly close, starlight from the distant hub glinting off the garish paint on their hulls. She scanned for her target, black hull against black sky. Movement to starboard caught her eye, but it was merely *Freedom's* boat blazing at full thruster as the narrow ship raced in close behind.

That small boat was callsign *Rapier*, if she remembered – way more badass than her own boat's callsign *Dagger*. *Freedom* got all the cool stuff, she thought with a smirk.

Even as Amelia watched, *Freedom* began to stow her huge bowsprit sail and the sheets on her port and starboard masts. Looking back to port, she saw that *Daring* was also beginning to retract her side masts. Battle was upon them.

"Do you see our target?" she asked Hunter.

"No…" He was carefully scanning left to right.

The Theropod ships were now in motion, turning sharply as they no doubt spotted the incoming boats. Sails fluttered and flapped as the Theropods turned into beam winds, their simple rigging not designed for quick manoeuvres. *Emerald Crown* pivoted upward and began retracting one mast, cannon ports already opening.

"Evasive!" Amelia ordered.

The boat lurched to starboard as Faith worked the thruster controls, trying to create a difficult target for the Theropod gunners. Amelia kept an eye on all the ships, but could still only see the sloop and two escorts.

Spouts of fire erupted from the sloop, but Amelia could tell the cannon shots weren't aimed at her. Most likely *Daring*, she guessed, or possibly Sky's boat, *Saber*. From what she could see, there was no damage. *Daring* was hauling to port to open her gun arcs as her starboard mast flattened against the hull.

"Hard to starboard," Amelia ordered.

The boat lurched again. Climbing to the gunnel Amelia just caught sight of *Daring's* broadside, and saw the puffs of impact against *Emerald Crown*.

"Hunter," she snapped, lifting her telescope again, "find our damn target!"

"Target in range," Sungate reported, hovering over the gunnery table.

"Fire."

She pulled down a single lever on her table, and *Freedom* rocked as her six port cannon fired as one. A deck below, sailors were now scrambling to reload the guns and get clear. Unlike *Daring*, where the gun crews themselves pulled the firing lines, *Freedom* was rigged to let the bridge have direct control of the weapons. They still needed to be reloaded manually, but these smaller cannon only needed a single trained sailor each.

Liam assessed *Emerald Crown*, spotting at least two hits but no appreciable damage. *Freedom's* guns were accurate, but lacked the punching power of *Daring's* heavy duty slug-throwers. His mission wasn't to damage *Emerald Crown*, however, and that opening salvo was merely a feint. He turned his attention to the escort ships, and the three Navy boats in play.

"Hard to port," he ordered. "*Rapier* is nearing its quarry. Ms. Sungate, target the vessel close to starboard."

"Aye, sir." She peered down her optical scope. "Ready."

"Fire."

Freedom shook again as her starboard battery unleashed. Liam spotted at least four impacts on the yellow-striped ship, including a sudden shift of one of its masts. A damaged spar?

"Reload," he ordered. "Fire at will."

Swift's boat *Rapier* was approaching from below, well outside the cannon arcs. Yellow Stripe was trying to roll and engage the boat, but the damage to its mast made its movements clumsy. The deck shook as Sungate fired again. More impacts rocked the target vessel. Fifteen seconds later, another broadside burst forth. Yellow Stripe fired a disorganized series of shots that sailed harmlessly between *Freedom* and *Rapier*. Swift was on final approach.

Liam looked forward, noting *Daring* dead ahead as the frigate steered straight into the melee. Her port guns fired at the ship with the blue scales and her starboard continued to pound away at the fleeing sloop. Liam lifted his telescope and scanned for the boats. There was one between him and *Daring*, weaving as it continued to close Shordar. He just caught sight of the other boat diving below *Daring* to follow Blue Scale as the Theropod ship evaded. That would be Sky in *Saber*, he surmised.

Unable to spot the third escort ship, he checked his tactical table. The information was old, but last seen it had been in the center of the pack. He lifted his telescope again. Where was that ship?

"*Rapier* is alongside the target," Sungate reported, "far side."

"One more broadside to keep them rattled while we board," he ordered. "Then shift target to support the other boats."

"Yes, sir."

Freedom shuddered again. At this range the cannon could hardly miss, but Liam knew the cannonballs would cause more distraction than real damage. Broadsides were blunt instruments as cannon crews knew only to aim at a ship rather than at any particular point on it. But all he had to do was buy Swift time to get aboard, and any distraction would help.

He checked the tactical table again, then scanned with his telescope. *Emerald Crown* was fine on the starboard bow, turning away. *Daring* was crossing ahead in pursuit. Yellow Stripe was close to starboard, falling astern as its sails floundered. Blue Scale was low off the port bow, trying to open the distance as *Saber* pursued, with Chief Sky and her team. *Daring's* second boat, *Dagger*, the one with Amelia aboard, continued to weave low on the starboard bow. The last escort ship, the one with the black hull, was…

Amelia's boat suddenly flipped upward, dust and gas streaming from its bottom side.

"Roll to port," Liam shouted. "Stand by to engage!"

———•—•———

"Breach! Breach! Breach!" Amelia shouted.

Hedge dove forward with a sealant patch, throwing it over the series of cracks in the bottom of the boat. Hunter was moments behind her, hands fumbling with a tube of sealant that he started squeezing out around the patch. Narrow and Song frantically spread the sealant with their hands around the patch.

Amelia scanned the space around her, desperately trying to spot their attacker. Ships and cannon fire were everywhere. But the impact had been beneath them.

"Roll to port!"

Faith heaved the boat over. Amelia hung on and scanned the sea of stars that swept past her eyes. There! Just in the glow of the distant Hub, she saw the outline of a ship.

"Hard about," she ordered. "Our target is astern."

The boat swung around. Amelia stabbed her hand out on a bearing of their ship, trying to keep it in sight as Faith made rapid, random course alterations. The black-hulled ship lit up with cannon fire, but nothing struck her boat.

"Full thrusters," she ordered. "We have to close."

Fire spewed forth in her peripheral and she caught afterglow of cannon fire from *Freedom's* hull as the ship soared into view, huge and close. *Freedom* rolled and cut in front of the boat, putting herself between Amelia and her target. Another faint glow indicated a broadside from the guns Amelia couldn't see.

"Watch out!" Faith cried, hauling the boat upward to stay clear of *Freedom's* top mast as it swung by.

"Stay behind *Freedom* if you can," Amelia said, "but close our target!"

"Fire!"

Liam felt a grim satisfaction as *Freedom* shook again, watching as the shots impacted Black Hull. The Theropod ship returned fire. Hard clangs against *Freedom* indicated the accuracy of their guns.

"I'm going to keep rolling," he said. "You maintain a steady barrage with alternating broadsides."

"Yes, sir," Sungate replied, face shining with perspiration as she stepped from port to starboard to control her guns.

Ahead of her, the starscape moved in a steady circle as *Freedom* rolled. Every fifteen seconds the deck rumbled with another barrage. Liam had lost sight of Amelia's boat, but he knew he was between her and her attacker.

No, he reminded himself. Her and her *target*. He had to let her approach. He scanned the tactical table again, realizing that his current, corkscrewing path was taking him away from the main battle.

"Hard to starboard," he ordered.

Freedom strained under his order as the crew fought to turn the ship even as she continued to roll. Loose equipment crashed around the bridge.

"Full thrusters," he gasped, hanging onto the console. "Flatten us out."

Finally, *Freedom* turned enough to catch the winds firmly in the sails of her two masts and started to pick up speed. Liam spotted Black Hull still Hubward, ripples indicating various hull breaches. He scanned ahead and saw the flash of Amelia's boat still jinking to foul any further cannon attacks.

In the distance, *Daring* was pushing toward *Emerald Crown*. Swift's boat was firmly locked alongside Yellow Stripe and Blue Scale was even now turning back into the fight. He couldn't see Sky's boat, but he had no doubt the assaulter was still closing her quarry. A port broadside shook the deck and he scanned Black Hull with his telescope.

He grabbed the ship-to-ship comms. "*Dagger*, this is *Freedom*."

Amelia grabbed the handset, still clutching her seat as Faith jinked them again. "This is *Dagger*."

"*I've softened up your target,*" crackled Liam voice, "and *will continue to draw their fire. I assess you can safely approach.*"

Freedom was turning back toward her boat with frightening speed, cannon fire still blazing between her and the Theropod ship. Maybe Liam was a little protective sometimes, but in moments like this she wasn't going to complain.

"How's the breach?" she asked Hunter.

"Sealed," he replied. "And far enough from the airlock that I'm not worried about us docking."

"Air pressure?"

"A little low." He grinned. "Like we're on a mountain hike."

"Full thrusters," she ordered, "high-speed approach. We're going straight in while *Freedom* can cover us."

"Yes, PO," Faith said, straightening his tiller and pushing his thrusters to max.

"*Freedom* this is *Dagger*," she said. "Thanks for the assist."

"Freedom *this is* Daring," came Riverton's sudden voice on the circuit. "*Move at best speed to support Saber. They're under heavy fire.*"

"*This is* Freedom," Liam replied, "*on my way.*"

Freedom soared directly over them, fire bursting from her hull as she loosed another barrage. The Theropod ship was more visible now, silhouetted against the Hub with ripples of distortion. Amelia raised her telescope again and searched the enemy hull. It was already in bad shape – Liam had certainly done a number on it. There should be an airlock half-way down the hull, just forward of the masts…

"Airlock spotted," she said, raising her arm to point at the spot on the black hull she wanted Faith to aim for.

"Got it," he said. "Going low to stay out of the cannon arcs."

Amelia felt her stomach fly into her throat as the boat dove. The Theropod hull exploded in cannon fire again, but nothing hit her hull. The boat levelled out and started to climb, the target growing in her view ahead. She could see it was trying to roll, to bring its guns to aim at her, but another well-placed barrage from *Freedom* knocked the Theropod ship on its axis. And that was all the time Faith needed.

He kept up their speed until they were inside the swing arcs of the masts, then rolled the boat to position the hull toward the Theropod ship and fired his reverse thrusters on full. The boat roared in protest and Amelia sank in her seat at the deceleration. All movement ended with a slam as the boat impacted the ship's hull. Hunter scrambled to open the boat's hatch and Hedge was already charging through.

As Amelia checked her weapons she heard the hiss of pressure differential and felt warm, humid air flood into the boat. Barely a breath later she heard a quick succession of pistol shots, followed by Hedge's familiar battle scream. Flatrock was right behind her, then Narrow. Song tried to follow but Amelia pushed herself forward and crawled through the short airlock.

Falling into gravity she landed on the deck on her hands and knees, rolling swiftly to her feet and drawing both pistols. Flatrock was guarding the passageway aft while Hedge and Narrow were already pushing forward. Beyond, the screeches and roars of Theropods echoed over the clang of blades.

The deck was soft like wood, the lighting dim and red, and the air was thick like a heavy summer's day. Amelia stumbled as she strode forward behind Narrow, her thighs aching with the sudden effort. She paused as Narrow slowed and lifted his sword high, stabbing over Hedge's head as she raised her cutlass in desperate defence of an upswung tailsword. The blow lifted her clear off her feet and she crashed back into Amelia. Narrow hacked down at the attacker, holding the ground.

Hedge barely noticed Amelia as she pulled herself up. She tried to join Narrow at the front but the passageway was too thin for both of them. She stabbed low while he swung high, but there were at least four Theropods defending and the way was blocked.

Capture if possible, Amelia remembered her orders, or scuttle if not. She grabbed a grenade from her belt.

"Fire in the hole!" she screamed.

The threw the bomb underhand as hard as she could, watching as it sailed past the first line of Theropods and rolled past the second. She retreated back until she bumped into Song, reaching up to receive Hedge as she turned away at the last second.

The whoosh of air flattened Hedge against her, the screams of the Theropods lost in the cacophony of the blast in such a confined area. Then the air reversed and yanked them forward. Amelia fell to her knees amidst the bloodied remains of Theropods, her hands slipping on the slick deck.

Narrow's powerful hand hauled her to her feet. "Let's go!"

Liam hung on as *Freedom* dipped her bow hard to port, sails rippling as she fought the headwind. Blue Scale was dead ahead and *Freedom's* four bow cannon were peppering it, but the Theropod wasn't taking the bait. Its cannons were firing singly and at will, trying to pick off Chief Sky and her team in *Saber* as the boat desperately tried to close and lock on.

"Ready broadside," he warned, as Freedom turned again.

"Sir," Sungate replied, "with *Saber* so close I can't guarantee she's out of the arcs."

"Target the mast, then, on the far side of the ship."

"We've loaded ball, not chain shot."

"I'm not trying to hurt them," he roared, "I'm trying to distract them. Fire!"

Sungate relayed the targeting orders by voice to her crews, then yanked down on her level. Cannonballs crossed the distance and punched randomly through Blue Scale's sails.

"Shall I reload with chain?" Sungate asked.

"Yes, just keep firing."

Sky was almost there, Liam could see, but was under heavy attack. He'd already seen *Saber* rocked twice by impacts and he doubted the boat could withstand a third. He'd driven *Freedo*m right up into Blue Scale's face, but the stubborn Theropods knew where the real threat was. The broadside of chain shot tore through the Theropod sails. It would reduce its ability to manoeuvre, but the cannons were still as deadly as ever.

Saber took a glancing hit and staggered in space, spinning wildly as one of her thrusters malfunctioned. She fell out of the firing arcs, but the Theropod was already starting to roll.

"*This is Saber*," came Sky's desperate voice, "*we've lost control... We can't board...*"

"Full thrusters forward," Liam ordered, desperately trying to get his ship between Blue Scale and *Saber*.

"We need to stop their guns," Sungate said, staring through her viewer.

"I'm aware, Ms. Sungate."

Blue Scale's guns fired again, a rolling barrage that didn't seem to connect with Sky's tumbling boat.

"Sir," she said, straightening, "those flares you fired to light up Shordar's ship in Morassian orbit. Where are they controlled from?"

He pointed to the console next to hers. "There, why?"

"We can direct them precisely, can't we?"

He strode over to show her the simple directional controls. "Yes, but they won't cause any damage."

Her face was beaming with excitement. "Permission to take control of flares?"

Another form of distraction? It wouldn't hurt. "Yes, please."

"All guns," she ordered over her firing net, "load ball shot and target my flare."

She shifted to the flare controls and, using her gun viewer, aimed the flare. She fired, and a red streak of light rocketed across the open space, impacting the Theropod hull directly on the central gunport. She danced back to her gun control and heaved on the lever.

All six cannon fired as one. All six cannonballs slammed into the same open gunport. A silent explosion ripped outward from the center of the Theropod ship as the slugs pounded through the opening and lit up the stored powder within.

"Same target," she cried, "fire at will!"

Freedom's deck rippled as the six cannon unleashed as fast as they could. The cannonballs punched through the hole in the hull and through the interior bulkheads. Blue Scale rolled to protect the damage. At this range, there was no room to maneuver. Liam barely saw Blue Scale's top mast before it smacked into *Freedom's*.

Liam crashed down on the flare console, ears ringing with the impact as he fell to the deck. He saw Sungate on her hands and knees next to him, and barely had time to pull himself up when he saw the flash of Blue Scale's cannon directly above him.

"Brace!" he shouted as the first cannonball struck the canopy over his head. The ringing in his ears faded in time for him to hear an ominous crack.

The wind was getting stronger as Amelia and Hedge rounded the next corner. That meant only one thing: uncontained breach.

Hedge grunted and dropped, a dent in her helmet indicating a bullet ricochet. Amelia raised her pistols and fired at the dark forms of Theropods through the swirling smoke ahead. Ducking down she grabbed Hedge and dragged her unconscious form back around the corner. Narrow appeared from the other direction, sword out and eyes wide.

"They've sealed off the bridge," he said. "If we blow any other bulkheads there won't be any more ship to take."

Amelia tried to lift Hedge, but her legs collapsed with the effort. She crashed down to the deck, noting with sudden unease that the soft surface was getting warmer. She tried to rise, but the wounds in her thighs ached in protest.

"We're outta here," she gasped. "Carry Hedge and follow me."

Clawing her way up the bulkhead, Amelia noted how easily Narrow hefted Hedge's limp form over his shoulders and advanced behind her. Up ahead, Song held the last intersection they'd cleared. He gestured for them to hurry.

"Air pressure is dropping rapidly," he shouted over the wind. "We have to evacuate."

"We're doing it," Amelia gasped. "Lead the way."

With sword and pistol out, Song hurried forward, ducking under the wreckage of the grenade blast and jumping across a tear in the deck that was visibly widening.

"Holy stars," he shouted. "She's coming apart!"

Amelia leaned against the bulkhead again, catching her breath and giving her legs a moment's rest. But she could see the deck starting to separate, Song being carried away from her by several inches a second. All around them, the bulkheads began to creak and groan.

Narrow was stopped beside her, staring in shock at the widening gulf.

"Go!" she screamed over the rising cacophony. "Get Hedge to safety!"

"What about you?"

"I'm fine."

"You're not."

"Come back for me, then!"

He considered for barely a moment, then nodded in determination. Stepping back several paces, he thundered forward and leapt across the opening, landing heavily and collapsing forward into Song. All three sailors tumbled to the deck in a mass of limbs and armor, and as Amelia tried to straighten she saw the first glimpses of space to her left. She sucked for oxygen, realizing that the very ship was coming apart.

Narrow was the first to his feet, staring helpless across the gap between them. The tear was opening on her left, that part of the ship separating faster than on her right. Bulkheads were snapping and cables and pipes breaking as the hull separated. He gestured at her to jump.

She looked at the gap. It was more than a man's height and still widening. Her legs could barely keep her standing – they'd never get her across.

<hr>

"Roll to port!" Liam ordered, even as he staggered to the damage control locker and grabbed a tube of emergency sealant. He sprayed it up onto the cracks in the canopy, watching the view outside spin as his orders were obeyed and *Freedom* turned her damaged side away from direct fire. The cracking stopped and he sagged down against the nearest console.

Sungate picked herself up, eyes wide with fear.

"Get on those guns," he ordered. "Keep firing."

It seemed his efforts to draw Blue Scale's attention away from *Saber* had finally worked, as *Freedom's* hull reverberated with nearly constant single impacts. Sungate managed a single broadside in return, but Liam turned the ship to get the solar wind behind them and open the distance.

Ahead, he could see *Daring* pulling back from her close battle with *Emerald Crown*. The frigate turned her bow toward *Freedom* and tacked into the wind. Liam steered wide, giving *Daring* a clear shot at Blue Scale. Riverton obliged, turning her ship to port and unleashing a full, sixteen-gun broadside. The battering assault on *Freedom* ceased as Blue Scale turned away.

"Freedom *this is* Daring," Riverton signalled. "*What's your status?*"

Liam scanned his damage control table, sailing table and tactical table.

"Shaken, but still in the fight. I've lost tracking on *Saber* – she needs recovery."

"*I see her.* Daring *will recover as we chase off this target. Support* Dagger."

Liam scanned ahead, spotting Black Hull easily as flames started to burst free from its hull. He grabbed his telescope to see if *Dagger* was moving away. He spotted a pair of lifeboats thrustering away at speed and even rigging sails, but of Amelia's boat he saw no sign. He checked his sailing configuration: they were in a beam wind that they could tack into, but the bowsprit sail was no use. He couldn't go any faster.

"*Dagger*, this is *Freedom*," he signalled. "I'm closing your position. What's your status?"

Static was the only response.

Amelia eased her way to the edge of the gap, looking across the widening distance. Flatrock had joined the others, helping Song to carry Hedge toward the waiting boat. But Narrow still shouted to Amelia, his words lost in the rush of escaping air, gesturing for her to attempt the impossible. Metal was breaking apart, sparks flying as cables snapped.

The thunder of fading pressure filled her ears, and the first frost of the vacuum was seeping into her. Another few moments and the entire ship would break in half – even now only the last frames to her right were still holding, bending against the force that was pulling the ship apart. Another pipe burst, spraying liquid into the gap that started to freeze within seconds.

She ducked as a thick black cable tumbled toward her, still sparking as the last of its power escaped into the vacuum. It slapped against the bulkhead across from her before tumbling outward with the escaping air. Another cable fell toward her and she shuffled clear. It knocked against the bulkhead and hung there for a moment before starting to drift toward the opening cracks in the hull.

Without thinking, Amelia grabbed it, hanging on to its warm, smooth surface. It was still attached to the other side of the hull, she saw, caught in a single bracket two decks up. Clinging to the cable, Amelia looked across at Narrow. He nodded frantically, gesturing her to come.

There was no room for a run-up, so Amelia took barely a step back before pushing herself forward with the cable. Her feet left the deck and she sailed into open space, feeling the frost of vacuum ice up her skin. The cable slipped as it broke free of its bracket, but in the gap she was in zero-gee and her momentum carried her forward before gravity took hold of her and she crashed down into Narrow's waiting arms.

He pulled the cable out of her failing fingers and helped her up, running down the passageway to where Flatrock still waited. They shoved her through the tube and she fell into the boat. Song and Hunter pulled her clear as Flatrock and Narrow climbed in after her.

"That's everyone," Narrow shouted. "Cast off!"

Amelia felt the shift of the deck and sucked in the oxygen-rich air around her. Hedge was just coming to, managing a weak grin as she tapped her dented helmet. Amelia glanced around the boat, realizing all eyes were on her.

"Well," she managed, "I think drinks are on me."

Liam finally let out the breath he'd been holding as *Freedom* clamped against *Daring*. Both ships had taken damage but thankfully none of the mooring links had been compromised. He took a careful look around *Freedom's* long, narrow bridge, assessing the status of this tough little ship he'd been entrusted with.

Sungate was busy signalling to the various outstations their securing instructions. *Freedom* was to be shut down, but also to be ready to deploy immediately. *Emerald Crown* was still out there, along with Blue Scale, and both had made good their escape while *Daring* rescued the stricken *Saber* and *Freedom* had escorted *Dagger* home.

Shordar's voice crackled over the radio again in yet another taunt.

"Thank you for a most amusing display of clumsy sailing, Human Navy. It allowed me to gather in all my lifeboats with ease. Please feel free to try and board my ships again. I assure you: we'll all be ready and waiting."

Riverton hadn't deigned to answer any of his signals, and now that *Freedom* was securely alongside, Liam angrily switched the radio off.

Her orders delivered, Sungate turned exhausted eyes to Liam. "All stations acknowledge, sir. Is there anything else?"

"Not for now, Julia," he sighed. "Well done, today."

"Thank you, sir." He might have expected a radiant smile or even an expression of smug satisfaction, but all she managed was a nod. She frowned in thought. "Sir, was that a victory?"

"We reduced Shordar's force from four ships to two, and it's possible that Lieutenant Swift's boarding team recovered key information that will help us. So… It's a victory in that it moved us closer to our goal of recovering the Suncatcher."

"Forgive me, sir, if it doesn't feel like a victory."

CHAPTER 11

Liam put his weight into the door, marked *Chiefs and Petty Officers Mess*, finally sensing it move. With heavy creaks it swung inward, dust swirling past him as he peered into an unadorned closet of a room. A long, shallow staircase stretched down away from him, leading forward into the ship even as it descended several decks.

"I always wondered what a chiefs and PO's mess was like," he mused to Swift who loomed behind him. "I guess this leads straight to the brothel?"

"Straight through the heart of the ship," Swift replied, stepping through and shining his lantern down the stairs. "These access tunnels can be useful when we're bringing up sails in a hurry."

Liam started descending the stairs, noting the uncovered machinery and circuitry along both sides of the passageway. "Pretty crowded down here."

"Which is why I usually have sails brought through the regular deck passages – don't want sailors banging into things they shouldn't. But when needed, these tunnels can give quick access to pretty much anywhere in the ship."

Liam paused at a landing, cranking a round handle to open the next door. It opened to reveal the main sailing control room, bustling as always with sailors managing *Daring's* propulsion. A few of the nearest sailors glanced up curiously at the open door, but no-one seemed surprised.

"Your department uses these tunnels often?"

"There isn't usually a need, but they're useful for doing quick surveys of the ship when we're in battle. If sensors to a part of the ship go down – or I don't trust what they're telling me – I can send a runner through these tunnels without getting in the way of the rest of the crew."

The stairs continued down to Four Deck below, and Liam knew that there was another access tunnel on the far side of the sailing control room, angled opposite to this one.

"Well," Liam said, "these were built when *Daring* was a test platform. Good to hear they're still of use."

"They're more of a nuisance than anything," Swift growled, leading the way back up to Two Deck. "And they make structural calculations harder because *Daring* doesn't match her class specs anymore."

"These tunnels make us lighter, I suppose?"

"Slightly, but they've changed the way stresses move through the ship, and our center of gravity isn't what it's supposed to be."

Stepping back out into the Two Deck passageway, Liam held the door for Swift. "Is that a problem?"

"Generally, no, because I know my ship." Swift shut the door, and his hand ran along the bulkhead for an extra moment. It was a quick gesture, and Liam sensed the affection in it. But when Swift turned his face was set in a scowl. "But it *can* be a problem if we start messing with sailing configurations."

Liam nodded. His chief propulsor was always grumpy about change, but he understood why. Whatever great idea to make *Daring* go faster that Liam, the captain or anyone else came up with, it was Swift and his engineers who were on the hook to actually make it happen.

The senior mess was only a few strides down the passageway, and having just been in the former chiefs and PO's mess, Liam couldn't help but notice that the plaque on the door still said *Wardroom* – the traditional reserve of the officers only. As he opened the door he encountered a gale of laughter from within, and stepping through he saw Chief Butcher, Chief Sky, Petty Officer Narrow and Petty Officer Virtue all seated around one end of the dining table, a bottle of rum between them. Three of them had removed their uniform coats and Amelia's collar was unbuttoned. They barely glanced up at his arrival, their expressions greeting him with easy familiarity.

For just a moment, and he hated himself for it, Liam imagined these four senior sailors in their own mess, behind their own door, drinking their own rum to their hearts content. Since time immemorial the Navy had seen fit to separate the crew of every warship into three distinct groups and *Daring*, because of her unique internal configuration, had been forced to collapse two of those groups together. He knew in his heart it was a good thing, and that the cohesion of the senior leadership in *Daring* was like no other ship in the fleet.

His eyes lingered on Amelia as she laughed again, so obviously comfortable in her home. But *Daring's* unique configuration, Liam knew, brought complications.

He glanced at Swift. His friend's face was unreadable.

"*Lee-arm*," Bella said, appearing at his side, "the captain's meeting begins in five minutes. I'll go away and help *Sarhm* in the kitchen."

Liam turned to the Theropod, smiling without showing any teeth. "Thank you, Bella, that sounds fine."

As she departed the room with a swish of her long tail, Liam moved to his customary seat at the head of the table. The senior sailors, he noted, were clustered at the other end, with a small pile of rolled up parchments next to Narrow.

"Sorry to break up the fun," he said lightly, "but the captain will be here soon. Let's get the rum put away so at least she doesn't see it."

"Maybe we should move, too," Amelia said. Was that a slur in her voice? "Wouldn't want the captain to smell it on us."

"Good idea," Liam said, pulling out the chair on his left.

Sky cleared away the bottle and glasses as the others grabbed their coats and shuffled out of their chairs. Amelia plunked down next to him in the proffered seat, grinning at him.

"Hello, darling," she purred.

"Good afternoon, darling," he said quietly, mindful that Butcher and Narrow were both seating themselves across from her. "Been self-medicating, I see."

"It helps," she said with mock indignation as she struggled into her coat, "with the pain."

"How much have you had?"

Her eyes wandered upward in thought as she fastened her collar. "I don't know… My glass was just always full."

Swift took the seat on the other side of Amelia, across from Narrow, setting down a pitcher of water and a tray of glasses. "A round, everyone?"

He passed out waters as Sky joined them at the table, followed shortly by the newly arrived Brown and Sungate, both impeccably turned out in their uniforms, who sat at the far end of the table. The sublieutenants at least, Liam sighed, would represent well for the captain's visit.

Precisely as the clock chimed the hour, there was a sharp rap on the mess door. At Liam's call it opened and Captain Riverton stepped through. Liam rose to his feet along with everyone else, noting Swift's quick steadying of Amelia as she swayed.

"Good afternoon, Captain," he greeted. "Please, join us."

Riverton strode smoothly to the other end of the table, her dark eyes surveying the assembled sailors. Her expression was as unreadable as ever as she pulled out the chair and stood, facing them all, for a long moment.

"Sit, please," she said.

As everyone retook their seats, Liam felt the weight of his captain's gaze upon him. She had never approved of alcoholic indulgence in space, but had eventually accepted it as a reality in a working crew. It was an ongoing tension between them, but one he doubted she'd raise today. But that didn't mean she wouldn't raise it another day, in private.

"Captain, thank you for joining us," he said, eager to get her focus on the tactical situation. "We have some options to discuss."

"Very good. And as an update, we still hold Shordar's ships. They're barely visible, continuing to track toward the outer Halo. We're slowly overtaking, perhaps two days away."

"I have an idea on how we can close that distance faster," Narrow declared, leaning forward to sweep his eyes around the table before settling on Riverton. "Something that can give us better speed, even in these weakening Halo winds."

"Go on, Artificer."

"Think about how the other races construct their masts," he said, eyes alight. "The Sectoids have huge ships but tiny masts – but they have hundreds of them placed all across their hulls. Lots of little masts that on their own don't give a big push, but together can propel a behemoth!"

Swift made to speak, but Narrow pressed on.

"And consider the Aquans. They mount their big sails aft, where there's no interference from the hull and just pure pushing power." He looked around the table again. "I realize our ships are built for Human-style masts, but with a few modifications we could rig both Sectoid and Aquan sails. We could double our speed!"

Liam was impressed by the artificer's enthusiasm, but he immediately turned his gaze to Swift. The propulsor was frowning deeply.

"Lieutenant Swift," Riverton said, clearly noting the same body language, "your thoughts?"

"Sectoid and Aquan ships are built differently from ours, with different stress patterns designed specifically for their type of sails. *Daring* isn't built to be driven those ways."

"But that doesn't mean she can't be," Narrow retorted, rolling out one of the parchments resting next to him on the table. "I've made some drawings, showing how we could rig some semi-permanent masts-"

"With what?" Swift snapped.

"With our replacement mast planks," Narrow replied. "We have plenty in

stores, and what I'm talking about doesn't require anything big. Here, look…"
He went on to give a technical explanation of how he wanted to rig a "stern
mast" to support the equivalent of *Freedom's* bowsprit sail behind *Daring,* as
well as eight smaller "sub masts" interspersed between the four main masts.

Liam wasn't an expert, but he knew enough about sail propulsion to
know that Narrow wasn't talking nonsense. He'd clearly thought through the
problem from multiple angles. When the artificer finished his explanation
and sat back, breathless, Liam caught Riverton's eye and both turned to Swift.

The propulsor was frowning, but the intensity of his gaze showed that
he was deeply considering the proposal. Finally, he shrugged.

"There are a lot of unknowns here, and that makes me nervous."

"But do you think the plan is technically feasible?" Riverton asked.

"In theory, yes… But there are so many variables involved I wouldn't
even know where to start."

"Start with my analysis," Narrow offered, smiling as he indicated all
the descriptions he'd scribbled in the margins of his drawings. "I've gone
through every checklist we have and done the calculations."

"But have you considered all the factors we don't know?"

Narrow frowned in puzzlement, but then pointed at his sheets again.
"I've considered everything we're aware of."

"Yes." Swift was very still, mind clearly still racing. "But what about the
things we *aren't* aware of?"

"Sir, with respect, how can I?"

A long moment of silence hung around table. Swift and Narrow starred
at each other across the unrolled plans.

"That's the trick," Swift finally replied. "Isn't it?"

"Ma'am," Narrow looked to Riverton, "I realize there are unknowns here,
but I assess that the risks are minimal. And the potential for gain is huge."

"I agree," Chief Butcher intoned. "What's the worst case? We expend
some effort, we maybe break a few sails and planks, and we learn."

Riverton look down the table to Liam. "XO?"

Liam glanced down at the detailed drawings again, at Narrow's enthusiastic expression and finally at Swift's crossed arms. "I share the propulsor's reluctance to try something completely untested, especially this far from a support base."

"Quartermaster," Riverton asked, switching her gaze, "do we have the stores to spare?"

"The articif…" Amelia stumbled over the word, "PO Narrow has shown me what he needs. I have enough sails and mast planking to do this."

The captain considered.

"Artificer," she said finally, "if I was to authorize one of these ideas – the Sectoid or the Aquan – which would you say is the more likely to support our mission?"

"The Aquan, ma'am, definitely," he said immediately, pointing at the massive stern mast in his drawing. "This one will get us the most speed, and it's the simplest to rig."

"Very well. Proceed with your stern mast."

"Thank you, ma'am."

Liam glanced at Swift. The propulsor was silent as he stared at the drawings. Liam understood well the danger of taking unnecessary risks, but unfortunately their mission made risks necessary. Especially the next idea he had decided to bring forward.

"Ma'am, we've also been examining the problem of our cannon range. It's clear that Shordar's sailors know our max effective range and have used it to harry us without taking and damage. Sublieutenant Sungate has been working on an idea." He gestured to her.

"Thank you, sir," she said. "I've been examining the chemical nature of our powder and," she nodded to Brown across the table from her, "with a great deal of expert help from Sublieutenant Brown, I think I've come up with a way to increase the range of our guns."

"Go on," Riverton said.

"The liquid fuel in our missiles is highly potent and, if a tiny amount is mixed with our powder, it can increase the explosive power of the charge, thereby propelling our cannonballs further."

"Missile fuel in the cannon?"

"Yes, ma'am. But not just any random amount. Sublieutenant Brown and I will work very carefully to calculate the precise amount – and it will be mere drops."

"I don't want to defuel my missiles to serve the cannon."

"Agreed, ma'am. I assure you: mere drops. And we will clearly mark the powder bags that have been augmented, so that they're used only at the appropriate times."

"And training for the gun crews?"

"I'll supervise it personally, ma'am."

"Will it work for both *Daring* and *Freedom's* guns?"

"In theory, yes. We'll adjust based on the different firing characteristics. I recommend we do our first test firing aboard *Freedom*, to ensure *Daring* is at no risk."

Riverton cast her gaze around the table. "Thoughts?"

Liam held his tongue, knowing that as XO his opinion tended to sway others. The fact that Brown was involved in this idea gave him a lot of confidence, but he confessed he was increasingly impressed with Sungate's keen intellect. When no-one spoke, he finally replied. "I support this idea, ma'am, and I'll personally oversee it."

"Very well." Riverton nodded to Sungate. "Proceed with your test aboard *Freedom*."

"Thank you, ma'am."

Amelia took a sip of water, realizing that her head was starting to spin. She was fascinated by Ethan's sailing ideas and felt that he'd explained them really well – both earlier when it had just been the four of them, and then again now to the officers. His passion for his trade was endearing and she really appreciated that he'd thought to ask her about stores. Nobody ever thought to ask about stores.

That tart Sungate had just described a neat idea about how to make the cannon fire better, and the captain had just given the go-ahead. Pretty quickly, actually. And Sungate hadn't even presented any cool technical drawings. It was probably all Charlotte Brown's idea, anyway, but they'd agreed to let the noble present it as hers. Poor Charlotte… Amelia leaned forward to look down the table at her friend. Then felt the table bump hard against her breasts.

A hand on each side suddenly righted her. Mason helped lean her back on her left, and she smiled at his scowling face before turning to Liam on her right. His expression was also stoic, but she knew he was just being the stern XO right now. And, she admitted, she was pretty drunk. Way too drunk for a formal briefing to the captain.

They were both so awesome, she thought. Liam was just the most amazing man she'd ever met, and Mason really was kind beneath his crusty exterior. It was so typical of them both to help her out when she was being silly. The meeting was continuing but she couldn't focus on the topic anymore, so she sat back in her chair and tried to hide from the captain behind Mason's bulk.

She cast her eyes around the table. Across from her was Chief Butcher, who was turned to listen intently to what the captain was saying. Next to him, Ethan was quietly rolling up his parchments and nodding along with the conversation. He noticed her gaze and gave her a wink.

He was a really nice addition to the ship, too, she decided. He was friendly, smart and had an infectious enthusiasm that inspired the crew. And, she couldn't help but think as she winked back at him, by the Abyss he was cute. She could feel the giggles rising up in her chest like a swarm of schoolgirls and she dropped her gaze, focusing on her fingers wrapped around the glass in front of her.

She heard a deep rustle of movement around her, then felt Mason and Liam each hook their fingers under her arms to haul her to her feet.

Everyone around her was suddenly standing at attention. She leaned into Mason's shoulder, focusing all her will into remaining motionless as the captain departed. She squeezed her arms against her body, imagining that she was perfectly straight like one of the mast planks stored below. Then she realized that Chief Butcher across from her was slightly askew. Or maybe she was just standing on an angle. The schoolgirls fought their way up her throat, and her lips sputtered as she held them back.

The door shut behind her and the strong hands holding her dropped her back into her seat. She burst out laughing, holding her gut at the release of energy. Her eyes went to Liam, who smirked down at her.

"You're cut off," he said, the amusement finally creeping onto his face.

"That's not fair," she protested, frowning at Liam's overprotectiveness. She could drink him under the table any day.

"Coxn," he said, "take charge of the quartermaster, if you please."

"Yes, sir," Butcher laughed. "Sorry, sir. A quick spot of rum at dinner carried on for a bit, I'm afraid."

Good ol' coxn, Amelia thought. Always backing her up. Liam shook his head, still smiling, and gave her shoulder a quick squeeze before departing. Swift disappeared on her other side, and Amelia shared another conspiratorial wink with Ethan as he gathered up his papers. Beyond him, Julia Sungate cast her a cold glance before departing the table. Pompous strumpet. Amelia briefly considered smacking Julia with a pillow this evening, just to see how she reacted. It would definitely be more fun than attacking her old cabinmate, Chief Sky, with a pillow. Amelia snorted with laughter again. Oh, she should probably have a nap. But maybe in the stores office, so as not to offend Lady Julia.

She downed her glass of water, listening to the chatter of her shipmates as they made their way to the door. She sensed excitement in their voices, and wondered vaguely what the rest of the briefing to the captain had included. She poured herself another water and drank it.

"Hey, Amelia," she heard, as a hand squeezed her shoulder.

She looked up and saw Ethan towering over her, rolled parchments tucked under his arm. His friendly smile made her smile.

"Hey, Ethan." Then, on an impulse. "You're awesome."

"Thanks. You're pretty awesome, too." He offered her a hand. "Do you have time to go to the stores office and start planning how we're going to build this stern mast?"

"Sure. I was just heading there."

She took his hand and hauled herself to her feet. The room swayed once, but she hung onto his hand and righted herself. She appreciated his firm grip around her palm as they headed for the door.

"Quite a storm we're riding," she said with a giggle.

"Stick with me," he laughed. "I'll get you through it."

As they stepped out into the main passageway she slipped her hand out of his, focusing completely on keeping one foot in front of the other as she made her way to the ladder down to Three Deck. She paused at the hatch, frowning as she assessed how she was going to get down this very steep set of stairs.

"I'll go first," Ethan offered.

She nodded gratefully and watched as he carefully worked his way down – he clearly wasn't sober either, she realized with satisfaction. Then she eased herself onto the first rung and started descending, careful to keep her hands on the railing and ensuring three points of contact at all times. Basic sailorship, she thought to herself triumphantly. The fact that her butt was being steadied by Ethan's hands didn't hurt, either.

The stores office was closed and she unlocked it with only a bit of trouble, and more giggling.

"I'm glad it's only you seeing me like this," she said as she pushed open the door and stepped through. "None of the officers would think it was funny."

"Oh, stars no," he said in a terrible exaggeration of a noble accent. "Most unbecoming, Quartermaster. Now run along and get me some chilled wine, what?"

She scoffed, dragging her hands along the console to where she could bring up her stores records on the screen.

"Did you notice how quickly the captain approved Lady Sungate's crazy plan?" he asked suddenly.

She paused, suddenly interested that she wasn't the only one to notice. "Yeah, I wondered that. I think it's actually Charlotte's plan, but she's savvy enough to know that anything presented by a noble will get a better reception."

Ethan scowled. "I figured. I mean, I had to making technical drawings and run down every line of thought to even get a hearing. Princess Julia swans in and just says her idea. Both captain and XO agree with her without question. And the XO even spoke against my plan."

Amelia knew that Liam was not that shallow, and that he always gave equal weight to ideas from commoners and nobles alike. She knew that she should defend him, explain what an amazing man he was. But she looked up at Ethan, looming quite close to her and gazing down at her with those bright, clever eyes. And said: "Yeah."

"We're about as lucky as we can be," he said, "being senior sailors in the Navy. We actually get some respect from the nobility, at least while we're in space."

"Some of the people we've fought against," she heard herself saying, even as the months and months of ruminating welled up in her mind, "wanted to overthrow the whole Imperial system. Wanted to give power to the commoners."

"Sounds good to me," he said.

"But it's never that simple," she protested, remembering all the pain and suffering she'd seen and experienced. "Revolution means war. And you know who suffers most in war: us."

"Hey, hey," he said, smiling easily as he slipped his arms around her and pulled her closer. "I'm not talking revolution. Sorry, this is too intense a conversation. I just wanted to say that I feel really lucky to be here, with you."

His body was warm and solid against hers, his smile so sweet. It was nice to have a peer close to her own age on board, somebody she could really talk to without any baggage of rank or background. She let her arms come up his back, appreciating his closeness. When he leaned down to her, and his lips met hers, it just seemed so innocent. Just a kiss. Not a good idea, but no big deal at all…

"I see I'm interrupting."

She knew that voice, and it snapped her back to sobriety in an instant. Breaking the kiss with Ethan – how long had they *been* kissing? – she brought her hands around to his chest and pushed herself away. His arms still held her close, though, as they both looked toward the door.

Liam stood in the opening, cold as ice. His eyes were fixed on her, and her heart sank at the hurt she saw in them.

"Oh, sorry XO," Ethan said breezily. "We'll shut the door next time."

"Allow me." Liam grabbed the handle and disappeared. The door slammed behind him.

"Oh, no," Amelia said, trying harder to push her way out of the embrace.

Ethan's arms loosened, but he didn't let go. He just gave her a shrug and a grin. "Whoops. I guess we'll just have to be a bit more discreet."

"No, Ethan," she said with more force, "let me go."

"Don't let some noble officer spoil the mood," he said, still holding her. "He's gone. And we're alone, with a closed door."

"Let. Me. Go."

He released her, staring down with genuine confusion. "What's the problem, Amelia? I like you, you like me. I thought this was going somewhere."

"It's not," she said, desperately trying to clear her head. "I made a mistake."

"No, I don't think so. I think you were just doing what you really want to do."

She stepped back, wondering if maybe she'd led him on a little bit. She really didn't think so.

"I'm sorry," she said. "I've given you the wrong impression."

"Not buying that," he said, moving closer. "I think you just need a bit of convincing."

He grabbed her by both shoulders and kissed her again. She tried to back away but bumped up against the console. His body pressed into hers as he kissed her. One strong hand gripped her shoulder and the other started to reach up her shirt. She fought to get clear, but his grip intensified as he started to pin her to the console.

Her knee was in his crotch before she could even form the thought. He released her, backing away with a gasp. She swung her fist upward into his face, and her knuckles burned with the sick crunch of impact. He tumbled backward, collapsing to one knee.

She straightened, putting herself between him and the door.

"Don't you ever, *ever* touch me again."

He held up a placating hand, shaking his head. "Okay, okay. Whatever."

Throwing open the door she ran out into the corridor, her hands and feet propelling her up the ladder and launching her onto Two Deck. She ran past a trio of startled crewmembers and ascended to the Gun Deck, then finally to the Quarterdeck. She was knocking on Liam's door before she even knew she was there.

"Come in," Liam called to the knock.

He was just settling down heavily into his seat when the door opened, and Amelia peered cautiously in. A tempest of emotions stormed through him, but he couldn't even muster the energy to rise. He simply stared at her.

"I'm so sorry," she said.

"I'm sure." He closed his eyes. Even looking at her was almost too much. He listened for the usual sounds of her entering his cabin and shutting the door, but there was nothing but the creak of the deck as *Daring* rode the winds. He opened his eyes. She was still mostly outside the doorframe, gripping the handle nervously. "What more do you want me to say?"

"Nothing," she breathed.

"Are you going to come in?"

"I don't know. What… What do you want me to do?"

He leaned his head back, stretching out his legs in front of him. He tried to look deep inside himself to answer her question, but all he saw was chaos.

"Amelia… I have no objectivity when it comes to you. If you need me to be the XO, I can't. If you need me to be your beloved… I can't. I just…" Any attempt to rationalize what was raging inside him was pointless. "I can't."

"I didn't mean for any of what you saw to happen," she said slowly. "I thought we were going to stores to count sails and mast planks."

"And yet," he heard himself say, "there you were. Tongue down his throat."

"He caught me off-guard," she continued, almost babbling. "He totally surprised me when he kissed me. I didn't want it at all."

"That's not what it looked like to me."

She pursed her lips in silence, then finally stepped in and shut the door.

"It's not like you haven't kissed another woman in front of me. And I believed you when you told me it meant nothing."

"Oh," he snapped, hardly needing the reminder, "let's bring that up. But let's remember how different the context was – or was your kissing PO Narrow in fact all part of a grand plan to complete our mission? Is Narrow really just Shordar in disguise?"

"Don't be stupid!"

"Don't deflect."

"I'm just saying… We've both made questionable decisions at times. And when you did, I didn't interfere. I trusted you."

"I trust you."

"No you don't!" Her face twisted in frustration. "You watch over me, you guard me, you second-guess me, you try to *keep me safe*. But you don't trust me."

The accusation stung, but it merely fuelled his anger.

"I didn't even want this to happen…" she continued. "I even told him to stop – had to kick him in the crotch."

"Are you saying," Liam said, sudden energy surging through him as he rose to his feet, "that he forced himself on you?"

His vision tinted red as the blood surged through him.

Amelia's eyes widened, and she desperately raised both her hands. "No, no, no… I mean… I kissed him, but it was a complete mistake."

Liam could barely hear her words for the blood pumping in his veins and he took another step toward the door. "Just say the word, Amelia…"

"Liam, no," she said, both hands on his chest. "Please, put your sword down."

He glanced to his left hand, where his scabbard had found its way into his grip. He carefully placed it back down, forcing himself to sit again. His fingers tapped the armrests as he glared at her.

"Right now, Amelia," he said carefully, "I'm incapable of being your XO or your beloved."

"So what does that mean?" she whispered.

"I don't know. But I want you to leave."

"Liam…"

Her anger still burned even as her eyes welled with tears. Warring instincts battled within him, to fight with her, to comfort her, to… protect her. It always came back to that.

"Please leave," he said quietly.

She nodded, tears streaming down her cheeks. "I'm sorry."

A hundred things burst into his mind to say, but he pressed his lips tightly shut. Finally, she departed.

Liam sat in his cabin for a long time, listening to the steady creak of the deck. His thoughts were too jumbled to even make sense of. He tried to push all thoughts of Amelia out of his mind, to focus on the mission. But every tactical idea came back to manoeuvring the ship, which meant propulsion, which meant sails, which meant that damned artificer. Or he turned his attention to how long *Daring* could stay out here in the Halo, and where she could replenish, but that brought his mind to stores, and the stores office, and that damned artificer.

He stared at his sword. Imagined the feel of the hilt as he drew it from the scabbard. He'd fought alongside Narrow, seen how inept the man was with a blade. His mind flashed with images of his saber punching through

Narrow's chest. Or slashing his neck open. He'd be dead before he even realized what was happening.

He shook his head, driving the images out of his mind. He was the executive officer aboard His Majesty's Sailing Ship *Daring*. He was in control of the situation.

But he knew that was a lie.

He didn't know how long he sat there, but no matter how he tried to tackle the problem, every thought process led to the same conclusion.

He rose from his chair, grabbed his scabbard from the deck and hooked it to his belt. Hand on the door he closed his eyes and took a deep breath, willing himself to find another way.

There was no other way. For him, or for Amelia.

Opening the door he stepped out, resigning himself to his decision and the consequences it would bring.

He knocked on the captain's door and, hearing her call, entered.

Riverton was seated at her desk, gaze lifting to greet him as he entered. Her eyes missed nothing, though, and she immediately rose to her feet and faced him.

He drew his sword. And, holding the blade flat with both palms, offered it to her.

"Captain Riverton, I regret to inform you that I'm no longer fit to be your executive officer."

CHAPTER 12

Captain Riverton stood in silence. Her eyes searched his, but he could make out nothing specific in their depths. The two of them stood in tableau for far too long, as he held his sword horizontally between them.

"Why?" she asked finally.

"I'm incapable of being objective when it comes to Petty Officer Virtue. Because of her, I have made mistakes that have risked our sailors and I fear that I will do so again. She is a fine member of our crew and doesn't deserve any sanction for my mistakes – I accept full responsibility and I offer my resignation as executive officer."

She studied him further, even folding her arms as her head cocked slightly.

"It takes great character to recognize one's own failings," she said. "And even greater character to accept responsibility for them."

She reached out both hands and lifted the sword out of his.

"I accept your resignation."

The blade lifted from his grasp, an inconsequential weight that represented all the burdens that he'd carried for so long on his shoulders. It was the end of his career, he knew. But better his than Amelia's.

"Please, Commander Blackwood," Riverton said, gesturing to her dining table. "Sit down."

He did. She sat across from him and laid the sword between them.

"I'm sorry for creating this problem for you," he said. "But I hope you agree with my recommendation that Lieutenant Swift take my place."

"Yes," she said dismissively, "there's no question it's Swift. I'm not worried about that. The real question is: what to do with you?"

He nodded. "I'm happy to take meals in my cabin and generally stay out of the way. Of course, I'll always be available to offer counsel-"

"That would never work, and you know it."

Having a spare commander just sitting around on a ship this small, especially the former XO, was a recipe for confusion, mixed loyalties and a general breakdown of discipline. If they were back home, he'd simply leave the ship at the next port, but *Daring* was deep in space, nowhere close to civilization.

"I need you to get off my ship," she stated plainly.

"Agreed, ma'am… But where?"

"It just so happens," she said, leaning back and steepling her fingers, "that we have another ship lashed to our hull. One capable of independent sailing and operations."

"*Freedom*? But… Wouldn't the Emperor object to you accepting my resignation and then sending me to another one of his vessels?"

"*Freedom* is not a commissioned warship – she is simply the greatest prize we captured during our letter of marque days. It was impossible to physically split her between all parties, so I paid a fair price in gold to everyone due a share."

Liam remembered the complicated accounting that he and Amelia had overseen as the captured assets of their vanquished enemies had been divvied up. The amount of gold Riverton had paid for all the shares of *Freedom* had been enough to set many sailors up for life.

"*Freedom*," she concluded, "is my personal property. And I can do with her as I wish."

"Yes, ma'am." He didn't dare guess where she was going with this.

She stood, lifted the sword and offered it back to him. "I would like you to take permanent command of *Freedom* and take a small selection of sailors from my ship to crew her."

Liam rose, stunned. "Ma'am, are you sure? Considering…"

"Considering your complicated relationship with Petty Officer Virtue? I assure you: I will be keeping my quartermaster aboard *Daring*." She lifted her hands fractionally, offering the sword again. "Without her to distract you, I have every confidence that you will once again be the outstanding Naval officer I have come to respect."

Slowly, gratefully, he took his saber back.

"Thank you, ma'am. I accept this command."

"Good. I can't imagine sidelining you when we're in the middle of chasing down the most notorious thief of our lifetime." She gestured dismissively at his sword. "Now put that thing away – we have work to do."

Amelia's eyes were leaden as she tried to open them. She shifted on her bunk, struggling to understand what all the noise around her was. When she finally opened her eyes, she saw Sungate moving efficiently about the cabin, grabbing what looked like the last of her things and placing them carefully in a bag.

"What's going on?" Amelia asked, propping herself up on an elbow.

"Oh, I'm sorry to disturb you," Sungate replied, "I was trying so hard to be quiet."

Amelia looked around the tiny space, saw that it was filled with Sungate's baggage. "Are you leaving?"

"Yes, I'm afraid so." The excitement in her eyes belied any real sense of regret. "Commander Blackwood has been given command of *Freedom* and he asked me to join him as part of the permanent crew."

Amelia lay back on her bunk, sighing as she processed this news. Liam was leaving. He was leaving the ship.

"Are you staying close to *Daring*, or does Commander Blackwood have new orders?"

"We're staying close," Sungate said with a warm smile. "I think Captain Riverton just wants both ships crewed and ready at all times."

"Who else is going with you?"

"Sublieutenant Brown, Master Rating Flatrock and a handful of sailors. We're going to be running very lean."

Amelia swung her feet down to the deck, fighting through the dizziness she recognized only too well as a nasty hangover, and eased her way past Sungate's bags. "What time is it?"

"Just an hour past supper. We missed you."

"I needed a rest." She was still dressed from earlier and she quickly found her boots.

Ignoring the pounding in her skull, Amelia forced herself up and out of the cabin. The main passageway was unusually active for this time in the day, no doubt as the crew responded to Riverton's sudden orders to crew *Freedom*. Her instinct was to head for the senior mess, but she wasn't ready to face Narrow if he was there. Her second instinct was to head for Liam's cabin, but she doubted she'd be welcome there – not if he was already running away to another ship. Almost without thinking, she climbed down the ladder and headed aft to boarding party stores.

Sure enough, Chief Sky had the stores locker open and was handing over satchels of gear to Flatrock. She glanced up at Amelia's approach.

"*Freedom* is taking six sets of our boarding gear, PO," she said.

It was a simple statement, but somehow there was always a challenge in her words. Amelia had no doubt who was in charge when it came to her and the ship's assaulter, but Sky always needed to assert that dominance.

"That's fine," Amelia replied. "I can do an inventory later to confirm what was moved."

"I have it all detailed right here," Sky replied, holding up a parchment.

"Sorry to be taking your stuff, PO," Flatrock said, although the sparkle of excitement in his eyes said otherwise.

"Are you the senior sailor heading to *Freedom*?" she asked. "I guess that makes you the coxn."

A toothy smile split his beard, and his gaze suddenly moved over her shoulder. "Hear that, Coxn? It looks like you and I are equals, now."

Amelia turned to see Chief Butcher grinning wryly as he strolled up. "I look forward to seeing you grow into a responsible leader, Master Rating."

"What?"

"Discipline, scheduling, setting the example… That's what being a coxn is."

"Hmm." Flatrock's face fell. "I thought it was mostly yelling and getting my way."

Butcher smiled at Amelia, but she couldn't muster any enthusiasm to join in the needling.

Sky loaded another satchel over Flatrock's broad shoulders. "Take these over to *Freedom* and find a good place to store them. Easily accessible, but secure. I'll come and check in half an hour."

"Yes, Chief." Flatrock lumbered away.

Amelia found herself alone the passageway with the ship's two chiefs. It was, she decided, not the most comfortable place to be. But they were both watching her expectantly.

"What?" she finally asked.

"How did your afternoon go?" Butcher asked. "It looked like you and Ethan were getting along just fine."

Her stomach churned with such force that she doubled over, hand rushing to cover her mouth.

"Quartermaster?" Butcher's voice was still light, but there was a sudden touch of concern.

"Back off," she hissed, forcing her gaze upward to glare at both of them. "Stop matchmaking. And stop encouraging him."

"I thought you two were…"

"So did he. A bit too much."

Butcher and Sky exchanged a glance.

"Are you okay?" Butcher said carefully.

She didn't answer right away, her mind whirling as all the emotion of the entire afternoon came rushing back. She felt no need to relive any of it.

"It's nothing," she muttered. "I don't want to talk about it."

"You don't look well."

"I'm just…" Now she just wanted to get out of there. She didn't need the whole ship to know her personal drama. "I'm just hungover, is all."

"Amelia." It was Chief Sky's voice, surprisingly gentle. And she *never* used Amelia's first name. "Did something happen with Ethan?"

"He…" she let out a heavy breath. "He kissed me, more than I wanted him to. And he didn't stop when I told him to."

"He didn't stop?" Sky's voice was like ice.

"Well, yes, he did. Eventually. He didn't… Nothing bad happened. He just kissed me more than I wanted."

"How many times did you say no?"

She looked up in surprise, having never heard this tone from Sky before. The assaulter's eyes were afire, but there was kindness in them.

"How many times," Sky repeated gently, "did you say no?"

"I don't know… Three or four." She glanced down the empty passageway, suddenly embarrassed. "I don't want everyone to know. I just want to put it behind me."

"Thank you for telling us," Butcher said quietly. "We believe you."

She felt a sudden rush of emotion from deep down. It had been there for hours, she realized, but pushed to the bottom of her soul. It was an ugly mixture of guilt, rage and shame.

"I'm so sorry that we encouraged the two of you," Butcher said. "I had no idea this would happen."

"Me neither." She shrugged. "He seemed so nice."

"We'll sort this out," Butcher said. "It won't happen again."

She looked between them. "What are you going to do?"

They exchanged another glance.

"What," Sky finally replied, "do you want us to do?"

"I just… think he and I need some space." She wrapped her arms tightly around herself. "I don't want to see him for a while."

"Maybe I could get him sent as part of the *Freedom* crew," Butcher suggested.

Remembering Liam's eyes when he'd heard of Narrow's misstep, she knew that was a terrible idea. "Don't do that, please, for his sake. I just want him to stay away from me – I don't want him dead."

"Very well."

There was a pause, and Amelia eventually realized that the ship's coxn and assaulter were patiently waiting for her to speak.

"I think I'll be okay," she said finally.

"Sungate is moving to *Freedom*," Sky said, "which means you'll be alone in your cabin. Do you… want me to stay with you for a couple of nights?"

Amelia looked up at that. She looked at Sky's powerful frame, coiled and ready for action. She looked into Sky's dark, penetrating eyes. And all she saw was kindness.

"Yes," she said, unable to stop the tears as the emotions flooded through her.

Sky didn't hug her – even Amelia in her current state knew that would be weird – but she laid a calloused hand on Amelia's shoulder.

"Why don't you go help Sam and Bella divvy up the food stores?" Butcher said. "It'll keep you busy and with friends for a while."

"Don't worry about anything else," Sky added. "We'll take care of it."

"I'd tell you not to worry," Subcommander Mason Swift said as they strode down the passageway, "but there's no point."

Liam managed a smile for his newly promoted friend, inviting him to descend the ladder first. Activity on Two Deck was picking up as stores were transferred to *Freedom* and the select dozen crewmembers moved their personnel effects over.

"Likewise," he replied. "I might tell you not to worry, but…"

"There's no point."

Three Deck was busy. The doors to the cargo bay connecting *Daring* and *Freedom* were constantly transited by sailors and Liam felt a twinge of guilt at all the extra work his own weakness had caused. But it might work out for the best, he reminded himself, treating *Freedom* as a full fighting ship rather than an oversized boat.

"I'm not worried about your ability to be executive officer," he finally replied as they weaved their way past a line of sailors shifting foodstuffs. "I'm just worried that you have enough on your plate as we prep this crazy new sailing configuration."

"Yes," Swift said with a new frown. "But thankfully I have an enthusiastic sailing artificer who can take charge of all that for me."

Liam pushed down the anger, realizing again that he needed to disappear to *Freedom* as soon as possible and put all this behind him. He was tempted to make his break from Swift right then and there, and stride across the cargo bay to *Freedom's* waiting airlock. But then he noticed Chief Butcher standing at the far end of the passageway, seemingly without purpose. Curious, he led Swift aft to greet the coxn.

"Good evening, sir," Butcher said smoothly. His expression was mild, but Liam could see the iron behind it. "I expect *Freedom* to be ready to slip within the hour."

Liam glanced around. There was no-one else with the coxn, who just seemed to be loitering outside the boarding party stores. There was a sudden shout of pain from within stores, and he gave Butcher a sharp glance.

"What's going on, Coxn?"

"Chief Sky is giving some remedial training," he replied. There was another cry of pain, and Liam realized it was a man.

"Anything we need to know about?" he asked.

From behind the door, he distinctly heard Sky's voice.

"Do you want me to keep going?"

There was another shout of pain.

"Oh, I didn't understand you. I thought 'no' meant 'yes'."

"Nothing you need to worry about, sir," Butcher said coldly, his voice almost covering the sound of a continued beating. "Everything will be fine moving forward."

"So we get each other? 'No' means 'no' right?"

Liam steeled himself, staring into the hard eyes of the coxn. Behind their resolve, he saw sympathy.

"Sir," Swift said quietly, "we probably shouldn't be here."

"Very good, Coxn," Liam said, spinning on his heel. "Carry on."

They moved away, neither speaking until they were well into the cargo bay and away from any ears. Swift turned to face Liam, reaching out to grip his shoulder.

"I will take care of the ship, sir," Swift said. "And all who sail in her."

"Should I go back?" he whispered. "Should I at least find her and say goodbye?"

Swift gripped him tighter. "For your sake, no. You should just go… But I'll tell her that you wanted to say goodbye."

Liam nodded, noting that the line of foodstuffs had ended, and that sailors were starting to clear the cargo bay.

"Well, then," he said, looking around at nothing before finally meeting his friend's eyes. "Fair winds, XO."

Swift shook his hand. "Following rays… Captain."

CHAPTER 13

"Our family is not the same," Bella said, her tiny, clawed hand removing Amelia's breakfast plate and replacing it with a fresh coffee. "I am sad."

Amelia reached up and squeezed Bella's free hand, feeling the cool, leathery skin as the three fingers squeezed around her own. "Me too."

"It's quieter around here," Templegrey agreed. "I didn't think I'd ever miss having noble ladies around, but Julia was an excellent conversationalist."

Ava was already showing signs of fatigue as she and Swift stood one-in-two bridge watches. Both Butcher and Sky had volunteered to stand short watches just to give the officers a break, but neither chief was qualified to take charge of the bridge and Riverton had spent most of those watches in her command chair. It had only been seven days since *Freedom* had separated from *Daring*, but it seemed like a lifetime. The smaller ship was visible through a telescope, and Amelia had found herself wandering up to the bridge often just to peer through the lookout's instrument.

"It's weird," Amelia said. "We now have a majority of commoners in the senior mess."

"Oh, yes," Ava said, adopting a particularly snooty expression. "So why aren't you all massaging my feet more?"

Amelia managed a laugh, but her sadness had too much inertia to shift.

The days had thankfully been very busy as the whole crew turned to in order to construct a whole new mast projecting out of the stern of the ship. Petty Officer Narrow had barely slept as he supervised the operation, logging more time in a spacesuit than most sailors did in a year. He'd barely come into the mess, other than to shovel down food and get back to work.

And that suited Amelia just fine.

It had been weirdly like old times, having Sky bunk above her again, and while the assaulter had made no efforts to kindle a friendship that had never existed, just her presence in the darkness of the cabin had made Amelia feel safe. She would far rather it be Liam, but she knew enough not to wish for what couldn't be.

"How long until Shordar reaches his hideout?" she asked.

Amelia had been too drunk to listen when Swift had reported the information his team had recovered from their captured Theropod ship, but apparently *Daring* now knew where Shordar was headed: a deserted world nearly at the edge of the Halo that was one of his main hideouts.

"At least three days," Ava said. "At our current speed we can't catch him in time, but if the new stern sails work…"

"Here's hoping."

The door to the mess opened and Narrow slipped in. He moved no further than the coffee tray, barely glancing at Amelia and Ava at the table. He smiled gratefully as Bella handed him the sugar, then, after a moment's hesitation, he turned to face the room.

"Good morning, ladies," he said, gaze resting on Ava. "The first trial of the new sails is ready to go. Captain wants everyone to close up at their battle stations."

"Oh, really?" Ava said, hauling herself to her feet with a sigh. "I suppose I shouldn't complain – it's been at least ten minutes since I was last on the bridge."

"I guess it's the best way to have us up and ready to respond if something goes wrong," he said.

"Is something going to go wrong?"

A hint of Narrow's old confidence shone through his careful expression. "No, ma'am."

"Then I guess I better get up there to watch nothing go wrong."

"Thanks, ma'am." He downed his coffee and left the room.

True to their word, Butcher and Sky had clearly taken care of things on that front. Narrow had kept well clear of Amelia since the two ships had parted, speaking to her if necessary but always at more than arm's distance. She didn't know what they'd said or done, but it had worked.

Amelia drained her own coffee and rose from her chair. Bella was already stowing the various crockery and Amelia gathered up the dirty dishes from breakfast.

"I'll take these," she said.

"*Arr-meh-ley-arr*," Bella said suddenly, reaching out to rest claws on her arm. "We are very sad for you. It is one thing to have our family broken up. It is much more to lose your mate."

It was amazing to look into those vertically slit, alien eyes and see complete understanding. Theropods couldn't cry, and Amelia knew she shouldn't. Now wasn't the time.

"Thanks," she whispered. "Hopefully we'll all be together again soon."

"Yes."

She looked around the empty mess, then gathered up the net of dishes and departed.

———•———

"It's my turn to do the dishes," Charlotte said, gathering up the breakfast plates.

Liam sat back in his folding chair, trying to stretch his legs to the side of the little table that had been erected at the back of *Freedom's* dark bridge.

With only three officers on board there was no point in isolating himself as captain, and with all of them standing watches the bridge was the only place they could ever be together. It had only seemed natural to set up a way to eat here.

"Thank you, darling," Julia said, rising gracefully from her seat. "I think I've neglected my watch long enough."

She stepped forward the few paces to the officer of the watch station, reaching for a telescope and scanning the dark skies around them as she quietly asked her single bridge crewmember for routine updates.

"Let me help you," Liam said, collecting the glasses as he rose.

"Nonsense, sir," Charlotte said, tapping his hand away. "You're the captain – this is beneath you."

"Charlotte…"

"Sir," she gave him her best glare, "we've already compromised enough Naval discipline to make our ship work. You must be seen to stand above."

"I think it humanizes me for the crew to see me help out."

"Exactly. But you must be superhuman, so that when this ship is in peril and all hope is lost, the crew know they can look to you to deliver them. Because you are more than any of us."

He thought to protest, but bit his tongue. Not only was he too tired to wade into a battle of wits with Charlotte Brown, in this case she was correct.

"Your understanding of Naval psychology is astute," he conceded finally.

"I take it seriously, sir."

Rising from his chair, Liam moved leisurely to join Sungate. *Freedom* – his ship – had been sailing smoothly for the days since they'd detached from *Daring*, and under his careful guidance his skeleton crew had figured out how to run the daily routine effectively.

For normal watches *Freedom* was treated like a merchant ship, with minimal crewing and only the simplest of maintenance. Once a day, though, for an hour or so, the crew would muster for an all-ship event, be it to fire the guns, change the sailing configuration, or just to clean.

"Can you see *Daring*?" he asked.

Julia handed him the telescope and pointed to the left. "Broad on the port beam – her new stern mast is coming together."

He lifted the viewing device and searched the deep black of the outer Halo, finding his target in moments. She hadn't moved, relatively speaking, in more than two days, but the construction on her stern had altered her profile. She was too distant for Liam to see details, but the awkward spars jutting out of her stern were too large to miss.

"Today should be the day she tests her new rig," he said. "We should ready the spritsail in case we need to keep up."

"Then it will be a great day of experimentation," she said, eyes lighting up. "My improved powder is ready to test."

Liam scanned ahead, eventually spotting the starlight flashing off the distant sails of Shordar's two ships. They were far enough away that any experiment should be invisible to them.

"Very well, Ms. Sungate. When would you like to begin?"

"Sublieutenant Brown will relieve me on watch shortly. I can make my preparations then."

"I look forward to seeing your ideas in action."

"Sublieutenant Brown is a gifted officer and her help with the chemistry has been invaluable." She offered a sad smile. "I regret my early attitude toward her."

"The Navy is unique in its ability to give everyone the chance to shine equally bright."

"Yes." She reached out to rest a hand on his sleeve. "And I'm surrounded by some of the brightest stars in the galaxy. I only hope that one day I will shine with equal brilliance."

"I think you're well on your way, Julia."

She gazed up at him through her eyelashes and smiled. It wasn't the first time she'd done it, and Liam was no fool in reading the courtly manners of a noblewoman. He knew she wasn't interested in him for his title or wealth – as the second son of a minor Halo lord he'd rank barely above peasant in her eyes – and he had little power to advance her career. If she wanted something from him, he couldn't imagine what.

So was it possible, he wondered, that she just admired him for him?

"Will you be staying with us, once this mission is complete?" he asked without thinking.

"It depends on His Majesty's whim, I suppose." Her smile broadened. "Are you making me an offer, sir?"

"At the moment I serve at Captain Riverton's whim," he replied, "so I won't make any promises I can't keep."

"Perhaps you could accompany me home, at least, to return the Suncatcher in person?"

That was a bold offer, if ever he'd heard one. Her gaze was intoxicating, but he forced himself to break it, casting his eyes toward the dark skies. He was still figuring out the complications of his first ship-borne romance – he had no appetite to encourage a second.

Still. He was surprised at how much he enjoyed spending time with a noble new to Naval life. It was strangely refreshing to be able to talk about something other than the service. It was freeing to talk about the challenges of running an estate, or about the latest political rumors, or even the newest fashions, without feeling guilty that he was lording his status over his companion. And, if he was very honest, he was tired of hearing about the daily suffering of the common person. Sometimes it was nice to just reside in a place of comfort.

"I'm sure a visit to Homeworld would be breathtaking," he heard himself say, taking a step closer.

"I would do my very best to make it so," she purred.

A torrent of emotions coursed through him, and he reminded himself angrily of why he'd wound up in *Freedom* in the first place. There was no room for him as captain to even entertain such ideas. And, he finally admitted to himself, he had no interest in replacing Amelia with anyone.

Sungate was still staring up at him.

"You flatter me, Lady Julia," he said quickly, forcing a charming smile to his lips as he stepped away. "And I'm distracting you from your watch."

She bowed her head slightly. "Captain."

He stepped away, fighting down any thoughts of romance and focusing on his duty to his ship.

Climbing down the hatch to the main deck, he spotted Master Rating Flatrock giving calm instructions to a pair of sailors. Watching the big man with his big beard speaking so quietly and carefully, Liam marvelled at how most sailors, given the opportunity, could rise to the occasion. Everyone in *Freedom* was being asked to do a role beyond their level of expertise, and yet he'd sensed no problems so far. There were questions aplenty, and more than a few hesitations the first time a sailor tried a new task, but in general they all seemed to love the ability to stretch.

Flatrock noticed him and, having tasked the sailors, hurried over.

"Captain, sir," he greeted, knuckling his forehead, "I've just briefed the oncoming watch on deck. They'll be reporting to their stations shortly."

One bound for the bridge and the other for sailing control, Liam knew.

"Very good, Coxn. Did you have the chance to eat breakfast yet?"

"Yes, sir," Flatrock said with sudden relish. "Who knew a boatsman could cook?"

Able Rating Hunter had revealed hidden talents in the first few days aboard, especially after the initial rotation of shared cooking had produced some truly awful meals. Liam was frankly relieved that Hunter had volunteered to be the full-time cook before Sungate had been rotated through. His stomach still churned when he remembered Ava Templegrey's one attempt to brew coffee.

"Good. I never thought I'd have to tell you to eat, but no more skipping meals."

"Yes, sir. There's just… so much to do, sir."

"I'm glad you're taking personal responsibility for the ship and her crew. Just remember to take care of yourself as well."

He nodded, brow furrowing. "Is this what it's like to be a petty officer, sir?"

"Yes…"

"Knew there was a reason I never went above master."

"It's a mental shift, thinking about others first." He clapped a hand on Flatrock's broad shoulder. "But you're doing it magnificently. Keep it up, Coxn."

"Yes, sir."

"And, just a heads up, we'll be doing our first augmented powder gunnery trial this forenoon. I suggest we use that as our all-ship evolution today."

Flatrock frowned as he processed this new information. "Yes, sir."

Liam paused, waiting for more. When it didn't come, he offered a little nudge.

"I suggest we close up at battle stations."

"Yes, sir. Thank you, sir." He turned to go, then turned back. "Very good, sir."

Liam stood in the passageway as Flatrock hurried off, no doubt to start rousing people. His crew was small and young, but they had heart. For the first time in days, he felt new optimism for the mission.

———·——

"Is this going to take long, PO?"

Hedge's voice range through the doorway and Amelia looked back into the main passageway, where Chief Sky and the rest of the boarding team stood or sat in varying degrees of boredom. They were at their battle station, but with no actual threat Sky had seen no need to pull out all the gear and suit up. Amelia had already passed the time counting the remaining boarding stores and had wandered to the next compartment aft.

"I have no idea," she called back. "But asking that question over and over will, for sure, speed things up."

Hedge stuck out her tongue and slumped down where she sat, folding her arms.

Amelia counted the emergency space suits hanging in the aft damage control station, which was no more than ten paces astern of boarding stores. She didn't know how far she could officially wander from her battle station, but since her team was spread at least ten paces in either direction, she figured she was still technically on station. At least here there were new things to count, and she found counting always made her feel better.

The damage control station was always crowded, but it was even more so now that a huge brace had been bolted to the after bulkhead. Beyond that wall, Amelia knew, was the aft thruster compartment, and beyond that was open space. The new mast was braced against the stern at three points and Amelia guessed one of them punched through the hull right by the thrusters. She gave the new brace a quick shake – or tried to: the heavy mount didn't shift.

Approaching footsteps caught her ear and she peered out through the doorway into the main passageway. Mason Swift was nearing, his mouth set in a grim line.

"Morning, XO," she greeted him, taking every opportunity to use his new title. The more she said it, the easier it would get.

"Morning, Quartermaster," he said absently, striding past the sailors who obligingly pulled in their legs or stepping over those who didn't. He nodded to Chief Sky, ignored Hedge's wink and peered in through the doorway where Amelia hovered. Then he stepped through to check the brace.

"Just did that," she said. "It feels solid."

"Never hurts to check again," he said. He tried to move the mount and then, when it remained still, cast his eyes around the entire space.

"I'm surprised to see you here," she said. "I figured you'd be in sailing control."

"Yes," he snapped, then lowered his voice and leaned in. "And if I was still the propulsion officer I would be. But as executive officer I need to keep a visual watch on the new mounts."

"Well, I'm going to be here the whole time," she said, pointing vaguely at boarding party stores. "I can keep an eye on things."

He frowned and made to reply, then stopped himself. His gaze moved restlessly.

"Yes, thank you. You'll be a useful second set of eyes. And it will give me a chance to at least pop in to sailing control."

"Happy to help. Not like I'm doing anything else useful."

He paused, finally turning his full attention to her. Fatigue lined his face, and he clearly had a dozen things on his mind, but for one long moment he just looked at her. And she felt seen.

"He really did want to say goodbye," he whispered.

"Then why didn't he?" she whispered back, aware of the dozen or so sailors sitting just outside.

"Because… I told him not to."

Whether Mason was lying or not, and whatever he was lying about, Amelia knew it came from a place of support. Liam was his best friend, and now Mason had to try and take his place. In that moment she saw him, too.

"Thank you," she said.

He nodded, mind already moving on to his many responsibilities.

"Clear a path!" he snapped as he stepped back out into the passageway.

Sailors obliged, but Amelia caught more than one withering glare in his wake as he strode off up the passageway, disappearing through the distant door into sailing control.

"I liked him better when he was the sailing officer," Hedge opined.

"Really?" Faith asked from the opposite wall.

"Okay, no, not really."

"Shut up, you cretins," Sky growled.

No-one, not even Hedge, dared to oppose the assaulter, and a sullen silence returned to the group.

Amelia stepped back out into the passageway, scanning the familiar faces and trying her best to ignore the fact that some of the most familiar faces were absent. Flatrock was in *Freedom*, being forced to finally accept some responsibility for someone other than himself, and Hunter was with him. Swift and Narrow were both in sailing control, and she didn't want to think about the most obvious absence of all.

Suppressing a sigh, she wondered if Liam was happier in his new ship. He had Charlotte and Julia to keep him company. Julia probably wasn't too unhappy to get some quality one-on-one time with Liam, that opportunistic tart, and Amelia wasn't blind to her beauty, intelligence and charm.

She felt her cheeks flush, but immediately fought it down. She had no idea where things stood between her and Liam, and what right did she have to comment if Liam decided to dally? To be honest, Julia Sungate was probably a better match for him than she was. Maybe that mistaken kiss with Narrow was just the first step toward the inevitable.

The deck swayed, forcing her to steady herself against the door frame. Sailors glanced up, suddenly aware of their surroundings.

"Here we go," Sky said. "They're unfurling sails on the new mast."

The deck lurched, and Amelia could definitely feel *Daring* accelerate.

"How many sails are they using?" Faith asked.

"Most of our spares," she replied, steadying herself against the bulkhead. "This one mast can carry the sails of about two and half regular ones."

"Wow."

The bulkhead creaked behind Amelia, and she wondered if the ship was turning. She straightened, getting her feet solidly under her as the deck shuddered and the hull groaned in the distance.

"Is that supposed to happen?" Hedge asked, sitting up and wrapping her arms around her knees.

"The ship often creaks when we pick up a stiff breeze," Amelia said.

A jolt sent Amelia stumbling, and she fell against Faith. Scrambling up, she pulled herself along the wall to the nearest door frame. Damage control was a mess as some equipment had toppled. The after bulkhead groaned.

"Here," she said, "if you're just sitting there, help me tidy this up."

Sailors were most unhappy when they felt helpless or useless, and even the simple task of picking up gear seemed to ease their fears. Hedge and

Faith both joined her in the cluttered space, rehanging space suits and vacuum plugs.

The after bulkhead suddenly pranged, and the huge brace shifted forward several inches.

"Is *that* supposed to happen?" Hedge cried.

A long, low shriek rumbled through the deck. Amelia gasped as she fell to starboard and Hedge's solid form landed on top of her.

Faith yanked Hedge up. "Do you feel that?" he shouted.

"Do you hear that?" Hedge replied over a rising roar.

Strong arms hefted Amelia to her feet and she leaned over the rattling brace. The after bulkhead was cracked, and through the growing wind she could see glimpses of blackness through the bulkhead beyond.

"Breach!" she screamed, grabbing the nearest jug of sealant.

Hedge was faster, opening the jug and throwing the sealant at the widening crack. The gel was sucked through the opening, disappearing through the gap in the hull.

"It's too big," Amelia shouted. "Get those plugs!"

Faith grabbed for one of the cone-shaped plugs on the deck, flexible devices made specifically to ram into gaps in the hull and stop the egress of air. But before he could move, Sky lurched into the space and grabbed him by the shoulders, hauling him out into the passageway.

"Everybody out!" she roared.

Amelia climbed over the fallen gear and followed the others through the door as the bulkhead behind them released a deafening groan. Hedge slammed the door behind her and dogged it down, desperately trying to create a seal.

"I say again," Sky shouted into the sound-powered phone, "breach on Three Deck! We've lost the aft damage control locker to space."

A deafening crash saw the door to damage control buckle outward dangerously.

"The brace has come loose," Amelia gasped.

"Copy," Sky said before slamming the phone down. "Everybody forward – evacuate!"

Amelia sucked in desperate breaths as she turned and sprinted, unsure if the air rushing past her was caused by just her own movement, or something much, much worse.

———•———

"The target is in place, sir," Brown reported.

Liam confirmed with his telescope that the hunk of trash was indeed holding station on the starboard beam. It wasn't terribly far away, but for this first test he just wanted to prove the new powder. Testing maximum range was for later.

"All right, Charlotte, are you happy?"

Brown turned from the officer of the watch console to give Liam a sly smile, readjusting the weapons belt. "My happiness is irrelevant to the safe gunnery operations of *Freedom*, sir. But I'm comfortable with proceeding with this test."

"Very good," he replied, appreciating her smarm. "I'll head down to the gun deck to supervise the firing."

She nodded and cast her eyes out toward the starry backdrop. He headed for the hatch, only to stop as she called him.

"And yes," she said, her smile blossoming with genuine warmth, "I am happy, sir."

He couldn't help but smile back, feeling his own mood lift at the sight of her beaming face. Was getting out from under the glare of Captain Riverton really that much of a relief to her? There was no time to ponder, though, as he descended the ladder and moved forward to the gun deck.

Freedom's sleek, narrow passageways were visually appealing, but they did make for tight quarters when multiple sailors gathered together. As Liam stepped outboard through the first airlock, he spied Sungate standing in her crisp uniform surrounded by a clutch of crouching sailors. All eyes were on the open airlock door leading to the first gun bay. Liam couldn't physically get past them and had to lean over the crouching Hunter to peer into the bay.

"I've already prepared the mixture," Sungate was saying through the door to Rating Leaf, who wore heavy gloves and eye goggles. "You just need to load it like normal."

"Yes, ma'am," he called.

Her eyes were alight with excitement, a feeling clearly matched by those around her. "This should double our explosive power," she declared to everyone.

Leaf glanced back, then grinned as he packed the powder bags into the breach. The cannon itself was polished brass, smaller and more delicate than *Daring's* brutish guns but still as large as a man.

Liam rested a hand on Sungate's shoulder. "You double-checked your mixture?"

She turned fully to him, expression serious. "Absolutely, sir."

"Rating Leaf," Liam called through the door, "are you clear on what you're doing?"

"Yes, sir," the young gunner called. "The ma'am was quite clear."

"All right then. Once you're loaded, get back out here and we'll fire remotely."

"I'd kind of like to do it from here, sir," Leaf said. "I'd love to see this baby in action."

"Next time, Rating," he said. "Let's try safety first."

"Yes, sir," he said, hooking the remote trigger to the gun and climbing out of the bay.

The gun bay airlock slammed shut. A single porthole allowed a glimpse inside, but Liam didn't bother fighting for a view. Leaf was pressed up against the glass and Sungate had knelt down amidst the sailors to try and watch. Liam took a few steps aft to grab the internal comms network and call the bridge.

"*Bridge, officer of the watch,*" Brown replied.

"This is the captain. Proceed with gunnery test with gun eleven, remote firing."

"*Yes, sir.*"

Liam hung up the phone and turned back toward the anticipatory crowd.

"I can't believe we're firing a cannon with twice the usual powder," Leaf commented.

"Twice the power," Sungate corrected.

"Yeah," he replied, nodding his confirmation. "Twice the powder gives twice the power."

"I didn't say-"

An explosion ripped through the hull. The gun bay door buckled as the blast punched holes through the bulkhead. Liam staggered back, ears ringing. He fell to the deck, vaguely aware of shouting all around him. He forced himself up, spinning in place to see his sailors heaped and mangled before him. There was blood everywhere, and as his vision wobbled he thought he saw shredded clothing flapping in the breeze.

The breeze. His spacefaring instincts kicked in and his head cleared. The gun bay door was barely attached to the mangled bulkhead and beyond was nothing but open space.

"Move!" he said, grabbing the nearest sailor and hauling him to his feet.

The mass of bodies was starting to stir as people came to and realized the situation.

"Everybody out!" Liam shouted, barely able to hear his own voice over the ringing in his ears.

Sungate was on her hands and knees, spitting blood. Leaf was motionless next to her, most of his head red and wet. Liam grabbed her under the arm and pulled her up. She stared at him, stunned and unseeing. He hustled her toward the airlock and then dragged Leaf after him. Other sailors were staggering forward to clear the wreckage, their movements ghoulish in the flashing red lights signalling pressure loss.

Liam grabbed Leaf's deadweight and heaved.

———•———

Amelia practically fell through the door to sailing control, fumbling in the shadows of emergency lighting. Shipwide power had failed moments earlier, plunging the crew into darkness before the torches lit themselves. Sky was headed to the bridge and Amelia wanted to help the propulsors, but as she regained her feet she came up short as a tidal wave of noise washed over her. She grabbed the nearest railing and hung on, trying to make sense of the chaos as *Daring's* deck tilted ominously.

"Reef the lot," she heard Swift order.

"No, no," Narrow protested, waving his arms to stop the mast monkeys from responding to the previous direction. "It's stabilizing! It's just settling, sir."

"Damn your eyes, man!" Swift roared. He slammed his fist on the console and glared at the entire room. A tense hush descended as all eyes went to him.

"Pull down every stern sail," he commanded. "And reef all four masts."

Sailors flowed around him, some scrambling into the mast access tubes while others dashed up the special access ladders cut through *Daring's* innards.

"Quartermaster," Swift barked, noticing her in the gloom, "what's the situation aft?"

"Three deck up to boarding stores is sealed off," she replied. "Damage control lost to space and the door was damaged when the stern mast brace broke loose."

"Shoring party," he snapped, gesturing a master rating to him. "Assess the door to after damage control and reinforce it if you can. If not, fall back to the airlock forward of boarding stores and secure it."

The sailor nodded and ran past Amelia into the passageway, a team of three carrying anti-breach gear in tow.

Sailing control emptied as sailors ran to fulfill their duties, but Amelia winced as *Daring* groaned again. She eased her way forward to close Swift and Narrow, who were leaning so close their heads were nearly touching.

"It's just some settling damage," Narrow was saying quickly. "Yeah, it sucks that we lost a couple of compartments, but we can adjust for that."

"We can't *adjust* to losing parts of the ship."

"But it worked! You felt the speed we were picking up. Look, what I recommend–"

"I recommend you shut your mouth," Swift snarled. "I'm trying to save this ship and everyone on board. Nothing else matters right now."

Narrow's gaze was pleading. "But we almost have it."

Swift looked away. "Shoring party!"

Another sailor hurried over.

"Conduct a rapid survey of the starboard side aft, especially around the lower mount. If you find nothing, report to boarding stores and help with the reinforcement efforts there." He glanced at his artificer. "Petty Officer Narrow will supervise."

"Yes, sir," the sailor said, knuckling his forehead and gesturing for his team to follow. He looked questioningly at Narrow.

Narrow, stunned, turned and stormed out of sailing control.

Swift glared after him, then gave the room another hard look to ensure no other sailor felt like arguing. Then he leaned in toward Amelia.

"How bad is it back aft?" he asked.

"Bad," she said, unable to suppress a shiver. "The entire brace broke free – do you know how much pressure that takes?"

"I have an idea. Which is why I was opposed to this whole scheme."

"I heard you object."

"Yeah, but I apparently haven't learned the noble skill of charm good enough, yet." He clenched his fist, hovering it above the console before forcing himself to relax.

"How bad is it overall?" she asked.

"Bad. Stress fractures all along the stern. One trunk of the stern mast punctured the hull where you were, and another smashed in our primary generator."

"Can we get power back?"

"My priority is keeping the air inside the ship. I don't even know where all the breaches are."

"If we find them, can we fix them?"

"In drydock, sure. Out here..." He gave her a worried glare.

"What can I do?"

He gathered his thoughts, eyes scanning the damage control table.

"We're going to need every last tub of sealant and reinforcement bar you have. If we've lost after damage control, that's a lot of gear no use to us."

"I'll go and check stores," she said. "And I can always suit up to recover what's in the vacuum."

He nodded. "Just be careful. I don't think we can handle any more surprises."

Liam guided *Freedom* through another gentle turn, reassuring himself that the hole in her hull wasn't affecting her ability to maneuver. Now that the breaches were sealed and there was no more air pushing outward, the ship seemed to have regained her agility. He'd taken the watch himself to free up Brown to help with the wounded, and as he stole a glance at the scared expression of the young sailor with him on the bridge, he thanked all the stars that he hadn't lost anyone in the blast.

It looked like the gun deck blast doors were holding, but the entire starboard side was cut off from the rest of the ship. He'd have to check their minimal stores, but he doubted *Freedom* had the necessary material to repair an entire gun bay. His new course was a slow intercept of *Daring*, and he wasn't too proud to admit that he needed help. A bit of expertise and gear from Swift's damage control teams and *Freedom* could be functional again – just minus one cannon.

He shook his head, replaying the last moments before the explosion. Leaf had obviously misunderstood Sungate's comments, and he hadn't the experience to question it. She, likewise, lacked the experience to properly supervise. Assumptions had been made, ambiguities left unchecked. Like almost every accident in space it was a chain of small errors, each one difficult to see until after the fact.

He lifted his telescope again to confirm *Daring's* relative bearing, noting that she'd apparently completed her stern mast trials. All of her sails, on all four – no, five – masts, were reefed. Odd… He adjusted *Freedom's* course toward a new intercept.

Habit made him scan toward the Theropod ships. His grip tightened around the telescope. Both ships had come about and were aggressively tacking into the winds. He suddenly wasn't the only one on an intercept course.

"Hail *Daring* with an emergency signal. The enemy is approaching."

CHAPTER 14

The only sound was her own breathing as she moved carefully along the hull, steadily reaching one hand after the other to pull herself across the rugged surface. But with each grip, Amelia felt the rumble of the ship beneath her, the groans and ripples as *Daring* struggled against the shifting pressures moving through her damaged body.

Her spacesuit was tight against her and Amelia had enough flexibility to glance "down" at the rope trailing behind her, slowly being let out as she moved aft. It was both her tether and her tool for the upcoming task, a string of hooks bouncing along its length. She looked "up" and saw a looming horizon where the hull dropped off, approaching faster than she'd like. She quickly grabbed at the surface, gently slowing herself. She stopped just as she reached the corner of what she knew was the transom, the flat stern of the ship, but what looked like a cliff opening out toward an endless plummet into darkness.

She forced her eyes to rise, taking in the towering frame of the stern mast that, even from here, was clearly off-kilter where the starboard brace had failed. The nearest strut of the tripod mast plunged down into the hull only a few paces from her and as she gripped the cold metal she felt another ripple of stress bleed up into her fingers.

She focused on her breathing, keeping it as slow and steady as she could, then she carefully turned herself to slip over the corner and grip onto the transom. She closed her eyes and forced her brain to reorient itself, so that the stern mast was now "below" her, and she eased her way down.

The rope resisted for a moment, then started to pay out again. Amelia watched the hull drift upward past her, then gasped as her feet pressed against something hard. Her knees buckled and she gripped at the hull, steadying herself as she came to rest on the stern mast's loose strut. The ship's biggest planks had been bolted together to form a giant support frame, and as Amelia lowered to her hands and knees on it she could see the splits in the heavy material. Crawling along the planks, she traced them up to the massive face of the hull, and the shredded gaps leading inside.

"I'm at the breach," she signalled. "There's enough room for me to go inside."

"*Hurry*," replied Swift. "*Just got word the Theropod ships are closing us.*"

Amelia suspected her suit carried her muttered curse back to sailing control, but she didn't care. Shuffling forward, she slipped through the tear in *Daring's* hull.

The thruster compartment was lost in shadows, and she flicked on her helmet lamp to guide her as she followed the cracked mast further into the ship. The breach into the damage control locker wasn't as wide, and she paused on the mast to assess movement. As she gripped the strut, she watched the tear in the bulkhead slowly move up and down. There was room when it widened, but not much. She inched forward until her helmet was almost level with the mangled surface. Watching, waiting, she got a sense of the timing…

She hauled herself through, sliding into the locker and tumbling down as artificial gravity took hold.

Fighting down panic, she got to her hands and knees, feeling the solid deck beneath her and listening for any tell-tale hiss of a leak in her suit.

She stayed frozen for a long moment, confirming that her suit wasn't tightening anywhere and there were no sudden sensations of freezing. She was good.

"I'm in the locker," she reported. "Give me some slack."

The rope obligingly loosened and she hauled in a few yards' worth, pulling the hooks toward her as she started grabbing shoring plugs and attaching them to the line. Next were the stacks of sealant jugs, then the half-dozen emergency spacesuits. It was tricky in her gloved hands to connect both suits and matching helmets to the hooks, but as her support team back at the airlock slowly reeled in the line, she managed to get them streaming outward.

Her headlamp scanned the cluttered space as she searched for any other useful equipment. The deck shifted in what she recognized was a turn, but she gasped as the loose mast suddenly swung toward her. Diving for the deck she felt the impact of the giant strut against the bulkhead.

"*Petty Officer Virtue*," Swift signalled, "*it's time to go.*"

"No argument here," she sputtered, climbing onto the strut and shimmying herself back through the gap. Gravity faded away and she drifted off the surface, but she gripped the rope and pulled herself back out through the tear in the outer hull. "Reel me in, if you please."

The line tugged her up and away from the broken mast. Her breath caught in her throat as she slipped free of the hull as she rounded the corner from the transom, watching in sudden terror as *Daring* started to shrink in her view. But with a snap the rope went taut and started hauling her in again. The airlock was only a few yards away, a dark gap in the mottled, dusty hull.

Tufts of dust suddenly danced to life in her peripheral, all along *Daring's* curved surface.

"*We're under attack!*" Swift warned.

Helpless to do anything but watch as she was reeled in, she saw the sixteen gunports open, and the black, round noses of Navy guns emerge.

"Suns and stars!" She grabbed the rope and started pulling herself hand over hand.

A silent, blinding flash indicated *Daring's* own broadside, and through hazy vision she just kept reaching for the rope.

"They're surrounding her," Brown reported, eyes on the tactical display.

Liam could see the ship movements with his own eyes, perplexed at why *Daring* was still showing no sails, even as the Theropod ships moved in on either side. *Freedom* was pointed right at the smaller enemy vessel, closing with all speed.

"*Daring* this is *Freedom*," he signalled. "Come up in speed. I will cover your withdrawal."

"*This is* Daring," came Riverton's icy reply. "*Flag hoist imminent. Close and engage. Out.*"

"Confirm port battery ready?" he asked.

"Yes, sir," Sungate replied from forward. "With the extra gunners we should be able to reload faster."

Well, Liam thought, that was one advantage to losing half his weapons – at least he had spare sailors to use. And he was able to keep his starboard mast extended. It made for an unbalanced course, but extra speed.

He lifted his telescope, scanning for the flag signal Riverton had promised. Radio signals could be monitored during battle, but the Navy had secret codes that could be transmitted visually if ships were in range.

As he watched, a series of colorful flags and pennants were hoisted up a line suspended up the after face of *Daring's* top mast. He read them, his stomach tightening as he interpreted the code.

Daring had extensive hull damage and was unable to use any sails or thrusters. She was dead in space.

"*Daring* can't maneuver," he said. "We need to cover her. Full speed, Ms. Brown, if you please."

"Yes, sir." She started issuing orders to sailing control.

"Load chain shot, Ms. Sungate, if you please," he ordered. "We're taking out their sails."

As Sungate passed the order, Liam assessed the battle geometry. The smaller Theropod ship, Blue Scale, was his closest target. Only her top and bottom masts were extended as she fired at *Daring* and aimed her opposite guns toward *Freedom*. *Emerald Crown* was on the far side of *Daring*, even now closing for a point-blank engagement. He made his decision.

Daring's guns could deal with a sloop. Blue Scale was *Freedom's* to disable.

Come hard right," he ordered. "Prepare broadside versus nearest Theropod ship, top mast only."

"Hard, right, aye."

"Guns ready," Sungate reported.

Freedom turned, and Brown steadied her with the target on the beam.

"Fire."

The cannons unleashed their chain shot, the impacts ripping through Blue Scale's top sails. The Theropod returned fire. *Freedom's* hull thudded with impacts.

"Guns ready."

"Fire."

Another broadside tore through the rippling sheets as *Freedom's* speed carried her ahead of her target. A series of flashes from *Daring* were followed by tufts of impact against Blue Scale's beam. Liam brought his ship hard to port, crossing Blue Scale's bow and leaving her sails wide open.

"Guns ready."

"Fire."

The mainsails of Blue Scale's top mast started to disintegrate, shredded by the onslaught. The Theropods no doubt had spares, but it would take time to pull in the tatters and get fresh sheet. *Freedom* was still ahead of her and out of enemy gun arcs.

"Shift target. Bottom mast, if you please."

"Guns ready."

"Fire."

The first of *Freedom's* chain shot tore through Blue Scale's lower sails. The enemy ship was noticeably slowing, debris spinning away from her hull as another of *Daring's* broadsides impacted.

"Shordar is continuing to close *Daring*," Brown reported.

"*Daring's* guns will hold her off," Liam said, eyes still on Blue Scale. "Fire."

Freedom shuddered with another broadside, but Liam felt Charlotte's hand on his arm.

"Sir," she said, "Shordar is closing *inside* gun range."

He looked to starboard, unable to see *Emerald Crown*. He grabbed a telescope and scanned the space around *Daring*, finally glimpsing the fluttering sails of a bottom mast just beyond *Daring's* bulk, very close. Then the hull of the sloop appeared, hugging the lower curve of the frigate. Liam lowered the telescope.

"He means to board her."

* * *

Amelia listened through her open helmet as another starboard broadside unleashed two decks above her. The guns had been firing consistently, port battery then starboard, the entire time she'd cycled through the airlock and helped to drag all the damage control gear into the shadowy main passageway. Sailors had disappeared with much of the gear, and from the faces of those around her she sensed that hull integrity was still very much in question.

The starboard battery fired again, and she suddenly realized that the port guns had been silent for two cycles. She glanced at Hedge, who stood nervously holding another shoring plank while Song and Faith eased open the airlock door leading aft. The sensors that still worked indicated that there was pressure beyond the door, and that the shoring of the damage control locker was holding, but in the darkness nothing was certain.

The deck shuddered, a huge ripple going through *Daring* as the entire ship shifted to starboard.

"That was no cannon fire," Amelia said.

"What was it?" Hedge asked, twitching with nervous energy.

Amelia had sailed in ships for too many years to be uncertain. That sort of all-encompassing thump was only felt when a ship came hard alongside a jetty. Or another ship.

The starboard guns fired again. But the port guns were silent.

"Shordar's alongside."

Hedge stared at her, then hefted her plank with a snarl. "Then I'll smash his little head into pulp."

"Get that door open," Amelia ordered, striding toward Song and Faith. "We need the boarding gear."

"But the pressure might be too low," Faith argued.

"Not for me," she snapped, closing her helmet's faceplate.

The lock released and Song snapped up all the dogs. Faith grabbed the door handle and tried to pull it open. The door resisted, lifting from its combing an inch before slamming back. Song braced himself against the bulkhead and pushed the frame while Faith heaved on the handle. They pried the door open, And Amelia felt the drag toward the opening. Hedge dropped her plank and grabbed the edge of the door, joining the struggle to pull it open against the rush of air. It finally fell back and locked open, all three sailors gasping for breath as they struggled forward.

Amelia stepped through, shining her headlamp between the emergency torches that still burned. Ahead, the damage control locker door had buckled inward, held in place by a frame of shoring that looked far too loose for Amelia's liking. But her target was the door forward of that, which she ripped open and scanned with her lamp. Armor, weapons, everything they needed.

She grabbed as much as she could carry and ran to the open airlock door, throwing the gear to the waiting hands of Faith, Song and Hedge. When she returned with the second load all three sailors were throwing on breastplates and helmets, and by the third load they were buckling on swords and pistols. They were also breathing comfortably, she noticed.

She lifted her faceplate. "Air's okay?"

"It's equalized," Faith said, even those words leaving him gasping. "Breathable."

After the fourth relay of equipment she dumped on the deck, Amelia realized she had more gear than sailors.

"Get to sailing control," she ordered Song. "Tell the XO to send as many people as possible to get armored up."

"Yes, PO." He ran off down the passageway.

"Lay this stuff out," she told Faith and Hedge. "Get it ready for quick donning."

She hurried back into the thin air of the damaged section, snapping down her faceplate again as she carried two more loads of gear out. Closing the airtight door behind her and sealing it, she saw Swift emerging from the shadows, a gaggle of sailors behind him. She unhooked her helmet and dropped it to the deck, slipping a loosened breastplate over her form-fitting spacesuit.

"Shordar's clamped onto our port side," Swift said, throwing on a breastplate with practiced ease. "They're breaking through the cargo airlock."

"Then we'll be ready to meet them," she snapped.

"Hedge, Faith, Song," Swift barked. "You're ready: get to the port cargo bay and hold any intruders there."

The trio disappeared into the shadows. Swift fastened a helmet and grabbed a weapons belt. He handed Amelia a second one. She loosened it and wrapped it tight around her suit.

"You'll have to lead the defence," he said. "Until I can get word to Sky to join you."

"I need you there, too," she replied.

He hesitated, just for a moment. "I need to be in sailing control. Gotta get that power back."

"You're the executive officer," Amelia countered. "We need you to defend the ship."

"But without power–"

"Can Narrow handle that on his own?"

Swift frowned. "If I order him to ignore his damned stern mast under pain of death… Yes, he can get us power back."

"Then do it."

Swift shook his head, still debating.

"Delegate, sir," Amelia hissed, gripping his arm. "And trust your people."

He nodded. "Go. I'll get word to the bridge, get Narrow going in the right direction, then join you."

"Yes, sir."

Amelia slammed an armored helmet onto her head, hooked her suit helmet to the back of her belt and motioned for the rest of the sailors to follow her.

"We have to get in there," Liam said, bracing as Blue Scale's latest broadside knocked *Freedom's* hull. "Stop the boarding."

Sungate glanced up from her console, brow furrowed in confusion.

Brown leaned close to Liam. "Sir, we still have an active target out here."

He looked over at Blue Scale, at the shredded sails and damaged hull. "She's out of the fight."

The Theropod ship clearly disagreed as it loosed another volley of shot and Liam was forced to hang on again. Frustration grew in his heart as he weighed his tactical options.

"That ship is weakened," Brown pressed, "but still dangerous. *Daring* will have to take care of herself."

He glared at her, and she stared back with pleading in her eyes. She'd said the name *Daring*, but they both knew who she was talking about.

"Fire at will," he ordered Sungate. As she continued her onslaught against Blue Scale's sails, Liam brought his face right next to Brown's.

"*Daring* is being boarded by Theropods," he whispered. "And that ship has clearly taken a lot of internal damage if none of their propulsion is available. They are in dire straits."

"And what, precisely," Charlotte countered, "will we do? We have barely a dozen crew on board, and a third of them are already injured. We can't join a melee."

"But we have to help."

"Absolutely, sir. But charging in to personally rescue one person, no matter how awesome she is, is not the answer. And you know this."

Her words pinned him. His cheeks flushed with indignation, but he fought it down. It seemed the entire senior mess was aware of his weakness. And now here he was, a commander, being reminded of his duties by a sublieutenant.

He pretended for a moment that Amelia wasn't aboard *Daring*, and reconsidered his tactical options. Suddenly, everything became clear.

"Switch to ball shot," he ordered Sungate. "Let's break up that hull."

"Yes, sir."

"Come hard left," he ordered Brown. "Bring us across her stern."

"Yes, sir."

With few functioning sails, Blue Scale was floundering. *Freedom* was literally sailing rings around her, keeping her port guns on target.

"Guns ready."

"Fire at will."

The deck shuddered as *Freedom* launched a broadside of ball shot. The heavy slugs tore into Blue Scale's outer shell, sending shards spinning away with each impact. It was a slow process, punching through a sailing ship's hull, but *Freedom* was at point-blank range and her guns were accurate. With *Daring's* cannon still pounding away at the helpless Theropod ship as well, it wasn't long before Liam spotted cracks forming beneath the shimmer and vapor of air escaping. He saw three lifeboats scrambling away from the stricken ship, and he ordered Sungate to cease fire.

"All right," he said, as Blue Scale began to break up and he turned his eyes to the sloop clinging to *Daring* like a parasite. "First problem solved. Let's work on the second."

———

Amelia staggered back as another tailsword slammed into her defending blade. The sheer force of the blow knocked her back several steps and her opponent rushed forward to fill the opening. Around her, sailors were struggling to hold the passageway leading to the cargo hold as Shordar's attack team pushed into the ship. There was movement everywhere, and just so much noise. Theropod screeches mixed with Human shouts, punctuated by the constant clang of steel on steel. At least the lights were back on, and she could see the carnage.

The tailsword swung again, but this time she deflected it upward and ducked low to get inside. She stomped on the brute's foot, throwing him off balance as the last energy of his tail swing tried to carry him forward. Her blade slashed down against armor and she pushed with her whole body, sending the Theropod tumbling backward. Amelia swung her sword again, finally catching flesh as the brute was forced to retreat.

There were already three more attackers facing her, teeth dripping with saliva as they roared at her. But she was inside their tail arcs and she pressed forward, stabbing into the first target with her blade and hacking at a second even as the first one fell.

Something heavy slammed into her back and she staggered, raising her sword in defence. A Theropod raised his tail and twisted it to bring his blade to bear, but then leapt back as Hedge and Song charged in, their battle screams loud enough to wake the dead. Amelia scrambled back, gasping for air, as more sailors pushed into the fray.

From several paces back, she assessed the situation as she caught her breath. The Theropods had easily fought their way through the cargo bay, where their superior speed and huge reach had overwhelmed the defenders. But now that the battle had spilled into the narrower passageway, the quick, short strikes of the Human swords were proving deadly. The Theropods were still pushing forward, though, holding two lines forward and aft of the cargo bay.

And in the middle of it all, she saw a single Theropod standing at the cargo bay entrance. Dressed in exquisite armor over green skin that almost seemed to shimmer, this brute surveyed the battle with a cool detachment. His eyes suddenly met Amelia's and his lips pulled back into a hideous smile.

She knew she should get back into the fight, but those iridescent, vertically slit eyes held her enthralled.

Shordar.

He roared. The Theropod mob roared in reply. He roared again, and they echoed his call, louder. He roared a third time, and the Theropods surged forward, hacking down the Humans and pushing them back. Shordar strode toward Amelia behind the battle line, pointing a dagger at her.

The interior bulkhead behind him suddenly slid open, disgorging Swift and a gaggle of sailors. They charged both Theropod lines from behind, hacking and slashing at their undefended flanks. Shordar ducked under a mighty swing by a big propulsor, rising only to plunge his dagger into the man's chest. The blade slipped out with a gush of blood and Shordar danced away from another attack.

The battle descended into chaos as Humans attacked the Theropods from all sides. The brutes went quick and low, leaping back from the battle and retreating toward the cargo bay doors.

From his belt, Shordar pulled out two small, round objects, holding them high with his small arms. Staring at Amelia again with that deadly grin, he threw one at her and the other at the opposite line of defenders.

"Grenade!" Amelia screamed, diving backward.

The bombs went off, but not with the concussive power she expected. She looked up into a thick haze of smoke that obscured most of her sailors as they coughed and staggered back, lifting their swords in defence. There was a clatter of feet, but suddenly an eerie quiet fell over the battle. Those grenades weren't meant to attack, she realized, but to distract.

"Press up," she ordered, scrambling to her feet and joining the line again. "Find them!"

Flanked by Song and Hedge she surged forward, meeting the opposite line of *Daring* sailors led by Sky. Through the choking smoke they spilled into the cargo bay, and she just caught sight of the last of the brutes fleeing into the airlock. They'd dropped some of their gear in their haste to retreat, and Amelia frowned as the cargo airlock doors closed.

"Get more rifles up here," Sky ordered. "They might make a second attack."

Sailors poured through the smoke to set up a new defensive position, coughing and waving away the caustic cloud that hung over the passageway.

"Use these as cover," Sky said, grabbing a crate and slamming it down on the deck. "Build a wall here at the door."

Sailors hurried to comply, setting up a defensive perimeter just inside the door as rifles arrived.

Amelia jogged forward, hoping that some of the dropped gear might be of use. She spotted a clutch of backpacks scattered close to the outer bulkhead. Ripping open the first, she saw that it was filled with bombs. She smiled, realizing that these would be very useful indeed.

Then she heard the distant hiss of the cargo bay's outer airlock closing. And felt the deep thud of Shordar's grapples releasing *Daring*. The Theropods were withdrawing, she realized, looking down at the bag in her hand. And they'd left behind all these explosives… right next to the airlock and outer hull.

Dropping the backpack she ran, waving at all the sailors crouched and ready to defend on the far side of the bay.

"Run!" she screamed. "The whole place is going to blow!"

The sailors were still staring at her in shock when she felt the blast from behind her. She flew forward on the wave of air. Then started to fly backward as *Daring's* hull burst open.

"The sloop is breaking free," Brown reported.

"Then she's all ours," Liam replied grimly. "Load ball shot."

Above the canopy, he could see the close form of *Daring* as *Freedom* passed beneath. Dust scattered as *Emerald Crown* pulled away and began to dip downward, clearly trying to stay out of *Daring's* gun arcs. But the Theropod couldn't evade *Freedom*.

"Guns ready."

"Fire."

Freedom rocked again as her guns unleashed, and Liam saw the satisfying puffs of dust and debris as the cannonballs struck the sloop.

But his eyes were torn away as a new flash erupted from *Daring*. He recognized that it was no broadside, and watched in shock as pieces of *Daring's* hull spun outward. He grabbed a telescope as *Freedom* came around under *Emerald Crown* and up onto *Daring's* port side. Shards of hull were tumbling away from a clear hole in the hull, as well as other objects.

"There are people in the wreckage," he said with growing horror.

"Oh, by the stars," Charlotte breathed next to him.

He continued to scan with the telescope as *Freedom* rose to meet the debris, and his heart caught in his throat.

———

Amelia felt the hard surface of the deck slam against her, then rush upward as she was sucked down by the very air around her. Her ears were roaring, face burning from the cold. She saw the outer hull flash by, watched in disbelief as the familiar hull of *Daring* revealed itself before her.

Then silence. Absolute silence as debris flew all around her away from the gaping hole in *Daring's* side. Light still burned from the cargo bay, but as much as she reached for it she couldn't grab hold.

Her lungs were burning. She couldn't breathe.

Like that pond so long ago, she watched the faint light of safety retreat from her.

She felt the crushing cold of the vacuum close in around her. She kept blinking to stop her eyeballs from freezing solid.

All was silent.

But she had to *breathe*.

She wrenched the armored helmet from her head. Reaching back on her belt, she gripped her suit helmet and slammed it down. She switched on her suit air and gasped as warm, moist, life-giving breath returned to her.

But *Daring* was still sailing away from her. And there was nothing she could do.

***

"One of them has a spacesuit on."

Even as Liam watched, the figure donned their suit helmet as they flailed away from *Daring*, riding the ejection of air.

"Sir," Sungate prompted, "shall we continue to engage Shordar?"

"Cease fire," he barked. "All stop – reef all sails."

The tumbling, suited figure was heading right for them, along with dozens of debris shards.

"Sir," Sungate pressed, "Shordar is getting away!"

"Half astern all thrusters," he ordered. "Get us stopped."

The sloop was already extending her port and starboard masts and was beginning to gain speed. Liam glanced at it once, then focused on the spinning figure falling toward them. *Freedom* was beginning to shudder under the force of her bow thrusters, but she was finally slowing.

"Is there anyone else with a spacesuit?" he asked, scanning again.

"I don't see any," Brown said.

Liam flicked on the internal broadcast. "This is the captain. Coxn, suit up two sailors at Airlock One and prepare to recover… an incoming survivor."

"What are you doing?" Sungate snapped, straightening and pointing beyond the canopy to port. "Shordar is right there. We can stop him today."

"We're picking up our fellow sailors," he replied, judging *Freedom's* motion to ensure she caught at least the suited figure.

"The Suncatcher is aboard that ship," she hissed. "It is my family's ancient heirloom and it is more important than any sailor!"

Liam set down the telescope, turning hard eyes to this impudent sub-lieutenant who was, it seemed, finally showing her true colors.

"You are welcome, Ms. Sungate, to don a spacesuit and go after Shordar yourself." He rounded the console, bearing down on her as his anger rose.

"And when you do, think about how much you'd appreciate keeping your life because your shipmates come and rescue you."

She bit down her angry response, but her eyes blazed.

"The life of any of my sailors," he stated, "is more valuable than any of your heirlooms."

Her lips pressed together in impotent fury and she couldn't help but glance at the sloop now fast diminishing off their port beam. She said nothing and turned back to her console.

"Ms. Brown," he said quietly, "do you see any other sailors in spacesuits?"

"No, sir," she replied. "Just the one."

"Then that's one life saved. A worthwhile effort, don't you think?"

"I do, sir." She examined her console. "Airlock One is open."

"Very good."

He surveyed the scene again. *Daring* was still dead in space, an ugly new hole marring her port side. *Emerald Crown* was showing her stern as all four of her masts caught the winds and carried her further into the darkness. He activated the external comms.

"*Daring* this is *Freedom*. We're holding station on your port side and recovering a survivor. How can I assist?"

"Freedom," Riverton replied, "*this is* Daring. *Hold position and assess the damage, if you please. How many survivors?*"

"Just one, I'm afraid."

"*Thank you for that.* Daring *out.*"

The bridge hatch swung upward and Liam turned to see Flatrock emerging, a grin splitting his bushy beard.

"We got us a wanderer, sir."

A second person climbed the ladder. They were in a spacesuit with the helmet still attached, but the movements of the small form were only too familiar. Even before she lifted her head and smiled, Liam knew exactly who stood before him. Steeling himself, and ignoring the sudden, overjoyed touch of Charlotte's hand on his arm, he walked aft to greet his visitor.

"Hello, Petty Officer Virtue." He couldn't quite suppress the grin. "I'm sorry I rescued you."

She pulled off her helmet and shook out her hair, eyes shining as she smiled at him.

"It's what you do, sir. And I love you for it."

She was clearly exhausted, injured and shaken. But she was also unbowed. She lifted her chin and ran her hand along his cheek.

"Just maybe," she said, "Let me rescue you next time."

Suddenly not caring who was watching, Liam leaned in and kissed her. Not with passion, not with urgency, but with quiet love. Her fingers pressed into his cheek as she kissed him back.

"Hey," came Flatrock's voice, "any more of that action to share around?"

CHAPTER 15

"This is crazy," Brown muttered, glancing nervously around the bridge. Liam gave her a silencing look, then made a point of strolling casually forward, almost right to the narrow cone where the canopy was close enough to touch. He smiled at Master Rating Flatrock and Able Rating Hunter, knowing that he had his two most experienced sailors to guide the ship this morning. Looking aft through the canopy, he could see *Daring's* wide transom rising slowly above *Freedom's* stern, close enough to block half the sky.

"We're in position," he decided, noting the trio of hawsers trailing behind *Freedom* to wrap around the struts of the stern mast still protruding from *Daring's* punctured hull. "Signal to *Daring* that we're ready to commence, if you please."

Brown nodded without hesitation, her anxiety melting away as she reported in a low, cultured voice to *Daring's* bridge.

"*Understood*," replied Templegrey over the radio. "*Commencing low power thrusters.*"

"Dead slow ahead rear thrusters," he ordered.

Hunter repeated the order and gently nudged the controls, Sungate hovering watchfully behind him. There was barely any change, but Liam felt the slightest of pressures in the deck as *Freedom* and *Daring* gently opened the distance. The lines stretching back grew taut, still connected to the frame of the stern mast. The angle was good, with *Daring* still slightly high on the stern. The strut punching into the frigate's starboard quarter was the biggest concern and Liam watched carefully, trying to appreciate the geometry. He'd seen vessels come under tow before, but this was something truly unique.

The deck wavered. Liam sensed a loss of momentum. "Is *Daring* opening?"

Brown hefted a distance meter to her eye and rolled the instrument's viewer. "No, sir."

"Ask Captain Riverton if she wants to use more power."

The signal was passed and after a few moments the reply came: affirmative.

"Slow ahead rear thrusters," Liam ordered.

Hunter complied. Almost immediately, *Freedom* started to strain. Faint creaks echoed through the hull as the deck vibrated. Then the entire ship surged forward, and everything became quiet.

Outside, Liam saw the stern mast break free of *Daring's* hull as the frigate started to pull away. He let out a sigh of relief.

"Well done," he said. "We've pulled the wreckage clear."

"Well done, the thrusters," Flatrock echoed with a grin. He then made a big show of blowing Hunter a kiss.

"Thanks, Coxn," Hunter replied with a laugh. And then blew a kiss back.

Liam rolled his eyes and smiled, walking away from the sailors. It was a disrespectful joke, but he'd rather they believe that he'd kissed Amelia in a moment of pure, innocent celebration than anything else.

"Signal to *Daring* that the mast is clear, if you please."

Brown did so, then reported the response. "The captain of *Daring* requests the pleasure of your company, sir, to pass on final orders."

"Very well," he said. "Able Rating Hunter, secure from thrusters and prepare the boat."

"Aye, sir."

"May I accompany you, sir?" Sungate asked suddenly. "I… would like to collect a few things from my old cabin that I left behind in my haste."

"You didn't think to collect them yesterday evening?" He'd sent her and Brown over for supper just the day before.

"I'm sorry, sir," she replied, face darkening in a blush. "I promise I won't delay you."

"Please don't. As soon as we return, we set sail to capture Shordar."

"Of course, sir." Her eyes sparkled with new excitement. "Thank you, sir."

He turned to Charlotte. "Sublieutenant Brown, you have the ship. Recover our towing hawsers and make all preparations to get underway as soon as I return."

"Yes, sir."

———

Amelia was relieved to see Mason Swift nod inside his helmet. He'd just returned from a survey of the damage to the aft damage control locker and thruster compartment and even now more shoring plates were being carried through the passageway door.

He lifted the helmet clear and ran a hand across his bald head before ringing the bridge. "Captain, ma'am, XO," he reported, even as he met Amelia's eye. "The break is clean. We can get underway immediately and I'll have the puncture patched within two watches. I assess we'll have the thruster back by the dog watch."

He nodded to whatever Riverton said, then hung up the phone.

"Sorry you had to move all that stuff," he said to Amelia as he started to wriggle out of his suit. "Just to have to move it all back again."

"No worries at all," she said, tugging the suit off his lean frame. "Just happy *Freedom* was here to pull the wreckage out of us. How would you have solved this otherwise?"

Anxiety flashed across his features as he clearly considered the other options. "I don't know."

"But I guess we don't have to care, either," she said brightly.

"Except," he said quietly, ensuring no-one else was in earshot, "I still have a propulsion artificer who's telling everyone who'll listen that there was nothing wrong with his design. That the strut puncturing the hull was just a shift in pressure that stabilized the whole system."

She shook her head, having heard a few sailors repeat that theory amongst themselves. "If only we hadn't been attacked, they say, everything would have been fine."

He scoffed, but his expression darkened. "Sailor gossip is one thing. But that is just not true."

"If they keep hearing the lies over and over," she agreed, "people assume they must be true."

"What, as XO," he said carefully, "do you think I should do?"

"You have any doubt? I assumed you'd put Narrow in his place."

"I have doubts... About where my role as XO ends and my own personality takes over." He sighed, his expression softening as he looked at her. "He's determined, and on this matter I disagree with his ideas. But that doesn't give me license to abuse him in my position."

"Well... Why don't you ask an experienced XO? Commander Blackwood has just come aboard to meet with the captain."

"And that's why you're way down here, idly watching me as I check damage?"

It was her turn to sigh. "Maybe."

"Did you talk aboard *Freedom*?"

"We only had a few moments."

"Whose choice was that?"

"Both, I think," she admitted. "But at least we weren't shouting at each other."

"I'm going to talk to him," he said, starting aft along the passageway. "I suggest you do the same. Afterward."

She didn't try to keep up with him, her mind whirling as she slowly made her way up the ladder.

Liam was on board. Right now. And everyone knew that when he departed the two ships were going to truly be separated. He and Riverton had concocted a plan to catch Shordar and it wasn't going to be a line of formation. Nor was it a plan likely to succeed. The two captains had even allowed most of *Freedom's* crew to join their friends here in *Daring* for supper last night, a clear sign that the ships were going their own ways. This might be the last time she ever saw him. Did she want their final parting to be the cool, professional farewell it had been?

Honestly, she wasn't sure.

Finding herself on Two Deck, she wandered into the senior mess. It was empty except for Bella, who was polishing silver. Gazing around the room, she smiled at the recent memories. Yesterday evening Charlotte and Julia had been boated over to dine with *Daring's* senior mess. Liam had stayed behind in *Freedom*, and Captain Riverton had even taken the watch here in *Daring* to give everyone a chance to relax. Having Charlotte back had been wonderful, and Amelia had to admit that Julia Sungate's presence had lightened the room. She still wasn't sure if she wished Liam had been present or not.

"Where is everyone?" she asked.

"The XO and coxn are both checking damage," Bella replied matter-of-factly, "and the artificer is in sailing control. The assaulter was here but recently left to relieve the doctor on the bridge."

Mention of the doctor made Amelia smile. Thanking Bella, she retreated and headed for sickbay. Now that Amelia knew that Liam wasn't Ava's type, she'd come to appreciate what a nice friendship the two nobles had. They understood each other in ways few could: if anyone could offer her sound advice on her Liam relationship, it was Ava.

Sickbay was quiet. Master Rating Song looked up as she entered, the empty beds around him a rare sight these days.

"Good afternoon, PO," he said. "Can I help you?"

She stopped in the doorway, waving away his query. "No, no. I was just looking for Dr. Templegrey – on a non-medical matter."

"I think she's on the bridge."

"I heard Chief Sky had relieved her."

He shrugged. "I don't know then, PO."

"Thanks anyway."

"No problem." He blew her a dramatic kiss, grinning.

She rolled her eyes, cursing the enthusiasm with which sailors gossiped. No-one seemed upset that Liam had kissed her, and everyone had just assumed it was in the heat of the moment of her life being saved. And maybe… that's all it was. Another question to ponder with Ava, if she could find her.

With a bit of puzzlement she retraced her steps forward and found herself outside Ava's cabin. She heard a laugh through the door and realized that her friend must just be taking a break from the bridge. She knocked and pushed open the door.

"Hi, Ava, I just wanted to quickly ask-"

A pair of startled cries froze her. She looked up to see Ava standing in her uniform shirt and trousers, shirt untucked and half-unbuttoned. Her coat was discarded on the deck by her feet and her hair was messily coming out of its careful, braided coils.

And trying her best to hide behind Ava, in a similar state of undress, was Julia Sungate.

Oh…" Amelia managed. "Oh, crap."

A tense silence hung in the cabin.

Then Ava burst out laughing. "Shut the door at least, darling!"

Amelia did so, then found herself facing the two young noblewomen. Julia rested her arms around Ava's shoulders as Ava shifted her weight to one hip. They stared at her, almost expectantly.

"I… I didn't know," she managed.

"Of course you didn't, darling," Ava said. "Noble ladies pride themselves on their discretion."

"It's recent," Julia added.

"I thought you two didn't like each other."

"We discovered a mutual interest."

"You were coming to ask something?" Julia prompted.

"Oh! Umm, yes. Uhh… Liam's on board, and I figure this is the last time I'll be able to talk to him. Things are okay between us, but not exactly great. Should I try to talk to him while I can, or just let things be?"

"Are you two happy with how things stand?" Ava asked.

"What are you talking about?" Julia interrupted.

"I'll tell you later." Ava turned piercing eyes back to Amelia. "Are you two happy?"

"Not really."

"Then you should talk."

"But, based on our last few talks, it might make things worse."

"Darling," Ava said, stepping out of Julia's embrace to squeeze Amelia's hands, "never miss the opportunity to tell someone you love them. That is never wasted effort."

"You're right," she said, squeezing back.

Ava released her and stepped back again. "So you'd better hurry. He won't be here much longer."

"Yeah…" Her mind was starting to race about what she was going to say to him.

"And, not to put too fine a point on it," Ava continued, "but Julia also has a boat to catch. And I have to get back on watch."

"Right." Sudden realization struck her and she reached for the door, blushing. "Right. So happy for you both."

She stepped out of the cabin, shutting it quickly to cover the sudden gales of laughter that followed her. Taking a deep breath, she headed for the quarterdeck.

"I think you should give a technical presentation to your entire department," Liam said, leaning against the desk as Swift sat back in the chair. "Make it clear exactly why Narrow's plan didn't work and show how you'd do it next time."

"But isn't that just encouraging him?"

It was strange to be in *Daring's* XO cabin. He'd barely vacated it a fortnight ago and already it seemed like a foreign place. It was Subcommander Swift's cabin now, and while the new XO had hardly spent time redecorating, there were enough subtle changes that it no longer felt like Liam's home.

"Not at all. If you present your talk as professional development for all your sailors, you can make out the stern mast concept to be a good thing, which he and his followers will like. But then you can, in excruciating detail, explain why his design failed so completely. And then, you can offer your own recommendations for how to do it better next time, ending the talk on a positive note."

"I sense the cunning strategy of an aristocrat at play," he said with an admiring frown. "Kill them with kindness, and all that?"

"Lower their guard with kindness," Liam corrected, "then eviscerate them with facts. And then package it all up with a warm smile."

"Beautiful. As long as I don't have to compliment him."

"Not at all. Just compliment the *concept*. He can hardly argue with that, since it was his."

"And I don't look like a petty bully."

"Not to the crew, anyway. I'll know the truth."

Mason scoffed, and Liam let himself laugh. It was good to have these moments with a friend. They'd already had a strategy council with Captain Riverton, and then adjourned to go over any last questions Mason had about running the ship. Liam was thankful he'd brought up his worries about Narrow. And as silence fell he sensed they both knew perfectly well what the last topic of conversation needed to be.

"So the crew," Mason began, "has developed this new habit of blowing kisses to each other."

"Yes… Mine as well."

"Any idea why?" The attempt at an innocent expression on Mason's face was laughable.

Liam sighed. "I'm sure you've heard the story."

"What I want to know is: will there be another kiss? Like, today?"

"I'd be happy to," he admitted, folding his arms as he leaned against the deck. "But I don't know if it's a good idea. She's a distraction, and I can't afford that right now."

"And I promise to keep her safe, so when you go back your ship, you don't have to worry about that. But right now, you're on *her* ship."

"Well," he forced the words from her mouth, "maybe she and I aren't meant to be together. It was always a long shot, considering everything stacked against us."

It was the first time he'd said those words out loud. He didn't like how they sounded.

"And since when have you shied away from long shots, if they're worthwhile?" Mason apparently didn't like them either.

"I think Julia Sungate might be interested in me," he said, avoiding the question. "That would be a more appropriate match."

"Do you like Julia more than Amelia?"

"Well, no. But-"

"Mia Hedge has been trying to get her hands on me ever since Sapphira," Mason retorted. "But I don't *like* her, so I don't do anything about it. It's not hard, Liam."

"It is for the nobility. We have other pressures."

"And you told your family to stuff those pressures up their arses years ago. Don't try and talk yourself into something just to avoid the real problem."

Liam stared down at his friend. "And what is the real problem?"

"You love Amelia Virtue."

He couldn't help but smile.

"And that," Mason added, "is a pretty classy problem to have."

There was a knock at the door. Mason's eyes were almost expectant as he called out a reply. The door creaked open and Amelia poked her head in.

"XO, sir…" Her eyes met Mason's, then went nervously to Liam. "I was hoping to speak to *Freedom's* commanding officer."

"Perfect timing," Mason said, jumping out of his chair. "I have many XO things to do, so I'm going to go and… XO. You can use my cabin for your discussion."

"Subcommander Swift," Liam said quickly, "thank you for everything."

Mason extended his hand. "Until next time, sir."

Liam ignored the handshake and wrapped his friend in a hug. "Until next time."

Amelia squeezed in the door to let Mason pass. He gave her a look, then blew her a kiss. She smacked him as he slipped out the door.

"Hello," Liam said, turning to face her fully.

"Hey," she replied. Her posture was shy as she kept her distance, leaning up against the far bulkhead, but her usual smile lit up her face. "I'm glad I caught you."

"Me too."

There was so much to say. And he could see the turmoil of emotions in her eyes. A dozen different statements rushed through his mind, a dozen different ways to approach the minefield that their relationship had become. He decided to just plunge in.

"I love you."

She stared at him, her lips parted to speak, and then her face dissolved in tears. She stepped forward and wrapped herself around him, quiet sobs melting against his chest. He closed his arms around her, loving the feel of her body against his.

"I love you, too," she said, finally lifting her head. "And I think we both know that's why you have to go."

"For now," he agreed, hating the words even as he said them.

She squeezed him, then stepped back, hands still on his waist.

"Captain of your own ship," she said with a smile even as she wiped her eyes. "Very impressive, Lord Blackwood."

"Lady Riverton's elegant solution to a tricky problem."

"She may be an ice queen, but she has quite the insight." She made a fist and punched him lightly in the stomach. "Too bad she's right about this, though."

"Let's finish the mission. And then we can go home and talk about the future."

Her eyes widened. "You… want to talk about the future?"

"With no expectations," he clarified quickly.

"No devious plan?" she teased. "No cunning trap to lure me in?"

"Never. Whatever we decide, it'll be what we both want." He gazed down at her, appreciating anew her many qualities. "I know that it's challenging, with you and I coming from different ranks and different backgrounds."

"Well, maybe I'll just take my commission, marry some handsome high lord from the Hub, and then greet you as an equal. I believe young Lord Highcastle is still available."

She was teasing, he could tell, and he relaxed.

"If you do, I'd have to find some high lady to match." He made a show of considering. "I believe Lady Sungate is also available."

"Oh, she's lovely," she gushed. And then laughed. "But you'd be competing against Ava Templegrey for her affections."

He couldn't stop the shock from showing. Amelia's eyes were sparkling and he knew she spoke the truth. "What? When did that happen?"

"A while ago."

"How did you know?"

"I'm a woman," she said smugly. "I just know these things."

"Well," he breathed, with more relief that he was willing to let on, "I'll need another plan, then."

"Happy to help you figure that out," she said, leaning in for a kiss, "when we get home."

"I look forward to it, darling."

"Until then, you stay safe." She tightened her grip on him. "And trust that I will too."

There was so much behind those bright, friendly eyes, he knew. Intelligence, resilience and savvy. It still pained him to let her go, but deep in his heart he knew she'd be all right.

He held her close, losing himself in one last kiss.

CHAPTER 16

This far out in the Halo, things were truly dark. As Liam scanned the skies for any other vessels, he noted the utter lack of stars in his field of view. There was the local star, around which the planet they were fast approaching orbited, and astern was the faint glow of the Hub. But ahead, beyond the distant form of *Emerald Crown*, was a blackness so deep it chilled the soul.

"Is that," Sungate suddenly whispered next to him, "the Abyss?"

"That's the edge of it," he replied quietly. "We're approaching one of the last stars in the galaxy."

She shivered, unable to take her eyes from the sweeping vista of nothingness.

Liam raised his telescope again, noting the sails on the sloop rippling as Shordar turned. The master thief was definitely aiming for the planet, an uncharted world so far beyond the boundaries of the Empire that Liam wondered if any Human had ever laid eyes on it before.

"What's in it?" Sungate asked.

"Excuse me?"

"The Abyss." She turned to stare at him. "What's in it?"

He looked outward again, shaking his head. "Nothing."

"How far does it go?"

"As best as we can tell… Forever."

She took a shaky breath, and lowered her gaze to study the sailing table with sudden, almost frantic interest. When she finally glanced up, her eyes fixed on the one nearby star.

"Then I'm grateful for this one light in the Abyss."

Liam had seen the Abyss once before, as a young Lieutenant on a survey mission, and he understood Sungate's discomfort. In the average person's experience, there were *always* stars in the sky, a reassuring, eternal presence providing warmth, light, and the winds upon which Humanity travelled. As a child of the Halo he understood at least that there were great swathes of blackness between the stars, but even he'd been shocked when he'd first seen the Abyss. To a Hub denizen like Sungate, this must be terrifying.

They were alone on the bridge, with the ship's helm locked and steady against the dying winds. With the time for action almost upon them, Liam wanted to give his crew one last chance to rest. He'd tried to sleep himself, but his mind was too active and rest was elusive. And though the future carried many unknowns, there was one question he thought he might get an answer to.

"Your first time aboard a warship has proven eventful, Julia. I hope we've met your expectations."

"You have, sir," she said, looking at him with a sudden smile.

"And… Would you still like me to escort you home with the Suncatcher?"

Her eyes sparkled with new interest. "Very much, Lord Blackwood."

"Or would you rather Lady Templegrey have the honor?"

Her gaze dropped as a new smile crept over her features. When she looked up at him again through her eyelashes, he saw nothing but playfulness.

"Either would be exquisite." She ran her fingers shamelessly along his waist. "But you'd be easier to show off in court."

So he *had* understood her earlier intentions correctly, if not their underlying motivation.

"You think a minor Halo lord would keep the marriage offers at bay?"

"Oh, stars, no. But at least you'd keep drunken young fops at bay. Ava at my side would only encourage them to approach in pairs."

"And start gossip."

"That doesn't bother me." She slipped her other hand onto his hip. "If anything it would signal that I'm open to a variety of offers."

"Is that all we are to you? A variety of offers."

"Ava is a lovely person. And a lovely distraction in this stressful time." She glanced back toward the closed hatch leading off the bridge. "If *you're* looking for a distraction, Lord Blackwood, Charlotte will be here to relieve me soon enough."

He stepped back enough that her hands fell away.

"I'm not, Lady Sungate."

"Shame."

He studied her indifferent confidence as she held his gaze fearlessly. "People are like the suns in the Hub to you, aren't they? Warm, useful and too numerous to count."

She sniffed a laugh. "I suppose they are."

"Well, have a look out there." She followed his gesture out toward the blackness beyond the canopy. "We're on the edge of the Abyss, with only a single sun lighting the darkness."

"Don't remind me."

"And that's kind of how I am," he continued, realizing anew why he chose to socialize outside his class. "There's only one sun lighting up my darkness. Only one sun that can."

"And she's wonderful," Sungate replied. "If a little rough around the edges."

"She's my light in the Abyss."

"I'm happy that you're free to find that single light," she said with a sigh. "I, however, feel the pressure from all those suns beating down on me every day I spend in the Imperial Court. It's why I love being in a ship where my name means nothing."

"But your shipmates do."

"First rule of the Imperial Court: don't make attachments."

"Ava is very dear to me," he said firmly. "Don't toy with her."

"Ava's eyes are wide open," she said with a cool certainty. Then her gaze softened. "But yes… She's more than just a distraction."

"It seems we understand each other, Lady Sungate."

"We do, Lord Blackwood."

"Then I'll wish you a quiet rest of your watch." He turned and headed for the hatch.

"Thank you, sir."

Liam managed several hours of sleep, but it was far too soon that he found himself once again on the bridge, this time surrounded by crew.

"We're still gaining on Shordar," Brown announced from the sailing table, "and we'll reach him before he makes planetfall."

"He's run all this way," Sungate mused at the gunnery table, barely glancing up, "only to fail now."

"Remember to load chain shot," Liam said. "We don't want to risk damaging the Suncatcher."

"Nothing weighs more heavily on my mind, sir."

Freedom was still down a cannon, but *Daring's* hullwrights had managed to repair the starboard gun deck and seal off the destroyed bay. A few more carefully supervised tests had proven that Sungate's augmented black powder worked brilliantly, significantly extending the effective range of their cannon. Captain Riverton had generously offered to partially defuel one of her missiles in order to give both ships a few broadsides' worth of shots. It wasn't a lot, but Liam knew today's battle wasn't intended for long range. Today's battle was going to be close and brutal.

A clank of armor plates drew Liam's attention aft, to where Master Rating Flatrock was clambering up to the bridge. The big man's breastplate was clearly a custom job, with the stylized image of a tower emblazoned across the silver metal, and would have cost a pretty penny. Liam knew that

Flatrock had spent much of his fortune in taverns and brothels back home on Passagia – it was good to see he'd spent at least some of the money earned from their adventures wisely.

"Boarding party ready, sir," he reported, knuckling his forehead.

"Very good, Coxn. I expect you'll be needed shortly."

Flatrock squinted through the canopy. "Are we almost upon them, sir?"

Emerald Crown was clearly visible ahead, still at full sail with all four masts extended. Beyond, filling much of the sky, was the dark circle of the uncharted planet. As Liam watched, the local star rose against the planet's limb, light shimmering through the *Emerald Crown's* fluttering sails.

"Shordar is trying to maintain maximum sheet for as long as he can," Liam explained, "and get to shelter at that planet."

"We'll catch him first, though?"

"We will. Those sails of his that you see? They'll be shredded in short order."

Freedom was closing rapidly, her bowsprit sail still taught as she rode the weakening solar winds. Shordar was no doubt watching carefully, judging the range as the cutter closed his ship.

"But surely he'll retract his side masts to return fire, sir."

"Experience had taught him just how close he can let us get before risking fire, and he's pushing all four masts right up to the last moment. He'll keep his port and starboard masts extended for speed, thinking he's out of gun range."

"Will my boat be heading into a crossfire?"

"Not if you steer it properly, Coxn."

Flatrock chuckled, but his deep-set eyes revealed a touch of fear. This was his first time leading a mission, Liam knew, and he was doubtless feeling the new pressure of responsibility.

"You've done this a hundred times, Coxn," he said, clapping a hand on Flatrock's shoulder. "Trust your instincts."

"Yes, sir."

"On your way, then."

Flatrock retreated down the ladder. Liam turned his attention back to the quarry ahead. *Freedom* had closed the distance and he knew it was time.

"Ms. Brown," he announced, "come right to give us a broadside on *Emerald Crown*."

"Yes, sir."

"Ms. Sungate, target his top sail, if you please."

"Yes, sir."

"Roll the ship to bring both batteries to bear. Fire at will."

Liam watched as the view beyond the canopy turned, *Emerald Crown* drawing left as the crescent planet loomed in the distance. On *Freedom's* other side, *Daring* was head-on, looking enormous with all four masts at full sail. The frigate was slower, and Shordar assumed he could maintain his lead until safely in the shallows of orbit. Liam was about to dissuade him of that notion.

Freedom's deck shook as the first broadside unleashed. As Brown rolled the ship, Liam snapped up the telescope and tracked the sloop, noting with satisfaction the first tears in the upper mainsails. Shordar disappeared beneath them, only to reappear on the starboard side just as the guns fired. The slow roll continued and the port battery fired again.

"We're scoring hits," Sungate reported, "but the roll is decreasing accuracy."

"Steady us up, Ms. Brown, if you please. Port-side to."

Freedom rolled through another complete rotation before Brown thrusted them back onto a stable course. Liam could see with the naked eye how Shordar's top sails were coming loose from the onslaught. They were far from destroyed, but his ship would already be imbalanced and slowed.

"Target the bottom sails, if you please."

More shots thundered away, tearing into the mast beneath the sloop. The port and starboard masts were still holding strong, but Liam knew Shordar would have to stow them if he wanted to return fire. *Daring* was now looming large, just beginning her turn to bring her own guns to bear.

"Come hard up," he ordered, "get us clear of *Daring's* line of fire."

Freedom's bow pulled upward as she sailed above the plane between the sloop and the frigate. As Brown rolled to keep their port guns on target, Liam watched *Daring's* beam explode with fire as she loosed her first volley.

"*Emerald Crown* is wallowing," Brown reported.

With only two effective masts, the sloop had clearly slowed. The approaching planet now filled half the sky but was still a distant haven. Liam scanned *Daring* for the pre-arranged flag signal.

"I'm in normal range," Sungate said, "and switching to normal powder."

"Very good."

Daring had turned to keep *Emerald Crown* on the bow, then veered back to open the gun arcs again. Another hail of chain shot tore through Shordar's sails. Liam glanced at the damage, but kept his telescope focused on *Daring's* top mast.

The signal flags suddenly ran up the halyard: *deploy boats.*

"Launch the boat, if you please, Ms. Brown."

Liam listened as Brown sent the orders, and watched as *Emerald Crown* tried to maneuver with shredded sails both top and bottom. Shordar still hadn't retracted his side masts – still couldn't fire his cannon. Liam scanned *Daring* and saw both her boats launching.

He rubbed his chin, trying to get inside Shordar's mind. The master thief surely wasn't going to make it this easy.

"Sir," Brown reported, "three new ships inbound from the planet!"

⸻⸻⸻

Amelia crouched low in the boat. It wouldn't help, she knew, but somehow she just felt like the boat was harder to see if she and her team were lower. Hedge was beside her, legs jittering with excitement, and causing the extra pistols slung across her breastplate to rattle. Swift was in front next to Song, telescope up as he surveyed toward the planet. *Daring* had just reported three ships approaching, and Amelia knew well what danger that represented to a small boat.

"I assess we can make it," Swift said into his radio. "Recommend proceed."

"*Agreed,*" came Riverton's curt reply.

"Full thrusters," Swift ordered. "Full speed approach."

"Aye, sir," Faith replied, pushing his thrusters to maximum speed.

Amelia felt the acceleration, watching as *Emerald Crown* grew quickly ahead. All four masts were still extended so it was going to be a tricky approach, especially with *Saber* and *Freedom's* boat, *Rapier,* closing from other vectors. With three boarding parties, the plan was simple: get on board, overwhelm the crew and take control. But with three new enemy ships inbound, the margin for error was fast diminishing.

A puff of flame from the nearest ship made Amelia duck lower in her seat.

"They've got bow cannon," she announced.

"Steady as she goes," Swift ordered.

The boat continued to close *Emerald Crown* on a straight course. Amelia just hoped their speed would be enough. On their port side, *Rapier* began to weave as cannonballs rocketed past her. The serpentine course made her harder to hit, but it also left her exposed for longer. Suddenly, Amelia liked Swift's plan better.

The top and starboard masts of *Emerald Crown* filled her view on either side of the boat, stretching upward as *Dagger* closed to board. The top mast was practically bereft of sails and the starboard sails flapped uncertainly as *Dagger* herself interrupted the wind flow.

"Airlock spotted," Song cried, pointing at the rapidly approaching hull.

"Got it," Faith said, "hang on!"

Amelia grabbed her seat as the boat rotated, feeling herself get heavy as the thrusters reversed to kill its speed. Hedge slammed into her, grunting as the forces shifted and Amelia was thrown onto her. Then the boat slammed to a halt and Song dove to secure the connection.

Amelia pulled herself off Hedge and gestured toward the hatch. "After you."

Song wrenched open the airlock and Hedge jumped through, landing on the outer door of *Emerald Crown*. Her override tool was already in her hand and before Amelia could ever get out of the boat the enemy door pushed open.

Hedge's sword was the first through, blocking an immediate strike from a massive tailsword. She screamed and emptied her pistol in both directions, then pushed herself clear of the airlock. Amelia yanked herself through the tunnel and thrust her sword through the open door. Hedge was unleashing fury to her right so she climbed out to the left.

One Theropod was down, grasping at his torso from what she expected were bullet wounds. His tail lay flat against the deck, weighed down by the heavy blade, and he hissed angrily at Amelia. She lifted her own pistol and scanned beyond, through the warm, humid mist. She stepped forward to make room as Swift and Song entered the ship.

The fallen Theropod suddenly swung his tail. The strike was low enough that she leapt over it, then dropped her cutlass to block the vicious back-swing. The brute was struggling to his feet, but she stabbed into his torso. Blood sprayed as he collapsed in a heap.

"*Dagger* aboard," she heard Swift report.

"Saber *aboard*," Sky's voice sounded in her ear.

Amelia paused, glancing back to Swift. When no third report came, he frowned and gestured for her to advance.

"To the bridge," he ordered.

Leaving Faith to secure their escape route, Amelia led the team aft. Her orders were to take control of this ship, and that's what she intended to do.

———•—•———

"Two boats have linked up to *Emerald Crown*," Liam reported, lowering his telescope. "But I've lost sight of *Rapier*."

"There!" Brown said at his side, pointing to where two of the new ships were closing in, cannons firing wildly.

"Come left," he ordered, "get us in between."

Under Brown's direction *Freedom* leaned to port, her bowsprit sail momentarily obscuring *Emerald Crown* as the sloop struggled to make way. *Daring* opened fire again, fresh chain punching through *Emerald Crown's* starboard sails. *Freedom* continued her turn, cutting across the bow of Shordar's stricken vessel and right into the fire of the new Theropod escorts.

Liam scanned them visually. One looked like an old tender from an Imperial shipyard with gunports carved along its beam. The second, larger one was a tub of a vessel that had probably started its career as an in-system hauler. In the distance, still rising up from the planet was a ship that looked for all the stars like a Sectoid scout ship, except that the original tiny masts had been broken off and replaced with four rickety frames that looked ready to snap under the pressure of their sails.

Old Tender was clearly the fastest and even as Liam watched it swung sharply to port, bringing all its side guns to bear. They fired in a loose approximation of a broadside, and he spotted one clear impact that sent *Rapier* tumbling.

"Target the smaller enemy ship," he snapped. "Get us in front of her!"

Freedom banked to starboard, overtaking the smaller vessel.

"Guns ready."

"Fire."

Chain shot rattled through Old Tender's sails, but she continued to press forward, bow cannon firing again at *Rapier* as she turned.

"Reload with ball – destroy that ship."

Brown cut right across the bow of Old Tender, forcing the smaller ship to pull up.

"Guns ready."

"Fire at will."

The broadside was deeper with the bigger rounds. Liam saw multiple tufts of impact along Old Tender's starboard side. *Freedom's* speed carried her directly ahead of the target, into point-blank range, and the second, looser broadside punched holes through Old Tender's bow. Air shimmered amidst the debris tumbling outward.

Liam scanned the skies for *Rapier*. The boat had come hard about and was already inside the masts of *Emerald Crown*. Even from here Liam could see the boat's crew frantically tearing free one of the benches and pressing it down as a makeshift shoring plank.

Freedom continued her turn, strafing Old Tender's port side. Beyond, *Daring* loomed as she chewed away at Shordar's port sails.

Liam just saw *Rapier* slam into Shordar's hull. He lifted his telescope and watched the boarding party and the boat's crew scramble to safety. The boat went dark as it lost power, a bulbous growth on *Emerald Crown's* hull. For a moment Liam thought he saw *Daring's* boats high on the sloop's hull just forward of the bridge, but then realized that *Saber* and *Dagger* were on the far side. He raised his spyglass again. What was Shordar planning?

———•———

Amelia thrust forward again, driving the Theropod back through the door. The space was too narrow for his tailsword and he flicked at her with daggers in his hands. The first one pinged harmlessly off her breastplate and she slashed the other one clean out of the brute's hand. The dagger struck her side with a lightning strike, nicking her flesh through the padded armor at her waist. She spun to clear, smashing her elbow into the Theropod's face. The head snapped back on the neck, then lashed out with teeth bared. Her backhand fist sent several of those teeth flying as she turned back, hacking down with her cutlass to finally drop the enemy.

Stepping on that fallen tail to avoid any surprises, she felt the body go limp as she scanned the intersection she'd just reached. Movement saw her blade come up in defence, her pistol out of its holster again. She lowered both weapons as she recognized the burly form of Master Sailor Flatrock stumble into view.

"*Rapier* ahoy," she shouted.

Flatrock grinned as he spotted her, emerging around the corner with his team. Amelia glanced back as Swift, Hedge and Song arrived behind her.

"Sorry, sir," Flatrock grumbled to Swift. "Took a bit of fire on the way in."

"You drew it away from us," Swift said, eyes still scanning all four directions. "You have my thanks."

"We couldn't contact any of you," Flatrock said, tapping his ear.

"Comms are jammed," Swift replied.

He gestured Hedge toward the forward passageway, where a heavy, sealed door blocked any further progress. Amelia took up position facing aft, but she could see that this passage didn't extend far. This close to the stern, she suspected the two doors on either bulkhead led to cabins. Definitely worth a look later, but probably not where Shordar was hiding right now. The forward door, that Hedge was currently testing, led to the bridge.

"It's hard-sealed," Hedge called back.

"Flatrock," Swift said, "take your team down one deck and cover any access hatches up into the bridge. Cut off any escape route."

"Yes, sir. Where's Chief Sky?"

"Taking sailing control, I presume."

That had been the last signal Amelia or any of them had heard, before a piercing, non-stop tone had overwhelmed their radios. It had eventually faded, but now there was nothing but static.

Flatrock gestured to his team and they retreated down the passageway, turning forward at the next junction.

"I've got explosives, sir," Hedge announced, with the usual gleam in her eye.

Swift considered. Then he glanced questioning at Amelia.

"Sir," she said quietly, "our mission is to take control of the ship. We need to get on the bridge."

"But ultimately," he countered, "our mission is to recover the Suncatcher. Explosions in the vicinity of the treasure are not a good idea."

"Good point."

His saber tilted toward the after passageway. "Check those two doors. Just make sure we haven't missed anything."

"Yes, sir."

"Hedge," he growled, moving forward, "what's the minimum amount of force we need?"

Her reply was lost as Amelia kicked open the port-side door, sweeping her pistol through the opening with her blade up defensively. Dim lanterns revealed that it was indeed a cabin, low and cramped but clearly done up with luxury. The round bed was piled with sheets and pillows and the sideboard was full of expensive looking liquors. A low table was dressed in a white tablecloth and shelves beyond it displayed silver settings held in place. A desk was clear of any clutter, the locked drawers resisting her efforts to peer inside.

She scanned the bulkheads and even peered at the rafters: there was no treasure hiding here. But this was Shordar's own cabin – who knew what secrets she could find if she took the time?

"Fire in the hole!"

Hedge's screech made Amelia crouch instinctively. A moment later the cabin rattled with the force of a distant explosion. She was up and into the passageway in time to see the rest of her team picking themselves up from cover in the intersection. Hedge ran forward and tested the bridge door. It was still intact, but the bottom of the frame was warped and blackened. She grabbed the bottom of the door and heaved, to no avail.

"Use leverage," Swift ordered, motioning Song forward.

The medic handed Hedge a long crowbar that matched his own. They jammed the bars into the crack beneath the door and together started to push. Amelia heard the awful screech of tortured metal as the bottom of the door started to bend upward.

Then Song cried out in pain, dropping his crowbar and dancing awkwardly back to collapse around the corner.

"Bastard shot me," he shouted, gripping his ankle.

Amelia ran for cover as more flashes lit up the crack beneath the door.

She staggered as a bullet pinged off her shin guard, diving into the side passage next to Song. The medic gasped as he pulled off his boot to reveal a bloodied, swollen, purple mass.

"What do I do?" Amelia asked, ripping one of his medical kits from his belt.

"Get it wrapped," he hissed. "Stop the bleeding and hold it together."

She pulled out a bandage and fumbled to get it around the shattered joint. Her hand pressed against the wound as Song gasped in pain.

"Sorry," she said.

"Just do it!"

Ignoring his cries of pain, she tied the bandage as tightly as she could, ignoring the rapid discoloration of the cloth as it pressed against the wound. Holding it in place, she secured the wrapping as best she could, then looked up at Swift, who crouched in the other side passage to avoid the stream of bullets still flying past.

"How is he?" the XO called.

"He'll make it," Amelia shouted back immediately. But she caught his eye and subtly shook her head.

"I saw that," Song spat. "Just get me some poppied rum and lay me back. Elevate the leg."

She helped him lie back and then lifted his foot to rest against the bulkhead, gritting her teeth as he winced. The medical kit had half a dozen pre-poured shots of rum and she cracked one open to pour it into his mouth.

"I'm fine," he said, looking more angry with himself than anything. "Get those bastards."

Amelia crawled back to the intersection, spotting Swift still hunkered down across from her. The cracks of bullets had slowed, but enough projectiles zinged past that she stayed back. Swift motioned upward, rising to his full height. Amelia did the same, realizing that all the shots were low. She peeked around the corner.

Hedge was off the deck, her legs spread and feet braced against each bulkhead. She was facing Amelia, still slowly prying the broken door upward.

Amelia just caught a glimpse of Theropod feet beyond, then a wedge-shaped ahead appeared, followed by a pistol. She jerked back.

"I still got grenades," Hedge shouted.

Swift shook his head, mind clearly racing.

"Just hold there," he shouted back. Then he lowered back down and flipped his pistol around the corner to fire low. Sudden alien hisses were drowned by Hedge swearing at him.

Amelia staggered as the entire ship suddenly shook. She tumbled back against the rear bulkhead, feeling like the ship had suddenly flipped upward on its stern. Hedge crashed down from her perch, crowbar clanging along the deck as it bounced and rolled past Amelia. She reached out and grabbed Hedge's arms, hauling her into the side passage just as the acceleration dropped off. They untangled enough to get clear of the main passage and the cracks of fresh bullets.

Amelia checked on Song, who'd been thrown backward with the rest of them, and realized that he'd passed out. He was still breathing and his pulse was steady, but a combination of pain and poppied rum had done him in. She checked his shattered ankle again, then slipped his medical bags over her shoulder.

Swift was on his feet, pistol out as he peeked forward again. Hedge was unhurt as she climbed to her feet, reaching for her grenades.

"No," Amelia said, staying her hand. "We can't risk damaging the Suncatcher."

Hedge let go of her bombs and drew her extra pistols with a snarl.

"I am going to take that bridge," she snarled, "and piss in the Suncatcher."

———•———

Liam shielded his eyes as *Freedom* turned into the sun, trying to get a better angle on *Emerald Crown*. Both Old Tender and Fat Tub had positioned themselves between him and Shordar, peppering away with their cannon. *Freedom* had taken hits, but most of the Theropod shots had gone wild.

Julia Sungate and her team, however, never missed.

Another broadside smashed into Old Tender and the ship finally started to break up. It leaked air from a dozen holes and as its unbalanced sails continued to pull, it started to tear itself apart. Lifeboats launched amidst the growing wreckage, cluttering the view even more.

Liam grabbed the telescope and peered toward *Emerald Crown*, but the sloop was still half obscured by its escorts. It had suddenly thrusted forward with great speed, perhaps in a last gasp to reach the safety of the surface, but its sails were destroyed and the top mast was visibly bent from *Daring's* relentless onslaught. All three boarding parties had made it aboard, but no word had come for long minutes. *Freedom* still had comms with *Daring*, suggesting either that Shordar had erected a local jamming field… or that something very bad had happened aboard *Emerald Crown*.

He forced his fists to unclench. Amelia could take care of herself, he knew. His job was to deal with the pestering escort ships.

"Shift target to the fat tub," he ordered. "Ball shot."

"Yes, sir," Sungate replied, completely focused on her gunnery table.

"Fire at will."

The big old ship had turned sharply, forcing *Freedom* to haul to starboard and avoid a collision. It was easy enough for Brown to keep the cutter clear, but Fat Tub had successfully kept *Freedom* separated from *Emerald Crown*. On the far side of the battle, *Daring* was in a heavy exchange with Sectoid Scout and unable to safely close.

Sungate's shots bounced off the thick, curving bow of Fat Tub as the lumbering ship tried to close again. Brown rolled the ship to give both batteries a chance to fire, and tiny impacts shattered against Fat Tub's hull. A dozen rotations and Liam called a halt, having lost his positional aware-ness. As *Freedom* settled out and turned toward the sun again, Liam saw that the constant barrage had finally punched through Fat Tub's heavy hide, but the big ship was still pushing forward with the winds, moving between *Freedom* and the planet.

Beyond, he could see, *Emerald Crown* was drifting out of control. Her momentum from that last thruster blast was pushing her toward the planet, but her sails were still in tatters. The ship made way about thirty degrees off her bow, and already the first glow of atmosphere was building around her.

"Do you see our boats?" he demanded.

Brown studied her tactical table. "I see two boats near *Emerald Crown*... Heading planetside."

Liam raised his telescope again.

"Pursuit course!"

The passageway had been silent for a full minute, but the deck was starting to vibrate. It was slight but constant. Amelia looked to Swift.

He motioned Hedge forward. "Get that door open."

As he and Amelia covered with pistols, Hedge retrieved her crowbar, ran forward and jammed it into the gap between frame and door. Grunting with the effort, she pried the opening wider, until finally the door snapped loose, falling off its bottom hinges and hanging open.

Amelia rushed forward, pistol out. She raced past Hedge and onto the bridge, scanning for targets.

The bridge was small, with only three stations and a central command stool. The canopy revealed a crescent planet looming massive, high on the port bow, only a few strips of tattered sail fluttering wildly from the broken top mast. Amelia looked forward, down the smooth surface of the hull, just as two boats pushed off.

"*Farewell, my friends,*" came a sudden, translated voice over a bridge speaker. "*It's been a good chase. I hope you appreciate the hot finale I've arranged for you.*"

"Thrusters are out of fuel," Swift said, examining the various bridge stations. "And there's no time to rig fresh sails."

Amelia looked desperately around the bridge. "Do we have an anchor chute?"

Swift's fingers danced over the consoles as he checked.

"What's that?" Hedge asked, pointing forward at the flickering glow growing at the bow.

"That's the upper atmosphere," Amelia said. "And we're heading right into it."

CHAPTER 17

Shordar's taunt still hung on the bridge of *Freedom* as Liam searched the skies. He could just make out the two boats moving away from the stricken *Emerald Crown*, headed for the planet. From this angle he could clearly see one of *Daring's* boats still alongside the ship, with no sign of the others.

"Any response from the boarding teams to our hails?"

"Negative, sir," Brown replied. "Still trying."

"Continue to close *Emerald Crown*," he ordered. "There might be survivors to pick up."

"Yes, sir," Brown said. "Shall I shorten sails to bring us in close? We won't be able to hold for long before we lose winds in the shallows."

The planet's atmosphere blocked the solar winds, rendering their sails far less effective. *Freedom* could always use thrusters, but she'd be slow and heavy.

The deck jolted as fresh cannon fire struck the stern. Fat Tub, it seemed, wasn't giving up. Liam scanned aft, beyond the looming Fat Tub where *Daring* still pounded away at Sectoid Scout. Riverton was in no position to pursue Shordar, which left only one option.

"Maintain full sheet," he said. "Do a close sail past of *Emerald Crown* to scan for survivors, but maintain pursuit of Shordar's boats."

The mission, he knew, was everything. Shordar was getting away, the Suncatcher with him, and he was almost out of sight. If his boats could get to the surface and disappear, *Freedom* and *Daring* could spend years in orbit and never find him. Keeping those boats in sight was the only way to complete the mission.

He spared a momentary glance at the glowing hulk of *Emerald Crown* as it drifted past. Amelia and the others would just have to take care of themselves.

⁂

"We have no control of this ship," Swift declared, straightening from the bridge console. "We have to abandon her."

"But the Suncatcher!" Hedge protested.

"Is with Shordar," Amelia concluded, watching the two boats diminishing ahead. "He's headed planetside. We need to follow."

"We need to get everybody off," Swift retorted. "Come on."

They slipped through the wreckage of the bridge door. Swift and Hedge lifted Song together and started to retreat toward the boat as Amelia tried the comms again.

"*This is* Saber," came a crackling reply from Sky, growing clearer with each word. "*We have sailing control, but things are starting to come apart down here.*"

"Shordar has fled," Amelia replied. "Everyone, abandon ship. Get to your boats!"

"*Understood.*" There was a pause, then Sky spoke again. "Rapier *isn't space-worthy, we need to split their team between our boats.*"

"Okay," she said, gasping as she climbed down a ladder, "send half of them aft to *Dagger*. We'll wait for them."

The hull was beginning to creak, and Amelia could feel the air getting warmer. Carrying Song it took much longer than she liked to get back to the airlock, and as they hurried up Faith turned wide eyes to her.

"What did you guys do to the ship?" he asked.

"Forced our enemy to scuttle it," she replied.

Swift climbed through to the boat, then Song was guided through the airlock tube. Just as Hedge swung through the opening, Amelia saw Flatrock, Hunter and Leaf appear forward. They spotted her and increased to a run. Flatrock's face was shining with sweat.

"This thing's coming apart," he gasped.

"Then stop wasting time and get in the boat," she snapped.

The hull was groaning loudly now. Smoke was drifting aft in the passageway.

Flatrock and his team scrambled through the airlock, and Amelia finally abandoned *Emerald Crown* to follow, closing the airlock door and climbing into the boat. As she scrabbled into a seat, she could see the glowing cone of pressure growing around *Emerald Crown's* bow. The fiery air was spreading aft, already passing the tips of the masts.

Hunter snapped the boat hatch shut, sealed it, and finally sat back. "We're clear."

"Cast off," Swift ordered.

Faith needed no further encouragement and the boat leaped free of the hull, turning as fast as Faith could apply thrusters. The flames of atmosphere licked against the canopy of the boat for a moment, then faded as *Dagger* pushed upward toward the stars.

Swift was assessing Song's injury, so Amelia grabbed the radio.

"Any ship, any ship, this is *Dagger*, away from *Emerald Crown*."

"*This is* Freedom," came Liam's reply, the relief palpable beneath his crisp tone. "*Good to hear your voice*, Dagger."

"We have a casualty and need to come alongside."

"*Is the casualty life-threatening?*"

Swift looked up and shook his head, then gave a thumbs-up.

"No," Amelia reported. "Unconscious and immobile, but stable."

There was a pause, then Liam replied. "*Dagger* this is *Freedom*. Turn planetward and pursue Shordar's boats. We need to catch him before he disappears on the surface."

Amelia caught Swift's eye. As one of *Daring's* boats, they didn't actually have to obey an order from *Freedom*. But *Freedom's* captain was their superior officer. It was Liam, for star's sake! But Song needed medical attention quickly if he ever wanted to walk again.

Swift frowned in thought. He looked down at Song's shattered ankle, then up at the crescent planet looming over them.

"Alter course to go planetside," he ordered. "And find those boats."

Amelia grabbed a telescope and began scanning, noting Hunter doing the same.

She sensed Swift's hesitation beside her as he fiddled with the radio handset. Finally, he spoke again.

"*Daring* this is *Dagger*... We're altering course to pursue the enemy planetside. We have one serious casualty – stable, but at risk if not tended to promptly."

He wasn't openly challenging Liam's order, but he was ensuring Riverton knew the whole picture.

"*This is* Daring," came that icy voice, with the rumble of a broadside clear behind her words, "*understood. Continue your pursuit.*"

———•———

Liam let out the breath he'd been holding. Riverton was supporting his decision. He could see now that at least one more of the boats was away from *Emerald Crown*, as the ship began to disappear inside a fiery envelope of heat and pressure.

"*Daring this is* Saber," reported Chief Sky, obviously breathing hard under her words, "*we're away from* Emerald Crown. Rapier *unfit to sail and all* Rapier's *crew split between our two boats. We're joining the pursuit.*"

As *Daring* acknowledged, Liam turned his full attention back to Shordar's boats. It took a few moments to locate them again as they shrank against the planet's night side.

"Lookout," he called, keeping his voice calm, "do you still hold Shordar?"

"Yes, sir," she said, telescope up. "Forty degrees from starboard, ten degrees down."

"Keeping them in sight is everything," he said. "Your sole job now is to keep them located. Don't take your eyes off them. Understood?"

"Yes, sir."

He moved to stand next to her, using the line of her telescope as a guide for his search. It still took a moment, but then he spotted the two dim shapes against the dark background. The sun was rising and faint yellow light illuminated their hulls, but as they descended they chased the night and flicked in and out of shadow.

"Ms. Sungate," he said, "prepare a yellow flare, firing bearing forty from starboard, ten down, if you please."

"Yes, sir."

"Ms. Brown, signal the boats to watch for a locator flare, if you please."

"Yes, sir."

He listened as Brown sent the signal, watching Shordar's boats continue their descent.

"Flare ready, sir."

"Fire."

A dazzling streak of light lanced outward from *Freedom*, lighting up the night sky as it raced downward. Shordar's boats were lit up by the incandescent rocket, and for thirty glorious seconds their target was fully exposed.

"I got them!" Amelia shouted, peering through her telescope. "I got them!"

Under the light of the flare, Shordar's boats glowed against the dark surface below.

"Full thrusters," Swift ordered. "Close those boats."

Amelia lowered her spyglass to glance around. *Saber* was behind them, keeping pace. *Freedom* was above them, holding altitude. *Daring* was in the distance, cannons blazing at the two targets surrounding her. And dead ahead as Faith adjusted the boat's course, was their prize. They'd chased this thief to the very end of the galaxy – there was no way he was escaping now.

"He's shaping a shallow course," Swift mused, "trying to reduce the heat against his hull and stay hidden longer."

"Is that good news?" she asked.

He shrugged. "It means we can do the same, and not strain the boat too much. But eventually he's going to hit thicker air and his boats will glow for at least a few moments."

As the flare faded, Amelia kept her telescope on the target. "We'll be ready."

"What do you think's waiting for us on the ground?" Flatrock asked.

"Don't care," Hedge replied, "I'm still going to piss in the Suncatcher before today is done."

Shordar's boats were fading from view as they descended into full night, but Liam knew that *Daring's* boats were in hot pursuit. They had locator beacons, so Shordar's approximate position could be tracked on the tactical table. His lookout diligently maintained her vigil with the spyglass and he retreated to Brown's station.

"Status of *Daring*?" he asked.

"Still fighting two escort ships, that have now closed to point-blank range."

Daring was a warship designed for close-in combat, but it only took one lucky shot from these pirates to cause serious damage. And there were no friendly shipyards within weeks of here. As he scanned the utterly black surface of the uninhabited world below, Liam realized that HMSS *Daring* was their only safe haven – the only source of crew, material, stores and spares, and the only vessel here capable of making the trek back to civilization unsupported. There might be more *Freedom* could do to pursue Shordar, but the mission wasn't just to recapture the Suncatcher – the mission was to return the Suncatcher safely. Without *Daring*, that was impossible.

"Ms. Sungate, fire another flare, same bearing, if you please." He turned to Brown. "Once that flare goes, we're turning to engage the hostiles."

The flare rocketed away, lighting up the night sky again. Brown gave the orders to turn *Freedom* hard to port, and the view beyond the canopy shifted from the dark horizon of the planet to the blistering fire between three star sailing ships.

"*Daring*, this is *Freedom*. We're inbound to assist."

The second flare couldn't reach as far into the atmosphere, but its glow lit up Shordar's boats enough for Amelia to spot them again. They were closer now, still trying to run slow and shallow to avoid looking like meteors. Faith adjusted course slightly to point directly at them, struggling to keep the boat on course as the pressure outside continued to build.

"They're increasing speed," Hunter reported, telescope still up.

Amelia scanned ahead and saw the pinpricks of boat thrusters at full, followed a few moments later by the first wisps of superheated air.

"He's given up on stealth," she said.

"Keep pushing," Swift urged Faith. "We can't lose them now."

The boat descended into the thickening air with increasing violence. Amelia hung on to her seat, gritting her teeth as the turbulence pounded her craft. Flatrock and Hedge held Song down, his unconscious form moaning softly with each lurch of the boat. The air ahead started to glow, growing into a bow wave that curved half-way back on the boat.

"I'm cutting thrusters," Faith shouted over the growing din. "We have to coast through this."

"Yes, please," Swift said.

Amelia stole a glance aft and saw a similar cone of fire surrounding *Saber*. Looking forward she could only assume Shordar's boats were punching through the air with the same spectacle, but they were invisible through *Dagger's* own cone of fire. The roar from outside grew to a screech and Amelia shut her eyes against the white-hot gas blasting past the boat.

Then, finally, the pressure eased as friction slowed the boat. The flames died away and, for a moment, Amelia felt weightless as *Dagger* emerged into the first light of dawn far below. Up ahead, tiny points of light indicated Shordar's boats igniting their thrusters. She pointed.

"Got it," Faith replied, pushing *Dagger's* own throttles forward.

Despite Shordar's best attempts, the sun was catching up to them all. The ground below – suddenly not that far below, Amelia realized with surprise – was still dark, but the sky was lightening and a grey glow lit up Shordar's boats as they descended rapidly. *Dagger* pursued at full thrust, with *Saber* close behind.

As Amelia watched, Shordar's boats landed and reptilian forms poured out. The boats were partially obscured by jagged, rocky outcrops bursting upward from a rolling plain. She couldn't make out details from this distance, but she clearly saw four Theropods struggling to lift out a large, golden object and set it down. More brutes scampered into view from behind one of the larger outcrops with a broad litter and together they lifted what could only be the Suncatcher onto it. The litter was raised and it disappeared from view.

"Thirty seconds to landing," Faith warned.

"Set us down on the other side of that long outcrop from their boats," Swift ordered. "We need cover to assemble our forces."

"Check weapons and ammo," Amelia said to everyone. "We're going in hot."

She glanced at her own cutlass still strapped to her belt and reloaded her pistol. There were no more bullets after that. Looking around, she realized that her sailors were similarly low – the boarding of *Emerald Crown* was supposed to have been their only mission that day. They weren't ready for another.

"What about these?" Flatrock said, pulling up a pair of long rifles from the boat's locker.

"Bring them," she said. Everything helped.

The boat set down in a cloud of dust, thumping against the rocks. Hedge was out the door in a moment, followed by Flatrock and Leaf. Amelia was next, sweeping the landing zone with her pistol and shielding her eyes against the dust as *Saber* soared down to land. Within moments, both boarding parties were out and creating a perimeter around the boats. Amelia rounded the long outcrop to peek at where the brutes had landed. There were no Theropods in sight, but a multitude of tracks over the dusty rocks revealed their path into a nearby cave.

Swift joined her and surveyed the scene, motioning Sky to join him.

"Assaulter," he said, "this is your show. Recommendations?"

"Leave *Saber's* boat crew here as rearguard," she said immediately, eyes scanning the outcrops around them before focusing on the cave. She gestured for Narrow to join them and the big man trotted over. "The rest of us, four teams led by me, Virtue, Narrow and you, sir. Your team will be our top cover, using the rifles and maintaining the overall picture. I'll lead the main assault with Narrow and Virtue flanking me."

"We don't know what's in there," Swift said, gesturing to the cave.

"Which is why I'm keeping the plan simple," she snapped. "I go for Shordar, or whatever the biggest target is. Narrow and Virtue, watch my sides. Sir, if there's any way to get high, take it. Get under cover and shoot down from there."

"One addition," Swift said, turning to Amelia. "Virtue, your goal is the Suncatcher. Cover Sky, yes, but find that treasure, make sure it doesn't escape, and recover it if you can. Our mission is not to defeat Shordar – it's to get that damn bowl."

She nodded. Across from her, Narrow frowned but said nothing.

"Gather your teams," he ordered them.

As Amelia moved clear, she felt a strong hand on her arm. Turning, her eyes widened as she saw Narrow looming over her. She ripped her arm free of his grasp.

"I'm not a bad man," he said to her, eyes pleading for her to understand. "I'm sorry I made a mistake. I'll make it up to you today."

"You don't have to," she replied, stunned at his intensity. "We just have to get through this."

"I'll show them all," he said with a wink. Then he strode away.

Amelia motioned Hedge, Flatrock, and Faith to her. She ordered Leaf to Narrow's team and Hunter to Swift's team with the other good snipers. Amelia's three sailors clustered around her. She briefed them on the plan, then took up position behind Sky and her team as they started advancing along the edge of the nearest outcrop.

The entrance to the cave was broad and rough. It was easily big enough to get a boat through and torch light from inside made plain that it was inhabited. Low, reptilian forms were gathering at the entrance, huge swords swinging on their tails.

"Well," she said to Hedge, "at least it's not an ambush."

"Nope, just a killing field."

Up ahead, Sky kept close to the outcrop wall, sword up but pistol holstered. Ranged weapons were considered cowardly, Amelia remembered. These brutes intended for this to be an honorable fight. A bit of a surprise, considering their master was a thief.

Sky advanced steadily and the Theropods started shuffling forward, tails rising as they turned their bodies sideways to open their swings. There was at least a dozen of them, Amelia guessed, and she directed her team to flank left as Sky moved away from the wall and closed the center of the line. Narrow's team flanked right, snug against the rock and Swift's team brought up the rear.

The two lines were barely five paces apart when the Theropods suddenly dropped into crouches. Beyond them, from behind the rocks littered around the cave entrance, brutes with rifles popped up and fired. Amelia ducked for cover as bullets zinged past.

"My team," Narrow roared, "advance!"

He charged forward, sword held high and his eyes on the rifle-toting Theropods at the cave entrance.

"Narrow, get back!" Sky shouted.

"I'll take them out!" he replied with a sudden grin. "Follow behind me!"

"I said get back!" Sky was up again, thrusting out her arm to try and stop Narrow's team from following. Two of them hesitated but the other two charged forward with him.

Narrow swung his cutlass wildly as he reached the line of Theropods. They ducked under his strikes, dancing around him as he continued to run toward the reloading snipers.

Then one of the tailswords struck down, severing his leg at the knee. He collapsed in a heap, cutlass clanging on the rocks as he screamed and clutched his leg.

"Take position up there," Sky ordered the riflemen, pointing at the uneven ledges on the outcrop Swift's team still hugged. "Take out their gunners."

Another volley of shots exploded from the cave entrance. Amelia ducked again and heard at least one sailor cry out in pain. Then she was on her feet, charging forward.

———

Another volley of cannon fire slammed into *Freedom's* hull, but the cutter was made of stronger stuff than that. Liam watched as Fat Tub moved across his view, motionless beside *Daring* as *Freedom* dove past. Sungate fired another broadside, her gunners pinpointing the central gunport in Fat Tub's thick hull. The rounds slammed into the opening, and an explosion within indicated that at least one of them struck the powder bags. Another gun down.

Freedom rolled as she swept beneath the three ships and Liam saw another double broadside from *Daring* as Riverton continued her lesson in superior firepower. Fat Tub was holding up remarkably against the onslaught, but Sectoid Scout was a wreck, three of her four masts shattered and air leaking from multiple holes.

"Let's finish them," Liam declared. "Shift target to the Sectoid scout, ball shot."

"Guns ready," Sungate reported.

"Fire."

Freedom's barrage wasn't as mighty as *Daring's*, but her cannon were frighteningly precise and all five of her starboard shots struck the same hull plate. Liam saw tufts of dust blown swiftly free as air started escaping. Sungate fired again and the entire plate came loose, buckling as it snapped free of the hull. More air started to rush outward, shimmering in the vacuum. As *Freedom* soared upward past the beam of the enemy ship Liam braced for a volley of cannon fire, but the ports were quiet. Small boats began to launch as the crew abandoned ship.

"Cease fire," Liam ordered. "That's her out of the fight. Now let's deal with the fat tub."

Freedom was rising up *Daring's* starboard side and as Liam looked past the frigate's mottled hull he suddenly saw a broad form rising up its port side. Fat Tub was manoeuvring sharply upward, thrusters blazing, to clear *Daring's* gun arcs. Fat Tub suddenly turned hard to starboard, closing *Freedom* with increasing speed. On a collision course, Liam realized.

"Evasive port," he shouted.

His ship hauled to the left, rolling as Brown tried to open the distance. The canopy filled with the starry sky, but Liam knew every inch of *Freedom* – from stem to stern to the tips of her masts. And at the range Fat Tub was…

He staggered as the deck shook. An awful screech of twisting metal rattled through the hull, rising as if *Freedom* herself was screaming.

"Roll to starboard!"

But it was too late. Red flags lit up all over the sailing table as the bottom mast snapped under the force of Fat Tub's suicidal charge. The view beyond the canopy continued to spin as *Freedom* rolled.

"Steady us out."

"Multiple breaches on the lower deck," Brown cried even as she manipulated the thrusters. The roll slowed.

Liam raced to her side, scanning the tables. "How bad?"

"Five, no six compartments." Her eyes widened. "Seven!"

Freedom's lower deck was where all their food, water, spare parts and ammunition were stored.

"Get down there and seal them off," he ordered, grabbing the main broadcast handset. "All sailing hands, all starboard gunners, report to lower deck for damage control!"

Brown descended the ladder to the main deck, her voice ringing out with orders as she ran forward.

With a final wrench, the bottom mast snapped off, spiralling away like a broken twig as Fat Tub soared past beneath. Red flags were spreading across the sailing table and damage control table.

"Get below," he shouted to Sungate and his bridge team, fighting down his growing panic. "Seal those breaches!"

Freedom had such a small crew, he doubted they could stop the egress of air if the entire bottom mast mount had sheared. More red flags were lighting up as the damage spread. He grabbed the broadcast again. "All hands, all hands, report to lower deck for damage control."

The red flags were lighting up all down the ship's lower deck and yellows were appearing on the main deck. He reached for the external comms.

"*Daring* this is *Freedom*… We are out of the fight. Trying to contain the damage."

Daring sailed past, overhead, appearing to rise as *Freedom* continued to roll slowly. She altered to port and fired another broadside, but Fat Tub continued to open the distance.

Liam, alone on the bridge, scanned the rest of his consoles. Damage control and sailing were practically on fire with so many red and yellow flags, but suddenly tactical drew his attention. Fat Tub and *Daring* were opening astern, but the planet was looming ahead. With his entire crew desperately trying to keep the ship intact there was no-one to extend the port and starboard masts or get fresh sails up. He checked his thruster fuel levels: enough to slow the descent, maybe. The top mast was still functioning, and he had bridge controls to adjust sails, but the ship was badly unbalanced and sluggish.

Unless he could get her side masts extended and functioning, *Freedom* was going down.

—————

Amelia leapt back from another tailsword swing ahead of her, then blocked a heavy strike from the left with her cutlass. All around her Human and Theropod blades clanged together amidst grunts, snarls and the snap of bullets.

The Theropods were vicious fighters, but the sheer weight of their weapons kept them slow. It was nothing like when they attacked with their natural weapons, and a sudden rush of fear and anger at the memory gave Amelia's exhausted arm renewed energy. She pushed back the attacker on her left, dodged behind him and sliced down with her blade. It smashed through his back armor and through flesh and bone. With a gasp, the brute collapsed.

She wrenched her sword free with a shower of blood and faced the other opponent. The Theropod snarled and lifted his tailsword for another swing.

A shot rang out and the brute staggered, clutching vainly at a growing wound at the base of his neck. He fell, breath gargling. Amelia glanced up to the rocks. Hunter gave her a quick grin as he reloaded his rifle and took aim again.

Sky had reached the cave entrance and overwhelmed the remaining Theropod snipers, who dropped their weapons and ran inside. Sky ducked behind cover, dodging a few shots that were sent her way. She gestured for the three riflemen to climb down and join her. Swift gathered his only remaining sailor and did likewise. As a group of six, they disappeared into the cave.

Amelia scanned the battlefield. Six sailors were down, including Narrow with his severed leg, and twice as many Theropods. Some still lived on both sides, but there was no time for rest. Faith was barely on his feet, sword dropped from a mangled hand as he clutched at his midsection. Amelia ran to support him, slipping the medical bag from her shoulder.

"Here," she said, helping him to sit down. "Can you tend yourself?"

He nodded, eye bright and lucid through the pain. He took the medical bag with his good hand and opened it.

"Once you're okay," she ordered, "take care of our other wounded." She looked around at the carnage again, knowing some of her sailors had already breathed their last. "Triage those mostly likely to make it."

He nodded again, already cracking open a poppied rum to steady himself.

Amelia rose and saw Hedge and Flatrock waiting for her. Both were bloodied and haggard, but there was fight still in them.

"Come on," she said, leading them into the cave. "Let's find that Suncatcher."

The cave was surprisingly large and well-lit, looking more like a themed tavern than an edge-of-society hideout. Several long tables had been tipped over for cover, stools still scattered around them, and in the center of the room a cookfire smoldered under a large pot. Bedrolls were scattered in the shadows of the rugged nooks that made the walls impossible to define, almost like a maze extended in two dozen directions from this cavern.

Amelia kept to the middle of the room, watching for any ambushes from those nooks. She could hear the fighting deeper into the cave and could tell that Sky, Swift and their team had followed the main passageway that led deeper into the hillside.

"Come on, PO," Flatrock urged her. "They need our help."

Yeah," she said, jogging toward the noise of combat even as her eyes still scanned left and right. The many lamps cast many shadows around the cave, but she saw no movement anywhere. Most of Shordar's gang probably lay dead or dying at the entrance, but this thief was full of surprises. Who knew how many still guarded his treasure ahead. Based on the amount of roaring and hissing she could hear, a lot.

She increased speed, spotting the shadows of sword combat just around the next corner. If they could finish off the resistance, they could search this entire complex at their leisure. Shordar was making his last stand just ahead, she knew. And yet…

Amid the distant thunder of combat, she heard a distinct, nearby sound. *Tap. Tap.*

It was like a tiny hammer against a rock. But it carried with remarkable ease through the cavern.

She slowed as they left the main cavern and moved into the tunnel. Hedge and Flatrock did likewise, staring at her in confusion. She looked back at the still cavern, then motioned them to continue forward.

"Go help the others – and make noise doing it! I'll be right behind you."

Hedge and Flatrock exchanged a curious glance. Then Hedge shrugged and charged toward the corner, screaming some obscene battle cry. Flatrock hustled along behind her, adding his baritone roar to the noise.

Amelia tucked in against the wall, motionless as she surveyed the cavern. The only movement was the flicker of light off the sullen cookfire. The only sound was the deafening clatter of battle behind her. She knew she should go and help her shipmates. But she also knew that Shordar had been one step ahead of them the entire time.

Tap-tap-tap.

A glimmer of movement from one of the shadowy nooks froze her in place. As she watched, a single Theropod head peered out from cover, taking a long look and listen before disappearing again. Amelia dared not move, not even to glance back at the fighting around the corner.

Tap-tap… Tap.

Then, a Theropod reappeared from the nook, his green scales shimmering in the lamplight beneath a short cape as he skulked across the open space. Behind him, four more brutes carried a litter that supported a large object covered in a blanket.

Amelia gritted her teeth. They were five and she was one. Maybe two, if Faith could get his hands on a pistol. And maybe four if the two sailors guarding the Human boats happened to spot the Theropods. Not good odds, especially as she spied the pistols snug against every brute's chest.

But her mission was clear: get the Suncatcher. She rose into a crouch and started to run.

But her mission was clear: get the Suncatcher. She rose into a crouch and started to run.

Liam watched as the top sails shifted and caught the breeze, easing *Freedom* through the turn. Dawn had reached the planet's surface below and the greys and blacks were taking on new vibrancy as their sun shone down on them. It also meant the sun was on *Freedom*'s starboard quarter, giving Liam the best chance at manoeuvring his crippled ship into a stable descent. The first wisps of heated atmosphere were brushing against *Freedom*'s hull, but she was holding for now.

"Sublieutenant Brown," he said over the ship's broadcast, "report status of damage control."

Moments later, the internal phone whistled and he picked it up.

"*Lower deck is lost to space,*" she said, clearly panting. "*We're securing every hatch leading down and there are no leaks from the main deck.*"

Her matter-of-fact report chilled him. "We've lost the entire deck?"

"*I'm sorry, sir. We tried, but the damage was just too extensive.*"

"So we have holes in the hull?"

"*Yes, sir, big ones. But we've stabilized internal air and pressure.*"

The growing heat against *Freedom*'s hull wouldn't normally be a problem for a cutter designed for atmospheric entry. But the pressure alone would tear those holes apart, flood the lower deck with fire, and…

"I'm rolling the ship," he said, "to put our top side down for planetary insertion. I'm going to furl all sails. Get to sailing control and get that mast retracted."

He could well imagine the fear in Brown's eyes in the silence that followed. Then, "*Yes, sir. How much time do we have?*"

The first sparks of superheated gases flashed past the bow.

"None. Make it happen."

His fingers danced over the sailing table as he pulled in all the remaining sails. Even as he did he saw indication of the top mast starting to retract. Reaching for the thrusters he gently rolled the ship until the world loomed huge directly above him. He tapped the bow downward, trying to present *Freedom's* entire topside to the growing maelstrom.

"Freedom, *this is* Daring," came Riverton's staticky voice. "*What's your status?*"

"This is *Freedom*. I'm attempting a controlled insertion using thrusters."

"*Your aspect is incorrect*, Freedom." She said calmly. "*Recommend you aim with the bow.*"

"Apologies, ma'am," he said with a sad smile. "I may have scratched your ship's hull a bit too much for that. I'm shielding the damage as best I can."

"*Understood,*" she said finally. "*Fair winds, Commander Blackwood.*"

His smile widened. No judgement, no criticism. Just faith in him. "Following rays, Captain Riverton."

His thoughts went again to the life rafts, and the idea of getting his crew to safety. But *Freedom* was already too far into the atmosphere for rafts to safely launch. He could have sent them earlier, he knew, but had he done so they would never have been able to seal the damage or get the mast retracted. A thump above him indicated the top mast locking into place, its thick, round bulk obscuring the centerline of his view through the canopy. A view that was becoming increasingly obscured by the bow wave of fire.

He honestly doubted any of his crew would have gone, even if he'd ordered them. *Freedom* was their ship, now, and anything they could do to save her was worth it. He took one final look at his tables, and realized there was nothing more he could do. The ship was falling now, completely at the mercy of the elements. He sat down in his command chair – a seat he hardly ever used, he suddenly realized – and sat back to watch the show.

"All hands," he said, taking the ship's broadcast one last time. "Men and women of the cutter *Freedom*: thank you. Brace for shock."

A shot rang out just as Amelia reached the cave entrance, then a second. She emerged into the dawn light to see Faith falling to the ground, pistol dropping next to him. Shordar limped heavily, clutching his side with one clawed hand as the other still kept his own pistol raised.

Amelia's fury broke through her last attempts at caution and she screamed, raising her weapon and shooting the nearest Theropod. The brute stumbled and fell, and the litter carrying the Suncatcher collapsed down on top of him. Another litter bearer hissed in rage and charged Amelia. She shot twice, killing the beast.

A bullet pinged off her breastplate, knocking her staggering back. The two remaining litter bearers were struggling to drag their burden forward. Amelia emptied her last rounds into them. The Suncatcher crashed to the ground, a glimmer of gold peeking out from under the blanket.

Amelia raised her pistol toward Shordar. The master thief's lips parted in a menacing grin.

"You have no bullets left," his translator duly called. And then he raised his own weapon. "But I do."

Amelia dove for cover as Shordar fired at her. Bullets zipped past her head and her calf suddenly exploded in pain. She reached the cover of rocks and gasped as she looked down. Her left calf was bleeding through the padding.

"You're finished," Shordar said, stepping toward her on long, powerful legs coiled to spring.

"It's just a flesh wound," she spat, pulling herself up on the rock and drawing her cutlass.

Behind Shordar, none of the sailors still alive had the strength to rise. A few Theropods stared weakly as well, but none moved. Far behind her, she could still hear the fighting of what she knew was just one more distraction. But there, not ten paces away from her, was the damn thing this whole fight was about. The Suncatcher.

She forced herself to stand, ignoring the protests from her calf as she lifted her sword. She limped forward, eyes on the golden object barely visible.

Shordar drew his daggers and stepped between her and the prize. Lowering into an attack stance, his muscles rippled with strength as the breeze fluttered his cape.

She planted her feet, holding her cutlass in a guard.

His lips closed, hiding his teeth as his iridescent eyes bore into hers.

"You're impressive, Human. Perhaps there's no need for me to kill you."

"You can just walk away," she said. "Leave the Suncatcher and go. I won't chase you."

He barked softly. "How could I ever abandon my greatest asset?"

"Just walk away," she repeated, shuffling another step forward.

"Or," he said, "we could walk away together. Help me carry the Suncatcher to my boat."

"What?"

"Join my band of merry adventurers," he said with new enthusiasm. He yanked the blanket off the Suncatcher, revealing its golden magnificence. "I'll make you rich, and free from this Human prison called 'Empire'. Just drop your sword, take up these litter handles, and come away with me."

His eyes were intoxicating, their vertical slits fixated on her with surprising earnestness. Suddenly, she understood what Bella was talking about. Even across species, he was a charmer.

But Amelia had dealt with more than enough charmers in her life. She lunged forward, her cutlass stabbing at Shordar's heart.

He deftly sidestepped, her blade slashing through nothing but cape. He knocked aside her return strike with one dagger as the other slashed against her shoulder armor. She stumbled on her bad leg as she raised her sword in defence, but his tail was too swift. The slab of meat slammed into her. She flew through the air and crashed down on the rocky ground. She scrambled for her sword, but a three-toed foot kicked it away.

"Shame," Shordar said, the hiss of his true voice carrying real regret. "You might have been useful."

Amelia pushed herself backward on the ground, trying to get to her feet as Shordar steadily advanced. She screamed for help, but the wind was suddenly picking up and her voice was lost in the roar. Shordar's lips parted again, his teeth flashing as he lowered to strike.

An explosion to her side sent a cloud of broken rock and dust into the air. A wall of heated air knocked her sideways, and sent Shordar clear off his feet. He rolled back onto his legs, but his gaze left Amelia and stared upward.

The rushing wind was dying, and as Amelia looked upward she realized it was the sound of *Freedom* cutting through the air. The ship circled low, thrusters firing as it lowered to land. Another cannon fired, spraying debris just behind Shordar. The Theropod bolted at top speed, fleeing the battleground and disappearing around the bend, to where Amelia knew his boats were. She expected *Freedom* to keep turning and follow.

But then she saw the gaping hole midships on her bottom hull, and the smoke still rising from her blackened and tortured topside. *Freedom* could barely settle down on the ground, her savaged hull creaking as her weight settled down.

———•———

Liam watched as Shordar ran with inhuman speed across the ground, but his eyes went right back to the golden object resting at the mouth of the cave.

"Hull is stable," Brown declared. "Cargo bay doors are opening. Our medical team is deploying. I'll get some hands to bring in the prize."

Liam's gaze lingered on the Suncatcher as it caught the first rays of direct sun streaming in from between the rocky outcrops, but then he scanned the dozens of fallen figures on the ground, including one that was struggling to her feet.

"Oh, dear," he sighed, feeling a sudden sense of dread.

"What's wrong?" Sungate demanded from gunnery control. Her eyes were afire as she stared out the canopy. "That's the Suncatcher, isn't it?"

"Yes," he said. "And right next to it is a quartermaster who doesn't like to be rescued."

CHAPTER 18

The dockyards bustled with activity as carts and carriages brought supplies and people to the Navy ships lining the docks on both sides of the orbital structure. Cranes moved with graceful efficiency high above, loading stores into waiting cargo bays. A pair of battleships berthed at the far end of the docks, their three decks of guns enough to intimidate all but the most tenacious of foes. Several cruisers were berthed closer, smaller but still powerful ships that served as the backbone of the Imperial Fleet.

Liam always admired the hustle of the dockyards over his home world of Passagia. These certainly weren't the largest of His Majesty's port facilities, but the people who crewed them worked with heart. Much like the crew of the little frigate berthed off to the side, unnoticed by most workers and sailors who passed by with their eyes on the big ships. A single crane was in motion next to him, the arm reaching out of the air pocket and into the vacuum where *Daring* rested in her mooring. The crane reached clear over the hull and as it began to swing its load into view, Liam felt a rush of mixed emotions.

"You know," Riverton said, standing next to him, "I really should dock your pay for how you returned *Freedom* to me."

As the crane moved, *Freedom's* battered hulk appeared from behind *Daring*. The cutter was a mess, with hastily patched holes on her bottom side and a top side charred and scored. She was still missing her bottom mast and Liam didn't want to think about how mauled the top mast was. His gut swirled with guilt as he viewed again just how badly damaged Lady Riverton's property was, but at the same time his heart swelled with pride.

"She's a magnificent vessel, ma'am. And she served with honor." When her withering glare didn't falter, he shrugged. "I should think my naming a planet after you would compensate at least somewhat."

She laughed – a deep, musical laugh that surprised Liam each rare time he heard it.

"Fair enough, Commander Blackwood. And I think Shordar will cover the costs, anyway."

As the crane continued to carry *Freedom* toward a waiting drydock, Liam noticed the crewmembers working on the jetty next to *Daring*. Amelia was there, directing sailors as they moved sacks and unpacked crates. There was a skip to their steps, he could see from even here, and he knew it came from more than just coming home. Amelia had led them down a random tunnel inside the large cavern of Shordar's hideout, where they'd discovered a stunning treasure trove of stolen artifacts. Over the weeks it took to sail home their research had discovered the owners of almost everything and reward money was now pouring in. Riverton had agreed to share all proceeds according to the traditional split for prize money, meaning the crew had just earned a most unexpected windfall.

"I suspect we'll lose a few more sailors to retirement," he said.

"Perhaps. But let's see what Lord Grandview has in store for us. I'd like to think we've earned their loyalty and that they'll stick around."

The sailors could doubtless see the captains of *Daring* and *Freedom* standing on the jetty, but a wide gulf remained between them. No sailor wanted to fall too closely into the orbit of a senior officer on the prowl, especially when the sector commander, Rear Admiral Grandview, was on his way.

Liam wasn't nervous about the admiral's looming visit. The uninhabited world Rivertonia was now on the charts and HMSS *Daring* had earned the gratitude of the Emperor for recovering the Suncatcher intact. That prize had been taken under heavy guard as soon as *Daring* had reached Passagia. The intention had been for it to be spirited away without notice or ceremony, but many of the crew had made their own way to the jetty to catch one last glimpse of the most beautiful object they'd ever seen. Julia Sungate had served as escort to her family heirloom – alone, after all that – and was now on her way to the Imperial Armory to share her discovery of improved powder for the cannon.

"I wonder if we'll ever catch that thief?" he mused.

"If Sublieutenant Sungate has anything to say about it, we'll mobilize the entire fleet." Riverton's expression didn't shift. "I wish her well."

"She's one of the better ones," he agreed. "I'm sure she'll command a ship one day."

"If she does, it will be because she had a fine example," she said, eyes still on *Freedom*. "For some officers, bringing their first command home in that condition would be an embarrassment. But for you… I expect it is a source of great satisfaction."

She knew him too well. "I accomplished the mission and drove my ship and her crew to perform mighty deeds to do so. That is nothing to be embarrassed about."

"Agreed." She suddenly reached into her coat pocket. "And while I know you hate pomp and ceremony, please indulge me this small moment."

Her hand emerged with a four-pointed, golden star that fit in the palm of her hand: the symbol of warship command. She wore one on her left lapel, as did all officers who had held the honor of being a captain in space.

He stared at it. "But, ma'am… *Freedom* isn't a commissioned warship."

"You're an officer in His Majesty's Navy who commanded a ship crewed by His Majesty's sailors through multiple battles with His Majesty's enemies while accomplishing His Majesty's mission. Don't be pedantic, Mr. Blackwood."

"Yes, ma'am."

"You have taken on the highest honor," she said as she pinned the star to his lapel, "and the greatest burden anyone can in this fleet. You have earned this, and you should be so honored for the rest of your life."

He looked down at the command star, then back up at this most enigmatic of women. She wasn't smiling, but her eyes were filled with pride.

"Thank you, ma'am."

"Of course," she said, glancing one more time at *Freedom* as the crane slowly guided the cutter into the drydock, "I don't have a ship for you to command, at least for a while. Any thoughts on what you might do next?"

It had been weighing on him the entire trip home. He'd relinquished his position in *Daring*, but *Freedom* was no longer his. And that left him at loose ends.

"Petty Officer Virtue has suggested that I retire to my castle and become a dilletante."

Amusement lightened her expression, but it quickly turned serious again as her gaze drifted toward the brow. Liam turned and saw a familiar, burly form limp across the brow, heavy duffel slung over his shoulder opposite to his peg-leg.

The sailors handling stores all stopped as Petty Officer Ethan Narrow stepped onto the dock, a silent communication passing between them. He paused and watched as some of them drifted over to offer a few words. Even from here Liam could see his efforts to be jovial, but his broad shoulders sagged with more than just the heavy duffel bag.

Amelia approached him last, eyes wary. He stared at her for a moment, then offered his hand. She shook it, offered a parting comment, then turned away to start directing the sailors again. Narrow hefted his bag and limped away, eyes scanning the dock before noticing the two senior officers watching him. Without hesitation, he altered his path to approach them.

He was in civilian clothes, so there was no need to salute, but as he approached he dipped his head in a sign of respect to Riverton.

"Captain Riverton, Commander Blackwood. I'm heading ashore for the final time."

"Is all your paperwork sorted?" Liam asked, his instincts as XO always leading him back to administrative details. "Have you received all your pay?"

"Everything's good," Narrow replied. "Subcommander Swift was very thorough and ensured that I've been properly looked after."

"And did he make it clear," Riverton said, "that your wound does not require you to leave the Navy?"

"He did. And thank you, ma'am, for your offer to stay on. But I think my time in His Majesty's Service is done."

"I'm sorry to hear that," she said.

There was no sailor Liam wanted more to see off *Daring*, but his noble training kept his words civil.

"Your many talents will no doubt serve you well," he added.

"Thank you, sir."

There was a long pause. Narrow's expression was difficult to read, but it was clear he wanted to say more. He no longer wore a uniform, but a decade in the Navy no doubt still made it hard to address senior officers.

"Is there something on your mind, Mr. Narrow?"

His lips twisted in thought as his gaze moved between them. Finally, he sighed.

"This was a good ship. But we lost a lot of people on a mission that… that I don't really think needed to happen."

Liam stole a glance at Riverton. The captain's expression was unreadable, but her lips were pursed tight.

"I'm sorry for our losses as well," Liam said quickly. "In service there's always the risk that someone won't come home, but this mission was costly. Let's hope there isn't another one like it."

"Yeah… Well." Narrow shifted the bag on his shoulder. "I'm not sticking around to find out."

"Then may fortune favor you in your future endeavors," Liam said.

"And you, sir." He nodded to Riverton. "Captain."

As Narrow limped away, Liam felt no need to break the silence between him and Lady Sophia. She turned her eyes immediately away from her former artificer and studied the movements of *Daring's* stores team. Liam did likewise, heart warming as Amelia led her people with such easy confidence.

But Narrow's words stayed with him. The cost in lives had been high, and for what? An object? If he'd lost Amelia he suspected it would be him walking away on the jetty with a bag over his shoulder and bitterness in his heart. Why didn't he feel the same for the rest of the sailors he'd lost?

Because, he reminded himself as he stole another glance at Riverton's icy features, he'd learned not to. And if he was going to command his own ship again, it was a lesson he couldn't afford to forget. Sailors died in the service of the Navy and if he couldn't accept that, he should retire his commission now.

But what if it was Amelia?

"I'll be honest," Riverton said suddenly, "my new XO is good. But he's still very much drawn to his sails. Especially now that he no longer has a sailing artificer."

Liam was more than happy to see the back of said artificer, but he recognized the additional pressure on Swift.

But was it pressure? Or was it where Swift belonged?

"I wonder if Subcommander Swift would be happy to return to his sails?" he offered cautiously.

"He would." Riverton stated bluntly as her expression hardened. "But before we discuss anything further on this subject, let me be clear: I am not getting rid of my quartermaster. Any XO I take aboard would have to be at peace with that."

Liam nodded, a quick answer eluding him. He glanced again at Amelia where she casually directed her team. She made a comment he couldn't hear, but the sudden laughter from the sailors echoed across the jetty. She was so good at what she did, and his heart ached as he watched her.

"I understand, ma'am."

She remained silent beside him, also watching Amelia direct her crew.

"And yet," she said finally, "you offer no reassurance."

He turned back to her. "Ma'am… I have no honest reassurance to offer. My relationship with Ame- with Petty Officer Virtue is deep and profound. I value it greatly – I value *her* greatly – and I can't guarantee that this won't affect my judgement."

She regarded him. There was kindness within the cool depths of her eyes, but little sympathy.

"All I can offer," he said, "is that I'm aware of my own weakness, and that I'll do everything in my power to be objective when the time comes."

"Considering the situations we find ourselves in, that is a light offer."

Liam noticed a carriage approaching, sporting the pennant of Admiral Grandview. But his focus remained on Captain Riverton.

"It's the most honest offer I can make, ma'am. I'd be honored to serve as your executive officer again, but I take no offence if you consider me a liability in that position. I want what's best for you, for the ship and for the Navy."

The carriage pulled to a halt next to them. As the driver climbed down and lowered the steps outside the passenger compartment, Riverton's eyes remained fixed on Liam.

"That's a lot of risk, Commander Blackwood."

"I trust your judgement of my character, ma'am."

Only when the door to the carriage opened did she finally turn.

They both saluted as Rear Admiral Grandview stepped down. A broad, beaming figure, he'd been their commander and patron for many adventures. He smiled as he shook both their hands and his flag lieutenant climbed out of the carriage to wait behind him.

"Captain Riverton, congratulations on another successful mission for the crown. And Commander Blackwood, I see you've had your first taste of command – well done, lad."

"Thank you, sir," Riverton replied. "It's our pleasure to serve."

The admiral cast his eyes around the dockyard, lingering on *Daring* and on *Freedom*. "I won't waste words. The fleet is mobilizing to counter the Sectoid threat and we need every ship commanded and crewed by the finest people we can muster. There will be no room for mistakes in the coming months."

"I understand you have new orders?"

"Something a little unusual," he said, gesturing for his flag lieutenant to hand over a sealed scroll, "befitting my most unusual ship."

As Riverton took the scroll, Liam noticed the seal that bound it – not the usual Navy seal, but the mark of the Imperial household. Riverton cracked it open and unfurled the paper. Together they read the three simple paragraphs outlining the mission.

"As you can see," Grandview said, "a little unusual."

Riverton closed the scroll and, after the tiniest of pauses, glanced at Liam. He nodded.

She placed her hand on his shoulder and smiled, then turned back to the admiral.

"Lord Grandview, my executive officer and I," her hand squeezed his shoulder, "accept this commission."

ACKNOWLEDGEMENTS

It's great to be back in the swashbuckling universe of Blackwood & Virtue after too many years away, and I'd like to thank my author buddy Richard Dowker for all his support during that time. Thanks for keeping me accountable, for helping me to remember what a joy it is to write, and for how to grab those creative moments even when His Majesty's Side Gig takes me over the horizon for months at a time.

Thank you also to Marla for the gorgeous design work, and to Judi for bringing this book to the world.

Finally, to my beloved Emma: you are my everything.

ABOUT THE AUTHOR

Bennett R. Coles has a degree in naval history and has served as an officer in the Royal Canadian Navy and Canadian Army for more than twenty years. Once, very early in his career, he was back aft watching flight operations in the North Pacific and he thought: "This is really cool—but it would be even cooler if it was in SPACE!" Thus began his quest to write science fiction books with a naval theme. Along the way he has won an award or two, presented at numerous cons, and met many lovely people. This is his eighth book (that he'll admit to). He makes his home in Victoria, British Columbia with his lovely wife, two growing boys and two scheming cats.